The Gho

CW00432007

Contents

The Ghost Chaser

Chapter 1: Till death do us part

Steph

I look at the body and shudder. The corpse lies face up, the familiar mop of brown hair, cut shorter than I remember, has gleaming scarlet blood sticking to parts of his fringe and his head. Blood and brain matter seep from his violent head wound and drips slowly across the kitchen-diner laminate floor. His green eyes are open in that death stare that you never get used to. An iced chill runs through me. I take a deep breath as memories swirl through my mind, moments of joy when I'd first met this man. Of sunny days walking along the beach, hand in hand, as we laughed about the silliest things and licked our ice creams from their cones.

Memories flit through my mind and are soon replaced with a white wedding and an unplanned pregnancy. And then all I remember is heartache and pain.

Red marks cover his face, masking the handsome shape of his square jaw, straight nose and clear skin. He'd always been lucky with his skin I mused, and my heart fluttered in remembrance. This sallow, bloody lifeless face in front of me was the very one I used to dream about when we first began dating. Marks that look suspiciously like fingernail marks trailed across his skin. Had there been a struggle? I think of someone defending himself against him. He was strong, physically strong, and when caught in the moment, when his temper flared, he had the strength of an army of men. That, I could tell you from experience.

The memory of his green eyes which had once looked at me with love and admiration. Those eyes are now glazed and empty, in final slumber. He's wearing a white linen shirt, blue jeans and trainer-style shoes.

I take a deep breath. My name is Steph Rutland, and this is my first murder case since my fast track promotion four months ago to Detective Inspector, and for ease I'm usually known as DI Rutland. *Keep calm* I tell myself. *He can't hurt you, or another living person again.* I bend down, as close as I dare without touching him, to study the angle of his body and search for clues to what happened to this man. This is the closest I've been to him without him physically hurting me in a long time. What does that tell you? This man, who was my first love, my husband and father to our fourteen-year-old son Ben – he became a monster with a short temper who needed no excuse to use me as his punchbag. A temper that became his weapon to use at his will if I didn't meet some impossible standard that only he was allowed to set.

This was the devil himself.

I stand and walk around the kitchen area. The grey square wall clock says 1.15pm. There are two half empty wine glasses on the counter and a brown-handled screwdriver lies on the floor near the kitchen sink. I peer closely at it and see no obvious signs of blood. I'm sure the Scenes of Crime Officers, commonly known as SOCO, will use their equipment to glean any hidden blood particles and fingerprints. Questions rush through me. How the hell had he managed to move to the same county as us, without me knowing? Was this a coincidence? Why had he moved? Did he still own the car sales business in Basingstoke? Who was he with last night and where was that person?

There's a brown wooden baseball bat lying on the kitchen floor near the sink unit. About a quarter of it is covered in blood. It's not rocket science to assume that this is the murder weapon. I'm feeling more confused every minute. How did this man, my ex-husband and someone who I've not seen in eleven years, find himself lying dead on his own kitchen floor? What the hell happened here? And why leave the bat here for us to find? Did the attacker run out of time, or panic? Something doesn't add up. I can't understand why the bat would be left like that. Thoughts run through my head, it's spinning, and for a moment I scrape my hand through my long curly jet-black hair and briefly press my fingers against my forehead. This cannot be happening.

Follow the evidence, that's what you're taught in the Major Investigation Team, follow the evidence and do the leg work. It's not like watching a TV crime show where everything is condensed into a sixty-minute solvable time slot. Solving a crime takes a lot of patience, time and perseverance. And also, quite a bit of luck.

"Is there a wallet to identify him?" asks my colleague, Detective Sergeant Chris Jackson, his clean-shaven oval face scrunched in concentration. A wisp of dark-blonde hair falls over his brown eyes and my fingers tingle with the sudden urge to push it behind his ear. Must be my maternal instinct kicking in.

"No," says the police constable who was the first person on the scene. "Nothing."

I stand and look at them as the duty forensic pathologist walks in, suitably dressed for a crime scene in a white protection suit and matching disposable shoe covers and gloves. Jesus, what a mess. I should have known that today would pan out this way. I mean, I'm not the luckiest of people. Soon, I'll have to own up to them that I know this man and that he was my ex-husband. I know I'm procrastinating, but I need a minute to process what has happened. I think I'm in shock, I never thought I'd see him again, but he's here. Now. Dead on the kitchen floor. I just need a minute to get my head together.

"Hey, Dr Soames. Good to see you," I say, giving her a quick nod. Dr Daisy Soames – thirty-something, petite, fitness freak with short blonde hair which has a streak of purple across her fringe. She's been a friend of mine from my Hendon training days. It's on days like this I wish I were back there at Hendon, working hard to complete the training, forming friendships and enjoying the social interaction.

A sudden vision comes to me of Daisy and I celebrating another Hendon trainee's 21st birthday, Andy I think his name was. The memory of Daisy throwing back a pitcher of cider for a twenty-pound bet still brings tears to my eyes. I spent most of my time with her in the bathroom, carefully holding her hair back to keep it away from her heaving mouth, the twenty-pound note peeping out of the top of her jeans pocket. I couldn't believe how rough we both felt the following day. Gosh, was that really seven years ago now?

When I think back to how low I'd been when I'd walked away from my marriage my tummy still churns and my heart beats a little faster. It brings a feeling of apprehension, a blackness to my soul. Anyone who's experienced that feeling of extreme exhaustion, the kind that sends you into a trance-like state of despondency, will understand the desolation of accepting a situation that you know deep down is simply not right.

Well, that was me a few years ago, accepting cruel words and a quick temper from my spouse that often resulted in me dragging my sore, bruised body through the motions of looking after Ben. Yes, when you hit rock bottom and there's no place left to go. Struggling through each day as if in a dream. You will understand what I'm saying.

I am not that person anymore. I am the person I was before I met HIM. Well, I think I am. I've moved on and Ben, my son, is growing up fast. I need to pull myself together and find out what happened here.

Daisy's eyes light up and a smile forms across her face when she sees me. She is one of the kindest people I know. "Detective Inspector Rutland, good to see you."

"You too," I reply warmly, acutely aware of the dead body lying at my feet.

"Dr Soames," Chris greets her, a thoughtful look on his face. Daisy smiles, nods her head and lowers her eyelashes to the floor. Daisy shy? I think I'm missing something here. Does she have a soft spot for Chris?

"DS Jackson," Daisy mutters in a slightly breathless tone, meeting his gaze. She's usually so cool and collected, I rarely see this side of Daisy. I watch with fascination as a slow blush rises from her neck and makes its way up her heart-shaped face, covering her freckles.

"Boss. We need to identify who this guy is," Chris states blandly standing beside me.

"No need," I say, taking a deep breath and aiming for a steady voice. "This is my ex-husband."

"Ex-husband? You were married?" Daisy asks, her eyebrows shooting up.

"Yes. I got divorced ten years ago. His name is Ray Delossi."

I nod my head sadly at her. I wasn't sad that he was dead. I was sad because it had to be me of all people to be investigating what had happened to him. I stare down at his lifeless, bloody body and realise that somewhere well hidden, deep within me, is an emotion that I thought I'd dealt with a long time ago. Anger. Anger at Ray for hurting me. For Ben who had grown up without a father. At Ray who could easily have found me over the years. I had reverted to my maiden name. He could have taken me to court for supervised access of Ben. But he hadn't. I wonder why.

There are so many things I wish I could have said to him, to tell him how much he'd hurt me, physically and mentally. To show him the physical scars and to explain the loss of my self-confidence, the loss of the person I used to be, and the lack of trust I have in myself to make the right choice when looking for someone to share my life with. Hence, I don't. Share my life. Personally. With anyone. Period.

Fleeting dark thoughts envelop me, memories of visits to the doctor with hidden cuts and bruises, of Ray's shouting and his face so angry that spittle leaked from his mouth as he spoke to me. It became too much for me to bear. Then I do something that I haven't done for a while now. I start to chew on the inside of my cheek, using my teeth to nibble the soft tissue inside my mouth. It's the anxiety, the panic.

When I finally left him, I knew that there was no choice. He'd broken my arm and slashed me with a kitchen knife. It had hurt so much, and I thought I was going to die. I thought of Ben, how Ray had begun to make snide, nasty remarks to him – even started to call him a brat. And all because I had been catching up on some ironing and the noise irritated him while he was watching the television. I knew I had to leave him, for both of our sakes. And that's how I found my limit, my rock bottom.

I shudder when I think of the decision to leave Ray. It was a Friday. The morning after I found my limit. I waited for him to leave the house at 7.30am and then slowly got out of bed. I could hear Ben playing in his room and for once was glad that Ray had demanded that we put a safety gate on his door frame so that he was unable to leave the room.

My pale blue nightgown had stuck to the front of my bloody chest and neck. The over the counter painkillers had worn off and I needed to take more. I knew my arm was broken by the way it dangled uselessly at my side. I worried it was dislocated too. The pain of dressing was just too much, so I'd carefully lowered a loose-fitting dress over my head which opened at the front and left my damaged arm dangling inside. Some of the cuts around my neck and chest had reopened as I'd peeled the nightgown from my skin. I got Ben dressed as well as I could with one hand and called for an ambulance. When I arrived at the hospital with Ben snuggled into me, I knew at once that I would never return home.

For a few hours everything was a blur. We were given our own room. Doctors and nurses came and went as Ben and myself were examined and then, when they'd finished dressing and stitching the wounds on my chest, I sat waiting for the specialist to come and shift my shoulder back into place. As it happened my arm wasn't broken, but my shoulder was dislocated. The waves of pain were excruciating, so much so that I could taste bile at the back of my throat, and I couldn't stop the trembling motion making its way down my good left arm and working along my left shoulder to my fingers. Calling the ambulance was the right thing to do.

A short while later my shoulder bone had been put back into its socket and I'd been given stronger pain relief to help manage the pain. My arm was rested back into a sling. Ben was napping in the small bed in the corner of the room that one of the nurses had provided and I'd began to doze when two women came into the room.

"Hi, Steph," said the woman with the short brown bob-style hair and freckles, moving closer to my bed. Her tone when she introduced herself was soft but firm. "My name is Detective Sergeant Julie Leadbetter. I've been assigned to your case." She offered a smile of encouragement.

"I can't go back," I say quietly, wincing when I inadvertently move my shoulder.

"I know," DS Leadbetter reassured me, dressed in black trousers and a grey sweater. "This is Jenny Greyson and I think she can help you and Ben."

The blonde-haired woman wearing jeans and a long white cotton shirt steps forward and speaks in a warm, calming tone:

"Hi, Steph," Jenny says as Ben begins to stir in his bed, rubbing his eyes. He sits up, looking for me.

"Mummy, I woke up." His cheeks are flushed, and he begins to clamber out of bed. Immediately, I feel emotional and tears spring to my eyes.

"Let me," the woman called Jenny offers, waiting for my approval. Tears roll down my cheeks, I don't know where they keep coming from. I nod to Jenny and watch as she carefully lifts my three-year-old son and holds him firmly as she rocks from side to side on her hips.

"I know you're in pain, emotional and weary," Jenny says softly as she sways Ben.

"Yes," I whisper.

"I would like to offer yourself and Ben a place to live when you are released from hospital. A safe place. I run two refuge homes as part of The Lighthouse charity. I work with the police counsellors and the emergency social care team."

"A safe place," I mutter to myself, trying to make sense of what she was offering. "For me and Ben?"

"Yes. I think that we can help you. In many ways. Would you like that?" Jenny asked.

I close my eyes to block out everything for a moment. Then I open them and say weakly:

"Yes please."

DS Leadbetter moves the conversation to another topic.

"We will need a statement from you. Hospital records and photographs can be used as evidence to build a case of spousal abuse against your husband. How would you feel about going down that route?"

"You mean, he may be arrested, put in prison if I testify that he did this to me?" I ask. I can hear the trembling tone of my words. Would I be safe? Would he find me? Would he find Ben?

"Yes, but we will make sure that you and Ben are safe." DS Leadbetter's freckled face looks sincere and her words offer reassurance. There is something genuine about the look on their faces and tone of their voices that makes me believe that I can trust these people.

"OK," I say quietly.

***

All I wanted to do was to survive Ray's emotional and physical abuse and to keep Ben and I safe. Everything else was a bonus.

It's impossible to understand what it's like to live as if you're treading on eggshells, wondering what word, look or action would cause a person to erupt into fits of emotional and physical abuse, whether a partner, stranger, relative or parent. Yes, it's impossible to understand unless you've been through it.

I was granted a divorce from Ray Delossi on the grounds of unreasonable behaviour. He had little chance to petition the divorce thanks to my close friends, Stuart and Jenny Greyson from The Lighthouse charity. The Greysons started The Lighthouse charity because they wanted to help women and children who were victims of domestic violence. They work with their local authorities to home, support and nurture those in need. Short-term stays at the refuge homes sometimes turned into long-term placements as each case was taken on its own merit. You were welcome there until you felt able to move on.

Ben had just turned three when we'd found refuge at Shore House, one of The Lighthouse homes. We'd lived there for nearly four years while I got back on my feet. We were lucky to meet people such as Lottie, who ran Shore House, and Jem, who also needed somewhere safe to stay. Jem had become a good friend during those four years as we rebuilt our shattered lives. She was always drawing, sketching and painting. She had a gift for it. Ben and I used to watch her, the graceful way her petite frame folded as she leaned over her work, her mop of dark curly hair moving from side to side as she dipped her paintbrush, sweeping it across the paper. I found it very relaxing to watch.

Lottie, who managed Shore House, had a pretty face and a kind, quiet manner. With red wavy shoulder-length hair, she was always on hand to help but happy to give you space to do your own thing. She lived in the house next to Shore House, married briefly and widowed too soon by pancreatic cancer. She now had a four-year-old son, Harley. He's adorable. Between them all, Lottie, Jem, and the Greysons – they had enriched our lives and treated us as though we were the heart of their family. I firmly believe that without Stuart and Jenny's intervention, Ben and I would be lying injured or dead in a ditch somewhere.

Daisy raises an eyebrow as if to ask if this is something we need to talk about. I've known Daisy for a while now, she is the most kind and loyal friend, but there is one trait that shines above all traits and that's her stubbornness and eagerness to try to help you and solve any problems you may have. It drives me crazy.

The men look at each other as though they have some secret code that women aren't allowed to know about. Really? Is that all they've got to offer? I might as well return home and climb into bed now.

"Jesus, Boss." Chris runs his hands through his hair. I can almost hear his brain ticking away as he thinks of the complications that the death a Detective Inspector's ex-spouse will cause to the investigation.

My phone vibrates and I look at the text. It's Jenny, and she's inviting Ben and I to dinner on Sunday. I text back to confirm that we can make it and mention that something's happened at work and that I'll call them later tonight. Confidentially speaking and workwise, I need to be careful. I can't breach my professional ethics, but there has to be some flexibility in how I work this case. I trust Jenny and Stuart with my life, and I may need their help.

My day is not going well.

"Everyone! Stay calm," I say, taking the lead before things get out of hand. "Find, gather and analyse the evidence. That's what we do. Daisy, any idea of time of death?" I look at the body, keeping my gaze away from his open eyes, and feel nothing but pity that this is how Ray's life ended.

"I'll have a quick look at the body first," Daisy replies, dropping to the floor and kneeling over Ray.

Concentration is etched on her face. She touches various parts of his body then opens his shirt which has small blood splatters across the front.

"Can you give me a hand, DS Jackson?" she asks Chris, as he stoops to the body. Daisy takes a firm but respectful hold of Ray's right leg and shoulder, manoeuvring the body on to its side and toward Chris. With care he slowly lowers the body to the floor. Now that Ray is facing the floor, we can see that there is another injury to the back of his head.

"Ah. So, we have two head wounds," Daisy announces, peering closer to the injury.

"Is it the same type of wound?" I ask her.

"Not sure, but I think so," she replies, her eyes flitting across his scalp collecting information.

"There's a baseball bat over there with blood on it." I point to where it lies waiting to be bagged and tagged for evidence. "That could be the murder weapon."

Daisy reaches into her pocket for a small torch and looks at the blood and indention mark on Ray's head. "It could well be. Get SOCO to bring me the baseball bat and anything else they find so that I can check the impact site for size to see if it matches the shape of the bat. I'll analyse the blood on the bat against Ray's blood and dust for fingerprints."

Daisy checks for discolouration of his skin and lividity on the back. Sometimes bruises don't become visible for a few days. I watch Daisy and Chris turn Ray back so that he's facing the ceiling again. She moves swiftly feeling his body, looking closer at the colour of his skin and then looks up at me.

"You all right if I close his eyes?" she asks, waiting for permission.

"Please." I nod, feeling relief that I won't have to keep looking into the death glaze of my ex-husband. I watch as Daisy places her right hand over his face and slowly draws it down his skin, catching the eyelids as they are forced down to cover his eyes.

"I would say from the state of the body that time of death was approximately between 9pm last night and 8am this morning. I'll have a firm time for you when I get him to the lab."

"Who called it in?" Chris asks the young police officer standing next to him.

"I did. PC Tribble, Sam Tribble," the tall, lean officer with a mop of short red hair says. He shuffles slightly as he straightens his shoulders and stretches to his full height and I notice that this brings Tribble and myself to eye level. Jesus, he must be around five feet ten. He begins his statement. "We received a call from his next-door neighbour at 10.30am this morning. He had a parcel that he'd taken in for Mr Delossi at around 9.20am and there was no answer when he knocked on the door at 9.45am although Mr Delossi's car was there. The neighbour believed that Mr Delossi was possibly having a lazy morning due to it being the weekend and so tried Mr Delossi's door again at 10.25am. The neighbour, Mr Geoff Cross, looked through the lounge window and saw the victim's bloody upper body lying at the far end of the kitchen-diner floor. As you can see, there isn't a door between the lounge and the kitchen diner just an arched walk through."

Can I swap my life with someone else for a moment? Maybe Ben and I could spend a few days with Lottie and Harley in Lyme Regis. Their three-bedroomed stone cottage sits next to Shore House, my old refuge home in Lyme which nestles on the Jurassic coast of West Dorset. The salty smell of the sea air can rejuvenate my tired mind. I have sweet familiar memories of the town centre with its quaint shops and bright red, white and blue bunting, enticing locals and tourists into their brightly decorated shops. The harbour wall is famously known as "The Cobb" – it was here that Jem, Ben and I would walk barefoot in the summer to cool our hot feet. So many happy memories. I miss Jem. And Lottie.

Then it hits me. What do I tell Ben? The only thing he knows for sure about Ray is that his dad is not a good guy and that's why he doesn't live with us. It's not as though he's seen him recently and I rack my brain to remember when Ben and Ray last had contact with each other. God, it must be eleven years.

Chris stares at the white glossy lower kitchen units. His eyes scrunch slightly and focus on something that's caught his attention. I've seen that look before. Raised brows ask me a silent question as Chris glances my way. I shrug my shoulders to show him that I don't know what he's seen. An object glistens on the floor in the recess between the sink unit and the dishwasher. He steps toward the unit and lowers himself to the floor as he carefully studies the long, sleek shape. I move closer to see what he's found and watch with bated breath as he takes a photo of the object in situ before pulling out a large stainless steel carving knife. The hilt of the knife is the only part of it not covered in blood.

Jesus, what happened here? I stoop to the corpse so that Daisy and I can quickly double check Ray's body for puncture wounds. We can't find a thing. The same thoughts run through our minds as she confirms aloud.

"No knife wounds."

Chris bags the knife and looks at me. "Somewhere, there is a person walking around with stab wounds and no doubt drawing a lot of attention. Tribble, check the local hospitals and note any knife injuries that have come in over the past twenty-four hours."

"Yes, Sir," Tribble says, writing a quick note in his notebook.

"Tribble," I begin with my instructions. "You will also need to ensure that only relevant personnel come into this house. This is now an active crime scene and needs to be cordoned off, with a police presence monitoring the front and rear entrance until further notice. After that, I need you to canvas the neighbours to see if they have seen or heard anything unusual over the past forty-eight hours."

"Will do," he answers. Will do, what? I'd better break him in quickly, I haven't got the time for any funny business.

"Will do, what?" I ask.

"Will do, Detective Inspector."

"That's better," I say, making the point. I don't tolerate sloppiness in the ranks. People in my business work hard to get where they are, so it's imperative that the chain of command is understood and followed to the letter.

"Chris, are SOCO on their way?" He nods, so I carry on. "Leave them to get everything bagged and tagged. Let's keep looking for the missing wallet. I suspect from the state of Ray's face that there is another person out there, possibly a victim."

"Another victim?" Tribble begins to argue. "But this man is dead."

"I can see that, Tribble," I explain. "But we don't know exactly what happened here and we need to find who Ray was with last night as soon as possible. He or she may be the attacker, or they may be both the attacker and the victim," I say to him patiently. Tribble is beginning to irritate me with his comments.

I catch Daisy's blue-eyed stare and we share a quick eye roll. Rookies, when will they learn to listen and take note?

I walk to Chris, all the time checking the kitchen and dining room and peering into the lounge, looking for the parcel that the neighbour tried to deliver. I can't see it anywhere.

"Chris, can you put out a search on local hospitals for any knife wound victims? Also, let's get that parcel from Mr Cross, the one he was trying to deliver."

I need to get back to the office to set up the case file and begin the incident board, so I finalise with Chris what we need to do and move through the kitchen diner and into the lounge to the front door. Daisy stands up and follows me. We need to catch up soon over a drink because we rarely meet each other at work, and if we don't make a catch-up date now, we'll forget.

My eyes wander to a bookcase in the lounge. There are several photo frames of different sizes displayed on top of the unit. The largest silver frame stops me in my tracks. Shit. It's a photo taken about five months ago of Ben and I at a local pizza restaurant.

We're both smiling and about to take a massive bite of a delectable pepperoni pizza. I remember that night well. I'd managed to get off work early and had made the most of the unexpected treat by spending time with Ben, enjoying a meal out and a jaunt to the cinema.

Daisy looks at the photo frame I hadn't realised I had picked up and was now holding, and stares at the photo. A cold shiver runs down my spine. Questions are swirling around in my head. Her face looks as worried as I feel. "Holy shit, Steph. What's this?"

"I don't know," I whisper. "I haven't seen him in eleven years. He must have been following us. Jesus, for how long? Why?" I shake my head in disbelief.

I feel violated. I cannot believe that Ray had this photo so casually placed in his lounge, as though Ben and I were still his immediate family. I place the photo frame back on the bookcase and take a snapshot of it on my phone to use as evidence. I'll leave the SOCO to do the rest. There are answers that I need and quickly. I'm trying hard not to let the feeling of panic take over as my hands become clammy, my shoulders stiff.

There's only one person who I can think of to find information that others can't. The one person who can cross lines that I can't, or won't, because of my professional ethics. Jack Kinsey. He's the private investigator who works occasionally for Stuart and Jenny. He's good at fact finding and checking information, particularly when people want to go off the grid and disappear. Jenny and Stuart introduced me to him last year when I was involved in building a case to charge Jem's no-good alcoholic mother with blackmail. Jack is trustworthy, methodical and understands the importance of confidentiality. Jenny and Stuart cannot sing his praises highly enough whenever his name is mentioned in conversation. In the darkness, late at night, I can still hear his deep husky voice sometimes. When I feel lonely. You'd think I'd be used to the loneliness after eleven years.

It was a crazy time. I was making my name known at St. Aldates Police Station, Oxford, and had caught the eye of DI Jones, who pushed and supported me to take the Detective career route. I had passed the Detective Sergeant's exam just before the blackmail case, but with everything going on, I wanted to keep it quiet and keep my head down.

DI Brown was being head-hunted for promotion to Detective Chief Inspector and he needed someone he could trust and mentor to become the next DI. He wanted new blood, he'd told me, someone with integrity, not worn down by the job and ready to shape the unit into the new era of Thames Valley policing. With support from Stuart and Jenny, I had feverishly revised for and passed my Inspector's exam six months ago and, hey presto, before I knew it, I was heading up my own unit. I'm under probation for three months but with Mike Jones mentoring me, I feel that I can really make a difference. It was incredible, to think how I'd pulled myself out of those dark days to where I am now.

I feel a sense of sadness when I think about Jack. I had meant to get in touch with him when the blackmail case was closed following Joyce's death so that I could check that my friend Jem and The Lighthouse charity had not been left compromised by Joyce's actions. After all, she had been threatening to divulge extremely sensitive information about the charity and Jem's true identity. If details of the refuge homes had been released to the news and posted on social media a lot of already vulnerable people could be in danger.

Deep within me I'd also wanted to meet Jack in person, the owner of that husky voice. Where would that lead me? I'm not sure. I didn't even know if I was ready for another relationship. The fact that he had piqued my interest at all was very telling. Remember when you first meet someone, and you feel that instant connection? It's a bit like that but obviously without meeting the guy. Ben would be shouting with excitement from the rooftops if he thought I was remotely interested in another man. I'm pretty sure he thinks I'm going to be alone for the rest of my life, sitting in my armchair, a set of knitting needles and plain balls of wool on my lap and talking to myself.

What Ben doesn't realise is that I've erected walls of steel around my heart to protect me and ultimately to protect him. I don't want a repeat of Ray. I won't go through that again. That's the real reason why I hadn't contacted Jack after the blackmail case. I'm afraid. Finding Ray and the photo has unsettled me more than I realise.

Before I lose my nerve, I take out my phone, find Jack's number and send him a text:

Hey Jack, it's Steph. We were in touch last year regarding the blackmail case with Jem, Joyce and The Lighthouse charity. I need your help.

He's probably busy, or doesn't remember me, I tell myself and part of me hopes that he doesn't answer, because if he does then I have to face my fears. When all you have is what you know it's difficult to start again and let someone in, particularly if it's a man. Working with Chris isn't a problem because that's work. We banter and respect each other, but there's a fine line between being friendly, keeping focused and staying professional. This line is always carefully adhered to.

Daisy is watching me closely. Her forehead furrows with concern as she looks at me, her eyes asking a question. She reaches out to pat my arm.

"Drinks tomorrow? At mine or yours?" she asks.

"Sounds good. Mine OK? 7pm?" I say.

My phone vibrates. I smile at Daisy to confirm our catch-up and scan my phone.

It's Jack. Wow – that was quick!

> *Hey Steph, always happy to help a damsel in distress. Tell me where and when you want to meet.*

My tummy feels a little funny which is a sign that I'm feeling overwhelmed. The last time I had an emotional response like this was when I first met Ray. Being in an abusive spousal relationship doesn't encourage you to make new relationships, if anything, you can become paranoid and have an overwhelming sense of dread. The need to protect yourself and your child from pain, mentally or physically, fills every part of your body.

Despite this I need Jack's help, so I have to get over my feelings of anxiety and bite the bullet. Before I can change my mind, I send a reply:

> *Tonight, my place, 7pm?*

I take a deep breath and wait for his reply. It seems an endless wait:

> *I'll be there. See you tonight. Jack.*

I quickly type a thank you to him and give him my address before pressing send and putting my phone away. The deed is done. There's no going back and then, surprisingly, I feel some of the stress lift from my shoulders and a sense of calmness envelops me. I can't get out of this oppressive place fast enough.

Chapter 2: Waiting

Unknown, the night before

The hood from my coat covers my face but I can still see my target. The house across the road. His house. On this dark, cold night. I shuffle back behind the wall of the alleyway. It's ideal for lurking in the shadows. His house lights are on. A woman wearing a grey coat went in there thirty minutes go but I couldn't see her face. Another possible victim. Luring them into his home. Should I go and check on her? No, I'll give her three more minutes. My hand strokes the smooth, cold steel handle of the knife tucked safely in the inside pocket of my coat.

The front door is suddenly thrown open. I hear the woman sobbing as she runs through the small front garden and into the street. The first thing I notice is that she isn't wearing a coat. Her head is facing down and her long hair falls over her face. The second thing I notice are the blood stains and tears on her blouse. Her shoulders shudder as she runs on flat shoes towards the bus stop at the bottom of the road. The woman drags her handbag along the floor with one hand, the other clutches her chest as if she's in pain. What has the fucker done now? My hand fists in anger. That bastard does not deserve to live.

The woman stops as though she's not sure if she should keep running or wait for the bus. The running slows into a fast-paced walk. She keeps going.

My eyes search the area to see if anyone is around. The street is empty. I come out of the shadows, remembering to keep my head down and walk slowly toward his house. The door is not shut properly, the woman left it slightly ajar in her haste to leave his property. I force the knife further into my inside pocket to secure it and take out the pair of disposable vinyl gloves from my jeans pocket. I'm ready.

Carefully, I push the front door. I need to be invisible, keep my actions to the minimum. There's no sound apart from the slight creak of the hinge. I walk through the small hallway, noticing a woman's grey coat hanging from the black coat rack. As I reach the living room, I see him crouching on the laminate floor in the dining area. His head is down and he's holding his groin with both hands. There are blood splatters on the carpet. Shit. I scan the living room. There's a bookcase with photos and two small brown leather sofas. My eye rests on the baseball bat sitting between the armchair and the fake fireplace.

"Shit," the man mutters to the floor. "Fucking bitch. I'll get her for this."

There's also a screwdriver on the floor.

So, this is where the monster lives. A nice, ordinary semi-detached house. Hidden amongst normal people, where he can keep up the pretence of respectability. That's why I'm here, to even the odds. To make him pay. As I walk towards him his face crinkles in pain when he starts to move. What a wimp. I pick up the baseball bat before he has time to think. He's still rubbing his balls and his eyes are half closed. He's shaking his head. I bet he's never met someone who was willing to fight back before. Muttering an oath, he uses the wall to help him to stand.

When he's upright and looking straight at me, I study this pitiful excuse of a man. I see the scratch marks on his face and tiny speckles of blood dotted across his white linen shirt.

"No, you won't," I say, surprised at the lack of emotion in my voice. I pull back my hood to look at him fully, take a deep breath and use all my strength to swing the bat, aiming for the front of his head. I see the surprise in his eyes.

"You," he whispers, recognising my face just before the hollow sound of the baseball bat hits his head, breaking the silence. The sound reminds me of a hockey stick hitting a ball. I watch with interest as he grunts in pain, let's out a loud moan, then falls to the floor with a thud. Now he knows what it's like to be on the receiving end of a violent assault.

Seconds later he groans, holding his head and pushes himself to his feet again. Go on. Keep getting up. I can do this all night. I'm behind him now and aim for the back of his head. The sound of his bones cracking and the crunching as the wood meets his skull reassure me that this time he won't get up. I wait. Nothing. Not a sound.

I search the kitchen units for some bleach or similar. I twist the lid of the yellow bleach bottle and pour it over the handle of the bat, rubbing the sterile liquid briskly with my right glove. I'm not rinsing the blood off. That's proof to me that he's where he should be, on that cold hard floor. Alone and unloved. Something shiny catches my eye on the floor next to the washing machine, and I bend my knees to take a closer look and discover the handle of a large knife. Unsure of what to do, I decide to leave the knife where it is. I place the bat on the kitchen floor not far from the sink unit and walk over to him. I feel no guilt, just hatred. I grab his heavy shoulders to turn his body so that he's facing me, and for a moment I believe he's staring at me. Am I afraid? Do I shudder? Not a chance.

His eyes are glazed over. He's dead. It won't make a difference in the grand scheme of things. Still, there's a sense of peace that he won't hurt any more people. I pick him up by the shoulders and shuffle him around so that he's facing upwards toward the ceiling.

I stop to replay my actions and movements since arriving here and I question where I may have left any evidence. When I'm satisfied that the police will find no trace of me I walk to the front door. The only thing left to do is to take the grey coat off the rack on my way out. There's no point in someone else getting the blame for something I've done. She'll have suffered enough.

Job done.

Chapter 3: Meeting Jack

Steph

At the office, I start putting together the case file and attach Ray's photo to the centre of the incident board with sticky tape. I use this time to write my thoughts and questions in my A4 notebook. Collecting ideas and questions from my initial assessment is part of my usual work pattern when I start a fresh case. I place the book into an opaque blue folder so that I can collect any loose pictures, photos or notes as the case develops.

Ray's death has given me a feeling of catharsis, a huge sense of relief and closure because that part of my life is now over, and I don't have to worry anymore that he will one day turn up on my front doorstep. That relief is counterbalanced by the worry of having to share my past with my colleagues and other professionals. There are going to be hard questions to answer when we explore Ray's history, particularly when I am forced to acknowledge spousal abuse. There will be court judgements on file, hospital photos and medical records to show domestic violence within the marriage. My hands feel clammy, my head starts to pound and for a moment I put my arms on my desk and rest my head on my open hands. Don't let him win, face what you need to face and move on.

Images of Ray's violence fill my mind and I start chewing the inside of my cheek again, wondering if I will ever get over my sheer anguish of those days. I remember the absolute shock the first time he'd been violent toward me. I had burnt the chicken roast dinner because I'd been consoling Ben who was teething at the time. At ten months old Ben and his lovely angelic chubby smile had been replaced by despair, sore gums and rosy cheeks, and had been crying constantly through the pain of his back teeth coming through. During a short respite when Ben had found comfort from sucking a frozen teething ring, I'd managed to produce two rather unappetising plates of fishfingers, chips and peas.

When Ray had come home from work and sat down at the dining table, I'd put the plates of food on the table and took my place opposite him. The shock of watching him pick his plate up and hurl it with force at my face left me shaking as I automatically raised my arms to protect myself.

"Ray!" I shouted, through tears of panic and rage, my heart racing. I just couldn't believe it. There is nothing in the marriage manual that prepares you for the day when a dinner plate catches you on the side of the head, thrown hard enough to cause your vision to blur. Or prepares you for the impenetrable band of your husband's hand as he grabs your hair and yanks your head backwards. The pain feels like your neck is about to snap. I was facing the ceiling and couldn't see anything because my eyes were awash with tears.

"Please stop. Ray, stop!" I sobbed, begging him to stop, my cheeks sodden from the rolling tears. I kept begging for him to let me go. My hands were trying to push him away, but he was behind me and much stronger than I was. No, no one prepares you for the moment when your husband slaps you so hard that your teeth rattle and shoot out of your mouth. So hard that you and the dining chair you are sitting in are hauled backwards. I cannot explain the absolute fear, shock and the pain that gripped me from Ray's actions that probably only took a few minutes but felt like a lifetime. No, I am not looking forward to reliving my experiences. Not one bit.

I had put Ray and his abuse behind me many years ago and I'm now wondering whether I'll need to be recused from the case or even be marked as a potential suspect. I need to speak to my boss, DCI Mike Jones, to check if I'm able to stay on and oversee Ray's murder. What a mess.

I was on my own last night, binge watching a crime series on Netflix in my living room, dressed down in a purple sweat top and pants and my fluffy bunny slippers happily enjoying the company of a glass of red wine and a large bar of my favourite chocolate. I'd chilled out on the sofa and lost myself in the comedy-drama crime series. The dark blue three-piece suite had been chosen for its comfort and high framed back and sleek straight armrests. It goes well with the white painted walls and the solitary piece of artwork, one of Jem's paintings, a watercolour of the beautiful red and white lighthouse that stands proudly on Portland Bill. It's aptly called Proud and is signed by Jem. The painting sits pride of place over my mahogany mantelpiece instead of a mirror. This painting has huge sentimental value to me because Jem is an up and coming, much sought after artist and paints under the pseudonym of Marnie Lake. Two photos of Ben are placed side by side and adorn a lounge wall, and a black framed A4 photo of myself and Ben sits in the windowsill next to a glass vase of just opened daffodils. Yes, I can certainly vouch for the comfort of the sofa, it's great for lounging. If only the sofa could vouch for me. So, while Ben had been enjoying a sleepover last night at his friend Josh's house – two doors to the right of us – I was home alone. I don't even have an alibi. Fuck!

I quickly text Chris to ask if he's retrieved Ray's parcel from the neighbour yet. The ping comes back:

Yes. It's an Amazon delivery for a pair of Nike trainers.

I reply:

Anything odd about the delivery?

No.

I tap back:

That's good news. Let me know if you find anything else.

I wait for his response:

Will do. Speak later.

I pop my phone into my black trouser pocket, grab everything I need and head out to pick up Ben from Josh's house for 5.30pm. His mum, Amanda, has been a godsend when I'm working 9–5 shifts and don't want Ben to be on his own too much. He's growing up fast, but he's only just turned fourteen and I feel reassured that he's got someone nearby who can help him if there's an emergency. Of course, it's an added bonus that Josh, with his tall, slightly plump frame and almost red hair, also happens to be Ben's school buddy. I promised I'd call my Lighthouse friends Stuart and Jenny Greyson to update them about Ray's death and Jack is due here at 7pm, so I need to do something quick for dinner.

I pull out yesterday's beef stew from the fridge and reheat it in the microwave, put fresh vegetables on to boil and cut off chunky bread for dipping. I'm aiming to have dinner with Ben before Jack arrives. Ben usually spends his evenings in his room catching up on homework, chatting to friends on his phone and internet browsing – while I check on him every so often. I'd like to think that I'm a diligent parent because I closely monitor my son's social media activity and as a two-person family unit we're lucky that we're close and chat most of the time.

I can't help but smile. I'm probably showing my age now thinking back to my own teenage years and a time when we had to interact verbally in person, by letter or by using the landline telephone. My thoughts turn to Ben. I don't feel too uneasy about introducing him to Jack, after all, Jack is simply someone who is helping me with a case. I look at my watch, I think I just about have time to fit in that phone call to the Greysons.

I chat to Jenny while the veg is cooking, explaining about Ray's death and the possibility that there may be a victim out there with knife wounds who may have killed Ray in self-defence.

I hear a startled gasp from Jenny as I recite what we found at Ray's house and I'm not surprised to hear Jenny's voice rise a few octaves, shocked at the sudden news.

"Oh, my goodness, Steph!" she cries. "I can't believe it. Ray. Dead. Did someone kill him? Are you OK? Is Ben OK?"

Questions rush from her and I take a deep breath before answering. I'll try to be as honest as I can without stepping out of the realms of police confidentiality.

"I know it's sudden. I can't believe he's dead. I know he wasn't good to me, but he was Ben's father. I'm not sure if he's hurt someone or not, or if this was premeditated. We need to find who he was with last night, put a timeline together. Then we'll know more."

"Yes, of course. I appreciate that you can only reveal certain information at this stage." She has always been so kind, so understanding.

"I'm still in shock. I haven't seen him in eleven years. But I was once married to him and I loved him for a short while until he started hurting me. I haven't told Ben yet. I'll tell him tomorrow. I need to think about what to say to him. I can't just blurt it out."

"I know," said Jenny in a reassuring tone. I can almost feel the warmth of her words. "Take your time and do it when you feel it's right for Ben. Just make sure he doesn't hear it from anyone else first."

"I will." I hear the saucepan with the vegetables hiss and water bubbles over onto the gas hob and I quickly turn the control switch to a lower setting, all the while still talking to Jenny. When I tell her about the photograph I've found of myself and Ben on show in Ray's lounge she suggests that I ask Jack to look into Ray's finances and phone records, to see if they give an insight into who he was talking to and to see if he had any money worries prior to his death.

"I texted him earlier," I said, "he's coming over tonight to discuss how he can help."

"Really?" says Jenny, and I can hear relief inflected in her voice. "I'm glad. Stuart and I have worked with Jack for a few years now. He's been in involved in various projects such as checking the location, history, court arrangements and criminal convictions of abusive spouses to ensure the safety of women and children in our refuge homes. Their safety always comes first. He also chased financial information and the whereabouts of Jem's mother during her deplorable blackmail stint last year."

"I know," I say, and my shoulders sag and I suddenly feel weary. She's telling me nothing I don't already know. "And they should be protected from further harm or intimidation. I can't tell you how much I appreciate and care for you and Stuart. For saving me and Ben." My words come out husky with emotion, and my teeth subconsciously nibble the inside of my right cheek. I hadn't felt safe in my marital home for a long time, but I felt I couldn't leave, that I had nowhere to go, no one to turn to. Not until Shore House. That was my saving grace.

"Oh, Steph," Jenny speaks, her voice trembling with emotion. "I wish I were there to give you a hug right now."

"Me too, Jenny," I say sadly.

"Going back to Jack, he's one of the good guys, Steph."

"So you keep telling me."

"Maybe one day you'll believe it."

We say our goodbyes and hang up. I use a knife to check the vegetables. They're turning soft. I've overcooked them again. It's the story of my life. Overcooking things. I turn the gas off, set the microwave to heat the stew and begin laying two places at the mahogany dining table which seats four people in the spacious dining room.

"Ben!" I call. No answer.

I walk through the lounge and stand with conviction at the bottom of the stairs.

"Ben! Dinner's ready!" I call.

"Coming," calls a voice as Ben appears at the top of the stairs and makes his way down to me.

"I'm famished!" he states. Funny how teenagers are either always starving or always famished.

As we begin to eat the hot supper, I bring up the topic of Jack's visit to the house tonight.

"I'm on a case at the moment and I need the help of someone that Stuart and Jenny know. His name is Jack."

"Jack?" he asks, his big brown eyes catching mine across the table. "Do I know him?"

"No. I talked to him briefly last year when I was working a blackmail case. But no, you don't know him."

"Jack's going to come over tonight to help me with some aspects of the case. Are you OK with that?" I ask, trying to not to sound too worried.

"Sure." He chews a spoonful of stew carefully, then breaks off a piece of bread for dipping.

"He's not a serial killer or anything, is he?"

"No," I smile. "No, Ben. Jenny says he's one of the good guys."

I study Ben's features. He's tall for fourteen, almost as tall as me and I'm five feet seven. He's got dark hair just like me and Ray, and I think he gets the curls from me. He keeps it short because he doesn't want to get teased at school. I would venture to say that he's got Ray's distinguished narrow nose which reminds me of Branwell Bronte, brother of the famous Bronte writing sisters. To me, his mother, he's the most handsome young man with his full pink lips and a small cluster of freckles dotted below his big brown eyes. He has a few hobbies which include football, computers and cars. He also has the most caring and mature approach to life. I'm not sure where he gets that from.

That's me and my boy Ben, as we sit down to one last main meal together before I have to change his life forever, before I tell him that his dad has died.

Ben is in his room finishing his homework when the doorbell buzzes. *Goodness, calm down, Steph, be cool, you're thirty-five-years-old for goodness sake! Don't overthink this.* I open the door and my heart misses a beat. Jack. He's extremely easy on the eye. To be fair I haven't actually met Jack before, I've only spoken to him over the phone, therefore imagining what he looks like has varied from month to month. I close my eyes for a moment and recall the deep and husky sound of his voice. I'm not sure what I expected him to look like, but it wasn't this.

He oozes confidence, stands at least six feet two, possibly in his mid to late thirties and looks extremely lean and physically fit in his dark grey jeans and blue and white checked shirt. He's bald but it suits him and is very sexy, and the stubble on his oval jaw makes him look a little rugged. I close my eyes briefly to pray he's not married or in a serious relationship.

Jack smiles and I'm lost. His soft, soulful brown eyes are so clear and honest I find it hard to turn away.

"Hey, Steph, good to finally meet you. You going to invite me in?" His deep husky voice calms me and thrills me at the same time. *Keep calm. Keep calm.*

"Hey, Jack." I raise an arm to beckon him inside. "Sorry, please come in. Thanks for coming so promptly."

"No problem. Your text sounded important," he says walking casually through my narrow hallway and into the cosy lounge of my semi-detached house. "Stuart and Jenny once told me that you were one of the strongest people they knew, and if you ever asked for help it must be important."

"Stuart and Jenny are good people," I respond with a smile. "I wouldn't be here right now if it wasn't for them. Ben might be in care. Our lives could be totally different. I owe them everything."

"Then tell me what you need," he says with authority, making himself at home in one of the comfy, blue and very lounge-worthy chairs that completes my three-piece suite. I stand, hovering near his chair. I'm nervous. If I tell him about Ray and how he abused me he might look at me differently, and I don't want him to feel sorry for me.

"Before I tell you what happened today, I need to tell you about Ray, my ex-husband." I sit down in the second chair with the sofa separating us and clasp my hands together, my arms resting on my knees. I was about to explain Ray and my marriage when Jack's voice broke the looming silence.

"When Stuart and Jenny asked me to investigate Joyce's blackmail attempt last year, I knew there was a connection to you and to Shore House. Jenny revealed that you and Ben had stayed there for a while. I've done some work for the Greysons, I know about The Lighthouse charity refuge homes and how they help vulnerable women and children who have experienced domestic violence. That's why I work for them. To help make a difference and protect people."

"Jack," I sigh. "I still feel shame when I think about what I allowed Ray to do to me. I let him belittle me, beat me, hurt me. I became so despondent I struggled to look after Ben. Finally, after he'd tried to strangle me, had dislocated my shoulder and cut me continuously with a knife, I ended up in the hospital with my three-year-old son crying next to me. That's when I knew something had to change. I was introduced to Jenny Greyson and she took Ben and myself to Shore House."

"I'm so sorry, Steph," he says, standing to face me. He didn't move. His soft brown eyes held such sorrow and the grimace of his mouth and drawn eyebrows reflected a feeling of uncertainty. It was as though he wanted to give me a hug but didn't feel it was appropriate.

"No one should have to go through that." He sounds angry and I can see by the hard lines of his face that he's trying hard to rein in his feelings. "A man who uses his fists on a woman or child is the lowest kind of human being in my book, and I've met quite a few monsters."

I feel a little awkward, I'm not used to people feeling angry on my behalf. Even Stuart, who is usually so calm, doesn't let his emotions cloud his judgement. I swiftly move the subject on to how we found Ray's body this afternoon, the scratches to his face, the baseball bat covered in blood, the two bloody head wounds and the bloody knife. Finally, I finish with the strangest piece of evidence, the photo of Ben and me in his lounge. The silver framed photo taken of us at the pizza restaurant. Throughout my description my voice begins to shake until it's nothing but a whisper. I feel a cold shudder working its way along my shoulders and down my spine and I absently rub my arms for warmth.

"That's not good," he mutters. I can almost hear his brain ticking away as he tries to make sense of what he's hearing. I know how he feels.

"I know. He must have been watching me or having someone watch me and Ben. Just thinking about it makes me feel sick, let alone the fact that he displayed us both as his fake family in his lounge for everyone to see. To top it all, I don't have an alibi for last night as I was on my own watching TV because Ben was having a sleepover with a friend." I slump in the chair feeling demoralised.

"Jesus, Jack, yesterday my life was good. I had a sense of order in my life, living my quiet but comfortable existence with my son and enjoying my work. Now I feel as though everything is being ripped away from me bit by bit."

Jack walks to my chair and looks down at me. I can't bear to look up, I don't want his pity. I don't need his pity.

"Steph, Ray was a piece of shit, you know that. He did shit to people and who knows if someone decided it was time for payback. Then that's on him. And for starters, if you need an alibi, I'm your man. We were here throughout the night watching TV, just tell me what we were watching or if we were doing something else," he says with a quick lift of his eyebrow.

"Jack!" I admonish. I can feel myself blushing which irritates me because I don't usually blush. I tilt my head to look up at him and see the smile on his face. I think he might be flirting with me and I like it, but I feel out of my depth. I push my hair to one side, exposing the side of my neck and smile.

"We. Were. Watching. A crime series on Netflix," I say, the first thing that comes to my mind, and I punctuate each word to make sure I believe the lie just as much as he does. My heart is beating so fast and I can't take my eyes from his full smiling lips. They are so damn kissable. I want him to kiss me. I suddenly feel a warmth settle in my tummy and it slowly makes its way down to my groin. *Bloody hell, I haven't felt such an intense attraction since Ray.*

"I can't possibly use you as my alibi, Jack. It wouldn't work."

"Why not? Did you kill him?" He leans slightly toward me, his body relaxed. He carefully lowers his arm and his fingers touch my shoulder lightly.

His gentle touch sears my skin through my thin white blouse. Butterflies flutter in my tummy and leave when he withdraws his hand. The urge to throw myself at him, to tell him to kiss me as though it's the end of the world, even though I've only just met him, is overwhelming. I don't know why he's being so careful. I'm not made of glass.

"Of course not! What a stupid question!" I can't help but snap.

"Well then, you need to take yourself out of the suspect equation and into the let's work the evidence arena. It's the only way."

I stand up, move to the drinks cabinet and turn to him.

"I need a glass of red wine. Would you like one?"

"Please." His voice seems deeper, huskier. I take out two glass and fill them with the wine. I walk over to him and hand him a glass. His movements are sleek and confident, almost regal and they remind me of the graceful movement of a cat.

We clink glasses. "Here's to spending last night together watching a crime series," he says, taking a large gulp of the liquid while offering me the sweetest smile. My hand shakes slightly, and I jolt my glass and watch despairingly as red wine splashes onto the front of my white blouse. Great!

"Bugger!" I mutter under my breath.

Damn. I start to unbutton my high neck white blouse, forgetting that Jack is here and then I look up to see him staring at me and suddenly my hands are still. There's an old scar just below my breastbone that stretches across the top of my upper chest and stops just short of the right side of my neck. Usually I wear button-up blouses, high neck jumpers or wrap a scarf around my neck to cover it. I think he's noticed the scar.

He doesn't say anything, just looks at me with questioning eyes. I think he wants to touch me, so I nod slowly and watch as he reaches forward so that his fingers gently touch the top of the scar that peeks from my slightly opened blouse. The touch lasts seconds but feels like a lifetime. And just like before, his touch burns my skin and a warmth spreads through my tummy, a warmth that feels both alien and sexual at the same time. No man has touched me since Ray. It's been fourteen years since Ray touched me with kindness and love, that's a long time to be without close human contact.

"Did he do that?" he asks quietly, and I sense a shift of emotion as his whole body seems to stiffen. A frown appears on his forehead and his lips form a grim line.

"Yes," I whisper, feeling slightly unsteady on my feet.

"Are there more?" His eyes study my face, asking for honesty.

"Yes, a few, but some aren't on the outside. Some of them are in here and others in here." I look at him and touch my heart and my head with my hand. My lips tremble as I search his unsmiling face and try to lose myself in his eyes.

A memory surfaces of Ray coming with us to the play park one Saturday morning. It was early and the park was empty. Ben was two-years-old and he'd tripped when running to the swings.

"Swing. Swing," he'd called excitedly, before falling flat on his face on the black rubber play surface and giving a loud wail.

I was about to rush to his side when Ray had grabbed my arm.

"Leave him," he'd said. "He'll never learn to do things for himself if you're constantly going to help him."

"But he's only two, Ray, and he's crying," I'd argued, trying to pull out of his grasp. Ben was still lying face down, crying on the floor.

"Mummy, Mummy!"

I twisted and wrenched until Ray let me go. I knew I would pay the price for not doing as he'd said, but my maternal feelings were stronger than my need to survive. Ray did a quick check of the park, rushed forward, grabbed my long curly hair in his hand, marched me to the metal frame of the swings past Ben and smashed my head into the bar.

He was so quick.

"Ray!" I begged. "Ray, please." I panicked and tried to reach behind me to get his hands off my head. Tears were running down my face. I could feel the skin tear open on my forehead, stars were swimming before my eyes and the pain was almost too much to bear. Then, for good measure, he smashed my head into the bar again. I was sobbing and screaming.

"Please stop! Please stop!"

"Fuck you!" He suddenly let go of me and pushed me to the floor. I turned to see him storming out of the play park, anger rolling off him in waves and growling his final insult:

"Whining bitch!" he spat my way, before disappearing from view.

Holding my throbbing head with one hand and trying to find a tissue in my handbag with the other to wipe my nose, my bloody forehead and my tears, I turn to Ben. At some point during Ray's assault he'd stopped crying and was now standing. Ben took one look at me and tottered my way.

"Mummy. Sowwy," he said as he raised his arms to me.

"Hey, baby boy." I stooped low to gather his little body to me, wincing in pain as I stood to hold him in my arms.

"I love you so much, Ben," I whimpered, holding on to my young child, trying not to cry. And all I could hear on that silent Saturday morning was the sound of my choked voice as I soothingly told him that everything would be alright.

***

"Steph?" Jack's voice brings me back to reality, to the here and now. "You OK? I think I lost you for a moment."

"Sorry. It was a memory," I reply. I feel a single teardrop roll down my cheek.

"Can I?" Jack asks. His eyes calm me. Why, I don't know. Yet. But it's something I'd like to explore. I nod. Then I watch in slow motion as he reaches to me and his thumb softly traces the tear along my skin, drying it as he goes.

"I'm glad he's dead." He doesn't look glad, he looks angry.

"Me too."

"Now drink your wine," he says as he points to my glass.

"Why?" I ask.

"Because you've had a bad day and it might help you to unwind. And…"

"And?" I ask.

"Because we need to look into Ray's death objectively. Did Ray take the photo? If not, who did? Was someone hired to follow you guys? Was Ray in trouble? Financial or otherwise? And finally…" His heated gaze studies my face as our eyes lock. "Because I'm attracted to you and this is not the right time to be following up on that attraction."

"You're attracted to me?" My voice rises an octave. He's attracted to me. My pulse is racing, and I can't help smiling. He's attracted to me. I bite my lower lip and look at him, watching his facial reaction. Jack inhales sharply and his pupils dilate. What on earth is the matter with me? I don't even know if he's married, single or part of a commune.

"I'm attracted to you too, Jack," I say quietly, and the back of his hand gently brushes my cheek.

"Good, and before you ask…" He offers an almost shy smile, displaying a touch of vulnerability. "I'm not married or in a relationship. I'm not widowed or divorced. I don't have kids and I definitely don't do affairs."

I look at him, relieved and shocked by his sudden revelations. This man knows how to get straight to the point.

"I'm relieved to hear that. It was on my mind." I respect his honesty and find his frankness quite endearing.

"Now, do you have a copy of the photo you found of you and Ben?" he asks, turning and heading back to his chair.

I pick up my phone which is sitting next to the grey lamp on the small table between the sofa and the chair and begin to flick through the photos until I find the copy of the one at Ray's house. Something tells me this is going to be a long night. I sigh and rub my forehead as the door opens and the tall gangly frame of my teenage son enters the room. Ben brushes his fingers through his short black curly hair, looks at Jack and I, shrugs and asks:

"Mum, have you seen my black Nike trainers?" He looks at me, then at Jack.

"Ben, this is Jack. He's a friend of Stuart and Jenny."

"Hey," Jack says, and places the phone screen down so that Ben can't see the photo.

"Hey, Jack." Ben looks disinterested, as though there's a stranger in our home every night.

I find the former muddy, newly cleaned trainers on the mat by the kitchen door.

"Thanks, Mum. See you in the morning." He kisses my cheek and heads back upstairs.

Well, that was easier than I thought, I muse, as I begin to follow Ben up the stairs to my bedroom to change.

"Back in a minute," I tell Jack, "I'm just going to change my blouse."

Jack opens his mouth to say something. He changes his mind and stands up.

"I'll nip to the car to get my laptop," he says.

I can't help but feel that my day is getting better now that Jack's here. I hope he and I can find out what Ray was up to prior to his death so that my team and I can investigate his murder and move on with our lives.

Chapter 4: Fake families

Ray, six months ago

I was born Raymond James Delossi, the youngest of two sons to Elsie and James Delossi thirty-six years ago. I was just over six pounds in weight and wailed with the lungs of a tenor my mum, Elsie, used to fondly recall each year I celebrated my birthday. My wispy hair was blonde and slowly turned darker as I grew older, which seemed to match my green eyes. From the moment I was born my name was shortened to Ray.

My brother David, three years my senior, was taller than me, that is until I reached thirteen when I had a massive growth spurt. Everyone called him Dave because it suited him better. He wasn't a tidy person, he didn't keep himself clean, couldn't even put a comb through his dark straight hair and, unfortunately, he'd inherited Dad's fiery temper. There were odd things about Dave that worried me when we were growing up, such as the fact that he could be charming one minute and extremely arrogant the next. He was brilliant at manipulating people, including mum and myself by exploiting our good nature such as talking us into doing his share of chores around the house because he felt ill, explaining that we were helping him out or complimenting us that we would do the task better.

When I was ten-years-old I'd unwittingly discovered one of Dave's more serious traits one Saturday afternoon when, out of boredom, I'd found myself exploring the old waste ground at the back of our house. I'd been swishing a stick I'd found into the long grass looking for anything of value when I heard something crying. It sounded like a cat mewling in pain. I looked to where the sound was coming from and found Dave kneeling beside the creature and hitting it with a stick. The black cat lay on the wet grass, blood streaking matted lines along its fur as it cowered between each blow, crying. Yellow piercing eyes look pleadingly at him, and in that moment I was so angry with Dave for hurting this small animal that I pushed him hard on the shoulder and I shouted at him:

"You're hurting it! Leave it alone!"

"Bugger off! Go find your own fun. I like hurting it," he'd bragged in my face. My whole body shook with rage. I wanted to pound Dave in the face with my fist until it was bloody and sore. I chose to save the cat first and in my blistering fury I turned to Dave and pushed him hard to the ground, away from the defenceless creature. I kneeled to the cat's bloody body and lifted it gently into my arms.

"Stop being such a psycho, Dave, and pick on someone your own size," I told him as I walked away. The cat's blood began to seep on to my blue jumper and I was worried that mum would be mad at me. Then I felt a blow to my back, followed by a crunch as shooting pains seared my lower back and took my breath away. I placed the cat carefully on the ground, rubbing my back to ease the ache and turned to Dave.

"You bloody prick! Don't ever touch me again!" I screamed, as I grabbed the front of his brown jacket and pulled him into my face. My brain had shut down and I just wanted to hurt him the way he'd hurt the cat, so I pushed him back slightly, raised my fisted right arm and punched him in the face letting the pent-up anger out with my fists.

"Ray!" Dave seemed shocked.

"Don't bloody Ray me, you psycho! Touch me again and I'll kill you!" I could feel the blood rush to my face in anger. I guess I had a temper too. For the second time that Saturday afternoon I bent down to pick up the cat so that I could check if it was OK and take him home. This time my psychotic brother left me alone.

***

"When life doesn't go the way you want, you change it to make life give you what you want." That's what my dad always used to say when he was home from prison after being detained behind bars at Her Majesty's pleasure. My dad had been away from home for the best part of my life. In fact, it's surprising that he and my mum managed to conceive my older brother and myself during his short breaks from Her Royal Highness.

My dad, Jim Delossi. He was short, around five feet four, with his brown hair thinning around the side of his scalp and the top layer combed over to cover his hairless head. He had the biggest blue eyes I've ever seen and thrived on telling anyone who would listen about his Italian descent. He also used this as an excuse for his foul temper. His great-grandad had arrived in London with a pregnant wife in tow from a small obscure Italian village a few years back. Many of the family members had gone back to Italy and those who hadn't were now dead.

My dad, Jim, the not so successful shop burglar. He would try his hand stealing anything from jewellery to second-hand electronics and clothes. I don't think it helped that he was fat which meant he wasn't good at making quick exits from his chosen venues.

I watched my dad try to make a quick exit one time. I remember it well because it was interesting and funny at the same time. I'd been twelve years old when the police had knocked on the front door of our terraced house in Tower Hamlets, East London. mum had opened the door and dad had taken one glimpse of their uniforms and panicked, pushing his big body out of the scruffy old armchair and making his exit through the kitchen door and into the overgrown, messy yard.

"Jim!" Mum had shouted at him, her brown hair hanging limply on her shoulders and her tired-looking face seemed to age before my eyes. Her thin lips pulled together in a grim line as she wondered what my errant father had been up to now.

"Jim Delossi, what have you done now?" her usually soft voice raised in annoyance. "When I get hold of you, I'm going to smack you around the head with the frying pan. Knock some sense into you."

My mum was lovely. She stood taller than dad at five feet eight, had a slim frame and believed that working hard was the best way to get on in life. I delivered newspapers every morning and weekend from the age of thirteen. I gave mum ten pounds every Friday to help out with food and saved the rest. I lived frugally, never spent a penny. I was saving so that I could leave London and leave this miserable life.

Back to the old man, I'd followed him, watching with interest from the kitchen window as he'd waddled to the back gate, through the weeds and around the old black bike that Dave had left in the middle of the yard. Dad was still wearing his dirty white saggy vest, worn out black slippers, crumpled faded jeans and sported a balding mop of grey hair. It was comical, the waddling. He looked like a penguin. The two police officers scrambled into the kitchen, past the scuffed units and swiftly followed dad into the yard. Dad wouldn't get very far. He never did. He always got caught. All for a few pounds.

There was a noise as the back gate was kicked open and I saw Dad's white vested belly first. His hands were pulled behind his back, probably handcuffed. The police officers held on to each of dad's arms as they walked him back, escorting him carefully through the yard and into the open kitchen door to the house. Dad in the meantime had been twisting from side to side, trying to shake off the hands that were holding his arms.

"Bastards!" Dad's voice boomed, loud enough for the whole street to hear. "Bugger off and leave me alone. I ain't done nothing."

I continued to watch, open-mouthed, as the taller officer spoke to my dad:

"Jim Delossi, I am arresting you on suspicion of stealing goods to the value of £1000 from Cheyney's Jewellers."

"Their stuff is fake," Dad shouted as spit dribbled down his chin. "Why would I take it?"

The officer picked up where he'd left off:

"You do not have to say anything, but it may harm your defence if you do not mention when questioned something you later rely on in court. Anything you do say may be given in evidence. We're taking you to Bow Police Station."

"Let me put some shoes on. These slippers are knackered," Dad asked in his usual fashion, while mum went to the bottom of the stairs and picked up dad's dull black lace-ups. I watched the scene in fascination from the corner of the room. It was like living in your own soap opera.

My thirteen-year-old brother walked in at that moment, his gangly frame stooping slightly as he moved. With long, dark, overgrown matted hair, dirty clothes and unhealthy skin tone, I suspected that he used more of the drugs than he sold. He never went to school because he was busy making money and a name for himself as a minor drug dealer on the estate. He sold mostly weed.

"What's going on?" asked Dave in his deep baritone voice as he put his phone away in his pocket.

"Your dad's being arrested," mum stated. "Again."

"Shut your mouth, Elsie," Dad bellowed.

"Dad?" Dave looked at our father, annoyance showing on his sallow grey face. "What is the bloody point of nicking things if you always get bloody caught!"

"David!" Mum's stern voice warned. She knew that Dave's temper was no better than our dad's.

Dave stood taller than dad, most people did. He walked casually over to him, hands balled in fists at his side and spat in his face. Dad pulled at the officers, looked up into Dave's face and bellowed:

"You little bugger! Who do you think you are?" Dad kicked him hard in the balls. Dave crumpled into himself holding his privates, and then, before my eyes, he pulled himself upright, stepped forward, pulled back his arm and punched Dad hard in the face. Dad stumbled back several steps, his nose bloodied and sitting at an awkward angle.

"Oi!" The tall police officer stepped in. "That's enough!"

"I'm going get you for that, you little sod," Dad threatened. "One day I'll get you for that."

"What the fuck use are you to anyone?" Dave's face looked at Dad as if he was a piece of shit on the floor and stormed off.

"Bugger," said the police officer.

"Bugger," I said.

"Damn right!" Mum added.

"You going to be alright, Mrs Delossi?" asked the taller police officer.

"I'll be fine. It's better when he's out of my hair anyway," she shrugged. Then, as an afterthought, she asked:

"How did you know it was Jim?"

"His fingerprints were on the door handle and display cabinets," the shorter officer replied.

"Can I ask what he stole?" Mum was so polite, the opposite of my father.

"A selection of cubic zirconia necklaces, rings and earrings. The funny thing was he completely missed the real diamonds. He left their display case untouched." The taller officer's face flinched slightly in an attempt not to smile.

"Did you recover anything?" I asked, taking a step forward.

"A few necklaces he'd dropped on the floor as he left the premises. He left his fingerprints on those too."

"That just about sums him up," Mum stated wearily as she turned toward the kitchen. "Now, if you don't mind, I need to start the tea before I go to my cleaning job. Ray?" She looked at me. "Give us a hand, love. Then you can start your homework."

And that's why my mum gave up on my dad. She worked on the till in the local supermarket from 9am–4pm every day and four evenings a week she cleaned offices for cash. All of this to make ends meet when the man who should have been providing for her and us was languishing in prison with three meals a day, time to chill out, a roof over his head and no worries about paying the rent or paying the bills. One consolation though, at least she claimed benefits for being a single parent because dad was away for a lot of the time.

Eleven years ago, I had it all. The love of a good woman, a nice home and a child. I never wanted to turn out like my dad. I really wanted to turn my life around, but stuff got in the way. I've always liked school and Mum had made sure that I did my homework and kept my grades up. I wasn't overly bright in class but as I became older, I began to enjoy school more. English, history and physical education were my favourite subjects. The main problem was my temper, I felt like an explosive device set on timer that was stuck at two seconds. That was until something or someone set me off.

The move to Basingstoke came completely out of the blue. One minute I'd been having an eighteenth birthday pint of beer with my dad who had just finished a short stint at Wormwood Scrubs for stealing five gas barbeques from a local Do It Yourself superstore. Five barbeques? I can't be the only person in the world who realises that you can't fit five barbeques in a Ford Fiesta. Surely. And the next minute, during my pint, Dad introduces me to a man he met in prison, Danny Devlin, a man with so much dark facial hair that I had to stare a while to make out his small, brown eyes. He slouched his shoulders as he walked toward me, his hands deep in his pockets. He looked a bit younger than Dad who was forty.

"Ray, this is Danny," my dad said, pulling out a seat for Danny.

"Hey," I said, offering my pint up to him in acknowledgement.

"What're you drinking?" Dad pushed back his chair and stood up.

"Pint of lager would be good." Danny nodded to dad and watched him walked to the bar. He turned to me and said:

"Congrats. I hear it's your birthday. Happy eighteenth."

"Yeah. Thanks." I didn't know this man, so I didn't feel much like talking to him. I sat looking at my pint until Dad came back.

"Cheers, mate." Danny took the drink from Dad.

"Anyway," Danny said in his cockney nasal tone, "me and your dad, we've got a proposition for you."

Now they were beginning to worry me. Proposition? What the hell were they up to? No good, that's for sure.

"Yeah. I'm all ears," I said, finishing my drink and trying to sound confident.

"Well, son, it's like this. Basingstoke. We're going to send you to Basingstoke."

"Jesus! Basingstoke!" I wince. I had been intending to stay in London.

"Hear us out," Danny said, lowering his voice, putting his elbows on the table and leaning in toward me.

"So, we set you up in a small house in Basingstoke with a car sales business. Everything will be in your name. Your dad and I will each take twenty per cent of the business leaving you with the majority holding share."

"Sound too good to be true. What's the catch?" I was interested but wanted to play it cool until I'd heard the full story.

"The catch," Dad stated, his eyes lit with excitement. "It's not so bad. We need a caretaker we can trust to front the business because we need somewhere to clean money and cars on a regular basis."

"You're joking! Both of you. Are you mad? If I get caught it'll be all on me." I knew they were up to something.

"Calm down, boy." Dad raised his voice. "Think about it for a minute. You won't get out of this shithole any other way. Do you want to be living with your mum in that pokey house forever, with your brother bringing druggies home when she's at work? We're giving you an opportunity to get out. To move on."

I took a deep breath and stared into my empty pint glass. I didn't have many options, just the promise of some occasional work behind the bar at a nightclub in the city or working in the newsagent store I'd been working for since I was thirteen. If I stayed, I could take my chances to get a job, my own place and still look out for mum. Dave would do whatever the hell he wanted. He didn't care about anyone. Their offer of a house and business in Basingstoke didn't seem such a bad idea now. At least it gave me the option to move away and start afresh. I could make it work.

"OK," I raised my head and looked at them both and said, "I'll do it."

"Brilliant!" Danny quips with a smile. "I'll get a round in to celebrate."

And that's how I found myself living in Basingstoke managing Delossi Car Sales.

***

I met Steph four years later. It had been a Sunday morning and I was sitting on my usual bench in my favourite park with a takeaway cappuccino and the Sunday paper, when the quiet thumping of feet pounding the ground made me look up. The latest news stories were forgotten the moment I caught a glimpse of the owner of those feet. She was tall with a slender frame and her long dark curly hair was pulled back into a ponytail. Her tight black and grey jogging bottoms showed the sexy curve of her bottom and thighs and the matching long-sleeved top revealed the graceful, curvy shape of her breasts and shoulder blades. Clearly, she jogged regularly.

As she came towards me, she noticed that the supplement had fallen from the middle of the paper. She stopped, bent to retrieve it and held it out to me, smiling.

"Here," her voice was soft but firm, "you dropped this."

"Thanks," I smiled back, my pulse racing as I reached for the magazine with clammy hands. God, she was beautiful. I wanted to take her home right there and then. I'd been with a few girls over the years, but they'd never had this effect on me before.

"I'm Ray."

"Steph," she replied, and I was secretly pleased that she didn't seem to be in a hurry.

I didn't want to risk not seeing her again, so I asked the fated question:

"Would you like to go for a drink sometime?"

Silence hung in the air as she thought about it.

"Yes, OK," she smiled.

We made arrangements to meet for a drink in a local bar we both knew for the following evening. And that's how it began. From the moment I met Steph I knew she was different. She had luscious long dark curly hair that spiralled like a tornado. She was bright, full of life and blew me away with her enthusiasm for living. She revealed that she was twenty-one and that she worked as a secretary for a solicitor's firm on the outskirts of town. She said it had been hard at first because she hadn't any experience of working in that environment. She'd been there a year and had used that time to take driving lessons and to find a one-bedroomed flat a fifteen-minute walk from the War Memorial Park.

During the early days of our relationship I enjoyed being around Steph. We visited the Brighton beach and wandered along the shoreline hand in hand. Her smile could heal the hollow feeling inside me and make me feel contented, as though I deserved to be happy. I enjoyed history and visiting museums with their ancient artefacts and fossils. Learning about how people and animals used to live in places all over the world captivated my curious nature. Museums were one of the few places that gave me peace and let me just be me. I could lose myself.

I found myself struggling to cope with her stubbornness and positive attitude. One time we'd been visiting Mum one weekend and they'd been chatting in the kitchen. The lounge door was open so I could hear some of the things they were talking about. They got on well and I was pleased. That was until I heard them whispering about Dad who was back in prison. This time he'd been caught dragging a bench along the council car park. The bench had "Property of London Borough Council" printed on the top! It was too heavy for him to drag so a couple of police officers had given him a hand to put it back in its rightful place. It wasn't until they checked his car that they found several dog litter bins, and a solar fountain. They arrested him. Again.

"I'm in love with Ray," I heard Steph say as I sat on the sofa browsing Facebook on my phone.

"Oh, Steph. That makes me so happy." Mum's voice grew louder with her news. I could almost hear them hugging as low sniffles drifted through. Part of me was happy to hear this. But I wasn't sure if I wanted to be tied down just yet.

"I think Ray feels the same way." Steph's voice sounds hopeful.

"I'm sure he does," Mum replied, "he'd be a fool not to."

"He's such a good man," Steph said. "He's clever, kind and works hard."

Man. Is she really talking about me? I don't think she knows me very well. I should have been happy that Steph saw me this way.

Their conversation returned to Delossi Car Sales. They knew that Dad was involved in setting me up in it, and they knew that it was making a lot of money somehow. Dad's regular visits to Basingstoke and the amount of people working on the cars that suddenly came in before being driven off to pastures new were hard to explain. Mum and Steph knew something wasn't right but couldn't put their finger on what it was.

As usual I remained silent. It was none of their business. Still, it pissed me off that Mum and Steph wouldn't let it go. The less they knew about Delossi Car Sales the better. I'd always kept my mouth shut and turned a blind eye when it came to the business set up; as long as Dad and Danny kept me out of it I would continue playing their game.

On the way home Steph wouldn't stop talking. She told me how fond she was of my mum and how much she admired her. I was trying to concentrate on driving and trying to mull the dad and Danny situation over in my head, wondering if I would ever have the opportunity to buy them out so that the business and my house was mine outright. Steph kept talking, telling me her worries about the business and that she was excited about an account she was working on with her manager.

"Bloody hell, Steph," I snapped, giving her a curt sideways look. "Can you just shut up for a minute? I can't hear myself think."

I hadn't meant to sound so harsh.

"Ray! Please don't talk to me like that," she'd sniffed, obviously hurt by my comment. "I'm just making conversation, that's what people do."

"I know, but sometimes I need a bit of peace, space to think."

"OK," she began carefully. "Are you worried about the business?"

"Of course not!" I raised my voice. "Why the hell would I be worried?"

"Something's not right, Ray, you know it isn't." There was no mistaking the worry in the tone of her voice, quiet, unsteady words.

"Steph! Leave it."

"But, Ray…"

"I said fucking leave it! And give me some peace," I shouted, giving a warning stare.

The rest of the journey was spent in peace and awkward silence.

Unfortunately, after a whirlwind romance and a wedding that cost more than I could afford, I discovered it was her cheerfulness and ability to be honest with me, those characteristics which had attracted her to me, that led to her downfall. She was simply getting on my nerves. She couldn't help it.

She was twenty-two and I'd been twenty-three when we'd got married, and six months later she was pregnant. I guess I realised I'd had enough when Ben arrived. That was when I noticed the real change in her. She'd gone from being a happy person to an apologetic, exhausted bore. Ben woke every two hours and the tiredness could be seen clearly on her face. She stopped making any effort to look after herself. She stopped jogging and cracks were beginning to show in our relationship and I never realised the pressure that having a new baby in the house would create. I never understood any of this, so I used to stay late at the car shop, but eventually I had to go home. That was where the problems were.

I still cringe when I remember the first time I hit Steph. I couldn't believe I could do that to a woman, especially to a woman who is the mother of my ten-month-old child.

My day had been rubbish. The business was not going well, and I'd had to lay off Fred Livingston, my best part-time sales person. I wasn't in the mood for any dramas when I got home at 6.30pm.

Then I walked in and saw the mess in the kitchen of our two-bedroom flat. There was a smell of burnt food, crumbs and toys were scattered on the floor and there wasn't a clean worktop in sight. I looked across the room to see the dining table with two place settings. I didn't say anything as she tried to smile. Her face was pale and drawn and there was baby sick stuck to her sweatshirt. And there she was, nibbling the inside of her cheek. I knew she did it when she was worried and she couldn't help it, but it was bloody annoying.

"Hey, Ray. I was hoping to get this mess cleared away before you got home."

I said nothing, just walked to the fridge and helped myself to a Corona. I rolled my eyes, willing myself to take a deep breath, so I moved to the table and sat down. Ben was in his cot in his room. The baby monitor suddenly comes to life as a loud wailing burst through the speaker. Shit, that baby had great timing. The crying grew louder. It was doing my head in and a red mist began to float into my vision.

"I'll go see to him," Steph said quietly.

"No! Leave him be," I bit back at her.

"But, Ray," she pleaded. Her shoulders slumped as she pleaded for me to let her go to Ben.

The piercing crying had turned into hollow sobs. I pushed myself out of the chair, walked to the monitor and threw it at the wall as hard as I could. The noise stopped but I could still hear a distant wail as I went back to my seat. Steph was sobbing quietly, gulping back tears and wiping her eyes and nose with dirty sleeves.

Slowly, she placed my dinner plate in front of me and took her place opposite me at the table. I stared at the plate. Fishfingers, chips and peas. Fucking fishfingers. I'd been to work all day and in all that time all she'd done is look after the baby and cook fucking fishfingers, chips and peas.

I stared at the plate.

"What the fuck is this?" I said, my temper rising.

"Sorry, Ray, but Ben's teething. He's been crying all afternoon and I overcooked the chicken. It was like rubber."

"Sorry! Sorry!" My voice rises as I mimicked her, and before I could stop myself I'd thrown the plate at her head with such force that it cracked into three pieces as it caught the side of her face. She tried frantically to protect herself with her hands, but it was too late. I still remember the look of shock on her sobbing face at my action and the sound of her screeching and whimpering like an injured bird.

"Ray, please," she pleaded. She was sobbing uncontrollably. Big, loud annoying sobs that drove me insane. I couldn't stop myself. I was beyond reasoning with. I pushed myself out of the chair and walked across to her, watching her cower as I approached.

"Ray," she sobbed. "Please. Don't do this." She was sobbing and hiccupping, and her shoulders were shaking.

I grabbed her hair, that luscious dark curly hair that I had once loved with a passion and bunched it tightly in my right hand. She fought me, moving her body from side to side and flailing around trying to disconnect my hand from her hair. It was no use. I was much stronger than she was. Then I yanked her head back so that she looked up at me.

"Please," she screamed, looking into my eyes in between Ben's distant wailing. "Please."

"Fish fucking fingers, Steph!" I raged back at her. "Fish fucking fingers."

"Ray!" She was crying big fat tears. Then, letting go of her hair, I smacked her so hard across the face that her chair fell backwards and then I stormed out of the house.

I think back to that moment when everything started to unravel, and I became this monster. It's true that some men do feel that pang of guilt at what they've done. Promising never to do it again. But they just can't help themselves. I'm one of them.

When Steph eventually left me not long after Ben turned three, I almost felt a sense of relief she wouldn't be there to bring the monster out in me. I shouldn't have been surprised because she looked a mess and must have been in pain after one of my rages. She had a bad arm and knife slashes across her upper chest.

I walked through the empty rooms of the house at 7pm one Friday night. Nearly everything was left as it had been that morning, soft toys scattered everywhere, clothes ready for ironing, neatly folded on the dining table, but for Ben's nappy bag and Steph's handbag and their coats. I sat in the nearest chair I could find, my hands in my head. Do I let them go or do I look for them? Steph didn't have any friends that I knew of and had given up work to look after Ben. Pulling myself together I used my phone to find the phone numbers of my nearest hospitals and began to make calls. I told them that my wife was depressed and had left me.

Each time the receptionist had forwarded me to the Accident and Emergency Department. Each time they apologised and told me that no one had been admitted.

Over the years I moved on with my life and tried to keep control of my temper whenever I was in a relationship. It was hard because the older I got the more my temper flared and the less I tolerated. There were a couple of girlfriends over the years, Sue and Lily. Both were nice women in their own way. One lasted six months and the other ten months. Then there was that young one, the one with the dark hair and pretty face. She wore that cute silver butterfly necklace. Can't remember her name, Billy, Binnie or something like that. It was a nickname. She didn't like her birth name. It just didn't work out. They weren't Steph.

About ten years ago I was contacted by a solicitor because Steph had filed for divorce. I've thought increasingly about Steph and my son until finally, last month, I hired an investigator called Dave Lewis who has an office in Witney to find them.

The strangest thing is that I didn't want to see them. Not right now, anyway. Sure, I wanted to know where they were because that information gives me power. Maybe I could eventually have them back to live with me, everything would work out and we'd have a future together. I don't believe that things were that bad when we lived together. Steph probably wouldn't annoy me like she used to. I do love her in my own way. I enjoyed controlling her. It felt good to be in control of something. I missed it.

Would you believe that Lewis found out that Steph was in the police force, the bloody police! She'd done well for herself, climbing the corporate ladder. She's a Detective Inspector in the Thames Valley Police based at Oxford. I couldn't believe it at first, how ironic is that?

I moved from Basingstoke to Wantage in Oxfordshire a few weeks ago. I thought it would be good to live closer to Ben even if I never got to see him again in person. Who knows, maybe one day we will have a relationship of sorts. You never know. Then there was Steph. I toyed with the idea of getting in touch with her, but I don't think she's ready to start again. Yet.

I had Lewis print a few photos of Steph and Ben to remind me of them. In my mind they were still my family, and I know that may sound distorted in other people's eyes but it's what I want and what I need. To have them back with me.

It doesn't mean I can't have some fun while I'm biding my time with them. I'll put myself out there, start dating again. Perhaps I can find a way to make Steph love me again, to make her realise what she's missing without me in her life.

Chapter 5: Chasing ghosts

Steph

I feel the tear of material as my blouse is yanked open. The knife pierces my skin slowly, blood dribbles from my chest and runs in slow rivulets down my breasts. One of his hands is tightly wrapped around my hair holding my head back, his right hand holds the knife. This is not happening. Everything is in slow motion. And all of this because he had wanted sex and I didn't. I'd tried to placate him by saying that we'd have some time together when we were in bed. But Ray had wanted it there and then, started fumbling, grabbing for me. I'd told him no. It was 9pm for God's sake, didn't he realise I was tired. I was filling the dishwasher, that's when he'd picked up the carving knife from the knife block nearby. By the time I realised his intentions it was too late. The hard slap across my cheek stunned me, then his hand gripped my head hard bringing me out of my daze, and before I knew what was happening, he was dragging me by my hair to the dining chair. I was screaming, grabbing anything I could because I knew if he got me into that chair things would get much worse. My last thought as I slumped in the chair was thank God Ben was asleep.

The pain brings me back to reality. The sting of the knife as it cuts the skin is excruciating, and I begin to scream while my clammy hands try to grab his wrist to push the knife away from me.

"Wouldn't it have been easier to have just said yes to me?" he snarled. "What's the matter with you? Are you frigid? I'll make sure no man will want to look at you, let alone have sex with you." He pinched the top of my right breast. Hard.

"Ray… Argh!"

I'm screaming so loud the shrill sound hurts my ears. My shoulders swivel from side to side to try to get away from him. The pain travels across my chest making me breathless, making me panic, and I take a quick look and see the dark blood coming from my skin. I feel sick and bite back the bile that's threatening to come up. Again, I start to scream.

"Steph!"

"Stop, stop, stop," I shout and plead at the same time. Tears flow down my face. My head hurts and my vision blurs. For God's sake, make it stop. I flinch as Ray puts pressure on the knife to drag it up toward my neck. I can't stand it. I let out a silent scream as my voice becomes trapped somewhere deep inside me. I'm in absolute fear for my life. Sweat pours from me as the voice inside me keeps asking, when will he stop? What will he do next? I close my eyes for a moment, let my limbs go limp and give in to him.

"Steph! Stay with me. I'm not finished yet." He slaps my face hard, making me come back to him.

I begin to struggle again, my hands trying to grab whatever part of him they can to make him stop.

"Nooo! Get off me!" I feel a buzz of energy and grab his arm from my neck, pulling with everything I've got.

"Get off me, you little cow," he snarls, briefly letting go of my head to prise my fingers from his arm. Shit – he doesn't like that. The pressure on the knife increases as I grope for something, for anything. I feel like he's cutting me in half, cutting into my nerves, my soul. It's as though I'm having a surgical procedure without an anaesthetic.

The look on his face tells me that he is far from finished with me. He seems to have second thoughts about grabbing my hair again because he puts his large hand on my face, holding it over my nose and mouth. He studies me closely, a cold, detached stare that frightens me. There is no concern, no emotion. It's as though he's been taken over by someone else. It's Ray's body but not Ray himself. I make moaning, gasping sounds as I try to draw air into my lungs. My body fights for the need to inhale a breath and it feels as if my face is blowing up. Shit. This is it. I'm not coming back from this. Ben's face flashes before my eyes. *I love you, Ben. I'm sorry.* And then just as I give up and close my eyes in final defeat, he takes his hand away and I gasp air into my lungs. There's a quick movement as the knife is taken from the table. God, please make this end.

I blink and another dark memory fills my anguished mind. It's like watching a horror movie and you're the star. A movie that never ends. I watch in silence as the knife moves across the top of my breast and continues sideways to my neck. I worry if I struggle too much he might accidentally cut my throat. The sting as the knife slices my skin makes me feel afraid, panicked, angry. *Why would you do this, Ray? Why?* I lash out, trying to escape his hold on me.

"Please, Ray, stop. You're hurting me!" I half scream, wondering if my panicked heart will beat out of my chest. I need to calm down, but all I feel is a burning sensation across the top of my chest.

Ray looks at me and sneers. "You asked for it. I asked you to pick up my suit from the cleaners. Now what am I going to wear tomorrow?"

"I'm sorry. I don't feel well and haven't left the house."

"Steph."

"Please don't do this, Ray," I sob. The sting of pain is becoming unbearable as Ray holds the knife blade against my neck and continues pushing down until he can see a line of blood. I can see it too, dark red seeping down to my breasts.

***

"Steph! You were daydreaming." I hear a familiar deep husky voice and feel someone gently shaking me. I gingerly turn my head from side to side to clear the images inside my brain. I look into concerned, brown eyes that remind me of golden-brown autumn leaves just before they fall from the tree. A worry frown shows on his forehead. I think I frightened him. He's leaning over me and his hand sits on my shoulder.

I'm tired and try to remember how I came to be daydreaming. Jack had been sitting in his chair, his laptop on his knee. I was sitting on the sofa near to him with my laptop.

"Tell me what you can or know about Ray's business, Delossi Car Sales," he'd asked.

"I don't know that much," I begin. "Years ago I had my suspicions that the business was being used to front something. Drugs or similar."

I gently massage the scar on my chest to reassure myself that it's healed. I can almost feel a strange stinging sensation across it, a phantom pain.

"I'm sorry," I begin.

"Don't ever apologise to me, Steph." There's a glint of pain and anger in his eyes as he kneels in front of me, stroking my hair and squeezing my shoulder to comfort me.

"What he did to you, the abuse and the scars, is the stuff of nightmares," he says, taking his hand from my shoulder. He pushes up to a standing position and moves back to his chair. Then he picks up his discarded laptop and puts it on the floor.

"I haven't had a nightmare for five years," I say, more to myself. "I won't let my experiences with Ray define me because then he wins. I'm strong enough to chase away his ghost."

"I like that, the Ghost Chaser. I know you're strong, Steph, but seeing Ray's corpse must have brought all of those old memories back."

"But I don't want to feel afraid again, Jack, I don't want to have these nightmares," I say heatedly. "I want to have the safe life

I've created for Ben and myself back. The pizzas, the visits to the cinema, my job and my close group of friends. I don't want to be like this again because then Ray wins." I sit forward, my hands leaning on my chin. I look at him. We're close, our knees are almost touching.

"You're safe now, Steph. Ray's dead," he says, leaning forward in his chair, hands clasped together. His head turns so that he can look straight into my eyes and I hold his gaze in return. I want him to see me with all my faults.

"Thank you for being here, Jack."

"No problem. I will do whatever I can to help you," he says with a note of sincerity in his voice.

I could sit like this forever, simply enjoying this man's company. How can that be? How can this man so easily begin to break down my defences when my walls are made of granite? I didn't see this coming.

Something else has been playing on my mind since I saw Ray's body this afternoon. The claw marks. The bloody knife. My gut tells me that there's a victim out there. That someone got hurt defending themselves.

"Jack," I begin, "the scratches on Ray's face and the bloody knife are worrying me."

"Me too," he agrees. "Are you thinking the same thing? That he hurt someone and they retaliated?"

"Yes. We need to find them quickly," I answer solemnly. "If they're still alive."

My phone pings and I look at my watch. 9.15pm. Jesus. Where did the time go? My DS Chris Jackson has sent me a text.

You free to talk?

Yes, I type back.

"Chris needs to speak to me," I explain to Jack, and he nods, collects the laptop and places it on the table in the dining room. I hear the kettle being filled with water and then the rumble of the water heating as he switches it on to boil. Surprisingly, this scene with the familiar everyday sounds feels normal and comforting.

The ringtone, the phone coming to life, makes me focus and I answer quickly, never taking my eyes off Jack as he looks through cupboards in search of coffee and mugs.

"Chris," I say.

"Hey, Boss," Chris begins. "We've had confirmation that the fingerprints on the knife and the blood on the baseball bat belong to the deceased, Ray Delossi. Although a few marks have come up on the bat there's nothing conclusive, no fingerprints. The lab has found traces of bleach on the handle." Chris paused. "One lead has come up though. Danielle called earlier, she's been checking out Ray's phone. There are several recent calls and texts to someone on his contact list over the past month. They were to someone called Corinna James."

I give a sigh of relief. It's good to get an early lead on a case.

"Shame about the marks on the bat," I agree with him. "Unless we can place Corinna James in the house at the time of the murder, we've got very little to go on." My brain begins to calculate what we need to do next. "Good work, Chris, now let's follow up on Corinna. We need to ask her a few questions."

"I've checked her out," he continued. "She's eighteen and been in care since she was ten. She now lives in a housing complex in Abingdon purpose built for young people who have left the care system."

"Good work. We're making progress. So she's not on the fingerprint database which means she's got no previous criminal prosecutions or convictions. Interesting. Good work. Are you at home?"

"Yes."

"Text me her address and I'll meet you there," I say, walking into the kitchen to find Jack.

"Will do." Chris sounds a bit worried. "One more thing, Boss."

"Yes?" I answer, as my heart begins to beat faster.

"We found another photo frame of you and Ben upstairs next to Delossi's bed."

I shake my head and roll my shoulders. If only I had stayed in bed this morning.

"That's great! Just great." I can't keep the exasperation from my reply. "I have no idea why he has two photos of myself and Ben in his home. Thanks for giving me a heads-up on that. I'll see you at Corinna's." I nibble the inside of my cheek. There won't be much skin left there soon.

I disconnect the phone and walk slowly into the kitchen. Jack hears me come in and turns to me, waiting to hear what I have to say.

I tell him that the fingerprints on the knife were Ray's, about the inconclusive marks on the bat and that we've got a possible lead on someone called Corinna James.

"How did you find her?" Jack asks, handing me a coffee. "Not sure if you have sugar so I didn't put any in."

I add sugar to my coffee and continue explaining what we've got so far.

"We found messages and calls and texts to and from Corinna and Ray over the last month. Danielle, the Information Technologist on my team, found them on Ray's phone and they lead us to her. She's not on the database so has no previous convictions. The baseball bat has been wiped with bleach which means there are no prints, and without assuming too much it is possible that Corinna James may have attacked Ray. Though, I'm not sure if she did that in self-defence or not. I've got her address and I'm meeting Chris there in an hour. On top of that, they've found another framed photo of Ben and me in Ray's house, upstairs next to his bed."

"Shit." Jack nods his head as if he can't believe what's happening. I'm just grateful that he's not throwing a ton of questions at me right now because I need to be focused on finding Corinna.

"I know it's a lot to ask, but…" I hold my coffee close and face him.

"But what?" Jack asks, his eyes on my face and his hands casually sitting on the top of his trouser pockets. He doesn't look angry or worried. He looks ready to help. "Steph?" he asks softly.

I stand still, my coffee mug clutched to tightly to my chest, wondering if I'm doing the right thing. It feels wrong to keep asking someone who I've just met to help even though I know that I need it.

"Ray's death has made me really nervous and I would feel better if someone I trusted was in the house with Ben. Usually, I would arrange for a friend to stay if I have to work in the evening, but it's too late to organise."

"That's fine," he says in a low voice.

"Ben is very self-sufficient and shouldn't give you any grief. Can you stay until I get back?"

There, I've said it. It's not fair to ask him but I can't seem to help myself. For someone who prides herself on being independent and strong I'm not doing very well here, am I?

Did he just say yes? He said it so quietly. Maybe I misheard him.

"Yes," he repeats simply, and my heart misses a beat with gratitude. "Can you make sure that Ben's OK with me being here though. He doesn't know me."

I smile, thankful for his consideration of my son.

"I will."

We head upstairs to Ben's room. I'm not sure how he'll react to Jack staying here but I don't want to leave him alone. Leaving Ben here with Jack is a calculated decision. True, I don't know Jack, but I trust Jenny and Stuart with my life. And they trust Jack. The extended surrogate Lighthouse family has taught me that we need to rely on each other and trust each other. Besides, Ben's safety and my peace of mind comes first. I check my watch, it's 9.30pm. I'm sure he'll be awake.

I knock and then walk into Ben's messy room whilst Jack waits in the hallway. Ben's in bed, his hair falling over his eyes as his fingers busily tap on his mobile, probably checking his Facebook page or texting a friend.

"Ben, sweetie," I begin, "I've got to go to work for a few hours and I've asked Jack to stay here to keep an eye on you."

"But, Mum… I'm fourteen. I don't need a babysitter!" he begins to argue, his brows pulling together showing his annoyance.

"I know, sweetie, but there's something about this case that makes me nervous and I need to know that you're safe. I trust Jack."

Ben looks at me and rolls his eyes to the ceiling. He knows he's not going to win this argument.

"Jack will be downstairs. Do you want to have a quick word with him?"

"OK," Ben says, his eyes peering to the doorway.

Jack pops his head around the door.

"What's your favourite car, Jack?" my fourteen-year-old son asks seriously.

"Aston Martin," Jack quips back.

"Not bad," he muses. "Mine's a Jaguar F-type convertible. I'll have my own one day."

I smile. Ben has been crazy about cars for most of his life. The accumulated mass of die cast supercars are still boxed carefully in his wardrobe. I lean closer to Ben to kiss his cheek before telling him:

"Jack will be downstairs if you need anything. Lights out in five minutes."

"Yep," Jack says with a dry expression, his eyes twinkling. "I'll be binge watching some gripping crime series on Netflix." There's a moment when our eyes meet and neither of us are able to look away. We hold each other's gaze for the briefest of moments as a storm of emotions overwhelm me. I take a deep breath as the feelings of uncertainty, hope, curiosity and fear whirl through my newly awakened emotions.

I feel my cheeks start to redden. Maybe this isn't such a good idea.

Jack and I head downstairs in silence. I can't help feeling a little out of sorts and I hope that my cheeks have returned to their normal colour.

"You look cute when you blush." Jack looks at me as we reach the lounge, and I lower my eyes briefly. I'm not used to compliments, particularly from a man. Still, I find the beginning of a smile pulling at the corner of my mouth.

"Jack." I look at him. "I need to go." I grab my things and walk towards the front door.

"I know. Sorry, couldn't help it." His hand caresses my face briefly. "Be careful."

"I will, and thanks again for watching Ben." I touch his hand briefly and turn. It's time to go and discover what's happened to Corinna James.

Chapter 6: Looking for trouble

Steph

I park next to Chris's car in the designated parking area for the building known as Richmond Court. It's 10pm and I'm beginning to feel the weariness of this never-ending day. Jack's words fill my head, the way he told me he's attracted to me and that I look good when I blush. A warmth comes over me like a large pair of arms keeping me warm, keeping me safe. Thinking of him lifts some of my weariness. *Concentrate Steph! Keep your eye on the ball.*

Richmond Court is a new facility. It offers ten independent flats for care leavers turned eighteen who are on the lower level support pathway plan. The brown and red brick two-storey building has an inviting glass and wooden door entrance and entry is gained through the secure buzzer system. A landscaped communal garden with seating areas is featured in the quadrangle of the ground floor. There's a caretaker who lives on the premises who's on call twenty-four hours a day, that's Mr Jules Walker. In addition to this there's a laundry room. It looks like a nice place to live. Corinna James lives in flat number six.

I check the buzzer and press the relevant number. There's a crackle on the line and then Chris's voice answers:

"Hello?"

"Hey, Chris. It's me."

"Hey, Boss. Hold on a second, I'll buzz you in. I've got Jules Walker waiting outside the flat. I'll send him down to you. He'll escort you to flat six. See you in a minute." He disconnects the phone, presses the buzzer, and I push the door to enter the building.

I'm surprised by how nice it is. There's a lift and set of steps, plus there are plants, mirrors and artwork decorating the foyer. A man walks towards me. My brain immediately starts to assess his character as he reaches me. He's blonde, in his mid-twenties and is wearing faded blue jeans and a thin grey long-sleeved top. His blonde hair falls just below his shoulders and is tied back in a ponytail. It seems to compliment his angular face, straight nose and blue eyes.

"Detective Inspector Rutland?" He leans forward slightly, smiles and puts out his hand.

"I'm Jules Walker. I'm the onsite caretaker here." His voice is strong and the way he walks and holds himself displays a confidence I didn't expect. I guess I was expecting an older person, not a young, confident person who looks as though he should be exploring the far corners of the world as an archaeologist.

"Yes." I take his hand. It's warm and firm as I expected it would be. "I'm DI Rutland. Thanks for letting us in, Mr Walker." I offer my work smile. It's a cross between a smile and a grimace. It doesn't reach my eyes. I've fashioned it in the mirror at home. I want people to see me as professional but not unapproachable.

"Call me Jules," he smiles. "I'll show you the way."

My footsteps totter behind his big striding gait, trying to keep up. Questions swirl through my mind relating to Jules Walker. Why would he want to work somewhere like here, on call for twenty-four hours a day? It can't be an easy job.

"How many young people do you currently have living here?" I ask as I follow him up two small flights of steps to the first floor. The corridor has white painted walls and square brass wall lights fitted on either side of the door to each flat.

"We have ten flats and all of them are currently in use. So, there are ten young people living here," he answers, walking forward, his arm outstretched. "This is Corinna's flat. Number six."

"Thanks," I say, looking at the blue hardwood door with a peephole and note the brass door number six and a matching door handle. "Do they live here totally independently?" I ask him, as we stop in front of the door.

"Yes. They are each allocated a personal advisor on their individual pathway plan and he or she will visit them each week to see how they're doing. They check how each young person is coping financially and emotionally," he explains, staring at the number on the door. "Everyone is self-sufficient and I'm on site if there are any major problems."

"That's quite a commitment, Mr Walker. I mean Jules. You can't have much of a life if you're here all day, every day," I say, watching his face intently for any tell-tale signs of making up a story.

"I have cover on Wednesdays and Sundays. Just to give me a break. I live in flat ten. Lydia Darcey covers for me on those two days. She stays in the spare studio flat on the ground floor next to the garden. It's flat number eleven. I'm working here as an intern for six months to gain experience for my social work degree."

"A worthwhile occupation," I say, feeling relieved that he's not living his life in this building for the next twenty years.

"How long have you been here?" I notice his easy-going manner and the words seem to flow from him. It's hard to fathom if he's telling the truth. I sense that he's holding something back, not telling me everything. It's just a feeling I get. I may be wrong, but my instincts are usually bang on.

"Three months. I'm halfway through," he answers.

I look at him thoughtfully before asking my final question. "How long has Corinna been at Richmond Court?"

He shuffles slightly and lowers his gaze as though he's trying to remember. "She came here four months ago. I remember Lydia telling me that she'd been here a month before I started work." He stares down the corridor deep in thought. "I'll leave you to it.

73

Your DS is in there. Just give him a knock. I'll be in my flat if you need me." He gives me a brief smile and saunters along the corridor.

I knock on the blue door and wait for Chris to answer. The first thing I notice when he opens the door is the tiredness on his face. He's still wearing his white shirt and dark blue trousers, but now he wears a dark grey coat to keep out the chill.

"Hey," I say. "How are you getting on?" I follow Chris through the blue carpeted off-white painted hallway of the flat, looking briefly into the open rooms until I find myself standing in a small but functional kitchen. It's decorated in the same off-white colour as the hall and houses the usual white goods of a cooker, fridge and washing machine. It's clean and tidy. There's a pale blue vinyl covering the kitchen floor.

"The flat consists of this corridor at the end of which is the kitchen. Next to the kitchen we have the living room with a small dining table, and on the opposite side of the corridor there is a bedroom and a bathroom. I assume that all of the flats are of a similar layout."

"I agree. Nice place." I look around. "She keeps it clean. Jules Walker says she's been here four months," I inform him as I put on my latex gloves and look around the kitchen to get a feeling for the type of person that Corinna James is. My eyes stray to the blood splatters.

"Look at this." Chris chews his bottom lip and with gloved hands he picks up a large bundle of kitchen roll and several bloody tea towels from the draining board. We both stare at the scrunched materials. They look as though someone has been mopping up copious amounts of blood. Or staunching several bloody wounds.

"Shit!" I can't help but mutter under my breath.

Chris's face shows his professional persona, the one he wants people to see, but I notice the way he chews his bottom lip when he's worried or trying to hold back his emotions. I notice the stormy, angry look in his eyes when we talk. I guess he can see my personal coping strategies too, the ones where I nibble my inner cheeks or fight off a headache.

"Jesus. She must have been a mess when she came back here," he says, his lips set in a grim line.

"I don't know," I say, in answer to him. "But nothing good by the amount of blood we have here."

That's an understatement. There is blood splattered over the sink and taps and numerous bloody handprints on walls and door handles throughout the room. I'd bet a year's pay that these handprints and the blood belong to Corinna James. I watch Chris carefully replace the red bundle onto the draining board.

"Leave that for SOCO," I say, walking out of the kitchen into the hallway to locate the living room. Again, the off-white colour covers the walls and a sea of blue carpet follows from the hallway, however, the addition of furniture and furnishings adds a warmth to the room. There is a dark red two-seat sofa, a matching chair, a TV perched on a low beech coloured unit, and a small low matching table sits between the sofa and chair. I think these things are already provided for the young people, but I make a mental note to check with Jules Walker. I can see that Corinna has tried to add some personal touches by scattering grey knitted cushions across the two seating areas and casually hanging a matching grey throw on the arm of the sofa.

I walk to the low table and pick up two black photo frames sitting beside a large three-wick white candle. It would be good to know what Corinna looks like so we know who we're looking for. I look at the prints and freeze. One shows a pretty, happy young woman with long, dark curly hair. I think I forget to breathe. Jesus, she looks just like me.

"Shit, Boss! She looks a lot like you," says Chris, as his head turns my way and his eyes catch mine.

I slowly exhale, forcing myself to respond. "I can see that, Chris," I say, trying to keep the anger from my voice. "Thanks for stating the obvious. Anything helpful you can offer here would be appreciated."

The second photo reveals a romantic moment as she leans into kiss Ray on the cheek whilst smiling and trying to take a selfie of them both.

I take a snapshot of the two photos with my phone and quickly send it to Jack. He's going to love this. Chris also takes a photo so that we can use it for the incident board.

Further checks on the place reveal nothing unusual. That is until the notepad and pen sitting on the kitchen unit catches my attention. Slowly, I pick it up and find the horror movie that is my life swooping up to engulf me. Again. In blue ballpoint pen, neatly written in capital letters are the words STEPH RUTLAND. Holy Shit!

"Chris," I call to him, "you're going to want to see this." I hear steps coming my way.

"Fuck!" he says, standing next to me and reading the words I'm staring at in disbelief.

"Precisely!"

"I don't know this girl, never met her. Why would she write my name down? Let's get SOCO here and start processing the scene. Hopefully, they will come up with something to help us find her. For now check hospitals, minor injury units, etc."

Chris puts the notepad carefully into an evidence bag, seals it, records the details and puts it in his bag.

I need to get to this girl quickly before I officially bring her in for questioning. Where is she? If she's bleeding out and in need of help where would she go?

"We'll have to tell the DCI, Boss," Chris says quietly. He knows the links between this case and myself are becoming too big for either of us to ignore.

"I know. Give me twelve hours and we'll tell him everything. For now, let's find Corinna. Wherever she was last night, whatever happened, the blood in her flat suggests that she's injured. I'll call SOCO and get them here to start processing."

Following the call, I wander despondently around the little flat. I'm careful not to disrupt any blood splatters or any other items that are needed for fingerprints and evidence bags. Suddenly my phone buzzes. I check the text message. It's Jack.

Need you to come back. I stare at the words and think of Ben.

Is Ben OK? I quickly type.

He's fine. Come back as soon as you can, Jack replies.

SOCO have just arrived and I'm heading back now. Probably about thirty minutes.

I let him know and wait for his reply.

That's fine. See you soon.

His reply offers a little reassurance, but not much. Clearly something is wrong, and I try to ignore the shiver that runs down my spine. Jack wouldn't text me at work unless it was important. I can't help but worry. He said it's fine, and I'm sure he can cope with whatever it is until I'm able to get back. Chris walks into the room, takes one look at my face and asks if everything is alright. I nod and put my phone back in my pocket. The last thing I want is Chris becoming involved in my private business. We go through the motions of explaining what we've found to SOCO, pointing out key findings and then finally leave them to it.

"Let's meet up at 8am tomorrow," I say, making my way to the entrance. "Can you get Tribble on the team? We'll work through the incident board and set up actions. Hopefully the hospitals will flag up anyone who comes in with a knife wound."

"Sounds good. Goodnight, Boss," he calls as I open the door.

"Night, Chris," I reply, looking at my watch. It's 1am and an overwhelming tiredness takes over me as I take the stairs and make my way across the car park to the car. It feels like this night will ever end. There's no traffic on the road and as I drive my mind goes over everything that has happened today and yesterday. Seeing Ray's battered body, the photos in his house, meeting Jack. And now there's the complication of Corinna James. Where the hell is she? I'm sure I'll find her soon, but I can't help but feel anxious when I park at the side of the house next to Jack's red Mazda, anxious to know what prompted his urgent text. I'm about to find out.

Chapter 7: Blip

Unknown

I used to say to my little sister, Blip, that when she grew up the world would be her playground. She'd be able to fly to the hottest countries, trek over the highest mountains, sail to the most beautiful places.

I used to say a lot of things to her when we were young, and life was exciting. A time for believing in dreams that come true and the goodness that lives inside every one of us. Blip. I can't think of her without a lump coming to my throat. Obviously, Blip wasn't her real name. She was born Belinda Karin Walker-Mason at a healthy 8lb 3oz in the hospital formerly known as the North Staffs Maternity Hospital in Stoke-on-Trent, Staffordshire. I was six-years-old when she was born and, from the moment I laid eyes on her swathed in a white knitted blanket, a pink woolly hat sitting atop her tiny head and her pink face scrunched up as she slept, I knew I would love her forever.

My dad had helped me onto a chair and asked if I wanted to hold her. I nodded "yes" in awe. The moment was such a big one, she was three hours old, and she was the most precious thing I'd ever held. I'd waited with bated breath as Dad leaned down and gently laid Belinda in my arms. I moved my arms slightly trying to get comfortable without waking or dropping her.

"I love you, Blip," I said softly, looking down into her sleeping rosy face. "I'll always love you." I could feel the warmth of her through the blanket. A real, living person. And I thought my heart would burst with happiness.

"Blip?" Kerry, my radiant stepmother had queried. She looked thoughtful, her golden hair pushed behind her ears and her bright smile made her face light up, almost brighter than the sun. "I like that, sweetie. It suits her."

I smiled at her and her tired eyes began to water as she blew me a kiss. I didn't want to make her cry. Not on this special day. I took my hand off Blip and quickly pretended to catch her kiss. She wasn't my biological mother, but she treated me just as I'd imagined a mother would treat a child she loved. I knew I loved her. And I knew Kerry loved me.

My dad, Eric, was a good man. When I was little, he was so tall that I thought he was a giant. I used to run my fingers through his short soft brown hair and his wispy beard would tickle my cheek making me smile. Dad used to joke a lot, but when my biological mother had walked out on us, he'd changed. Sometimes I'd look at him when he wasn't watching and see the sadness in his eyes. I'd been three when my birth mother had told us she was visiting her own mother for two days because she was unwell. What we didn't know at the time was that Granny wasn't unwell and Mum wasn't going visit her to look after her. In fact, no one knows where Mum went. The only thing we knew for sure was that she never came back.

How can a mother do that to her child? I don't know. The feeling of being abandoned and not wanted is the worst feeling in the world. It's makes you feel like you're not good enough. That you don't deserve to be loved. I mean, if your own mother can't love you, how can you expect anyone else to love you? When I was little I felt as though my insides were crying. It sounds funny to say it that way, but I was little and the pain of not being wanted, of living with my dad who was always so sad, made me feel like crying. And I didn't want to make my dad more unhappy than he was, so I cried inside.

Dad tried everything to find Mum. We visited Granny but there was no sign. He placed a Missing Person advert in the local newsagent window with a photo of her. He put together a poster and nailed it to telegraph posts near our house. Granny had given Dad some information on where they'd lived when Mum had been a small child, places she would likely return to. We visited those places. We went to Anglesey where she'd been brought up and we scoured seaside resorts such as Rhyl and Llandudno where Mum had holidayed as a child. Nothing. It's like she disappeared off the face of the earth.

It's not like it is today. There was no Facebook, no internet.

When I was four-years-old Kerry came into our lives and the sun began to shine again. Kerry worked part-time at the Children's Centre in Milton before the centre closed due to government cutbacks. It was close to where we lived in Light Oaks. Dad used to take me there and Kerry would help him to sort out practical things such as applying for a school place for me at the nearest primary school.

Kerry and Dad fell in love over a cappuccino and a pain au chocolat she used to tell me. Six months later they were married and before we knew it Blip was on the way. She used to sit me on her lap and sing nursery rhymes to us both.

"Can you be my new mummy?" I shyly asked her one day. "Can you love me forever and never go away?" I'd stroked her cheek and she'd hugged me as close as her big belly would allow. Tears flowed down her cheeks and Dad had closed his eyes, savouring the moment.

"I would love to be your new mummy," she'd whispered, looking solemnly at me, the traces of her tears still on her cheeks.

"Promise me you'll never go away," I asked. I was sure she would disappear from our lives as quickly as she'd arrived. I was four and I needed a mummy.

"I promise," she'd said sincerely, kissing my forehead. "You're my little soldier. I love you."

It's funny how life has its ebbs and flows. Experiences so magical that you want to imprint them into your mind as a forever keepsake, something positive to sustain and distract you from bad thoughts, worse experiences and horrific nightmares.

Two years before I went to university we moved to Thame in Oxfordshire. Dad had updated his software knowledge and was now working for a large, well-known company who had changed the way vacuum cleaners worked. Mum worked as a Teaching Assistant at a primary school. And Blip, she settled into school life. I returned home regularly, like a homing pigeon because I missed my family.

The problems started when I came back home after completing my degree. Blip was sixteen, too young to be doing most things but old enough to believe that she knew what she was doing. She was getting good grades at school and was due to move on to the attached sixth form to complete her formal education.

Then she met Ray Delossi.

Chapter 8: Sentry duty

Jack

When I got the text from Steph out of the blue yesterday, I had no idea what I was getting myself into. I thought it was a simple problem that I could help her with, but something more complex and sinister is going on in her life than I could ever have imagined. The fact that Steph and Ben lived at Shore House a few years ago speaks volumes. She needed refuge, a safe place for herself and her son. I'm glad they found Stuart and Jenny. I've heard some of the things that Ray did to Steph from her own lips and from her daydream. It's not good. He was a real nasty piece of work.

Shit, Jack! How do you get yourself into these things?

I should have known better. Stuart and Jenny were right about Steph. She was Miss Independent, so if she reached out for help it must be bad. I'm a thirty-eight-year-old, easy-going kind of guy and I wanted to help her. That's why I said I'd look after her son when she was called in to work. I like my job as an investigator and consultant forensic psychologist, it gives me independence and makes my time pretty much my own. I love my cars – one of which is a red five-door Mazda CX-5. I like visiting my parents on Sunday evenings for dinner to catch up and to make sure they're OK. I like lifting weights at the gym, kickboxing and I love women. Overall, I haven't had many meaningful relationships. Guess I've just never found the right woman.

When the doorbell rang twenty minutes ago, I thought it was Steph and that she'd forgotten her key. I hadn't expected to find a bedraggled dark-haired, pale, younger-looking version of Steph staring back at me with eyes full of fear and pain. It was a surreal moment. They both even had clear hazel eyes. She was holding a thin black raincoat tightly around her, as though she was trying to keep herself safe and a long-handled casual black shoulder bag.

"Does Steph live here? Steph Rutland?" she'd asked me in a quiet voice.

I think of the photo that Steph sent me earlier and know that this is Corinna James.

"You're Corinna. Corinna James, aren't you?" I'd asked, trying to find out what she wanted. "Why do you want Steph?"

"Yes. I'm Corinna. I need her help," the woman answered, clutching her coat tightly.

"She had to pop out, but she'll be back soon." I studied her face. It had a pained, vulnerable look about it. Slightly scrunched in pain, weary. Could I trust her enough to let her into the house? Ben's in here.

At the mention of Steph's absence, Corinna had taken a step back as though she meant to walk away. She winced when she moved.

"Do you have any weapons on you? I want to let you wait in the house until Steph comes back, but I need to know that I can trust you." I look at her. She looks fragile and in need of help. If I stay close, I could easily overpower her if needed.

"No." She shakes her head. "No weapons, nothing. I'm just in pain and I need help."

I look into her eyes and see nothing but pure terror. At that moment I make a judgement call to let Corinna into Steph's home. I raise an arm to gesture for her to enter.

Corinna's pale face was drawn in anguish, her eyes had widened in panic, then closed as though she was talking silently to herself. She had hesitated briefly before walking gingerly towards me, into the house. I pointed to the living room seating area and told Corinna to sit anywhere she wanted, watching as she sat down slowly on one end of the blue sofa, hands still clutching her coat around her, the strap to her bag sitting on her shoulder. The way she winced when she lowered herself rang alarm bells in my brain, and I sat in one of the chairs watching her closely before getting out my phone.

"I'm going to ask Steph how long she'll be," I say, quickly typing a text to Steph asking her to come back as soon as possible. I press send and wait for a reply. The ping of the phone breaks the silence. Steph says she's on her way back.

"Corinna," I began. "Steph and I will help you if we can. I need to ask you something and it's really important."

Signs of panic reflected across her face as she sat up as if ready to run out of the room. I don't want to upset her, don't want her to leave.

"Are you hurt?" I ask.

Corinna's head falls to her chest in a sign of resignation and she clutches her coat so tight that her knuckles begin to whiten. Her shoulders start to move uncontrollably, and I can hear low wracking sobs coming from her downturned face, sobs that reveal pain, terror and desolation. I feel a bubble of anger begin to simmer at my feet and slowly make its way up my body until my hands are balled into fists at the side of me in rage. Did Ray do this to her? I tell myself to calm down as a slight tick starts to manifest itself on my cheek and I begin to grind my teeth.

I was pondering Steph's arrival when the key turned in the latch. The front door opened and a weary-looking Steph walks in. Thank God. Steph will know what to do. For a moment Steph looks unsure of what to do and I watch her push her long hair behind an ear. I can see she's chewing her inner cheek. Our eyes meet, locked together in a moment of understanding that we've found Corinna and need to help her. I turn my head to Corinna, her face wet with tears, she seems unable to take her eyes from Steph.

"Hi, sorry I'm late." Steph looks apologetically at me, wriggling out of her jacket and placing it over the arm of a chair.

"No problem," I respond.

"How's Ben?" Steph drops her bag on the same chair. "Anything from him?"

"Nothing," I assure her. "I haven't heard from him for hours."

"Good. I'll check on him in a minute."

Steph faces Corinna, and in a low voice she asks:

"Corinna? Are you OK? I've been looking for you."

"Steph?" Corinna stares at Steph. Her words tumble out like an avalanche of emotion desperate to be released. "It's all such a mess. It happened so fast. It was Ray, I met him a month ago. He told me about you, wouldn't stop talking about you. I didn't know where else to go."

Reacting to Corinna's outburst Steph's forehead crinkles in anguish, her lips drawn together. She looks almost as distressed as Corinna. Steph turns to Corinna and touches her arm gently before sitting in a nearby chair.

"It's OK, Corinna. We will get you medical attention and help you to sort this out."

The way Steph says "we" makes me feel unexpectedly pleased and a wave of affection for this woman sweeps over me. We hardly know each other and yet, from the moment she opened her door to me, I felt it. A connection. God. This is getting complicated.

Corinna looks dazed, her eyes are flickering from one of us to the other and I think shock is setting in. Steph and I know that Corinna needs an ambulance because we don't know the extent of her wounds and it's important that she is processed as soon as possible. Still, Steph sits, arms resting on her lap, fingers clasped together as she looks at Corinna.

I lean against the doorframe that links the living room to the dining room, fold my arms over my chest and say quietly to Steph:

"We need to call an ambulance."

She looks at me as if she'd forgotten I was here.

"Sorry, Jack. We do," she apologises. "Might be better if you do it in the kitchen. I can talk to Corinna then."

I nod but don't move. I'm mesmerised by this young woman standing in her living room, captivated by the scene unfolding in front of me.

"I know about Ray." Steph leans forward, a determined look on her face. "But first I need to know that you're alright. Do you think you can take off your coat? I'm not going to examine you, but I do want to see if you're visibly bleeding."

"I can't," Corinna murmurs.

"Why?" Steph asks.

"It hurts too much." At those words I look at Steph and her mouth forms a grim line. We freeze, dreading what we will find. Slowly Steph stands and holds out a hand to Corinna, silently asking her to stand.

For a moment I'm not sure if she will take Steph's hand, but after a moment Corinna sighs and takes the offered hand allowing Steph to pull her to her feet. Corinna takes the bag off her shoulder, undoes the belt to her coat, and then in excruciatingly slow motion she undoes three large buttons and lets the coat fall from her shoulders.

Corinna is wearing a pale blue button blouse over black leggings. There are torn strips on the blouse as if it has been cut with scissors or something sharp. Streaks of blood seep in a criss-cross pattern across the front like smudges of paint. The top two buttons have been left undone and you can see red fingerprint marks around her pale neck with a thin bloody line trailing down towards her chest.

Steph stares at the blood, the fingermarks and the slashes on the clothes, and for a second I see a brief glimpse of something akin to recognition shadow her face. She looks visibly shocked.

"Please help me," Corinna implores in a quiet voice, "it hurts so much."

"Oh, sweetie." Steph's voice sounds anguished as though she's about to burst into tears. She carefully holds the sides of Corinna's arms.

I look at them both and disappear into the kitchen to call for an ambulance. Once this is done and I'm assured that the paramedics will be with us as soon as possible, I put the kettle on to boil so I could make hot drinks. I needed something to keep me busy. I try to block out the sighs of pain and discomfort coming from the lounge. I am full of rage. It's a good thing that bastard is dead, or I would have been hunting him down tonight and doing the job myself.

I grasp the handle of my coffee mug so tight that I'm sure it will snap off at any moment. I cannot understand how a man can do that to a woman. Only a monster could hurt another human being in that way. My chest feels tight and I'm so wound up that I feel the need to get some fresh air into my lungs. I put my mug on the counter, stride to the white kitchen door, grab the chrome handle and throw the door open. I feel better as soon as I step over the threshold into the cool darkness that blankets the early hours of the morning.

I breathe in deeply, taking a few steps from the door as the cold air catches the back of my throat. I want to help Steph, I can't explain what it is but something about her and Ben makes me want to chase every nightmare, every painful memory, bruise and broken bone away. Don't get me wrong I'm not a hero in any shape or form, but I cannot abide bullies or men who use women as punchbags.

A movement from behind me catches my attention as I stare into the dark shadows of the garden.

"She's bleeding quite a bit." Steph's low voice breaks the dark silence as I feel her move next to me. "I've left her in the living room with a cup of sugared tea to give her some energy. How long until the ambulance arrives, do you know?"

I look across at Steph's profile and the brightness from the open door with its fixed ceiling light skims her face. I see the tracks of tears which have fallen on the side of her cheek. My need to comfort her overwhelms my need to keep my distance, and in that moment I can't help but reach for her hand and thread her fingers through mine. She tightens her fingers around mine. Warm and soft.

"They said they'd dispatch one as soon as possible," I reply.

"Good." She sounds relieved. "The sooner she gets medical care the better. Two things happened in Ray's house last night that we know for sure. One is that Corinna got hurt, and number two is that Ray died. I'll call Noah, Jem's solicitor husband, in a few hours. Corinna is going to need a solicitor. I'll also get Stuart and Jenny on board in case she needs a place to stay."

"That's a good idea," I say, gently squeezing her fingers.

"Jack?" Her voice seems uncertain. A question. So, I turn to look at her.

"Yeah?" I answer quietly, scared of what she's going to ask. She faces me and the glint in her eye tells me she's near to tears.

"Is this my fault? Should I have done more to try to put him away?"

"No. Steph." I stop her right there trying to keep the anger from my voice. There's no way she's taking the blame for what that bastard did.

"Don't you dare blame yourself for what he did. This is on him. Everything he did was on him. You pressed charges and it didn't go to court. That's on the justice system, but you are not to blame for his actions."

"But, Jack," she tries to argue, self-doubt evident in her voice. Her glistening eyes shine in the darkness.

"No buts, Steph. Please don't torture yourself like this," I say firmly, a pleading note to my voice. I place my hands gently on

89

her shoulders and watch for any sign that means she's not happy with me touching her. There's nothing. Of their own volition by hands move to tenderly cup her face.

"Not your fault," I whisper, holding her gaze. Her lips tremble and her shoulders begin to shiver. With the cold, I think.

The sirens bring us back to reality. They're getting closer. Probably in the next road. I take my hands from her face and wait for the noise to increase as the ambulance turns in to our road.

"Well, if the noise from the sirens doesn't wake Ben, I don't know what will!" she says.

"Why don't you go check on him and I'll let the paramedics in?" I suggest as we walk into the kitchen.

"I'd like to follow Corinna to the hospital, check she's alright. I'll need to notify the relevant people that we've found her and get one of my female DCs to meet us at the hospital," Steph says as we reach the dining room. Instinctively I know she wants me to stay but doesn't want to ask me. I know that she's used to being independent, so I defuse the situation by offering.

"I'll be here. I'll crash on the sofa."

"Thanks. I'll check on Ben and let him know that I've got to pop out again. I'll get you a couple of blankets." The relief shows in her face as her tired features relax, and I choke back the need to hold her and tell her that everything will be alright.

We walk into the lounge to find Corinna, her coat pulled tight around her, fast asleep on the sofa. She looks so peaceful. Steph smiles at me. It feels good to be helping her in any way we can. I smile back at Steph, watching her quietly climb the stairs. I hear her open a door, walk in and back out again. I guess Ben didn't hear the sirens after all. As she comes down the stairs with pillows, a sheet and a couple of blankets she's talking in a low voice on her phone. This woman never stops. Her independent life, her son, her work. It's everything to her.

Ten minutes later and the house is quiet again. Steph has followed Corinna to the hospital. This is going to be a long night. I look at the clock on the lounge wall. It's 2.15am already. I sink down onto the sofa, put my phone next to my head and pull the blankets over me. I need to get the spare charger from my car after I've had a quick nap, there's not much life left in my phone. But for now, I'm exhausted. Sleep claims me before my head even hits the pillow.

Chapter 9: A wolf in sheep's clothing

Corinna

How on earth did I get into this situation? I can't get comfortable in the patient transport chair I'm strapped into in the ambulance. I feel every turn in the road, every bump, every increase in speed and every time the vehicle comes to a standstill. I absently rub my neck and a shock of pain from the cuts Ray made with the knife takes my breath away. I wince, scrunch my eyes closed and count to ten, trying to block out the pain.

"Please don't do that," the male paramedic who introduced himself as Len tells me. He's the one looking after me in the back of the van. The woman paramedic, name unknown, is driving.

"Sorry," I say with a wince.

"I don't want you to pull the pads off," he says, his gloved hands adjusting the pads on my neck. He looks about forty, has a few strands of hair on his head and a brown moustache. He takes my left hand.

"I'm going to put a saline line in to you. Push some fluids," he explains, tapping the back of my hands.

"You've got good veins, Corinna." He swabs the back of my right hand with antiseptic solution and takes a cannula out of the sterile wrapper. "You'll feel a small pinch."

"Ah," I say, as the cannula needle is inserted into my skin. I try not to flinch as I watch Len swiftly tape the small device securely to the back of my hand. He takes a saline bag from an overhead unit and threads the tubing around a small hook on the wall near me before connecting the drip to the cannula.

"Well done." He smiles as we hit a bump in the road and my body tenses. I'm frightened, tired and in pain. I haven't eaten for at least twenty-four hours.

My mind wanders to Steph Rutland and her friend Jack. They took me in when I had nowhere else to go. It's strange, but I felt like I knew her before I'd even met her. The photos of her, Ray and their son were in his house. Ray was obsessed with her, loving her and hating her with equal passion until his distorted mind couldn't decide what it wanted. I'm glad I broke up with him. I've got more self-respect than to stay with someone who physically hurts me and is obsessed with his ex-wife. Why stay with a partner who measures you against his ex-wife? That's just wrong.

I don't know why but for some inexplicable reason I feel that I can trust Steph. Maybe it's because we have Ray in common or because we look alike. I just know that even though she's a police officer that she gets me.

The next few days are going to be hard, but if someone is watching my back, I believe I'll be strong enough to cope with the stress. I know I kicked Ray hard in the groin, I know I hurt him, but it was nothing compared to what he was doing to me and it was the one way I could think of that would allow me a chance to escape. He was like an animal. Feral. I can still feel the knife as it sliced through my skin, the pain so bad I almost passed out. The metallic smell of my own blood as it dribbled across my neck and down my chest to my breasts continues to haunt me. I smell it everywhere. Bastard. I hope he thinks twice before trying to hurt someone else.

"You OK?" Len asks, breaking into my thoughts.

"Yeah." I try to smile. I feel happier knowing Steph is following me to the hospital.

I remember her words before we left. The paramedics had been checking me over before finding me able to walk carefully to the ambulance and into the waiting transport seat. Steph and I had been sitting in the living room.

"When you get to the hospital," Steph tells me, "the nurses will check your wounds and take blood samples for evidence and elimination purposes. I will need to speak to my colleagues and update them. I'll need to take your statement describing what happened at Ray's house, including how you came to be injured. We'll probably do that tomorrow. One thing you need to remember though, Corinna…"

I looked at Steph taking in her every word, me sitting in the armchair and Steph on the sofa. I was unsure what she was about to say. I hold my breath. Waiting.

"I am here for you," she continues, "and I will help you in any way I can."

"Thank you," I say quietly.

The ambulance parks outside the Accident and Emergency Department and myself and the paramedics arrive to find it is relatively quiet. I hope fervently that I'll get some pain relief soon. My neck and chest feel like they've been ripped open, they're throbbing so badly. I think I've been running on adrenaline since leaving Ray's house.

There is something that I'm afraid to ask Steph. I want to know if they found Ray in his house. I don't believe that I've injured him too much. A knee to the groin can hardly cause significant damage, can it? I'm terrified what he might do to me when he finds me. He's going to go crazy.

Steph comes through the main doors, a purposeful look on her face as she sees me and strides my way. She speaks to the staff and then we're shown to a quiet treatment room to wait for the nurse. The room contains a small white table and chair. There are a couple of floor-to- ceiling store cupboards along a wall and a moveable hospital bed. Steph looks at me and motions for me sit in the chair provided. Len helps me to untangle the drip so that I can sit in the chair and the paramedics both say a quiet a goodbye.

"Steph?" I finally ask the question that's been plaguing me since I left Ray's house.

"Yes?"

"Is Ray… is he OK?"

She walks to me, leans down in front me and gently pats my shoulder:

"No," she says solemnly. "I'm afraid he's dead."

My vision blurs for a moment as though a heavy object is crushing down on my head. Dead! He can't be. I only used my knee to hurt him in his privates for God's sake. Panic starts to set in as my shoulders start to shiver uncontrollably.

"Dead?" I say in disbelief. "He can't be dead." I grab the hand on my shoulder in panic and squeeze tight.

"Corinna, I don't know what happened between you both. But when we found Ray he was dead."

"Jesus!" I say, as my mind tells me to keep quiet and say absolutely nothing until I've spoken to a solicitor. "How the bloody hell can he be dead? I only kneed him in the balls." My voice is angry now. How dare Ray attack me like that and end up dead! Leaving me as the main suspect.

"You only kicked him in the balls?" Steph queries, her face puzzled.

"Yes. Well, I used my knee actually. I thought he was going to kill me."

"Shit." She seems distracted, trying to work through things in her mind. "Obviously there's something going on here that we don't know about. Try not to worry, I'm going to take your statement tomorrow and we'll go through everything in detail then."

I sit quietly, resigned to waiting for what feels like the inevitably bleak outcome to this non-stop nightmare. Ten minutes later the heavy wooden door opens, and two nurses walk into the room. Both nurses look apprehensive as they move closer to me. The tall, blonde-haired nurse with kind eyes speaks first:

"Hello, Corinna. Is it OK if I call you Corinna?" I nod stiffly in response. The unknown is always the worst when you're not sure what is about to happen to you. I think it's the anticipation, the waiting. It's like the first time you have sex, you don't know what to expect but you hope it's not going to be too bad.

"Good," says the nurse as though it's normal to be standing in a cold hospital room with a chest full of knife slashes. "I'm Staff Nurse Briony and this nurse here is called Terri. We're going to help you. I'm going to detach your drip for the moment and then we will both help you to take off your shirt and the rest of your clothes so that we can see what needs attention first."

 I nod in response.

"Are you in any pain?" Staff Nurse Briony asks, leaning down to make eye contact with me.

"Yes." My voice has a quiet, hollow sound to it. I raise my head and meet her gaze. Surprisingly there is no pity there, just a need to work through the motions of what needs to be done.

"We'll get you some pain relief as soon as we can." She gives me a small smile. I don't think to this day that she realises how much that small smile meant to me at the time. I take a deep breath and close my eyes. Please let's just get this over with.

There's a brief knock at the door and a serious-looking woman sporting a short, pixie-style haircut enters the room clutching an iPad and a small black case. She nods to Steph.

"Boss." The voice is soft but holds a harsh, no nonsense quality to it.

"Justine. Thanks for coming."

"Of course," the woman named Justine replies.

I'm surprised when the woman turns her attention to me. She tries to soften her facial features by offering a faint smile.

"Hi, Corinna, my name is DC Justine Placker."

I nod shyly in response and listen as she continues:

"I work with DI Rutland. I'm going to take some photos of you if that's all right? The first thing I need is to get a set of fingerprints from you. I'll follow this with a saliva swab and take samples from under your nails." She looks at Staff Nurse Briony. "Is that OK with you?"

The nurse looks a little unsure. I think she wants to check my cuts first. She looks at Terri briefly before answering firmly:

"Yes, as long it doesn't take too long. She needs medical attention. Terri, can you detach the drip for the officer please?"

Terri moves forward to the storage cupboards. She's smaller than her colleague and needs to stretch her slender arms significantly to reach the higher unit, her brown ponytail draping down to her shoulders. Once she'd slipped on the gloves and collected a few things in a small tray she steps over to my chair.

"This shouldn't hurt," she says in a raspy voice as she pulls out the drip, keeping the cannula still attached to my hand. "There," she says. "OK?"

I nod. She was right, it didn't hurt.

"I'll be as quick as I can," DC Placker says to the room as she carefully puts her case on the table beside me. "This won't hurt, Corinna. We'll start with the fingerprints." She looks at me, opens the case and takes out a pad of ink and pre-printed paper sheets with space allocated for each finger on each hand.

"Are you able to stand?" she asks me.

I nod but I feel a little vacant as though I'm in the room but hovering outside of my body. I use the side of the table to push myself out of the chair. My injuries feel like sandpaper, tight, stinging. Every time I move, they become unbearable as if someone is throwing salt at them. The loneliness creeps into me.

DC Placker notices my sharp intake of breath as she gently but firmly picks up my right hand being careful not to touch the cannula, selects the thumb, rolls it in ink and pushes it into the designated paper space. She repeats this until all ten fingers are printed.

I look at DC Placker waiting for my next instruction.

"Are you holding up, Corinna?" the DC asks. "You're looking a little pale."

The nurses step forward. Staff Nurse Briony takes control.

"I think Corinna needs to sit for a moment. Can you continue your swabs while she's resting?"

"Yes, of course," replies the DC softly, her eyes fleetingly meeting Steph's.

The fingerprint equipment is returned to the case and evidence is recorded and sealed in relevant wallets. Details from Ray's attack flit through my mind making me shudder. I remember trying to get him off me during my futile attempts to protect myself. I remember reaching out to scratch Ray's face and I remember dragging my short nails down into his skin.

I sit like a shop window mannequin as the woman DC uses a thin wooden applicator to collect the evidence of Ray's skin from under my nails. And I sit, feeling cold and detached as she asks me to open my mouth and uses a long-handled cotton bud to swab the inside of my mouth.

I hear voices talking. The DC is telling someone that she'll send everything to the lab for processing. She's probably talking to Steph. My shoulders slump in surrender.

Someone pats me on the shoulder, and I wince. Don't they understand I'm in pain?

"We're nearly done now, Corinna," says Staff Nurse Briony. "We are going to help you to remove your clothes so that we can make an assessment of your wounds and how best to treat them. Do you think you can stand for a little while?"

With a nurse either side of me I stand and move until I am standing in the middle of the treatment room. I try to muster whatever energy is left in my exhausted, brutalised body. Let's just get this over and done with.

Staff Nurse Briony and Terri help me to take off my shirt. They see fingermarks around my neck and the cuts from the knife as Ray sliced my skin open from left to right over the top of my breasts and slowly moved up to my neck. The cuts are deeper on my neck. I look as if someone has tried to decapitate me. Briony tries hard not to flinch or look at her colleague, but her eyes turn to Steph of their own volition. Steph nods at her and stands there watching. There's no disgust, no pity, only a strange feeling of understanding.

My mind wanders back to the time when I first met Ray. I'd been visiting the Oxford University Museum of Natural History, scouting out the place because I'd applied for a job as a collections clerk there and had managed to get an interview. My long wayward curls had been left free to bounce in whichever direction they wanted, and I was wearing black cropped leggings with black flat shoes under a blue denim skirt to keep out the chill. A purple long-sleeved T-shirt kept me warm and went well with my wooden fish necklace and matching earrings. The top was thin enough to wear under my favourite three-buttoned black coat which I was now carrying over my arm. The fossilised remains of long dead dinosaurs from millions of years ago were fascinating as I meandered through the glass exhibits and the moulded recreations. This job, if I could get through the interview, would be amazing.

After my years in the care system at eighteen I finally became old enough to have my own place. Well, it was almost my own place. It was run by the local council as part of the government initiative to narrow the gap between children who had been bought up in care and those who hadn't. I had access to support if I needed it, the flats were a purpose-built independent living facility for young adults leaving care.

"It's an Iguanodon," a voice stated with confidence as I take my eyes from the display and search for the owner. A man with broad shoulders sits on a nearby bench studying the same display. His angular face and Grecian nose give him the look of a film star. I'm mesmerised by bright sea-green eyes which are marred only by the visible dark shadows beneath them. I can't take my eyes off him or his dark brown hair cut just below the neckline. He wears a black leather jacket and black jeans with confidence. I'm interested.

"They were plant eaters you know. They ate things like early flowering plants and conifers," says the man as he looks up from the fossils and gives me a warm smile. "They also grew to be thirty feet long and lived during the early Cretaceous period," he continues with some authority, making me wonder if he worked as a teacher or lecturer.

"They did? How long ago was that?" I asked, fascinated by his knowledge and wanting to know more.

"Between one hundred and twenty-five to one hundred and twenty-six million years ago," he answers without even having to think about it.

"Wow! That's a long time," I couldn't imagine that sort of time frame. I'm only eighteen. My life has been hard so far, I couldn't grasp properly what had happened to me in the past eighteen years, let alone hundreds of millions of years ago.

"It sure is hard to grasp. Want to sit down?" He moves along the bench to make space for me.

I briefly hesitate but my feet betray me by walking straight to the bench and sitting down beside him.

"I'm Ray by the way," he says, holding out his hand.

"Corinna," I reply, taking his warm, firm hand and wondering what it would feel like to walk hand in hand down the street with this man.

"Pretty name," he smiles, then his eyes become dark and begin to glass over as though he's thinking about something else. "Sorry, you remind me of someone I used to know."

"Oh no. In a good way or bad way?" I ask, hoping that it's in a good way.

"A bit of both," he muses, his lips twitching upwards. "Fancy a coffee? I know a nice place five minutes' walk from here. The coffee is good."

My usual reserved conscience stood up with her heckles rising and shouted, *No, don't you dare.* The adventurous side of my nature overrode the warning and before I could stop myself, I said clearly:

"Yes, sure. Lead on."

It's strange looking back as he was so much older than me, almost old enough to be my dad, but I felt lonely and tired of doing things on my own. Maybe I was looking for a father figure, someone to take care of me for a change. He left when I was seven years old. I wanted to get to know this man, the man who knew about dinosaurs, what they ate and when they lived. It was out of character for me, I'm quite a reserved person, but I smiled back at him.

And that's how I met him. We went for a coffee in a quirky little place on the corner nearby. I had a latte and Ray had an espresso as we watched the hustle and bustle of tourists and inhabitants of Oxford as they went about their business. Sitting comfortably in our eclectic mismatched chairs with a small table lamp between us, we chatted about everything to do with life and the universe for hours. In fact, we talked until the shop was about to close and I smiled sheepishly at the staff, feeling embarrassed about drawing attention to myself, to us. He seemed so nice. How was I to know that he was a wolf in sheep's clothing as we exchanged phone numbers? How was I to know that this cool guy would turn out to be my worst nightmare?

"Corinna, can you sit on the bed please?"

A voice breaks into my thoughts. I think it's Staff Nurse Briony. Before I have time to reply I am gently pushed against the bed until I can feel it touch the back of my knees.

"We're going to inject your wounds with anaesthetic because you'll need quite a lot of stitches," the voice continues.

I feel like I'm still in a dream. I just want to block everything out and get this over with. Then something happens to me that has never happened before. The room turns to a fuzzy grey and voices begin to fade. Spots float before my eyes, my head feels dizzy… and then there is nothing.

Chapter 10: Second time lucky

Ray, one month ago

History is important, we need to remember and learn from past events. The idea that someone or something lived on this planet before humans fascinates me. Dinosaurs, relics, skeletal remains, learning about what used to be and how people lived years ago – these are things that thrill and excite me. I swear if I'd had the right upbringing with parents who cared about me enough to push me to succeed that I would have become an archaeologist.

That being said, I hadn't done too badly for myself. I had my own house in a nice area in Wantage, Oxfordshire and the majority share of a car sales business, even if that business wasn't doing so well. And I drove a nice car. What more could I want?

While the car sales business began to slump a year ago, the cleaning business has grown significantly. Six months ago, we had a meeting – Dad, Danny Devlin and I in a local pub. I had an idea what they were planning because I'd noticed the increase in bodies around the place and the never-ending cars that needed new colours and registrations. It took me a long time to find the right staff who were willing to get on with their job and ignore everything else that was going on. I couldn't have chosen better with my manager Luke Pertwee and his assistant Reggie Flonder. They knew when to keep their mouths shut and took their monthly wages complete with the attached bonuses.

Over the years I'd kept to my side of the contract and stayed well out of the cleaning business. As we sat mulling over our pints in the pub, it was clear that Danny D and Dad wanted to pull out of the original contract so that they could buy a bigger company and premises. In the pub Dad had argued with Danny to let me continue to hold the majority of shares in relation to the business. Eventually, Danny had agreed but he knew that the business already had a question mark over it. Dad had rescinded on his shares and so I now held eighty per cent. That's eighty per cent of a failing business.

My head has been all over the place since the car sales business started struggling and resulted in me being unable to make last month's rent on the salesroom. I need five grand minimum each month to cover my costs. Therefore, I went and did the only thing I could think of at the time and asked Danny D to loan me five grand two weeks ago. I think the stress of it is getting to me. I've had a niggling headache for about a week now.

I've got until the end of the month to come up with the repayment plus interest or Danny D will send someone to my door with the pliers to start cutting off my fingers and toes. I'm keen to keep all my digits, thank you very much. Danny said it's nothing personal, just business. Jesus! What a bloody mess I've got myself into! I've had an idea of doing a job with Dad but he doesn't have the greatest success in his line of work.

I got a call from Mum two weeks ago. I'd been cleaning the car on a sunny Sunday, a bit chilly but not too bad. I hadn't called Mum in weeks, so my first reaction was to ignore it because I knew I'd get nothing but trouble for answering.

"Ray? Is that you?" she'd asked in her soft voice.

Well, of course it's bloody me, I thought. My trousers were wet from cleaning the car and I needed to finish the job so that I could change my clothes.

"Yep. Hey, Mum. How are things?" I asked. She'd always taught me to be polite on the phone.

"Not good, Ray. Not good." She began to sob.

"Mum, I'm in the middle of cleaning the car. Can I call you back in say… ten?"

I didn't get any farther.

"It's your dad, Ray." Her voice is quiet.

"What's he up to now?" I half joked. "Is he in prison again?"

"Yes, he was in prison. He was arrested for taking stolen televisions from Dodgy Eric from down the road."

There's a pause before she continues. She speaks in such a low voice that I have to strain to hear. "Your dad's been stabbed, Ray. By another inmate."

Fuck. I dropped the sponge into the dirty bucket of water. My stomach felt sick. The only sound I could hear was my mother's quiet sobbing down the phone line.

"Is he alright? How bad is it?" I ask her.

"He's gone, Ray," she said sadly.

"He can't be," I argued. "I only saw him a few months ago."

"The knife pierced his heart," she sobbed quietly. "He died instantly."

"Shit!"

"Ray!" Mum sobbed.

"Sorry, Mum. I'm so damned sorry. Cannot believe the old bugger met his end in prison of all places." My voice sounds strange, hollow somehow.

"Can you come over? I can't find your brother. I need you." She sounded so sad, so lost. I couldn't imagine how she felt married to a man who had spent most of his life in prison. He never loved her enough to try and go straight.

"Don't worry, Mum, I'll make a few phone calls tonight and drive up to you first thing tomorrow," I reassured her.

"Thanks, Ray. I knew I could count on you." Her voice sounds less shaky.

Like a dutiful son I went to Tower Hamlets and stayed with Mum, helping her through this tough time. I felt numb. We'd never had a close relationship me and Dad, but he was still my dad and if it wasn't for him and Danny D I would still be living at home with Mum taking on dead-end jobs. Dave never made an appearance.

He's probably lying in a dark room somewhere either high on drugs or dead. I stayed with Mum for five days but returned home to Oxfordshire where I needed to put some thought into sorting out my loan.

I'm now down to four weeks to get the loan money for Danny D. And, pardon my French, but I'm shitting myself. I'm reading the local paper at my desk the following Monday morning at work when an advert catches my eye. It's for a debt collector. The company paid two hundred pounds for each debt collected. In my mind I calculate that I would need to collect forty debts inside of two weeks. Is it doable? I ask myself. Possibly. I make a note of the job details on my phone to follow up this evening.

Suddenly, I have a brainwave. My love life has been non-existent, which is mostly due to the fierce need I have to reconnect with my son and my former wife. I'm so excited I almost have a hard-on. Shit. This could really work. I can literally kill two birds with one stone if I get this right. Part one of my plan includes emailing my son. Getting him on my side, meeting up. Pulling on his heartstrings. Who doesn't want to have a relationship with their father? Part two would be to decorate my second bedroom in the house and to turn it from a study into a young male teenager-style room. Part two would also involve kidnapping Ben, hiding him somewhere safe and blackmailing Steph for his safe return. I could even hide him here. I would make sure he wouldn't come to any harm.

Brilliant! I love that. I get to reconnect with Ben again which is something I've been wanting to do for a while, and if Steph doesn't want to be part of our new family unit then that's her problem. Still, having Steph back in my life might be just what I need to help me get back on my feet.

I climb the stairs to the study, kick the door open and I turn on my laptop to check my emails. Nothing interesting there. I take a piece of paper from my trouser pocket and stare at the email address handwritten in blue ink. Lewis, the private investigator who had been checking out my former family for me, handed it to me a few days ago and I've been wondering what to do with the information.

I look at the room I use as a study with new eyes. This would make a great teenage bedroom, there's plenty of space and it wouldn't take much to change it over. I carefully begin to type an email to Ben and begin with a couple of lines explaining that I'm his father. I say how much I've missed him over the past eleven years, and in an attempt cause mischief between Ben and Steph I tell him that his mum had kept me away from him for those eleven years because of her delusions that I was a bad husband and father. Well, she had. Sort of. I type the subject heading as "Catching up" and let my finger hover over the send button before pushing it down firmly. And the email is sent. There's no going back now.

I was still thinking about the kidnapping and ransom idea, trying to firm up some plans in my mind such as moving forward to arrange a meeting with Ben. Or perhaps I could wait for him outside the school gates, when I realised that I was driving my black BMW into Oxford. I was mentally working out the step by step kidnapping process as I walked through the city centre to the open doors of the Oxford University Museum of Natural History. If I was clever enough it was possible that neither Ben nor Steph would know it was me.

When I reached the prehistoric exhibits I sat on a low wooden bench, thinking. I begin to study the familiar skeletal remains of an Iguanodon including the related drawings, artefacts and information sheets surrounding it. I know this information by heart. It calms me, engages my mind so that I can immerse myself in a time and place long ago. I look up and there she stands. The woman takes my breath away. She looks just like Steph with long, dark wavy hair and her slim build. Her short denim skirt over her black leggings accentuate the shape of her hips and bottom. Perfection. She was younger than Steph, much younger, which excited me. I couldn't help but be drawn to her, like a moth to a flame, as she studied the information sheets, looked at the exhibits behind the glass cabinets and gently touched the historical moulded recreations of creatures of a bygone age.

I sit and watch her, waiting for the right moment to say something. "It's an Iguanodon," I'd told her to get her attention. It felt good to have an excuse to talk to her and, as she smiled at me and tilted her head, her hazel eyes lit up. In that moment I wanted to impress her so badly that words tumbled out of my mouth as I explained about Iguanodons, what they ate, how long ago they lived. I could see the interest in her eyes as I talked, recognising the slight blush, a quick swallow here and there when you know someone is attracted to you, and then I asked her to sit down. I introduced myself and she told me her name was Corinna, as her soft warm hand took my outstretched hand. Corinna, the name suited her.

When I'd asked her if she'd like to grab a coffee, I'd waited with bated breath unsure of what I'd do if she said no. She didn't though, and despite the fact that she'd looked so much like Steph it took my breath away. I gave myself up to enjoying the moment of leading her to the quirky coffee shop I knew on the corner at the end of the road. We'd chatted for hours until the shop was about to close for the day, and I'd forgotten how good it was to really connect with someone.

Determined to give my relationship with Corinna the best chance I could, I tried hard to keep my temper in check, to be the boyfriend I thought she wanted. Kind, courteous, interested. When we needed to go through a door, I held it for her to go through first – smiling and gently holding her lower back as she walked past me. I'd pull out a chair for her to be seated when we ate in restaurants, wanting her to think the best of me. I smiled and listened to her ideas, ambitions and problems. It wasn't easy to be honest. Unfortunately, I didn't find her overly interesting, so my eyes would droop a little or my thoughts would wander to Ben and Steph.

The first time my tempter reared its ugly head was about two weeks into our relationship. I'd taken her to the cinema to see the action film *Equalizer 2* with Denzel Washington. It was good, he's one of my favourite actors, and Corinna had said that she'd wanted to see it. Then, out of the blue as we'd strolled hand in hand through the dark streets back to the car, she'd announced that she'd got the clerk job at the museum. Her face was beaming with excitement. I know I should have been happy for her, but I didn't want to share her with anyone or anything. Including a job. Before I could control myself, I'd turned to face her, let go of her hand and slapped her hard across the face in the street. I didn't even bother to check if the street was empty or not.

I just couldn't help myself. I was livid. An old woman with grey hair and thick-rimmed glasses who'd seen what had happened from across the street had walked over to us to ask Corinna if she was alright – and then turned her angry face my way to shout at me for hurting her. Even the old woman's menacing threats didn't dampen my anger. It just made it worse. I was like a ticking time bomb; the fuse had been lit and was simmering. Waiting.

A few days later I found one of my credit cards missing from my wallet. I'd noticed it that morning when I was checking my cash card was in my wallet. I'd meant to ask Corinna when I'd picked her up from her flat that morning, but then I'd forgotten. It was a Saturday and we'd visited the New Forest for the day. During a pub lunch beside Lymington Harbour her lovely face had beamed with happiness as she watched a father and son try their hand at catching crabs with a bucket.

We had arrived back to my house around 4pm and I'd made myself a cup of coffee while she she'd opted for water. I'd casually asked her if she's seen my Mastercard. She'd laughed, shaken her head and denied seeing the card. Obviously, I didn't believe her. That's not in my nature.

My temper erupted. Before I could stop myself, my hands were wrapped tightly around her throat and I was pushing her head on to the dining table. The glass dropped from her hands and smashed into small fragments on the laminate floor, like small hailstones. Her cry of surprise and pain as my hands closed around her slender throat told me how frightened she was. I felt such a rush of power and excitement from her reaction that I needed more. The whimpering sounds, the begging for me to let her go and the fat tears that rolled down her cheeks really turned me on. The sound of her head cracking into the wood was magnificent. I felt like a god! The power was so great.

I felt a release of excitement as she begged for me to stop hurting her. Hurting her? If she thought this was physical pain, she was in for a rude awakening. And then the enjoyment, the feeling of power and excitement suddenly left me. It felt as though something had snapped, clicked back into place. I looked at my hands that were still around her neck and let her go. I couldn't believe the horror in her face as she shuffled backwards until she stood hunched against the fridge. Her eyes were red with tears, her throat marked with my fingerprints and her bloodied forehead reminded me of my actions. She looked at me with disbelief and anger emanating from every pore.

"What the hell, Ray?" Corinna screamed, her eyes flashing with anger as she rubbed her head.

I looked at her and felt huge shame. If I didn't get my shit together, I would be back on my own again. Billy no mates.

"Sorry, Corinna. I didn't mean to hurt you. I just wanted my credit card back," I'd apologised, moving towards her until her hand came up frantically warning me to keep my distance.

"Stop! Don't touch me," she'd screeched at me. I knew I'd frightened her, and I wouldn't blame her if she left me and didn't come back. I put up my hands in a sign of surrender to show that I was backing off to give her some space. *You are a stupid man, Ray. Why can't you keep your temper in check?*

"I'm sorry," I said again. "I need to go." With that I left her in my house, still hunched by the fridge in shock, red fingermark patterns still around her throat like a fragile ruby necklace. *You are such a dick, Ray,* I tell myself on the other side of the closed front door. I hit myself in the head with my fist. Stupid man. Stupid man. I hit myself again.

At that moment my grey-haired neighbour, Geoff, opened his front door and popped his head. "Mr Delossi, I need to speak to you." He opened the door wider and pulled his faded brown checked dressing gown around his middle with his arthritic misshapen fingers.

"What, Geoff? This isn't a good time," I muttered without looking at him.

"I wanted to give you this back. I found it on the ground by your car earlier today." And with that he handed me my missing credit card.

"Thanks," is all I can say, as the red flush of shame colours my face. Again, I've let my temper get the better of me through assumptions and impatience. I can't bear the thought of facing Corinna and seeing the panic on her face, so I head to my local pub for a pint. I need something to dull the pain of being a dick.

Chapter 11: The plot thickens

Steph

I sit in the car which is parked next to my house and look at my watch. It's 4am. I left Corinna at the hospital with Justine and the nurses. After Corinna's fainting spell Staff Nurse Briony began injecting her chest and neck with anaesthetic in preparation for stitching her sore skin together. She was going to be bandaged from neck to chest. She looked both mentally and physically drained, poor thing.

They'd taken her to a ward of four beds where she occupies a bed in the far corner. The nurses pulled the curtains around her for privacy. She was put back on the saline drip to give her fluids and will be given pain relief when the anaesthetic has worn off. Beside her bed is a cup of tea and a couple of slices of toast. I am hopeful that she will feel better after some rest. I am so mad. Mad at the world, mad at Ray for being such a bastard. Just plain mad. But I also need to look after my team, so I told Justine to catch up on some sleep too and come into work a few hours later than usual as she looked exhausted after being up all night.

I see my reflection in the car mirror, the frown lines etched deeply across my forehead, and the crow's feet around my eyes. These are the marks of anger, resentment and deep-rooted pain. The marks of Ray. And I wonder who else he had left his mark on besides me and Corinna. I get out of the car and try to shake some of this anger from me because I don't want to drag it into my home. The need to rest is overwhelming, even my head and shoulders feel as if they can't support my body any longer. I let the weariness take over and feel relieved as I allow pure exhaustion to smother the anger like splashes of water on burning wood.

As I walk in through the front door all is silent in the house. I hear Jack snoring softly, which is strangely reassuring. I take off my

112

black ankle boots leaving them in the shoe rack in the hallway and pad quietly into the living room and over to where Jack is curled up on the sofa. I gaze at him and smile. He looks so calm and restful and so damn handsome in his sleep; that soft jawline, the long noble nose, and those full appealing lips. I pull the blankets over him properly as he groans in his sleep.

For what's left of the early hours though, I need to crash so I turn and head upstairs to my bedroom, checking on Ben as I pass his door. I quickly undress letting my clothes stay where they land on the bedroom floor, change into my flowery pyjamas and dive under the covers. Sleep at last.

It feels like I've only been asleep for a short while when I hear voices. I slowly open my eyes to find Ben perched on the side of my bed in the semi-darkness of my bedroom. He's munching a slice of wholemeal toast.

"She's awake," Ben says in a low voice.

I close my eyes again for a moment. I really don't want to wake up yet because then I would have to face the reality of another day of working on Ray's murder.

"Steph?" Now that's not Ben's voice, it's too deep, too husky. It's more like Jack's...

My eyes fly open and I stare across the room at Jack's unshaven face before he pulls backs one of the curtains to let daylight into the room, and I rub my strained eyes as they accustom themselves to the change. I mumble a good morning even though I'm pretty sure it's not going to be a good day, and it certainly doesn't feel like morning.

"What time is it?" I ask wearily, raising myself slightly and moving my pillows to buffer the headboard. I force my aching body into a sitting position.

"It's 7am. Thought we'd better get you moving, or you'll be late for work," says Jack with a grin.

I can't help but break into a smile at Jack. He sounds so domesticated. I watch as he stands beside the tea tray perched on the chest of drawers at the bottom of my bed. Strong tanned arms move below the rolled-up sleeves of his slightly creased blue and white checked shirt as he picks up the white and red spotted teapot.

"Tea? Sugar?" he asks, holding the pot aloft before pouring the tea into a mug.

I could get used to this I tell myself, waiting for my sleep addled brain to clear.

"Yes please, one sugar," I reply, my attention turning to Ben. He seems surprisingly chilled out as he finishes off his toast and leans to my bedside table to pick up a half empty mug of tea.

"What time did you get in?" Jack's voice cuts in.

"4am," I mutter. God. I'm going to be worn out today.

"We made toast," Ben says with pride, watching me take the mug of hot sweet tea from Jack. I close my hands around the mug, blow gently and take a small sip of the hot liquid. This is just what I needed. Ben slips off the bed, picks up the plate of buttered toast from the tray and offers it to me. Not surprisingly, there's around half a loaf of toasted bread stacked one by one on top of each other on the small plate. I study the tower of food and can't help but smile at Ben for his thoughtfulness as I wait for the pangs of hunger to leave my tummy before taking a slice. I take a bite, savouring its salty sweet taste. At this moment in time nothing tastes better than hot buttered toast. I watch Ben lay the plate unceremoniously next to me and take another slice for himself, closing his eyes in satisfaction as he takes a bite. Jack helps himself to a slice and carries on sipping his tea. For a few moments there is a blissful silence, apart from the satisfying chewing and crunching of breakfast and the slurping of tea.

The food and drink are beginning to make me feel human again, so I sit back for a moment and enjoy watching this fledging relationship developing between my son and Jack. They haven't spoken so much as a word to each other, but they seem at ease in each other's company. A pang of guilt hits me as I think of how Ben has missed out on having a male role model in his life. He is such a good young man – no longer a child – and he deserves the best; he deserves to be loved.

Jack puts his mug on the tray and sits on the side of my bed opposite Ben. With the boys either side of me it feels a little like they're protecting me, trying to keep me safe. God knows what from, but I know that the next few weeks are going to be tough.

Jack's eyes meet mine and he asks solemnly, "How is Corinna?"

I look at him, then at Ben, telling him we need to be discreet about this if we're talking in front of Ben.

"I think she's alright. I left her with Justine and the nurses. I'll call Jenny from The Lighthouse charity in a while to see if she can come over to support Corinna, as her advocate or similar. It's important that Corinna fully understands what is happening to her and has someone to support her. There's a vulnerability about her and I think she'd benefit from a friendly face and good advice." I look at Jack to check his reaction, feeling the bed move slightly as he rises and walks to the tea tray to collect his mug.

His graceful form resumes its place on the bed. I watch his lips form a slight grimace as he takes a sip of tea. "You're doing the right thing. I've only met her once and got the same vibes," he said, his eyes catching mine.

God, it felt good having someone to talk to, supporting your decisions. "Corinna told me earlier that she never hit or injured the victim with the bat. The only injury she gave him was a knee to the groin to help her get away from him!"

"Bloody hell!" Jack almost chokes whilst he's drinking his tea. "Who killed him then? And why?"

"I don't know. That's something I need to address to the team this morning," I mutter more to myself than to him. "Someone else was in that house and that's our murderer, I'm sure of it. I can't blame Chris for freaking out about this case either due to its mounting connections to me and my life. After all, we did find those photos at his house and my name was scribbled in Corinna's handwriting at her flat."

I close my eyes to block out everything and take a deep breath, just for a moment, so that I can calm my mind. When I'm composed, I ask the boys to leave so that I can shower and dress. Jack and Ben both stand up, and Ben leans over and kisses me on the cheek. "I need to get ready for school anyway," he says.

A sudden thought hits me and, loathe as I am to do it there's a niggle that needs sorting. I ask the question that may or may not be significant. "Hey, Ben, what size trainers are you?"

"Why?" he asks.

"Nothing. Just thinking I may treat you to some new ones." It's only a little white lie. Jack looks at me, a question in his eyes, but I slowly shake my head. It can wait until Ben leaves the room.

"Ah. Thanks, Mum. I'm seven and a half," he says, walking to his room to get ready for school.

"Trainers?" Jack asks me as soon as we are alone. *Please don't let those trainers Ray ordered be meant for Ben,* I silently pray.

I rise from the bed and walk towards Jack. Padding slowly across the carpet until I am close enough to feel his body, I look up at him, still in my flowery pyjamas and hold his gaze.

"Ray ordered a pair of Nikes. The delivery guy couldn't get an answer at Ray's so left them with the neighbour."

"You don't think…?" he begins to ask the question that's been worrying me.

"I don't know what to think, but as soon as I get into work, I'm going to find out the size of those trainers and pray that they're not seven and a half. Because that means there's a possibility that Ray may have got them for Ben. More importantly though, I need to find the right time to tell Ben about Ray. He has a right to know." I rub my forehead. I can feel a headache coming on already.

Jack's hands touch my shoulders gently and his thumbs move in slow circles. It's comforting. I like it. I didn't think I'd ever say that again. The thought of a man's hands on me should feel strange, shouldn't it? Why doesn't Jack's touch feel strange? Instead, the softness of his touch calms me.

"Take your time," he says quietly. "Tell him when you get back from work this evening, then you'll have plenty of time to talk it through."

"That's my plan," I assure him. "I'm going to leave work early to make sure that we have some time together. Daisy, a friend of mine who happens to be doing Ray's autopsy today, is coming over for a drink later. We're having a catch-up night," I explain, trying not to think about the awkward conversation I need to have with Ben this evening.

"I'll make sure that you and Ben don't need anything before I go, and then I'm heading home to change before I start my own investigations into Ray, his finances and the people in his life. I want to find out if it's Ray who's been taking photos of you and Ben, or if he hired someone to do it for him."

"Thank you. I don't know what I would have done without you yesterday," I say, looking at him and feeling cross with myself when a warm flush begins to creep up my neck. Perhaps when all of this is over Jack and I can start concentrating on exploring our own feelings. I'm not sure if we're an "us" yet but the feelings fluttering around inside me tell me that something is happening. He's good, he's kind and he offers to help people he hardly knows. That means a lot to me. I'm drawn to him as a person, a friend and as something more. I remember this morning how at ease Ben and Jack were with each other, preparing breakfast and bringing it up to me. It felt, dare I say it? "Normal". That we were a normal family.

I think that Jack can read my mind because his next words shock and warm me at the same time. "When this business with Ray is finished, I'd like to take you and Ben out for dinner, somewhere special."

"Dinner? Somewhere special? Both of us?" I ask, my heart racing. My eyes light up and I can't help but nibble my lower lip as I stare at his lips, wondering what it would feel like if he kissed me.

"Yes," he says, giving me the brightest smile. "But for now, you need to get ready for work." The lightness in his voice is infectious and I can't help but smile back. Jack strokes my cheek gently, takes my shoulders and steers me towards the bathroom at the end of the hall.

"Off you go. I'll make coffee." And with that he heads downstairs leaving me feeling warm, cared for and ready to start the day.

The shower invigorates me, and I'm soon dressed in my customary black bootleg trousers, white high-necked blouse and black suede ankle boots. I'm ready for work. I kiss Ben and wave him off to school and tell him that I'll be home at about 4pm so that we can have some time together. To my surprise he asks if Jack will be there. Could it be that my son is enjoying having Jack around? The protective mum in me wants to err on the side of caution. I don't want him to get too used to having Jack around in case things don't work out, but my heart tells me to take a chance with Jack.

I feel replenished after my mug of coffee as Jack and I leave the house, Jack to his red Mazda and me to my dark blue Fiesta. Jack leans into me and I feel his warm lips touch the side of my cheek. Briefly. He kissed me, albeit brief and on the side of my cheek, but he kissed me. I try not to blush, but I feel it coming anyway. I can't stop it. As the red flush reaches and warms my face, Jack's eyes catch mine:

"Gotcha," he mouths with a lop-sided grin.

"Shit. How do you do that?" I cringe, angry at myself. "I don't usually blush so easily."

"I know. I'll tell you one day," he winks. "Keep in touch. I'll text you with any updates," he says, his face serious now as he gets into his car.

"You too," I call back, reaching my car, opening it and sitting down. I move my rear-view mirror so that I can check my face. The blush is fading, and my eyes are bright. I feel alive.

***

My team are in the incident room when I arrive. They're early. The office is modern and open plan with a projector, various desks dotted around in different states of organised chaos and a whiteboard focused briefing area which homes portable incident boards on either side. Within the large open space there is a small inner office for me to return to when focusing on paperwork and confidential matters. The top part of my office consists of glass panels until it connects with the wooden brass-handled door and the grey panelled units making up the lower part of the office wall. It doesn't offer much privacy.

Our office is situated in a large grey modern building built five years ago to cover the policing and protection across the Thames Valley which covers Berkshire, Buckinghamshire and Oxfordshire. It's a lovely, bright environment to work in, with plenty of allocated parking and a good restaurant.

I look at my team of specialists. DC Justine Placker, who's supposed to be catching up on some sleep, sits typing furiously on her keyboard at her desk. She is a conscientious worker, has a serious character and is a good team player. She's petite, well-dressed in her black trousers and green blouse, and wears her hair in a short pixie-style haircut.

Chris Jackson is my number one. I couldn't do without him. He's smart, considerate and great for bouncing ideas off. We get on well and have been working together for four months now. He's a laid-back type of guy who consistently gives everything to the job. My DS is a worthy sidekick and if today is anything to go by, he's got a thing for my friend Dr Daisy Soames.

DC Danielle Roberts walks into the room. As my Information Technology Specialist Danielle works on all things that are IT related, from laptops to phones to retrieving and analysing information. Wispy mid-brown hair is secured into a loose bun, tendrils falling down the sides of her cheeks to make her look ethereal. She's not fragile though. She's fierce and passionate in everything she does.

I see Sam Tribble standing at the back of the room. He's wearing his police uniform, shirt trousers and jacket, but no hat. He's as tall as me, lean and has a mop of short red hair. He annoyed me yesterday a tad, but I appreciate people who speak their minds even if I don't always agree with them.

I look at the team who will hopefully help me solve the crime of why Ray died so that we can bring his killer to justice. Several good mornings are muttered as I walk to my small inner office. Chris knocks briefly on the door, waits for me to nod for him to enter and walks in carrying two steaming coffee mugs, our usual first drink of the day. He puts his mug down on my light wooden desk next to my plastic cactus and a small silver photo frame of Ben at the play park taken when he was five.

"You alright?" he asks, handing me my coffee. He's not meeting my eye and his body language is stiffer than normal. He's uncomfortable with me which is crap because I really need him to be his usual self. I need to be able to rely on him today. I wrap my hands around the mug, enjoying its almost burning touch.

"I'm fine," I begin, wincing as the heat burns my skin. "And just for the record, Chris, I was with an old friend, Jack Kinsey, last night at home watching a crime series on Netflix." I look at Chris who has no reason not to believe me.

He offers a strained smile and shakes his head before muttering:

"OK, I appreciate your honesty, Boss," as he rubs his hand through his dark blonde hair making it look messy. "But you can't say that this case isn't bloody weird," he says, finally meeting my eyes.

"I know, Chris. I bloody know that. Let's just crack on with finding Ray's killer," I mutter as I place my mug on my desk and take out my A4 notepad and wallet which contains loose blank notepaper and other information. When I'm happy that I have everything at hand I pick up my hot coffee and take a long, scalding satisfied sip before carrying both into the main briefing area and announcing slightly louder than I'd intended:

"Let's get started."

There's a ruffle of papers and a whisper of movement as we begin the first briefing of the case. Chris walks by my side, his hair still slightly messy from earlier. He's wearing his usual white shirt with a grey tie slightly loosened at the neck, dark grey trousers and smart black shoes. He's a good-looking man. I like him as a person too. He's got his notepad and pen in his left hand and what's left of his coffee in his right.

Alongside Ray's photos and details on one of the incident boards on the wall, Chris has added Corinna's photo, a photo of the knife and baseball bat and, finally, the copy of my name from the notepad in Corinna's writing. Justine has added photos of Corinna's injuries and stuck them next to her photo.

I sift through my paperwork and pull out a copy of the photograph of Ben and myself which was found in Ray's bedroom. I add this to the board. The team look up from what they're doing and move closer to the board.

"Everyone, if you haven't already introduced yourselves to him this is Sam Tribble. He's going to be working this case with us." I look at Sam then nod to the rest of the group.

"And this is Justine. Chris you've already met, and Danielle is our IT person."

Heads nod in acknowledgement. I've only had three hours' sleep and I want to get as far forward into the case as I can today. More importantly I want to get Corinna interviewed, but I'll need to seek medical advice on that. I know Daisy will give me a call when she's started the post-mortem, so we'll get started while we're waiting to hear from her. I begin briefing the team on the events following Ray's death.

I continue to address everyone. "At 10.30am yesterday, Sam was called to a house on Burch Street, Wantage. The neighbour had taken in a parcel because the victim wasn't answering. The neighbour, Mr Geoff Cross, noticed the victim's car, a black BMW, was parked outside his house and tried to redeliver the parcel at 10.25am. Mr Cross looked through the living room window to find the deceased lying on the kitchen diner floor. He called the police. The deceased is Ray Delossi, aged thirty-six."

I point to the two photos of Ray's smashed head. The room is quiet, so I continue with the briefing. It's an integral part of the job to make sure that everyone has the latest facts and information, putting the jigsaw puzzle together one tiny piece at a time. My voice sounds hollow as I speak:

"I'm going to be as transparent as possible. Ray Delossi was my ex-husband. We divorced ten years ago and haven't seen each other for eleven years. Ray is Ben's father and he was a violent sadistic man. I divorced him on the grounds of unreasonable behaviour due to his consistent mental and physical abuse."

There. I've said it. I've let myself open to see the pity in their eyes, to process the personal information about me that once known cannot be withdrawn. I check behind me and perch my bottom on the nearby desk. Waiting. Silence hangs in the room like a heavy shroud as they all stare at me.

Justine puts her notebook and pen onto a nearby desk. She speaks first, her brows drawn together with sympathy:

"Boss, I'm so sorry. I don't know what to say. He sounds like a real bastard."

"He was, Justine," I reply, giving her a half smile. "That doesn't detract from the fact that he's dead though and that we need to find his killer."

"Sure," she agrees, nodding her head. She folds her arms and looks at me as though she's never seen me before.

Chris comes over to me and puts his hand on my shoulder. "Anything you want or need, let me know."

"Same here," Danielle speaks up, firm and in control, but there's no mistaking the storm in her eyes.

Sam shakes his head. Anger on his face.

"Thanks, all. But this was a long time ago. I've moved on since then and so has Ben. Let's get Ray Delossi's killer and close the case. Now, getting back to the body Ray had two head wounds, one to the front and one to the back. We don't yet know if this is the cause of death, but Dr Soames aims to do the autopsy first thing this morning. We have the baseball bat which could be the murder weapon, and it's confirmed that it's covered in Ray's blood." I point to the photo of the baseball bat on the board.

Chris and I exchange a look, and he takes over.

"There are no fingerprints on the bat as it's been scrubbed with bleach. One break we've got though is a young woman called Corinna James. There were numerous calls and texts to her from Ray's mobile. She was also in his contact list. It is believed that they were in a relationship. Corinna has been in care since she was ten years old and lives in a flat specially built for young people leaving the care system. We also found a bloodstained carving knife in the kitchen which we now know has Ray's fingerprints on it and possibly Corinna's blood. We're waiting on the blood results. Ray has no puncture or slash wounds."

I look at the group as they make notes throughout the briefing and watch Sam scribbling furiously away, which reminds me to get him to change his uniform.

"Sam, can you change into your normal clothes before you go off site, please," I tell him, noting his swift nod of the head. Looking at the incident board I study the photo of Ben and myself found in Ray's bedroom and feel a surge of anger. How dare the bastard take photos of me and my son! How dare he do that without my permission. I'm so angry that the plastic red pen I'm holding snaps into two in my hand.

"Bugger. Sorry," I say, offering a weak smile to the room. It takes a few seconds to calm myself before I continue:

"However, there are a few complications with this case. A framed photo of myself and Ben taken six months ago was found at Ray's house on his bookcase. It shows Ben and I at a local pizza restaurant. I'm not sure who took the photo, possibly Ray or an investigator he hired to find me. Another photo of us was found beside his bed."

I look around the room and see a few eyebrows rise in disbelief. Chris stands stoically beside me – my number one.

"Bloody hell, Boss. He was stalking you!" Danielle bursts out.

"Danielle," Justine warns, patting her shoulder to calm her.

Someone clears their throat and I look to see where the noise comes from. It's Sam Tribble.

"Boss," his brown eyes hold mine for a moment. "For what it's worth, it sounds like whoever did this to your ex-husband has done the world a favour."

"I appreciate that, Sam," I say, with warmth in my voice. OK, so it's not nice having work colleagues know too much about your personal life - but on the other hand, having their support as a boss or colleague makes all the difference.

"Secondly, at Corinna's flat we found a piece of paper with my name on it. Why I'm not sure. The third thing is that Corinna turned up at my home in the early hours of this morning with slash wounds, bruises and strangulation marks around her neck. She was in a bad way and has been admitted to hospital. Justine and I were there to make sure that everything was logged and recorded. Corinna revealed that she had injured Ray by pushing her knee into his groin during the assault and that he was definitely alive when she left his house."

"Kneed him in the balls! I like her already," Danielle says with a straight face, her eyes finally resting on mine.

I nod and muse over another thought:

"If Corinna only kneed him in the groin, who hit him twice on the head?" I ask, stretching my limbs to a standing position and looking at the sea of faces in front of me.

Chris steps into the conversation. He looks at me, the group, and finally his gaze rests on Danielle.

"Precisely. There's something we're missing here, something out of place," he adds, before continuing. "We've got Ray's laptop and phone and Danielle has started sifting through the data checking out his emails and texts. One thing that is missing is Ray's wallet so keep a look out for it."

"Sam," I say, "the parcel with Nike trainers the neighbour took in. Can you tell me what size they were?" I close my eyes and wait patiently for Sam to check his notes. There is a flutter of paperwork being shuffled and people scribbling comments and ideas as I continue to wait. Sam looks up at me, a sense of pride on his face.

"Seven and a half, Boss."

"Bloody hell!" I perch myself on the end of the desk. Chris looks at me and I shake my head. Where on earth will I find the strength to see this case through? It was bad enough when Ray was alive, and I found myself looking over my shoulder waiting for him to turn up on my doorstep demanding to see Ben. This man will be haunting me to the end of my days.

The plot thickens. Why was he ordering Nike trainers the same size that Ben wears? Were they for him? Was he trying to reconnect with Ben? I realise that the team are looking at me, waiting for an explanation and I've got no option but to put my suspicions on the table.

"Ben, my son, wears seven and a half Nike trainers. Either this is a coincidence or Ray was planning to get touch with my son after eleven years and was trying to encourage a relationship. We need to find out why Corinna has my address and how she got it. Was it from Ray? For now, Justine and Sam, can you go back to Ray's house. Take another look for his wallet and for any documents relating to Ben or myself. Find any utility bills, note any money problems and check if he was still in the car sales business. Where was he currently getting his money from? Finally, talk to the neighbours, especially Geoff Cross, who took in the parcel. What kind of neighbour was Ray? Did they witness any strange behaviour? I also want to know if any neighbours witnessed someone going into or out of the Ray's house between eight and ten at night. My gut tells me that someone else was there. Chris." I look at him. "Any chance that Corinna's fingerprints are on one of the wine glasses or something in the house? We need to confirm or eliminate if she was there around the time of Ray's murder."

Chris looks up from taking notes. "I'll get on to the lab," he says before turning his gaze to Danielle. "Dan, we need the usual stuff. I want to know who he's been dating, eating dinner with, working with and corresponding with. Look out for anything that suggests he's got financial problems on his electronic gadgets, phone, tablet and laptop. Any large payments he's made, or regular payments. We need to find out who took the photo of Steph and Ben. Was Ray stalking them or did he pay someone to follow them? We need to know who that person is and bring him in for questioning."

"Meanwhile," I say as I scan the faces of the team, "we're on the clock now. Once I've got Corinna in custody, I'm going to apply for an extension to hold her for ninety-six hours. Time is of the essence, so Chris and I will speak to Corinna at the hospital and if she's fit to do so we'll take her statement. Let's start putting the puzzle pieces together to build a timeline leading up to Ray's death last night." I feel a vibration as my phone buzzes.

I raise my hand slightly to motion to everyone to be quiet while I take the call.

"Hey, Doc," I say as I listen to Daisy tell me that she's begun Ray's autopsy and I tell her that I will be with her as soon as I've got Corinna's statement.

"Thanks, everyone," I add, addressing the room. "I'm sure you've all heard that. Don't forget to keep me in the loop. We'll meet back here at 2.30pm for a catch-up."

The team begin to disperse as I grab my phone and call Jenny. I update her briefly and ask her if she can offer support and monitor Corinna as an advocate during her time in the hospital and during initial station procedures. I also ask, should the court allow, if she and Stuart would be able to find a space for Corinna at Hope House, The Lighthouse refuge home near Newbury, where she can be looked after and given appropriate care. And thankfully, Jenny assures me that she will have a space available for Corinna whenever she needs it. Finally, I ask Jenny to contact Noah, Jem's solicitor husband, and ask him if he'll be available as legal representation. At least initially while we sort this mess out.

I finish my coffee, head to my office to grab my shoulder bag and coat and walk back towards Chris at his desk in the main office as he looks up from his computer screen.

"Ready," I announce, clasping my hands together.

He nods, picks up his coat, slurps what's left of his coffee and says with a wink: "My turn to drive?"

"Yes," I reply, before following him outside to the car park. "Let's see what Corinna has to say and what Ray's autopsy reveals."

Chapter 12: The colourless world

Unknown, four years ago

There's a beeping in my head. Beep. Beep. Beep. It won't stop. My eyes open and the world is still grey. There's no colour. Just grey.

I think back to the last time I saw Blip, her unresponsive, pale body attached to machines which bleeped continuously keeping her alive. She was there in body but not soul. Mum and Dad were sitting by her bed holding her hands and sobbing quietly.

I was standing by the window, arms crossed and staring at her lifeless body, willing her to wake up before we turned off the machine, silently seething and making pledges to find Ray Delossi and make him pay for what he'd done to her and to our family.

I close my eyes for a minute trying to remember how she used to be. Her shoulder-length dark hair, her heart-shaped face, her blue eyes, her smile so full of joy and innocence that made everything better no matter how your day was going. Her necklace, the silver butterfly pendant and chain which I'd given her for her fifteenth birthday, she'd never taken it off, not until Ray Delossi had ripped it from her delicate throat in a fit of temper.

She used to look so happy when she saw his smart black Audi pull into the drive to take her on a date. He was older than she was, perhaps in his mid-twenties. She was only sixteen years old, for God's sake. I know our parents tried to keep her in the house, they tried their best. They were constantly encouraging her to meet boys of her own age, to do stuff with her friends, stuff that girls of her age should be doing. Blip wasn't having any of it though. She was mesmerised by him.

One time, about three weeks into their relationship, I'd had a chat with him as he waited for her in his car:

"Look after her," I'd warned him trying to sound tough as I leaned into the open driver seat window. "She's young and besotted with you."

"Sure," he'd said, with the ghost of a smile. "I like her, she's sweet and kind."

"She's sixteen-years-old and a lot younger than you," I added. "She won't be like your other girlfriends."

His whole face suddenly changed into something really unpleasant. His green eyes almost bulged out of their sockets with temper and his voice held a threatening note when he began to talk. "How the hell would you know what my other girlfriends have been like?" he'd snarled, almost curling his lip. "Now, my girl's here so fuck off, kiddo, and leave us alone."

"You're a real big man with your mouth and your car. But take this warning." I met his eyes and waited for him to blink. There was no way I was backing down. "You hurt my sister and I'll fucking kill you."

Blip chose that moment to come rushing out of the house dressed in a short red and blue flower summer dress, while a blue cardigan gave her some warmth and her usual dark red tote bag was slung carelessly on her shoulder. The silver butterfly necklace hung dutifully around her slender neck as a protective omen and reminder that she was still so young and inexperienced.

"Sorry, Ray. Couldn't find my phone," she told him, getting into the passenger seat and blowing me a kiss.

"Don't wait up for me," she'd called.

I heard him mutter something to her as he drove off and watched as Blip's smile dropped. Bastard.

The necklace didn't protect her. My parents were unable to protect her. Neither was I.

No one heard her come back home that night. But come home she did.

Our parents had gone to work, and I checked in her room to see if she was OK. She was lying on her front, her arm over her face. The duvet was pulled up high, but I could still see a glimpse of the red and blue dress she'd been wearing the day before.

"Hey, sleepyhead. You alright?" I asked cautiously, standing with my arms folded by the door. There was a strange feeling in the room, not unlike the feeling you get when you watch something on the TV and you know something bad is about to happen.

"Yes," she said quietly. Too quietly.

"Blip. Look at me," I said, trying not to let my voice rise. I was worried.

"No," came her sullen reply.

"Blip. Please. Just look at me," I pleaded.

I thought she was going to ignore me, then there was a shuffle. Her arm moved and she shuffled into a sitting position.

My heart stopped. Fuck.

Her mascara had run. Red swollen eyes looked back at me with such sadness and humiliation that they shook me to the core. My little sister had been hurt and I hadn't been able to prevent it.

But it was the bruising to her cheekbone, her right eye and her neck that took my breath away. I swear I could see fingerprints on her neck. Immediately I moved to the bed and carefully sat down, ignoring the solitary tear that was rolling down her soft pale cheek. I opened my arms and she flew into them and I felt such anguish that I had to swallow a lump in my throat to stop the tears welling up in my eyes. I needed to be strong for her, but God it was bloody hard when your first thoughts include violence to the person who hurt your sister. Blip's head dipped low as she snuggled into my chest bringing me back to reality. Then the sobbing started.

"Oh, Blip!" I said, my voice rough with emotion, cradling her as softly as I could. Her arms tightened around me.

"I'm sorry," she hiccupped. "I should have listened. I'll never see him again."

"Damn right you won't!" I said, harsher than I should have. "Where does he live?"

"I'm not telling you. I don't want you to get hurt too. He's a psycho," she said firmly.

"Blip," I warned.

"No," she said in a low voice, her breath tickling my neck. "I'm going to draw a line under it and move on."

"You need to go to the police. I could go with you. Or Mum and Dad."

"No!" she said half sobbing as I stroked her hair slowly.

"Alright, calm down," I said, hoping that she'd change her mind. "We'll talk about it later. You're going to have to tell Mum and Dad, you know."

"I will. I can't hide this."

"Hey, where's your necklace?" I ask, noticing her bare neck.

"He ripped it off my neck." Her voice is so sad.

"Bastard! I'm going to kill him." I can't believe she won't tell me where he lives.

"Please don't say that. I couldn't bear it if you got hurt or was arrested for assault."

That night, together, we told Mum and Dad about what Ray Delossi had done to her and Blip had sworn she'd never see him again. Mum had broken down in tears and hugged Blip tightly.

"Oh, my baby girl!" she kept saying in between sobs. "We've got you. Everything will be alright."

Everyone could see that Blip wasn't Blip anymore. She became withdrawn, stopped eating, wouldn't go to college. Mum and Dad found her a counsellor called Jane who came to the house on a weekly basis to support Blip through her trauma. Mum wanted to take her to see the doctor, but Blip was adamant she just needed time to get back to how she was.

One day, about three weeks after Ray attacked her, I came into the house after visiting the local shops to pick up milk and bread because Mum and Dad had an appointment with Blip's Head of Sixth Form and Jane with a view to getting Blip back into studies. I'd been gone no more than fifteen minutes. The house was quiet when I returned. It was usually quiet. This time though it felt different.

I'd left Blip reading in her room. I went to check on her and found the bed empty. I slowly opened the bathroom door. My heart was beating so fast I thought it was going burst from my ribcage. And there she was in the bathroom, lying in the bath in a pool of her own blood. Her wrists were open and bloody, her eyes were closed. The small serrated kitchen knife that she'd used to hurt herself had fallen between her black leggings which were splattered in blood.

I'll never forget that sight. Or the day that colour left my world. How I managed to call for an ambulance or make the call to my parents I'll never know. Blip was kept alive in the hospital in the Intensive Care Unit by machines, their continuous bleeping keeping her alive.

"Goodbye, Blip. I love you. I'll always love you," I'd whispered into her pale, sleeping face the following day. It was my turn to say goodbye to my sister. I held her warm hand, stroking the back of it. I knew that her brain wasn't functioning, but I so desperately wanted her to flinch or move, anything to prove to me that I was wrong. I looked up at the ceiling, please let me be wrong, God. But there was nothing, no sign of life. I sat back in my chair beside Mum. I hadn't even realised that there were tears rolling down my cheeks until I felt the wet drops on my hand.

We sat quietly, Mum, Dad and me, each in our own private hell as the line on the monitor flatlined. The toneless noise. Mum and Dad each hold one of Blip's hands. Both are sobbing quietly.

"Belinda, we love you so much," my dad had sobbed, his drawn face wet with tears.

"Rest in peace, darling," Mum's low voice spoke to Blip before she took my hand and wrapped her soft hand around mine.

The day we turned off her life support machine.

My family was broken again. It couldn't be fixed. All three of us became empty shells of the people we used to be. The world was rotten, it had given my parents and I nothing but heartache and a lifetime of pain. To me that seemed ridiculously unfair when that bastard carried on living a carefree, painless life.

So, here's my pledge to you, Ray Delossi. Make the most of what time you have left on this earth.

Because the clock is ticking.

And I'm coming for you.

Chapter 13: Dig deep

Steph

Chris parks his silver Volvo in one of several busy car parks at the hospital and we make our way across the car park to the main entrance. Our destination, Reception on Level 4, Ward 7.

"So?" I ask, lifting my eyebrows to Chris as we take the lift.

"So, what?" he asks, shrugging his shoulders.

"You and Daisy?" I can't help but mention the tension between him and Daisy yesterday when she was at Ray's house.

"There's nothing going on," he mutters more to himself than me. He slides his fingers through his hair, gives me a quick glance and shakes his head.

"Really?" I say, "because you could fry an egg on the heat that was coming off you guys. With your shy glances, smiles and slightly flirtatious addressing of each other."

"Oh." Chris's eyes close for a second. When he turns to me, I see the tightened muscles on his face contorted into embarrassment and resignation. "I was hoping you wouldn't notice."

"Not notice. Why? Don't you like her?"

"Yes, of course I do." He sounds as if he's in pain, his voice is clipped as though he's angry with himself.

"Then why don't you ask her out?" I push for an answer. Daisy is a good friend, and from what I saw yesterday she likes Chris. A lot.

"It's not that simple. I don't want things to change, to become awkward," he replies, with uncertainty in his voice and eyes lowered so I can't see if he's telling the truth.

"It is. That simple I mean. I think she likes you too." I look at him and watch his eyes widen when I say she likes him out loud. "Just think about it. Life is short." I want him to know that it's important to take a chance every now and then.

The lift jolts to a standstill and the moment is lost.

"I'll think about it," he says, his voice holding a warmth that I hadn't expected.

I follow Chris, keeping pace with his brisk steps along the corridor, noting the blue arrow signage which directs us to Ward 7. The curve of the corridor leads us to a short blond-haired woman who is wearing a light blue coloured top and a stern face. She sits behind the reception desk on Ward 7 and squints her eyes in concentration at the screen as she taps on the computer keys. She doesn't seem happy to see us. I peer at the name on her lanyard which reads Registered Nurse Frances Glaterman.

"Nurse Glaterman," I begin, taking out my own lanyard and badge. I watch as the nurse looks up and scans my lanyard. "I'm DI Steph Rutland and this is DS Chris Jackson," I nod to Chris as he shows her his identity badge. "We've come to see Corinna James."

"Corinna James? Let me check where she is." She speaks in a deep Yorkshire accent and scans the computer screen. "Ah yes. Room 5. It's the first door on the left," the nurse replies without looking up at us.

"Thanks," I smile. "Can you find out if she's fit to be interviewed," I ask.

"Sure. I'll just check with the staff nurse." I watch as she presses a button on the phone, waits for someone to answer and asks the question. The nurse puts the phone down and looks at me.

"In the early hours of this morning she had fifty stitches across her chest and leading into her neck. She's still on the drip for saline but that should be taken off today. Painkillers are being given orally. She's eaten a little breakfast this morning, which is good. Staff Nurse says that Corinna should be fine to be interviewed as long as you take regular breaks."

We walked along the corridor to the first door on the left, Corinna's room, and I gave a brief knock before we entered. I'd expected to encounter the police officer I'd asked Justine to organise to protect Corinna's room, but the corridor was empty. This was not a good sign. Until I'd unravelled the full picture of Corinna's injuries and Ray's death, I wanted to make sure that she wasn't in any danger, from someone else or herself. The police presence should have been outside her bloody door. God, I know I'm tired but give me a break here, let something go right for once. I take a deep breath as the wooden door creaks open and we walk into the room, that is, until I realise that the room is empty. Bugger. Chris and I stare at each other in stunned silence. There is no sign of Corinna or the police officer.

"Where is she?" Chris asks, looking panicked. The bedclothes are thrown back and the saline drip left hanging. Corinna is gone. Has she been taken? Has she run away? People do strange things when they're under stress. They panic.

"I don't know," I say as I walk out into the hall looking for our missing patient. I catch a glimpse of Nurse Glaterman by the ward reception desk. She's about to walk in the opposite direction so I shout louder than I intended to. "Nurse Glaterman?"

The nurse turns quickly, her face unsmiling. "Yes?"

"Corinna James?" I say breathlessly. "Where is she?"

"She should be in her room." The petite blonde's face puckers into a frown as she puts a pen into her shirt pocket. She walks to Room 5 as if she hopes that Corinna will have materialised like a homecoming beacon. She sweeps the room with her eyes. "I don't know where she is. She's still on the drip and has a lot of stitches so she shouldn't have gone anywhere."

"Well she's not there! Chris, can you check the stairs? Show her face to security, see if they've seen her. I'll check the toilets, and where on earth is that damn police officer?" I scurry along the corridor looking for bathroom signs. It's like a maze. My phone rings. It's Justine.

"Hey, Boss. We've found the wallet. Danielle has it. It was inside Ray's kindle cover which had slipped down the side of his bed."

"Thanks, Justine. I'm just looking for Corinna. She wasn't in her room. You did get a uniform to guard her door, didn't you?"

"Of course," came the distant reply.

"Well, there's no one here now. If they've gone off site…" I try hard to keep the anger out of my voice. I know it's not Justine's fault, but I can't help but be annoyed that I need to chase Corinna James. Again.

My stomach is churning as I disconnect the call and swiftly follow the signs for the toilets. Left, right and first left. Bloody hell, someone could have pissed themselves in this place by the time they reach the toilets. Finally, I reach the female toilet door but there's a white printed "Out of Use" sign taped to the front. Shit. Now, where would you go, Corinna?

I try to retrace my steps and find a map of the hospital by the lifts. The next set of toilets are on Level 6, the floor below. I grab my phone from my pocket and call Chris.

"Any sign?" I ask, trying to keep the panic at bay as I take the steps as quickly as I dare.

"Nothing. You?" He sounds out of breath like me.

"I'm on the stairs heading down to Level 6, to the toilets. The ones on this level are out of order," I explain, spying the large double doors and Level 6 arrow sign.

"I'm by the main entrance, I'll head back to you now. Meet you on 6."

I push through the heavy wooden door and immediately search for a toilet sign. The simple arrow sign doesn't do the route justice as it's the best part of a five-minute walk down a side hallway and the Male and Female toilets are hidden in a recess some twenty feet away. I push the female toilet door with slightly more force than I intended to do and went in. Thankfully, I find a uniformed police officer standing straight with her arms at her sides waiting outside one of the cubicle doors. I flash my lanyard at the tall brown-haired officer before introducing myself in a rather out of breath voice:

"Detective Inspector Rutland. Is she in there?"

"PC Sheila Dawson," she nods. "She needed the bathroom and I wouldn't let her out of my sight. I've checked the cubicles for windows. There's nothing. She's in here." She turns her oval chin and blue eyes to face the nearby cubicle occupied by Corinna.

"Well done, Dawson," I say, texting Chris quickly to say I've got Corinna and letting him know where we were. The toilet flushes and I hear a shuffling as Corinna slowly unlocks the cubicle door. She's wearing a hospital gown and a blanket wrapped around her. Her feet are bare.

I breathe a sigh of relief. Thank God she didn't try to run. I look at her pale face and note her red rimmed eyes and nose. Corinna scrunches up the toilet tissue in her hands and dabs at her eyes and her nose in a vain attempt to compose herself. The maternal part of me wants to scoop her up and take her home.

"Sorry. I couldn't hold on any longer, needed the bathroom," Corinna says, her voice soft.

"That's alright." I try to talk in a softer more supportive tone. "You gave us a bit of a fright when we couldn't find you. Let's get you back to bed," I gesture with my hand pointing to the door.

"Wait. Can I have a moment?" She looks so fragile, so vulnerable and so alone. She reminds me of myself all those years ago. Of course, I had Ben, but I didn't have anyone to take care of me until I found Stuart, Jenny and Lottie.

"Sure. Can you give us a minute?" I ask Dawson. She nods, and without a word she quietly leaves the bathroom and gives Corinna and I some privacy.

As soon as she's gone Corinna bursts into tears and dabs scrunched tissue continuously at her eyes to catch them quickly.

"I didn't mean to kill him when I hit him in the groin. I don't want to go to prison." She puts her hands over her face in despair and leans over the sink. The blanket begins to slide off her shoulders.

I move forward and pull the blanket back in place.

"I know you didn't mean to hurt him. That's why I'm here," I begin, trying to make her understand that there are other things happening here. "There are things we need to sort out. The order of events that led to Ray's death. I've got my DS, Chris Jackson, with me and we're going to take a statement. You can tell us exactly what happened. I will do everything I can to see that you are treated fairly. The attack on you has been documented, photographed and recorded so that we have clear evidence of what he did to you. When we've taken your statement and you're released from hospital we will need to take you into custody, Corinna, due to the severity of the crime. I will apply for an extension for you to be held in custody for up to ninety-six hours before we need to charge you or let you go."

"Custody," she murmurs in a choked voice.

"Yes, custody," I repeat softly. "I will speak to my superior to get further guidance on whether, due to your circumstances and lack of previous criminal record, the court will let you stay at one of Jenny and Stuart's refuge homes pending further court proceedings. To be honest, despite the evidence of your attack, I don't believe that bail will be acceptable to the courts. Try to be strong. I've got you a solicitor. I know it's hard, but I need you to trust me."

Corinna shakes her head, tears falling down her cheek and I watch helplessly as she twists her hands together reminding me how young this woman standing in front of me is. I am full of anger and can't help but pace the floor with my head low, biting my lip to stop myself from muttering oaths, oaths that are desperate to be said out loud. I am angry that Ray chose a young innocent girl to violate, rather than a mature self-assured woman who wouldn't put up with his shit.

I reach out and rub her arm gently. "I have asked Jenny from The Lighthouse charity to sit with you until you are taken to the police station. Due to your background I feel it is necessary for you to have an advocate to support you and speak on your behalf."

Her gaze met mine, anguished droplets of tears rolling down her already wet cheeks. "Why are you doing this for me?"

"Because I've been where you are. Ray needs to answer for his violence, even in death. I need you to be strong and trust me."

Corinna tries to smile, so I pat her arm and pull open the door to let her through. We find Dawson outside and I catch her eye and nod as we walk Corinna back to her room.

Once Corinna is settled back into her room, I buzz the nurse to come and check her stitches are still in place and to reattach her drip. I quickly find the nearest drink machine, buy three lattes, and tell Dawson to take a break while we start the interview.

Chris takes one of the two green cushioned wooden chairs in Corinna's room, shuffling it forward to face her as she sits against thick white pillows with dark hair curling softly around her face. I decide to lean against the window. I feel fidgety, on edge. The situation is uncomfortably familiar.

"Corinna," I say to her, "we need to take a statement from you. We need you to tell us what happened with Ray. Take us through how you met him and lead up to what happened on the day he died. Can you do that?"

She looks down at her hands which are both clasping the white bed sheet which sits at her waist and nods.

"Good. Take your time, we can take as many breaks as you need."

Corinna looks at Chris, then her gaze moves to mine. *You can do it,* I silently plead with her. *You need to do it to protect yourself from prison and to let the rest of the world know what a monster Ray Delossi really was.*

After what seems like an eternity, a quiet voice breaks the silence as Corinna begins to speak.

"I met him in a museum in Oxford. He started talking to me and it went from there. He suggested coffee and took me to a lovely little place nearby where we chatted for hours. I was at the museum because I was going for an interview and wanted to find out a little about the place beforehand."

She pauses as she twists her curly hair around her fingers. "I quickly fell under his spell. He was charming, easy to talk to and good-looking. He was older than me and I was drawn to his confident manner and his knowledge of the displays in the museum. We talked about our previous relationships and he told me that he had been married to someone called Steph and they had a teenaged son named Ben." She suddenly stopped as if she was trying to figure something out in her head. Her eyes stared at the wall before moving around the room to focus on me. "Ray still wore his wedding ring, and this bothered me because I don't date married men. When I asked him about it, he just said it was there to remind him how mean women could be."

"Do you think he was talking about me?" I queried.

She nodded and gave a careful shrug. Her brows drew together as if the movement had caused immense pain. I watched her close her eyes to counteract the pain, her slender fingers threading together and rubbing skin against skin until her knuckles whitened. And an overwhelming feeling of sorrow for this young woman engulfed me that I had to cough to hide a sob.

Corinna opened her eyes and continued her story. "He said that you had left him and taken Ben with you years before and that he was trying to start again. I thought it was strange that he had a few photos of you and Ben placed around his house. I also thought it was strange that you looked a lot like me. Yes, he meant you," she said, rolling her eyes to the ceiling. "He made it clear from the beginning that you had let him down badly."

What a load of bollocks! Ray was a great manipulator and always led you to believe that the reason he hurt you was your fault. I felt my body grow taut and tried to suppress the simmering anger. I had to stay professional.

"When did he start hurting you?" Chris asked.

"We had been to the cinema and everything had been fine until I had told him that I'd got the job at the museum. He just stared at me with a shocked look on his face and said, *'Say again?'*" Corinna's face looked lost in the moment, recalling the unhappy memory.

"He looked at me with thunder in his eyes, then in the middle of the street he raised his hand and slapped me hard across my face. I remember an old woman came up to us and told him that he should be ashamed of himself."

I look at the floor, ashamed that I knew how it felt to be on the receiving end of a violent assault from him. Dig deep and find that inner strength I tell myself. I think of Jack and a calmness settles over me.

"Do you know what he said after he slapped me?"

I shook my head.

"He said, *'You are just like her.'* I will never forget it. I've never been hit by anyone before. I kept telling myself that I wouldn't see him again, but he kept apologising and saying that it wouldn't happen again."

Bloody hell, she didn't stand a chance, did she? He used her innocence against her, charmed her so completely that she couldn't see what he really was, a man with an appetite for hurting women. A quick-tempered, cruel bastard.

"A couple of days after that first time, he couldn't find his credit card and tried to strangle me while pushing my head into the dining table. By the time he'd finished hurting me I had a bloody gash on my forehead and had to buy wound closing plasters from a nearby chemist to help it heal. Ray later told me that his neighbour, Geoff, had found the credit card near the front door. I was a mess. I couldn't sleep because I was worried all the time. My new job began to suffer, I wasn't the same person I was before I met Ray. After each assault he apologised. But that didn't make it right, just because he said sorry. Two nights ago I went to see Ray and I'd planned to tell him it was over. Everything about our relationship was toxic and I needed to get away from him and look out for myself. I got to his house at about 9pm but he had been drinking, the stench of alcohol that came from him when you got close was almost unbearable. He poured two glasses of wine and handed me one. So, to give me courage I took a few gulps." She stops talking as though the memory was too painful to talk about.

"You're doing well," Chris says. "Take your time."

We both look at Corinna, her pale face, the cannula attached to the back of her hand, sore with stitches, fingerprints on her neck. She looked so fragile and yet there was a quiet strength about her, an aura of defiance to stand her ground and tell her story.

"Ray was agitated. He was annoyed at you for being in the police force and for doing well for yourself. He had your address lying around on a piece of paper. I slipped it into my bag. He raked his fingers through his hair, talking in riddles and pacing the carpet. He said he owed money to someone and needed to make some cash fast to repay him. Then he mentioned Ben and said he was going to use him to get out of a tight spot. I had no idea what he was talking about."

"Wait a minute. He talked about Ben?" I asked, an icy coldness coming over me making me shudder. I walk towards the bed and lean into Corinna. "What exactly did he say about Ben?" I ask, almost dreading to hear the answer.

Corinna looked down at the sheets on her bed. Her hands were clutching the crisp white sheet and blanket, turning it over and scrunching it.

"I don't know. Something like Ben was going to help him out of a sticky situation. I told you I didn't understand what he was saying." Corinna's lips begin to quiver in distress.

"It's alright, Corinna, calm down," I say, trying to get my temper under control. My palms were clammy, and I nibbled my inner cheek. Whatever Ray had planned for Ben was a moot point now that Ray's dead. Even so, I can't shake the feeling that we've both had a lucky escape from Ray's twisted plans. I walked back to the window then turned so that I could rest my bottom against the sill and folded my arms, waiting for Corinna to continue her story.

"I told him I wanted to end our relationship." She stopped and her gaze dropped to the bedsheet that lay twisted in her hands. "That's when he changed. It was as though a lightbulb inside him had been switched on and he'd turned into another person. A monster. *'What do you mean you want to break up?'* he'd said in a low, threatening voice. *'Who do you think you are? You're nothing but a common slut!'*

"I knew then I had to get out of there. 'Wait a minute,' he'd said feeling around in the pocket of his jeans, 'have you had my wallet?' He became manic and I couldn't get through to him that I hadn't seen his stupid wallet. I kept telling him he was frightening me. He threw me up against the fridge and I screamed, screamed as loud as I could for him to get off me. My back jarred from being hauled into the fridge and I was sobbing in pain, trying to push him away. Before I could scream, he'd wrapped my hair around his fist and pulled hard. Then, with my head yanked back and his face in mine, he spat at me. 'Where the fuck is my wallet? Have you put it somewhere? You're just like that bloody cow, Steph. Can't be trusted.' When he said that I knew that I was in real trouble. I kept trying to push him off, my arms were flailing all over the place and I managed to scratch his face. I was petrified. Through this his grip never loosened.

"He hit me hard across the face and I knew that if I didn't get away from him soon that he would kill me. One hand still fisted my hair, so he used the other to pick up something from the counter and pushed me onto the dining table. Then he grabbed my throat so hard that all I saw were stars and I couldn't breathe properly. I thought I was going to pass out. 'You're just a prick tease,' he'd told me as he slowly started cutting me with a large carving knife across my upper chest and up into my neck. I could hear the material of my blouse tearing as he cut through material and skin. There was blood everywhere. I could smell it. It was dribbling down my chest covering my bra and the top of my breasts."

Chris and I looked at each other. We'd both noticed how pale and distraught she was becoming. Her voice was wavering as she held back tears. She needed a break.

"Corinna," I said gently, walking towards her and standing beside the bed, "why don't we take a break for a few minutes? You're doing really well."

Corinna took a deep breath, lay her head on the pillow for a moment and closed her eyes.

"Thanks," she whispered.

"We'll leave you in peace for a moment. Would you like a cup of tea?"

"Please," she said in a low voice, her dark curls sprawled out on the pillow, her eyes still shut.

Chris and I left her to find a cup of tea. I think we all needed a break. I started walking briskly. I needed some air. Chris walked by my side, his plain black notebook in his hands. We didn't utter one single word to each other until we were out of the hospital main doors and in the cool fresh air.

"Boss?" Chris raises his eyebrows, asking a question.

"I'm alright, Chris. Just needed some fresh air." I look into his face. I can see he's struggling with Corinna's statement too by the crease of his forehead and the grim line of his lips.

"I'll never get used to this, to hearing people's pain," he mutters. "Sometimes this job gets to you. You try not to let it, but it does."

I lift my hand to pat his shoulder. My thick blue woollen jacket brushes against his arm.

"I think that's a good thing. That it still affects us. When it doesn't get to us it means we've become desensitised to the horror and the pain that people suffer." I look up into the sky, it's cloudy and grey, similar to my mood. I try to savour the fresh air before turning to my DS.

"Right. Let's get back in there and finish what we came here to do."

We return to Corinna's room picking up a cup of tea on the way and Chris resumes his seat on the green cushioned chair so that he can write down the statement.

I move Corinna's bed table closer so that she can still reach the hot drink when she's sitting up. I take up my interview position leaning against the windowsill. I look at her, still in her hospital gown, and feel such sadness for her. I see her bravado as she tries to show us that she's alright, despite the frown on her face and her red puffy eyes. I stare at the bed, not directly making eye contact and ask her:

"Are you alright to carry on?"

She nods and I hear a quiet, "Yes."

Chris looks at his notes. "You were saying that there was blood everywhere," he reminded her, staring at the words on the page.

Corinna shuffles a little higher and carefully picks up her hot drink, taking a short sip.

"The knife slicing into me was excruciating, and I think I tried to blank it out. I felt like I was going to pass out with white-hot pain and panic. Eventually, Ray got bored and said he'd got something special that he could use on me. He dropped the knife on the floor, kicked it aside and let go of me for a few minutes. I could hear kitchen drawers being opened and closed, so I pushed myself off the table away from him.

"I didn't understand what he meant until he turned to me. He grabbed my arm and pushed me so my back was hard against a dining chair. In his hand was a large screwdriver. That's when I screamed, holding my arms up against my face to protect myself. 'Let's play the slut game. You run and I catch you. Does that sound like fun?' The screwdriver was heading slowly toward my tummy and I found myself stumbling as I tried to move away from him.

"I looked around for something to use to defend myself with, but in my panic couldn't find anything. Everything starts to get a bit blurry here. I remember Ray coming toward me, I remember seeing the screwdriver, and then I remember moving forward. I used all my strength to bring my knee up and into his groin, and then I saw the surprise on his face as he doubled over in pain. He was moaning and swearing and began to crouch on the floor holding his groin.

"That's when I realised that I had a chance to escape. I know I should have called the police, but I panicked, was in shock. So, I grabbed my bag and ran for my life, covered in blood, wearing my ripped clothes, a slashed chest and neck, a bruised face, neck and a sore head."

"Jesus!" Chris whispers under his breath as he sneaks a glance my way. A flicker of a question floats across his face and he asks:

"Just to clarify, Corinna. The only thing you hurt Ray with was your knee?"

"Yes," Corinna says, looking up from staring at her clenched white knuckles and fingers.

"And," Chris continues, "you hurt him in the groin?"

"Yes." She stares at me as if to ask what is happening.

"You didn't hit him over the head with a baseball bat at any point?"

"Nope, I was nowhere near the bat. He usually keeps it in the living room."

"Why?" She looks at Chris and then me. "Why are you asking me this?"

"Because," I say, "someone hit him over the head twice with the baseball bat and we think that's what killed him." I watch her eyes widen and her face pale again as she processes what I've just told her.

"Holy shit! Someone came in after me!" she says, putting her hands over her mouth.

This is the first time I've heard her swear. Good for her to have some fire in her belly. It seemed a genuine reaction for someone who was hearing this information for the first time, the surprised look on her face, but I'm well aware that guilty people can be particularly good actors.

"One more thing." I move closer to Corinna so that I can take a closer look at her face to see if she's telling me the truth. The answer to this question may be crucial to revealing what happened to Ray. "Did you see anyone as you ran out of the house? Anyone at all?"

She looked blankly at me for a moment as if trying to recall a memory.

"No, I don't think so. I was running for my life trying to get away. Wait!"

"Yes?" Chris leaned in closer to hear what she had remembered.

"There was movement on the corner of the street. Possibly through the alleyway cut through. I thought it was something walking along the wall. A cat maybe," Corinna mumbled, her brow drawn together in contemplation.

"That's good, Corinna, well remembered." I smile, pleased that we have another piece of information to work on. I texted Justine and Sam telling them to check out the alleyway near Ray's home.

My phone suddenly rings and it's Jenny to say that she had arrived at the hospital and is asking where Corinna is. I give her the information and walk to reception to speak to the nurse. I need to find out when Corinna will be discharged. Dawson stands outside the room.

As I wait for Jenny, I send a quick text to Daisy to tell her we will soon be with her. I decide to call Jack. I feel the need to hear his voice. He answers after the second ring.

"Hey you. How are things?" he asks.

"I'm fine. We've finished Corinna's statement and Jenny's just arrived. I'll do a handover with her and the officer here so they're up to speed with things and then Chris and I will head across the grounds to the mortuary to see Daisy," I reply.

"Are you sure you're OK?" He repeats this as though he knows this case is bringing back an avalanche of bad memories.

"Yes. I just wanted to hear your voice. It calms me." I can't help but tell him the truth why I needed to hear him.

"That's the nicest thing a woman has ever said to me. I wanted to hear your voice too. Call me anytime, Steph," he replies.

"Thanks again. Speak later," I say, disconnecting the call just as the lift opens and Jenny steps out. For a moment I remind myself how lucky I am to have this tall, slim, blonde-haired woman in my life. She has a beautiful smile but don't be fooled by that, this woman has a fierce loyalty and determination to those she cares about. She's dressed in mid-grey trousers, black ballerina style pumps and a soft pink fitted jumper. She wears a dark grey bag that crosses over her middle and has a dark grey jacket flung carelessly over one arm.

"Hey, Steph." She opens her arms and we enjoy a brief hug before getting down to business. I lead her to Room 5 and introduce her to Corinna and Chris.

Jenny leans over to Corinna and offers her hand.

"Hello, Corinna, I'm Jenny. I run The Lighthouse charity and we offer a safe place for vulnerable women and children to live while they're getting back on their feet. I have a space available in one of our homes for you, anytime you need it."

"Thanks," Corinna says quietly. "I don't really want to go home."

I look at Corinna and explain that she will soon be discharged.

"The doctor will be discharging you in a couple of hours. The nurse will be taking you off the drip, then she'll check your stitches and prepare any medicines and paperwork. Jenny will stay with you as long as she is able to. PC Dawson will take you to the station where you'll be held for at least twenty-four hours pending further investigation."

Against all the rules that go with my job, I follow my gut instinct and hand Corinna my mobile number. "Call me if you need me or think of anything else to add to your statement." I give her shoulder a gentle pat before Chris and I head to the door.

"Thanks, Jenny. Speak later," I say as I'm leaving the room. I have a quick word with Dawson telling her to stay with Corinna until she is discharged from hospital, which will probably take a few hours and then to take her to the station. I make sure she's aware that due to Corinna's vulnerable person status Jenny will stay as long as she can once Corinna's in custody as her advocate.

Chris and I muse over our theories in the lift on the way out of the building.

"Do you believe her?" he asks.

"Yes, I think so. I mean, you've only got to look at the wounds and scars she's got. Do you believe her?"

"Yes. There's an innocent rabbit in headlights look as though she's waiting for the executioner to come and lop off her head at any moment."

"So, we've still got a murderer out there."

I nod in agreement.

The mortuary is also known as the Swift Centre and is about a seven-minute walk across the hospital grounds. It's a brand new, state of the art building made from glass and steel. It has a sleekness about it that oozes power, transparency and understated elegance. I've only been here a couple of times, but I am always in awe whenever I visit. This time is no different as I pass through security zapping my lanyard. There is a burly, serious-looking security guard with short blonde hair dressed in a tight-fitting, blue uniformed shirt and wearing black trousers who gestures Chris and I through all the necessary security obstacles. I sign us in to the visitors' book to see Daisy.

We walk to the main pathologist office and are escorted through to the autopsy suite. Daisy prefers us to be fully gowned, masked, gloved and hairnetted to avoid cross-contamination, so we take a few minutes to suit up. We pass the glass viewing area and one of the assistants uses the microphone to announce us. Daisy looks up from the body that she's currently working on and gives us a warm welcome.

"Welcome to my parlour said the spider to the fly," she recites. She's an extrovert, the total opposite of me.

"Morning, Daisy," I say, standing next to her and trying to acclimatise myself to the sight and smell of the open body. Ray's body. It's a shock seeing him like this with his pale, naked form on display, his sternum stretched open so that Daisy can pull out his organs to analyse. On closer inspection I see the blueish hint to his groin where Corinna said she'd hurt him with her knee, and I see the scratch marks on his face where she said she'd scratched him. I also see the front baseball wound to the right side of his head, and if I lower myself, I can see the back blow to the head.

"How are you getting on with Ray? Corinna said all she did was kick him in the balls."

"Really? That's interesting." Daisy looks at me before turning her attention to Chris. She drops her mask and smiles at Chris, tilting her head slightly. "DS Jackson."

Chris drops his mask briefly. "Dr Soames," he replies, returning her smile.

"Oh, for God's sake, you two! Chris, give her a call tonight and sort out a date or something. My heart can't take this kind of stress," I mutter.

"Mmm... Boss!" Chris stumbles over his words. I'm sorry if I've embarrassed him but this smiling sweetly at each other business needs to stop. And soon.

Daisy's face is a cross between anger and embarrassment as she puts her mask in place.

"Steph!"

I put my hand up to stop her. "Tell me tonight. For now I need to focus on Ray." I look down at the body on the table.

Knowing this is Ray's body gives me an eerie feeling. A part of me denies that it could possibly be him lying stone cold on this hard slab in the autopsy suite. He was always a larger than life character. Still, you reap what you sow sometimes. And Ray reaped plenty.

"First of all, I can confirm time of death as between 9pm and 8am. Ray didn't look after himself. In fact, his liver shows some early signs of cirrhosis. His last meal was burger and chips and his last drink was red wine. The head wound to the front left side of the head and back of his head are consistent with the shape of the baseball bat found in Ray's house. Marks on the handle of the bat are inconclusive. The blood on the bat is Ray's, though. There are no other marks or bruises apart from the scratches on his face which I'm assuming will turn out to be from Corinna."

"I'm just waiting on the results now but that's our theory," I confirm. I check my phone but there's nothing. Chris and I continue to watch in silence as Daisy professionally, swiftly and with the utmost care goes through the procedures and processes, taking photos, collecting evidence.

"He's still wearing his wedding ring," she says quietly. Our eyes catch above our masks.

I shudder. That's not a crime, I remind myself. It's odd, perhaps sad, but not a crime.

My phone vibrates. It's a call, not a text. The caller comes up as Ben's school. Jesus, I hope he's OK.

"I've just got to take this," I say rushing out of the room. The school office tells me that Ben is feeling unwell and I know it'll be a strain to go and fetch him while I'm stuck at work. My fingers have typed in Jack's name and pressed "call" before I've realised what I've done, and the fact that he was the first person I thought of is, quite frankly, bloody sad.

"Hey, you," the now familiar husky voice says.

"Hey, Jack. Sorry to bother you and please feel free to say no."

"Just ask me, Steph." I can almost see Jack's exasperated smile.

"Ben's not well and I'm in the middle of Ray's autopsy with Chris and Daisy. Is there any chance you can pick him up from school and take him home?" I ask, hoping he'll say yes.

"No problem, there's nothing I can't do from your house. Text me the school's address and tell them I'm on my way," he says quickly.

"I owe you. Big time." I sigh with relief.

"Yes, you do," his soft husky voice replies.

Chris is looking at what looks like a brain as Daisy pops it on the scales and looks carefully at it.

"Problem?" she asks.

"Ben's unwell so I've asked Jack to go and pick him up," I tell her, knowing that there will be repercussions from giving this personal information.

"Jack?" both say in unison. What are they? Primary school children? Still, I can't help but smile. Daisy peers closely at the brain.

"Look at this. There's quite a large lump on the left side of his brain pressing on the amygdala. I would say a grade three." She collects a measuring ruler from a nearby utensil trolley and makes a note of the size by recording it on the suite Dictaphone as well as scribing the information on her clipboard.

"This part of the brain that it's pressing against affects the emotion and decision-making process."

"Holy shit!" I say, disbelievingly.

"It doesn't mean that he gets off the hook if he hurt Corinna, Steph. Although it may explain why. It could have been very slow growing. Unless his medical records show that he was diagnosed with a brain tumour, it looks as though Ray may not have realised that he had it."

My mind is working overtime trying to make sense of this. It didn't excuse his behaviour, but it must have had some effect on him. I remind myself that he was still a monster, brain tumour or not. Then it hits me that Daisy still doesn't know about Ray and what he did to me. That's not a conversation I want to have when we meet tonight, but I have a feeling it will be unavoidable. I look at my watch and glance at Chris. We need to get back to the office for the team update at 2.30pm.

"We need to go, Daisy. Let me know if you find anything else. See you at mine tonight at 7pm?"

"Yep." She briefly looks up from studying the brain and gives me the brightest smile. "I'll bring a bottle."

"You always do!"

I can't help but smile in response. She has that effect on me. How she can do such a morbid job and stay so cheerful will continue to be a mystery to me. An hour later and we're back at the office with the rest of the team chasing and checking information, having picked up a sandwich and crisps on the way in. I don't know where the time went today. We wolf down our food as Sam Tribble brings two steaming mugs of tea. Despite first impressions Sam is turning into a good team player and I'm beginning to like him.

I think it's about time that the team understand what kind of man Ray was, particularly now with the new development of the brain tumour. I know it will make me vulnerable and the situation more subjective, but I'm going to print off some of the evidence photographs from my case taken years ago during various visits to the hospital when Ray cut me with a knife, punched me in the face, broke my ribs, dislocated my shoulder, my nose and tried to strangle me. I looked like I'd been in a boxing ring.

I use the printer in my office to print off four different photos of a person; they look a lot like me, but I feel disassociated from them. It's me from another lifetime. Chris and I take our coffee mugs through to the main room and I start pinning my photos to the incident board next to Corinna's.

As everyone moves closer to start the meeting, I can see the realisation in their faces as they study the photos. I wait for, and dread what I am about to see from my team, a sea of pitying faces. This is me at my most vulnerable, when I was nothing but a punchbag for a bully. This is me at my most naked.

"Jesus, Steph," Chris says.

"Is that you, Boss?" Sam asks.

"Yes," I say with conviction. I need to own this and not let it, own me. Justine and Danielle look at me with sadness. Justine comments first: "Boss, I don't know what to say."

"There's nothing to say, nothing to be sorry about. This happened a long time ago. I know they're hard to look at, but these reflect what kind of man Ray Delossi was. Note the criss-cross knife slashes, the finger marks on my throat. These match what he did to Corinna James. This shows a *modus operandi*."

I look at the team. Their faces look distressed, disbelieving, and they look at me as though they're seeing me for the first time. I don't want their pity. I don't need their pity. I grab my A4 notepad and a pen, place a chair near the board and sit down. "Now, let's make a start and see what we've been able to find out since this morning. I need to be home for 4pm because there are conversations that I need to have with my son tonight about his dad, notwithstanding the fact that he's dead. Danielle, what did you find on Ray's laptop, phone, etc?"

Chapter 14: Honesty is the best policy

Ben

Biology. I just can't get excited over it. When it comes to biology and listening to my teacher, Mr Baxter, I know the day isn't going to go well. From the moment he starts talking in that nasally voice of his, I can't help but sit staring out of the window and daydreaming. I'm in the process of choosing which subjects I want to study for my General Certificate of Secondary Education. I'm not totally sure what I'll choose for my GCSEs but one thing's for sure, biology won't be on that list.

"Ben Rutland!" A nasally sharp voice jolts me back into the lesson. "You need to pay attention to this. I know learning about cell structures, their function and germination may not be your idea of fun, but it is part of this year's curriculum, therefore I would appreciate it if you could at least look as if you're paying attention."

"Sorry, Mr Baxter," I say, turning my head to stare at his shabby checked brown suit with trousers so long that they drag on the floor as he walks towards me. I can't look at his face because then I'll see his nose which is so big and gross that I'll start laughing uncontrollably. It reminds me of a parrot's nose, long with a downward curve. Some kids call him "Beaky" behind his back, but not me, I keep quiet. I don't like nicknames, sometimes they aren't very nice.

"I feel really sick." I grimace pretending to be in pain and put my hand over my mouth as though I'm going to be sick, anything to convince Mr Baxter to send me to the office so I can go home.

He peers at me with narrowed eyes. "If you're ill you need to go to the school office so that they can send you home."

"Thanks, Sir. Sorry, Sir. I felt alright when I woke up this morning," I explain, slowly shutting my workbook and putting my pens and pencils away into my pencil case and into my schoolbag and shuffle out of the classroom.

The office staff are kind, especially Miss Cato, the office manager. She's got long, blonde hair, gold-rimmed glasses and a kind smile. She wears a simple plain grey jumper and a thin gold chain with a gold cross. I know that Miss Cato will send for Mrs Hedges who is the school Special Educational Needs Coordinator and doubles as the school nurse. If Mrs Hedges thinks I should go home, then depending where I live and how unwell I am, I'll need to wait for a lift or possibly be allowed to walk home. On a good day it will take me and a couple of friends thirty minutes to walk to school. I probably won't be allowed to walk.

"What's the matter, Ben?" she asks, peering down through her glasses that always sit perched on the end of her nose. She nods her head for me to sit in one of the three office chairs perched against the wall.

"I feel really sick, Miss," I say, sitting down in the nearest one and dumping my bag on the floor.

"I'll call Mrs Hedges to come and have a look at you. How were you when you woke up this morning?"

"I felt fine. I had breakfast and a cup of tea; then I started to get pains in my tummy about an hour ago and kept hoping they would go away." I try to look sorry for myself, so I let my shoulders slump and keep my head down.

Miss Cato picks up her phone and presses a number on the switchboard. I hear her talking quietly to someone and put the receiver down.

"Mrs Hedges is on her way," she says kindly, her voice soft.

I feel bad about lying to Miss Cato. There's a pang of regret in the pit of my stomach, but I have things to do today and being at school is not one of them. I hear the swishing of skirts and a figure strides into the office as though on a mission. Mrs Hedges is here with her long grey hair and pair of red-rimmed glasses hanging on a chain at her throat, a blue knitted short sleeved top looking slightly tight on her plump frame. She knows the name of most of the children in the school.

I'm not surprised when she looks at me, her eyes squinting.

"Mr Rutland? Unwell I hear." She's abrupt and comes across as brisk, but underneath she's as soft as they come.

"Yes, Miss. I feel sick. Started getting tummy pains about an hour or so," I reply, hoping that she can't see through my façade.

"How often are the tummy pains?" she continues, popping her glasses onto her face.

"About every five minutes. I keep wanting to go to the toilet."

"Not good, Mr Rutland. Not good at all. Sounds like a bug. Is there someone who can collect you to take you home? Your mum?"

"I'm not sure," I answer honestly for the first time.

"No. She's at work. If you phone her, I'm sure she won't mind if I walk home on my own," I suggest helpfully.

Mrs Hedges shakes her head as Miss Cato looks away from her screen and stares at me. "You know we can't do that, Ben. School policy. I'll just give her a call."

I sit quietly and hope that Mum answers quickly so that I can get this over and done with. I've got things to do today.

Miss Cato brings up my contact details on the screen and presses the buttons on her phone.

"Hello, is that Miss Rutland? Sorry to bother you. It's Miss Cato from school."

Mum must be panicking asking if I'm alright, because the next words from Miss Cato are:

"No. It's nothing to worry about. Ben says he feels sick and per school policy I wondered if you could collect him."

There's another brief silence as Mum speaks to Miss Cato. I think she may be busy. She's always busy.

"Oh, I see. Yes, of course. Speak to you in a moment." Miss Cato disconnects the phone and places it back on her desk.

"She's got something on at work she can't get out of." Miss Cato swivels around to me. "She's going to ring back in a minute."

A few minutes later the shrill ringing of the phone breaks the silence and I watch with interest as Miss Cato picks up the receiver, puts it to her ear and says the usual phone greeting.

"Good morning, Oakworth Secondary School. You're through to the office. Oh, hello, Miss Rutland, thank you for calling me back. Yes, of course. Jack Kinsey will collect Ben. That's absolutely fine."

I try not to show my excitement. *Yay! Jack's coming. Jack's cool!*

Miss Cato swivels her chair so that she's facing me and smiles reassuringly.

"Someone called Jack is coming to collect you. He'll be here in approximately fifteen minutes. Let me know if you think you're going to be sick and I'll get you a bowl."

I nod to Miss Cato and murmur in a low voice:

"Thanks, Miss Cato. I will," and half sigh with relief that I'm finally going home. I sit with my hands together and move my ankles up and down to pass the time.

Mrs Hedges says, "Hope you feel better soon, Ben. Please call the school tomorrow before 8.30am if you're not coming in. I do hope it's not one of those nasty viruses that's doing the rounds. If you are sick today, we have a forty-eight-hour sickness absence policy, so do let us know."

"OK. Hope I'm alright though," I mutter, looking at my feet.

My phone is on silent, but I feel the vibration buzzing through my thigh as it comes to life. I take it out of my pocket as subtly as I can and it's a text from Mum:

Sorry honey. Stuck at work. Jack's coming to get you. X

That's fine. X I reply.

I feel a bit guilty as I sit back to wait for Jack, playing a game on my phone. The clock on the wall ticks louder. I need to check my emails. There may be one from Ray. I haven't told Mum about his emails. For one thing, she told me he wasn't a very nice person when they were married, and I know it will upset her to know I've been in contact with him. He said a few things in his email about Mum being delusional, but I think he's just angry with her for taking me away. He's promised to buy me some trainers which is weird as Mum mentioned getting me some new Nikes this morning. All of a sudden people are falling over themselves to buy me trainers!

The buzzer comes through from the intercom and I sit up and peer over to the window. I see Jack standing by the entrance intercom wearing a black leather biker jacket, red T-shirt and black jeans waiting to be admitted. He sees me through the glass and I give him a quick wave as he is buzzed into the school. Miss Cato looks at Jack and smiles. I guess she thinks he's cool too.

"Hey, Ben."

"Hey, Jack. Sorry you had to come. I think Mum's busy looking at dead bodies."

Jack smiles at Miss Cato who can't take her eyes off him. *Hands off, Miss Cato,* I warn silently. *I think he's interested in my mum. She hasn't been interested in anyone since forever, and I get the feeling that she might like him back. He would make the perfect dad.*

"And that sentence sounds wrong in so many ways," Jack muses. He gives me a quick wink and moves towards me to pick up my school bag. I smile at Jack feeling comfortable that he's so chilled and confident at the same time. It's nice to have another guy around to talk to. Don't get me wrong, I love my mum to bits, but sometimes I just want to talk boy stuff.

I stand and thank Miss Cato as Jack and I make our way out of the building and across the car park towards his car.

"Thanks for picking me up."

"No problem."

Jack presses the key fob to unlock his red Mazda, throws my bag in the backseat, opens the passenger door and motions for me to get in. I like his car. I like the sleek and laid-back shape of it. It reminds me of Jack. I'd like to be like him one day.

"I'm going to take you home. I'm presuming you have a key?" he asks quickly, waiting for me to nod before continuing. "Then you can chill for the afternoon. I'll keep an eye on you."

"You don't have to, I'll be fine," I say, hoping that he'll leave me alone so that I can check to see if I've got an email from Ray.

Jack starts to drive out of the school car park and heads towards home. I'm wondering whether to ask his advice on Ray. I don't want to upset Mum, but Ray started emailing me a month ago telling me that he was my dad and that he wanted to get in contact again. I don't know much about him because Mum never talks about him, but I remember she told me a while back that he's not a good man and he's got a violent temper. Ray said that he hadn't hurt my mum when they were together and that she was making it up. I don't believe him. I'm not sure if I want to call him Dad or not. For now, Ray will do. Still, I'm bound to be curious about where you came from and who your parents are.

"Jack, can I ask you something?" I say before I can stop myself.

"Sure." He looks quickly at me before stopping at a red traffic light.

"Forget it. It's nothing." I don't want to get my dad into trouble. Perhaps I'll just keep replying to his emails and leave it at that.

"I'm thirsty. Do you fancy a McDonald's milkshake?" Jack asks without looking my way. He carries on as if it doesn't matter whether I talk to him or not. I like that, it takes the pressure off.

"Sure."

"Good. It just so happens that we're five minutes away. They had better have chocolate flavoured milkshake or I'll be most annoyed."

Once we're in the McDonald's restaurant my appetite comes back with a vengeance and before I can say "I'll have a quarter pounder" we've ordered a Big Mac, two lots of fries and a Chicken Legend with mayo to go with our chocolate milkshakes. I follow Jack as he takes our tray to an empty booth, takes off his leather jacket and settles in the red leather style seats. I shuffle into the booth so we're sitting close but not touching. I'm cold so decide to keep my school blazer on. I thought I might feel uneasy sitting here with someone I don't know, but I don't. It feels good as we just sit in silence eating and drinking.

"Mmm," Jack says, munching through a mouthful of chicken and bun as the lettuce and mayonnaise slither out from the bun. "I forgot how good these were." He grabs a paper napkin and dabs it to the corner of his mouth.

I'm enjoying my Big Mac, licking my fingers, sucking chocolate milkshake through the straw and feeling more like myself, relaxed. I ask Jack the question that I wanted to ask earlier in the car:

"If you know something but you think it will hurt someone you love to know that you know it, do you think you should tell them anyway?"

Jack was quiet for a moment as he studied me. He wiped his hands on the paper napkin and leaned his bare arms on the table.

"I guess that depends on what it is you know," he said carefully. "In my experience most of the time it's best to be upfront with someone, even if you know that it will hurt their feelings. Has this got something to do with your mum?"

"Yes. And Ray," I confide quickly. There, I've said it.

"Ray?" he queried.

"My dad, Ray. He emailed me a month ago. I don't know how he got my email address, but he did. He said he wanted to get in touch, to meet me. He also said that Mum made things up when she said he'd hurt her. I don't believe him. I think he's angry because she took me away."

"Quite possibly," Jack agrees.

"Mum doesn't talk about him." I spill my secrets before I can stop myself. "Except when I was little. She once told me that he'd hurt her when they were married and isn't a good person. I haven't seen him in years. I'm not even sure whether I want to call him Dad or Ray."

For a moment there's silence as Jack processes what I've just told him. I see something dark and stormy in his eyes before he says:

"I'm glad you feel able to talk to me, Ben. What you're feeling is completely natural. I'm glad you don't believe what he said about your mum. You don't know him well enough to know if he's telling you the truth."

I nod. I know he's right. Now I've opened my worries up to him. I can't seem to stop myself from saying:

"He's still my dad though, Jack. You know what I mean?" I look across at him and see him nod in understanding. "I haven't met him or anything, just answered his emails. He said he was going to buy me some new trainers. I think he wants to meet me, but I don't want to hurt Mum's feelings."

Jack pats my arm briefly and pauses. "We all want to know about the people who bring us into this world. They are part of who we are, who made us, although they don't define who we become. That's up to us."

"Do I tell Mum?" This is the crucial question, the thing that's been worrying me the most. I'm relieved when the words are out. Then it's not just my decision. My fingers pick at the empty straw wrapper, scrunching it, rolling it, folding it.

Jack stares at the table, his rugged face and stubble beard dipping slightly as he slides his leftover fries along the table to me. His brown eyes look at me intently and his deep voice answers: "I think that would be a good idea."

Deep down I knew that's what he'd say. It's what I needed to hear. "Can you be there when I do it?" I ask, taking one of the offered fries and popping it into my mouth.

"If you want me to be, I will," he says as though we're talking about buying a packet of sweets from a shop.

I finish my mouthful and look at him. I like him. "Thanks, Jack," I say, feeling glad that I had the courage to confide in him.

"Thanks for telling me, for trusting me," Jack replies, taking a final slurp of his chocolate milkshake. "That's a very grown up thing to do."

I smile and help myself to more fries. I think things are going to be OK. Jack slips his arms into his leather jacket and we pile our rubbish onto the tray and empty it into the bins on our way out the door.

"You didn't really feel ill today, did you?" Jack suddenly asks as we reach the car.

"No," I reply. "I just feel a bit anxious, what with Mum going back to work last night and Ray's emails. I hate keeping secrets from her. I've got a strange feeling that something bad is about to happen."

"That's a lot of worry for one young person to carry on his shoulders. What you need is to chill out with a good movie and some popcorn."

"Sounds good, but it's a school night and Mum won't let me stay up too late."

"Leave your mum to me. If you manage to catch up on any homework you have this afternoon that would be great," he says with a knowing smile. "I will use my vast charms on your mother and have her wrapped around my little finger in no time."

"You're funny, you know that?" I say, laughing at the thought of Mum wrapped around Jack's little finger. "I think that's why Mum likes you."

"Likes me, does she? Well, it's definitely not for my hairstyle!" He rubs his hand over his bald head, and I can't help but laugh.

We arrive back home and I'm thirsty, so I grab a Coke Zero from the fridge and head to my room while Jack makes a phone call. I kick off my shoes and lie on my bed, arms behind my head looking up at the ceiling. I hope Mum won't be too mad with me.

I don't hear Jack until he appears by the open door. "I've spoken to your mum. She'll be back about 4pm and she's bringing popcorn. Her friend Daisy is coming over later so we thought we could call out for pizza, have dinner together and then you and I can hang out in here eating popcorn while we're watching our film. When you've caught up on homework browse through your Netflix and choose one you like. How does that sound?"

I smile at Jack and feel emotions so strong that they make me want to cry. I gulp down a sob to hold myself together. I know he's trying to make things better, to help me and Mum. If I had a permanent Dad, I would definitely want one like Jack.

"Yeah, sounds good."

"I'll be downstairs if you need anything."

"OK, thanks. I'm going to try and do some biology catch-up reading." I sit up, grab my bag and take out the massive textbook and my notepad. Why do school textbooks have to be so big and heavy? It's like they're specially designed that way to make carrying them to and from school nothing but a misery. I open the biology book, read the first sentence and then my eyelids start to droop, and I fall asleep.

Chapter 15: Trading Secrets

Jack

All is quiet upstairs. I think Ben has fallen asleep. Poor lad, he's going through some stuff and feels lonely. U2's "All I Want is You" is playing softly as I sip my lukewarm coffee and sit at the dining table in Steph's house staring at my laptop. The screen clearly shows activity and history in Ray's three bank accounts. Luckily, I have certain skills which enable me to hack into different accounts. I'm aware that's illegal. Make no mistake, I never intended to be a computer hacker when I was young, I simply found that I had a talent for finding information such as bank account details, account numbers, and once I had the login details I could easily work out people's passwords. They are usually such dumb passwords that I'm surprised they haven't been hacked into before. One account I was looking into for The Lighthouse charity, off the radar, the person's password was 123456789ten.

Something doesn't add up. Ray's been gradually losing money from the car sales business over the past couple of years. On top of that he'd been putting money aside each month into a savings account for eight years up until a month ago. The other thing that seems strange is that he deposited a one-off payment of five grand into his account last month. God knows where that money came from.

My mind wanders back to Steph and what she's doing. She is one of the strongest people I know and despite the chaos of the past few days it was good to hear her voice when she called earlier. I like this new relationship, or whatever undefined thing this is. I'm thirty-eight-years-old and didn't think I would ever find a woman who appeals to me on every level. This thing we have, Steph and me, the calmness, the working things out together, it's corny I know, but our connection has a natural vibe to it. It makes me happy.

And it is weird. I'm watching over Steph's son whilst digging into her ex's finances and paperwork because he was murdered a couple of days ago, and I'm now developing strong feelings for her. And spending time with Ben, watching a film and visiting McDonald's has brought out a paternal instinct in me that I'd never realised I had.

The front door opens, and I look at the wall clock. It's 3.55pm. Steph's made good time and I will be nothing but glad to get the next few hours over and done with. There are things that she and Ben need to say to each other, things that won't be easy for either of them to hear. I know Ben asked me to be here when he told his mum about the emails, but it feels like I'm intruding on something private.

Upstairs there is movement. Ben must be up and about. I hear the sound of jingling of keys as they're being put down on the hall table.

"Jack?" Steph calls.

"In here," I answer from the dining room.

She walks through the lounge and dumps her briefcase, two bags of popcorn and her handbag on the dining table and smiles shyly.

"How's Ben?"

"Fine," I reply, "he was having a nap upstairs."

I stand up and before I know it, I've moved towards her and caressed her cheek with the back of my hand. Her eyes close and she leans into my hand.

"I'll pop the kettle on while you go check on him," I say softly.

She nods and disappears upstairs. I can hear movement and voices, but I can't make out what they're chatting about. I hear the stairs creak with footsteps and continue putting tea in the teapot and getting the cups from the mug stand whilst the water boils in the kettle. I look around the cupboards hoping to find a packet of biscuits and settle for an unopened pack of shortbread which I open and put on a plate.

They come into the kitchen and stand, bemused, watching my tea making skills as I smile at them both. Ben's changed from his school clothes into dark blue jeans, a red Superdry sweatshirt and trainers.

"Why don't we sit down at the table and catch up with some tea and biscuits?" I say, and they both nod with a smile.

Once we're seated at the dining table, I stir the tea in the pot. God, when did I become so domesticated? This is so not me. I pour tea into the cups and look at Ben as we quickly acknowledge that this is the perfect time to be upfront with his mum. I'm about to prod Ben into action when they both speak in unison.

"I need to tell you something."

I can't help but smirk. These two are like peas in a pod, I muse, as I watch both laugh at the same time.

"You go first," Steph says.

"OK, Mum. I need to tell you that my dad, Ray, started emailing me about a month ago. I didn't reach out to him. He found me. But I replied to his emails and we kept in touch." He bites down on his bottom lip.

Steph moves forward to him, puts her arms around his young shoulders and says quietly, "I know, sweetie. Thank you for telling me."

"You know? How?" Ben looks at me and I shake my head to show that I don't know what she's talking about. I can't really ask her in front of him in case it's got something to do with the investigation into Ray's death.

"I'll tell you in a moment." She keeps one hand on his shoulder. "But I need you to know that wanting to have contact with your dad is natural. You are such a great kid that I'm surprised it's taken him this long to get in touch with you."

"I was so worried," Ben sighs with relief. "I didn't want to hurt your feelings, especially after you told me he wasn't a nice person, and I remember going to the hospital with you when I was little when he'd hurt you." He splutters out his words as though he's been trying to hold them in for a long time. "I wasn't planning on meeting him, honest I wasn't, but he was trying to buy me treats so that I would like him more, I think. That's what dads do, isn't it? Buy their kids treats."

"Of course, they do sweetheart," she says softly. "Of course, they do."

Steph reaches out to Ben to pull him close. Her eyes are bright with unshed tears and her face reflects the love she has for her son. If she has Ben she can deal with anything thrown at her. I wondered, not for the first time, if I should leave them to it, when suddenly Steph tilts her head up, her eyes focus on me and she mouths "Thank you." That smile is all it takes for my heart to finally find its home. That smile is what I would give anything to see at any time of the day or night. That smile settles me, warms me and makes me realise that I have a place here within this little family.

I feel a lump in my throat and an overwhelming sense of emotion, so I try to disguise it by leaving the table and helping myself to a glass of water. The cool liquid trickles down my throat as I watch the tableau of Steph and Ben as they go through the motion of trading secrets.

Steph pulls away and looks at Ben.

"Ben, I need to tell you something."

Ben looks at his mum, his eyes wide open, wondering what she is going to say.

"The case I've been working on. It's to do with your dad." She takes a breath as she watches Ben's reaction.

"My dad?" Ben asks, his voice momentarily steady. "What about him?"

Steph's words grow softer. "I'm sorry to have to tell you, Ben, but your dad has died."

I feel a pounding in my ears as Ben tries to process the news about his dad. This must be one of the hardest things that a child has to endure. The death of a parent.

"No!" Ben says steadily, looking at his mum "That can't be true!" His voice becomes louder, more strained. "I've only just started speaking to him again!" he shouts at Steph.

"I know, Ben, and I'm so, so sorry," his mum says in a quiet voice. "That's how I know about the emails between you and your dad. We've got his laptop and phone. A colleague has been going through his history and its content, checking his contacts so that we can find out what happened to him."

"No!" Tears fill Ben's brown eyes, and the freckles sitting high on his cheekbones crinkle as he scrunches his face. Shaking his head, he looks in disbelief at his mum.

"I'm sorry, Ben. I'm so, so sorry," Steph says as she reaches out to console her son. Without any warning at all he pushes his chair back, stands and almost throws himself at me, wrapping his arms around my back. The water in my glass swishes so much I think it's going to spill onto the kitchen floor. I hastily place it on the nearby counter.

I look at Steph as she accepts her son's need to be comforted by me. Her nose is red and there are silent tears falling down her cheeks, but this moment belongs to Ben and his grief for a father he hadn't known for most of his life. I do the only thing that seems natural and gently hold him through his pain.

I stroke his head but remain silent. The sound of intermittent sobbing fills my ears as his shoulders shake against my chest. I don't let go. After a few moments there is the sound of a chair scraping as Steph stands, and without saying a word she walks over to us both and encases us in her arms. After a few moments I look into her dark brown eyes and shuffle an arm so that she can slip hers around Ben. I use this opportunity to hold her too, keeping them both safe.

"I've got you both," I say, my voice breaking with emotion. In response I feel arms tighten around me and know somehow that if these guys became my family that we could cope with anything life throws at us. "Does anyone want pizza?" I ask after a while, hoping to distract Ben and Steph from their thoughts. I'm relieved when Ben nods his head to indicate a yes.

"Can we order, Mum? Please?" he says, pulling on the sleeve of her shirt.

Steph gently disengages herself from Ben and me and smiles. "Of course. Why don't you go find my laptop, bring up the page and we'll make a start on the order?"

Ben heads to the lounge to seek out the much-needed silver laptop and Steph looks into my eyes and gives me such an intense look that I'm momentarily stunned. It's as though she can really see me, see the person I become when I'm around her and Ben. There's an attraction too but I'd better rein that in. Steph will probably run a mile if I make a move on her.

"Jack?" Her voice is soft.

"Yes?" I hold her gaze. "What?" I ask, and before I can say another word, she surprises me completely by cupping my face with her hand and leaning her forehead against mine.

"Thank you," she whispers, before stepping back.

Ben rushes back into the room and I'm thankful we're no longer touching. I don't want to embarrass him. "I'm having large thick crust pepperoni. What are you both having?" He looks at his mum and then turns his gaze to me, a small grin on his young face.

"I told you she liked you," he says to me, putting the open laptop on the dining table and tapping quickly on the keys.

Steph looks at me, her eyebrows raised in query, but I just smile and shake my head. "Pepperoni sounds good to me," I reply.

While we wait for the delivery, I head back to my work area at the dining table. There are a ton of things to do, but my main priority is finding out what Ray was up to. I have found some information from his bank accounts regarding regular payments to a company called Lewis Investigations. That must be the private investigator Ray was using to get his information.

I know I'm not a police officer, but Steph asked me to get involved because I have some flexibility in finding out information. That means I don't always follow the letter of the law, but I'm OK with that. That's on my conscience. The women and children that Jenny and Stuart work with at The Lighthouse charity aren't there out of choice, they're there because someone hurt them, manipulated them, tried to kill them. Those people, the manipulators, and abusers don't often play by the rules. Neither do I. If I need to find out a former spouse's finances and details to make sure that they aren't being represented by the best lawyers or paying someone off to turn a blind eye to an assault charge, then so be it.

I google Lewis Investigations, and this turns out to be a small one-man investigative firm based in Witney. I make a note of the details and plan to give them a visit tomorrow. Hopefully this Lewis will be able to give information on Ray's state of mind and what he was investigating. I can be very persuasive when I want to be.

Amidst making a mental list of things to do, I spy Steph coming through the lounge door dressed down in a pink long-sleeved T-shirt, grey loose jogging bottoms and pink slippers. The mug of tea which I'm sure must be cold by now is in her hand and her hair falls in loose dark curls spiralling in all directions. My heart misses a beat at the sight of her. She's beautiful and sexy even in her dress-down state. I tell myself to keep my passion and thoughts to myself until this case is over. This is not the right time to let my hormones take over. Her phone pings, it's probably work. I watch her check her text, frown, press a quick reply and pop her phone back in the pocket of her jogging bottoms.

Steph checks her watch and looks out of the window for the pizza delivery. There's a vulnerability in the way Ben walks up to his mum by the window. His shoulders are slumped, and his eyes are red as he hugs her, his tall lanky body holding her close.

"How are you, honey?" she asks him. "I'm here if you want to talk about your dad."

"I just feel a bit out of it, you know?" Ben replies. "I can't think of anything but him and the fact that he's dead, even though I hardly knew him." Ben sighs. "I never got to know him, to know what I meant to him and find out if he loved me."

"I know, honey, I know," Steph says, holding him close. "You know my friend Daisy the doctor is coming over at seven? Jack asked earlier if you both could chill out in your room, watch something on Netflix and have popcorn. Do you still want to do that? I'm sure he won't mind if you've changed your mind."

I half listen as I tap away on the laptop keys. My stomach is growling and I'm trying to find local Oxfordshire loan sharks to see where the five grand came from that suddenly appeared in Ray's account. Hopefully, his phone contacts should come up with some mention of where he asked for the money, how the transaction was made, and acknowledging the repayments put in place. Nothing is flagging up here.

Thankfully, there's a knock on the door and the food arrives, and it's a welcome distraction from our current worries. We eat at the dining table, pizza boxes open, glasses of water and Diet Coke strewn across the wooden table. Conversation is kept light as we eat dinner and topics are steered away from dead bodies and murder enquiries. Ben and I decide to watch Taken 2 and I think we'll both enjoy the movie. I'm reasonably sure that whatever we watch will help distract Ben for a few hours.

Steph's phone rings while she's got a mouthful of pepperoni pizza and I raise my eyebrows in question, washing her shrug as she hands it, to me to answer. It's probably work-related anyway.

"DI Rutland's phone. Can you hold the line for a moment? Or can I take a message?" I ask.

"Hi, it's Corinna," a quiet, unsure voice says.

"Corinna?" I repeat. "It's Jack. How you doing? One moment, I'll just pass you on to her."

On hearing Corinna's name Steph's face tightens as she reaches to take her phone. She's in work mode immediately.

"Who's that?" Ben asks, pepperoni peeping out of his open mouth.

"Just someone to do with work," she answers in a low voice.

"Hey, Corinna." She stands up and walks to the kitchen. "I know what you mean. The nightmares are the worst when you're exhausted but you're too frightened to close your eyes. I understand."

There's silence as she listens to Corinna.

"It's natural, Corinna. You need to remember that you are not a victim, you're a survivor. You are strong. Don't let him have control over you. He's dead and you need to chase those fears away, stamp on them and kick them out the door. I've been where you are now. You can do it. That's OK, sweetie, anytime. I'm here."

Steph comes back into the room and I can see the wrinkle of her brows and the corner of her mouth is drawn downward in a frown. She's not happy. She sits on her chair and picks up a slice of pizza.

"How is she?" I ask, taking a sip of water.

"She's OK. Finding it hard to sleep," she replies in between bites.

"Having nightmares?" I look at her, hoping that she'll look at me, that she'll share her worries. It's not good to have to take the weight of everyone's problems on her slim shoulders.

"Yes." She puts the pizza slice back in its box and pushes it away from her. She leans her elbows on the dining table and looks at me. "She's having nightmares, she's in pain, she's tired and she's traumatised."

There is such sadness in her eyes that I want to scoop her up, hold her tight and tell her that everything will be alright. But I don't. Ben is here, this is not the right time. One day though, I hope that we'll find the right time.

"Not a good place to be. It will probably get worse before it gets better. We just need to be there to help if we can," is all I say.

A little while later Steph's friend Daisy arrives, a short, blonde bubble of happiness and smiles. She is slightly earlier than expected but brings a very welcome cheerful vibe to the house as well as a bottle of Shiraz. Steph brings her into the kitchen to meet me as I make myself a cup of tea.

"Daisy, this is Jack," says Steph introducing me to her friend. She's wearing a long, flowing dark blue skirt, a tight purple T-shirt and a grey cardigan. Her silver dangly flower earrings swish from side to side every time she moves her head. I watch as Daisy gives me a bright smile. She's pretty.

"Jack, lovely to meet you," Daisy says, shaking my hand in a firm grasp. "I've heard very little about you, but knowing Steph as I do, she rarely has male company. You are one of the chosen few. Fair warning though, if you hurt my friend, I will be checking out isolated places to bury your body."

I laugh nervously, not sure if she's joking or not. I think I must have passed some sort of test because she turns to Steph and says loud enough for me to hear, "He's a keeper."

Steph's rosy cheeks are a sight to behold as she watches Daisy open her kitchen cupboards looking for the wine glasses. I could tell her that there are some in the living room because we used them last night, but I hold my tongue, some things are better kept quiet. If she decides to tell Daisy about us, that's up to her. I have to say that I'm relieved her friend likes me.

Ben wanders into the room and offers Daisy an easy smile before saying, "Hey, Daisy, how are you doing?"

"I'm good, Ben. I can't believe how grown up you are!" She gives him a quick pat on the shoulder.

Ben's face lights up at her comment and he mutters a "thanks" as he saunters over to me. "I've got Taken 2 set up and ready, Jack."

"OK, just need to get us some stuff. You head up and I'll be with you in a minute," I tell him as I grab the bags of popcorn and a couple of cans of cola from the fridge. I hear heavy footsteps taking the stairs quickly and know that Ben's gone to his room. I stand beside Steph and Daisy before joining Ben for the film.

"I'll leave you two ladies to your catch up because Ben and I have a film to watch," I say to Steph as our eyes lock and I wonder if she feels the same way, that there are words left unspoken between us. At some point we will need to be open and honest with each other about what we're doing. If we take this further, she could get hurt; Ben could get hurt; fuck – I could get hurt. Perhaps it's best if I distance myself. Perhaps I should watch the film with Ben, go home and keep in touch with Steph via text.

"Great to meet you, Daisy," I say, as I move to follow Ben upstairs. When I reach the bottom of the steps I'm caught by surprise as Steph grabs hold of my arm to keep me still.

"Jack," she says breathlessly, "don't go getting cold feet on me now."

How does she do that, read my mind? I like her. I like her a lot and I'm just trying to do the right thing by her. I don't want to take advantage of her vulnerability and I don't want to be the rebound guy. My eyes stray to the point where her fingers are wrapped around my arm. Her touch feels good. She smiles shyly, lowering her eyelids to keep me from seeing her feelings. Which is a shame because she seems to be focused on my lips.

"Cold feet?" My voice is husky and low as I raise my hand to gently lift her chin. I want to make sure that she can't hide from me. Our eyes connect in the semi-darkness and my doubts of keeping my distance from her disappear. In a quiet, confident voice I tell her, "not going to happen."

I put my hands on her hips and slowly manoeuvre her backwards so that she's leaning against the coats hanging from their rack on the wall. I desperately want to kiss her, want to feel her soft lips on mine, her tongue touching mine as we explore each other. I feel myself harden and know that this moment isn't the right time. I know that there will be a right time, and in my heart, I know that Steph is worth waiting for.

So, I gently press a kiss to her soft cheek and silently pray for the right time to punch me in the face so when it comes, I don't miss it. Did I really think that I could leave this woman and move on with my life? I think it's fair to say that ship has sailed. Too late, mate, you've been swiftly caught hook, line and sinker.

"Go and have drinks with your friend. I have no intention of getting cold feet, tonight or any night."

I let go of Steph and see the pink flush of her face, reassuring me that I've done the right thing. I watch as she walks into the lounge and I can't help but feel that life is good.

"Please don't tell me that Jack is just a friend," I hear Daisy say as I walk up the stairs with a grin.

Chapter 16: A question of self-defence

Corinna

I sit and listen to the distant hustle and bustle of the police station, sipping my coffee from a mug that tells me "Don't Worry, Be Happy" and stare at my reflection in the huge frameless mirror which covers the top half of the wall facing me. I shudder and use my hot coffee mug to warm my hands. The police interview room is not cold, but I feel chilled. The off-white walls remind me of the dull cupboard under the stairs at home when I was a child. A room that is insignificant, it's just there to serve a purpose.

There's nothing in the room apart from my chair, a wooden table and two chairs on the opposite side of mine.

Annoyingly, the white metal and wood chair that I'm sitting in squeaks every time I move, which is a lot because my foot won't stop tapping on the floor, filling the silence with an intrusive repetition of "tap squeak, tap squeak". The cuts where the knife pierced my skin are sore, and when I move there is a pulling from the stitches which sets me on edge.

PC Dawson stands guard in the corner of the room, silent and poker-faced. Suddenly she breaks the silence and asks quietly: "You OK?"

"I think so," I say, my body shaking as I speak. "I'm frightened though and I can't stop shivering wondering what will happen to me. I know I hurt him but I was defending myself because he was assaulting me. I swear he was alive when I left him."

"Keep your chin up. Your solicitor should be here soon."

I nod without looking up from my coffee. I think about when Jenny, PC Dawson and I arrived at the station from the hospital about an hour ago. PC Dawson was carrying my white paper bag of painkillers and a five-day course of antibiotics to counteract

181

any infection. I was told by the hospital that someone will check my stitches and wounds while I'm here, but I'm not sure who that will be. I've been booked and held in custody by the Duty Sergeant; my personal belongings have been confiscated and I'm wearing a grey sweatshirt and jogging bottoms. That's when I was introduced to my new temporary home, the prison cell.

I hear PC Dawson open the door and talk quietly to someone in the corridor. Moments later the door opens again, and PC Dawson gently places a blue woollen blanket over my shoulders. I look up at her with both shock and appreciation.

"Better?" she asks.

"Much. Thanks." I try to smile.

The prison cell I have been assigned to is cold and stark. There is one metal-framed single bed, complete with a thin blue plastic mattress and a matching pillow and a grey blanket. In the corner of the small room sits a metal toilet and sink. It's dire, but then I guess that's to be expected for a cell.

I know I did wrong. I know I hurt Ray but there's no way that I killed him. I don't know how he could have died from a knee to the groin. I deserve everything I get if my knee killed him. Steph says that I need to be strong, but how can I when every bone in my body is screaming that I should pay for hurting the man I used to love? A man who tried to kill me.

I'm relieved that the cold metal handcuffs no longer encase my wrists. For now. The short, bald police officer with the unsmiling face and harsh voice who'd collected me from my prison cell had put the cuffs on me and then told me in an unfriendly manner that he was taking me to an interview room to meet my solicitor. Thankfully, PC Dawson was already here in the room when we arrived and explained to the police officer that she was assigned to take over and watch me during my briefing. She had brought me a coffee, sugar sachets and a plastic spoon to stir. and finally, thankfully, she took off the restricting, cold handcuffs.

I hear a noise behind me. The door opens and I can hear voices talking quietly. I turn my head and see Jenny walking towards me with a smile on her face. The cuff of her blue blouse rises slightly as she raises her arm to give me a quick wave of her hand. A tall man walks behind her, he's good-looking and has short dark hair. There's an air of confidence about him as he strides forward in his smart navy suit and crisp white shirt. A blue and white thin striped tie has been loosened around his neck a little giving a to hell with the rules vibe, and he's holding a black briefcase. He offers me a friendly smile. I try to return the smile but I can't seem to make the corners of my mouth turn upwards.

"Hi, Corinna, I'm Noah Robinson, a friend of Jenny's," the man introduces himself, as I look into the deepest blue eyes I've ever seen. "I'm going to represent you if that's alright with you?" He holds out his hand for me to shake. I place my mug on the table and take his outstretched hand in mine. His grip is warm and strong.

"Hi, Noah, I appreciate your help," I say quietly, tapping my foot and holding the blanket on my shoulders closer to keep warm.

"No problem," he says lightly. His tone seems sincere. "I'm happy to do whatever I can to help."

Noah takes one of the two seats opposite me across the table, lays his briefcase down and swiftly opens it. I watch his actions, mesmerised as he takes out pens and a large notepad. Jenny picks up a chair, places it beside me and sits.

***

All my life I've felt set apart from others. I've never had much of a family. Dad left when I was five and Mum's often fragile mental health meant that she couldn't look after me as well as she should have, so I was taken into care when I was ten. Medical tests undertaken by doctors on Mum two years following my dad's departure revealed that she had bipolar disorder. People may think that I should have already been monitored by the social care system, but Mum's mental health could be good at times if she took her lithium to stabilise her moods. I didn't become known to the system until I was nine. Gradually I took on more and more household stuff until the fateful day I'd arrived at school unaccompanied because Mum wouldn't get out of bed. Mr Oakworth my form teacher had noticed and taken me aside during my morning break period and asked how things were at home. As I sat next to him wearing my creased yellow school dress and scruffy green cardigan, I stared at him, with his serious-looking face, slightly crooked nose and almost black eyes and decided to tell him about Mum. Within twenty-four hours my mum and I were being supported by the social care system.

If you've ever been put in an extreme situation as a young child, you'll understand that when life changes you have to adapt quickly. You mature before you're supposed to. It's not about being brave or confident, it's a matter of survival. A matter of resilience.

And that's how I survived, this scrawny young thing with big brown eyes and dark hair, still at primary school, who spent her time worrying what food was in the house, what bills needed to be paid and what clothes needed to be washed and dried. Our only saving grace was Mrs Prince, our next-door neighbour, a thick-set woman with big dimpled cheeks, a double chin and a warm smile who popped in to see us every day to see if we needed anything from the shops.

From there on in Mum and I had a family social worker called Jude who would check in with us once a week to see how we were doing. It was about a week after my tenth birthday that Jude last visited. Mum had been almost catatonic for two days because she was refusing to take her medication. This didn't unduly worry me because it happened sometimes. Three months before she'd suddenly stopped taking the tablets for two days and everything had come to a standstill until I'd ground some tablets into her mug of tea. I usually gave her three days to see how her depression was manifesting itself before contacting Jude.

I remember my first residential care placement well. It was in a large red brick Victorian house – a bit like a children's home. The home was clean and tidy and apart from me there were nine additional young occupants. The best part was that we each had our own bedroom with a lock on the door for privacy. The worst part was that it took me a long time to get used to the noise level and constant movement around the house, especially with Sid and Eric around.

It's amazing how many people want to foster or adopt babies or young children, but sadly very few people want to foster or adopt a teenager. It's just the way it is and I accepted that as a teenager my bad cards in life were dealt a long time ago. I can hardly believe that meeting Ray in the museum has sent me down this path of no return.

Noah breaks into my thoughts. "Corinna, can you start at the very beginning and talk me through everything, from your life in care, to how you met Ray? Then can you tell me about the events leading up to and including your injuries, past and present, and the attack on Ray? Take your time."

I tell Noah everything I remember about my life, from being in care to the halfway flat. I explained how I had applied for and was offered the job as a collections clerk at the museum. I tell them how I met Ray and when things started to go wrong between us. I let it all out, including the comments from Steph and DS Carter about Ray. That he had been bashed on the head twice by a baseball bat. I tell them that the police think that that's what killed him. There's someone out there walking free who killed Ray Delossi.

Tears roll down my face. I'm annoyed at myself for being such a fool to have trusted Ray and wished for a future together. And I'm angry with the world for imprisoning me for something as vital as defending myself by kneeing Ray in the groin. I clasp my fingers together and wriggle them. I want to yank at my stitches and pull them out, all fifty of them. One by one. Jenny sits quietly beside me and pats the top of my hands.

This whole thing, being hurt, in the hospital, the police station and now talking to a solicitor – it all seems so surreal. It feels as though I'm talking about someone else. Another person's life, not mine. The feeling of detachment is something that I'm familiar with. I've felt detached for most of my life.

When I've finished there is silence. I hold my breath and look across the table at Noah, waiting until he finishes writing up his notes. The light catches his wedding ring as he rests his hand on the notebook. The silence lasts for a minute longer before Noah puts his pen down and looks up and across to me.

"Well, I think we've definitely got grounds for a self-defence case," Noah states, looking down at his notes briefly before returning his attention to Jenny and then myself. "I'll collect the autopsy report, lab results and police records, including your statement and any witness statements to corroborate it. The point is that we have a good place to start with your documented injuries. The fact that he attacked you, that you came to the police station voluntarily – even if it was via DI Rutland at her home.

"That's the first step done," he continues. "I've spoken to DI Rutland and she's put in a request for an extension for the maximum of ninety-six hours to hold you in custody. At that point the police need to formally charge you or release you. Serious crimes such as murder do not allow bail, pending charges or court dates."

"You mean, I may be released if there's not enough evidence to say that I've killed Ray?" I ask, my voice hopeful.

"Yes," he says carefully, "but at the moment the only evidence of someone in Ray Delossi's house on the night he was killed is you." He looks at his watch to calculate how much time I've got left. It's now 5pm.

"I was booked in at 2.30pm," I say, trying to be helpful. Noah's brows are drawn in concentration as he writes yet more notes in his pad.

"Thanks." He looks up. "So, we've got until 2.30pm on Monday to find out who the murderer is so that you can be released. Failing this, you will be charged for Ray's murder and we will need to go before the Magistrate's Court and then on to the Crown Court where a trial date will be set.

"I can and I will help you and support you wherever possible," Noah offers in a softer tone. I think he can see that I'm losing faith in everything that matters. The only real things I had was my work, my flat and my freedom, now they will all disappear in one swift swoop. Noah's voice cuts into my thoughts, kind and thoughtful. "I can be your advocate when we get to that stage, if you would like?"

"Yes please," I say softly. "You and Jenny have been so helpful. I would appreciate your continued support." I offer a weak smile.

"There are several people," Noah folds his hands on the table, opposite mine but not touching, "including myself, Jenny and Stuart who are going to work hard to support you and to build you the strongest defence case we can. My wife Jem and I know that Jenny and Stuart are the best people to have on your side when you need support. They will do whatever they can to help you. Try to be strong."

Tears fall down my cheeks. I hope I am strong enough to get through this.

"Corinna, it will be alright," says Jenny soothingly as she gently hugs me. "Tell her it will be alright, Noah," she pleads.

"I'm sorry, I can't promise you that, Corinna. But I can promise you that I will do everything in my power to help you."

As Noah and Jenny take their leave PC Dawson leads me back to my cell. I feel drained, my bones ache and I just want to sleep. I think of a passage from a Dr Seuss poem I used to read when I was young, and I tell myself:

"You have brains in your head,

You have feet in your shoes,

You can steer yourself in any direction you choose."

That will be me one day, despite my current situation. I need to remember that there are people who are trying to help clear my name. That I am not alone. I hear the door lock behind me and huddle under the blanket on the metal bed. I will do my time and I guess I will move on.

Chapter 17: Going through the motions

Unknown

I hoped I would feel better after killing him. The weight hasn't lifted though. It continues to sit heavily on my shoulders. The world is still without colour. I knew killing Delossi wouldn't change things. Blip is still dead. My parents are still heartbroken, Dad had to give up work due to depression and Mum works as a Teaching Assistant at a primary school. They live their lives going through the motions, but it's clear to see that a piece of them is missing. When I visit, they put on a united front of forced smiles to hide their pain, but I watch them when they're not looking. I see Mum's tears when her eyes catch a framed photo of Blip hanging on the wall or sitting on the windowsill. My dad is a broken man. He brushes his face with his hands when something reminds him of Blip, shakes his head and closes his eyes. His way of coping is to retreat within himself and hide from the world.

One thing I know for sure though, there's no coming back from committing cold-blooded murder, even if that person deserved to die – which Ray Delossi did. I did the world a favour, took him off the streets and away from young women, so that he couldn't hurt anyone else.

The springs are broken in my brown suede sofa so it's like sitting on a carpet of pebbles. I shuffle across the seat cushions trying to find some comfort. I haven't slept since I killed Ray Delossi. Exhaustion is crashing down on me like a bucket of iced water and it's strange, but every time I close my eyes, instead of seeing the bloody dents in Ray Delossi's scalp, my mind focuses on the persistent beeping of that damn life support machine. I run my hands through my hair, twisting it through my fingers and pushing it behind my ears.

I get up and move around the living room, stretching my spine and hips as I go. I reach for the remote control to turn on the TV, flicking through the channels until I find the local news. I turn the volume up when a small photo of Ray Delossi comes up on the screen saying that he's been murdered. The reporter goes on to say that they have someone in custody and to my horror Corinna's face stares back at me from the TV. Shit. Shit. I stare at her photo. I didn't take a good look at the woman as she came out of the house and ran out into the darkness that night. I'd been too focused on not been seen. Hiding in the shadows. I should have known, paid more attention to what was happening in the house. I can't believe they've arrested her.

I pace the blue carpeted floor. Christ, what a mess. My arms bend at the elbows as I clasp my hands behind the back of my head. I walk around in circles. "Corinna, shit." I mutter. "That's why that Detective and her Sergeant were here last night. Shit. Why didn't I realise that's why they wanted to get into her flat? Stupid, stupid man." I hit my forehead with the palm of my hand. Twice.

I am so mad at myself for not realising that the woman I'd seen bleeding and sobbing as she ran out of Ray's house was Corinna James. What the hell was she doing seeing Ray Delossi? I thought she'd have more sense than to go out with an arsehole like him. I know he was a charmer and a bastard, but I can't believe she fell for him. Come to think of it, I hadn't seen much of her over the past month. Jesus. I can't believe she's been arrested. God, I need a drink.

The whiskey burns my throat, but I take another gulp anyway. How can I help Corinna get out of this mess without giving myself away? There must be a way. I can't let her take the blame and spend the rest of her life in prison for something that I did. I need to think about this. If only there was some way of pushing the spotlight away from her, of ensuring that any evidence of her being in the house was overshadowed by the fact that someone else was in the house around that time Ray was killed.

I'd rather write a confession and take my own life than let an innocent person take the blame for something that they didn't do. There's not much left for me here anyway. Nothing of value.

Chapter 18: Stuff happens

Steph

Daisy sits in the comfy chair in the living room. I sit in the other chair at the far end of the room. The sofa is between us. She stares at me in silence. Her eyebrows are raised, and her oval chin is pointed in my direction as though she's willing me to tell her about my relationships with Ray and Jack. I don't want to tell her too much that's for sure, because if I do, I'll probably talk myself out of getting involved with Jack in the first place.

"Alright, I give up," I say, putting my hand up, acknowledging her non-verbal persistence. I raise my red wine glass to her in mock surrender.

"What do you want to know?" I ask, wondering what I'm letting myself in for by telling her about Ray. I nibble my inner cheek. Bugger. This is awkward.

"First of all. Ray? Spill the beans," she answers, almost immediately and with enthusiasm, her blue eyes bright with excitement.

"There's very little to tell," I explain. "We met nearly fifteen years ago. We were together for six months before Ben arrived and got married two months before he was born. Ray liked to be in charge a lot when we started going out. At first I liked that about him, I liked being looked after, protected. By the time Ben was born I realised that Ray's character had several serious flaws, two of which were his short temper and bouts of physical violence toward me."

"Jesus, Steph!" She looked so stunned, the shock of my declaration showing on her face. "I'm so sorry. I wish I'd never asked you about him now!"

"It's alright, Daisy." I soften my voice to reassure her and take a big gulp of my wine. I'd make a good poker player, hiding my feelings to people so they don't realise how upset I am.

"No! It's bloody well not alright! How can you sit there and talk about it so calmly as though it happened to someone else?" she says passionately, resting her arms on the sides of the chair.

I watch her as a teardrop rolls down her cheek. I put down my wine glass and slowly walk over to her. I put my hand on her shoulder and say: "I'm calm because it was such a long time ago and I've put it all behind me. That was until yesterday when Ray turned up dead."

Daisy pats my hand and gives me a sad smile.

"You are one of the strongest women I know. You deserve to be treated well. To be happy."

"Thanks, sweetie," I say as I move back to my chair and, more importantly, my wine.

"I'll carry on telling my tale of woe if that's all right? Once you know the truth then I can start getting on with my life again." I look at Daisy and see the slight nod of her head before continuing my story. "I was constantly tired because Ben never slept through the night and I was breastfeeding. I lost interest in looking after myself. Did you know I used to jog? Quite a lot actually. That's how I met him. Ray."

"I didn't know," Daisy says with sadness in her voice.

"I gave up jogging about a month after I met Ray because he was annoyed that I had a hobby which took me out of the house. His controlling manner spiralled from there." I didn't mention that I hadn't jogged since. That would be too revealing.

"Oh, Steph," Daisy cuts in, "I almost can't bear to hear what he did to you. What a bastard," she says, looking at the floor. One of her silver flower earrings shines in the lamplit room and it reminds me that there can be brightness in a world full of dark shadows.

"I know." I rub my clammy hand down the length of my thigh to my knee. The jersey material is soft and comforting. "It was a vicious cycle of violence, remorse, violence, remorse and always swearing he'll never do it again. He often manipulated me into believing that it was my fault for provoking him, until one night he attacked me so badly I thought I was going die. He cut me with a knife, his hands were around my throat and he twisted my shoulder socket and arm until it dislocated."

"Oh my God!" Daisy's anguished words fly across the room. Both hands cover her mouth as if she's going to be sick.

"I remember sitting on the hospital bed with Ben by my side deciding that there was no way we could go back to Ray. Ben had just turned three and Ray was already picking on him, so I figured that we weren't safe at home anymore, either of us. I asked the police to help us and before long Ben and I were taken to a refuge home for women and children. A safe place where you can recuperate from domestic abuse. Shore House is a beautiful detached property in Lyme Regis. It is a peaceful and safe place. The people who own the home, Stuart and Jenny Greyson, run The Lighthouse charity. Its manager, Lottie, and friends such as Jem, they all saved me. But for them, I don't think that I would be alive today."

"Oh, Steph, I wish I'd known. I wish I could have helped you," Daisy says fiercely. "I wish Ray were still alive so that I could hurt him for you."

"No, you don't!" My reply is equally passionate. "You don't want that on your conscience. Besides, it's not something I'm proud of. I didn't want anyone to know because I didn't want to be defined by it. I didn't want people to look at me and see a victim, the type of person who let a man like Ray use her as his punchbag."

We both take big gulps of wine until our glasses are empty, and Daisy reaches for the half empty wine bottle that sits idly on the small table next to her chair. She tops up her glass and walks over to my chair to refill mine. I wait until she's resumed her seat with her legs tucked comfortably underneath her before I go on

"Stuart and Jenny were brilliant. As my injuries started to heal, I was able to focus on what I wanted to do for myself and Ben to rebuild our lives. I needed to plan for our future. That's when I joined the police force. Stuart and Jenny supported me by offering childcare and access to legal representation so that I could start divorce proceedings. I also decided to press charges against Ray for grievous bodily harm.

"For some reason the charges against him didn't stick. Some of the evidence was disallowed and the bastard got away with it. I tell you, Daisy, I haven't seen Ray since the day I went to the hospital with Ben when he was three years old. I never went back to the house."

The mixture of emotions shadowing Daisy's face floors me. I can't help the tears that roll down my cheeks, mirroring hers. There is pity in her eyes. I can't think straight. I feel as though I've been stripped naked for the whole world to see. This is why I don't open up. People look at you differently, define you as a victim.

"Jesus. Don't cry, Steph. That piece of shit isn't worth it. He's dead now," she says through her tears. She returns her wine glass to the table, about to come over to me.

I don't think that I can handle her touch, so I put my hands up to ward her off. "No, Daisy. It's OK. Just give me a minute." I use my sleeve to wipe my nose and eyes. It's not ideal, but it'll do.

"I knew there was something in your past. I've caught sight of the scar on your neck a couple of times. But this…" She leans forward looking at me, her hands clasped, elbows resting on her knees. "This is a can of worms I never expected."

"I know. I'm sorry," I mutter. My head is beginning to ache with all this talk about Ray.

"Don't be silly. I was the one who pushed you to tell your story. Please don't blame yourself," she pleads. And then, as though a thought hits her, she asks. "Does Jack know? About Ray I mean and what he did to you?"

"Yes. He knows what Ray did to me," I say quietly.

"Ah." Her voice has that know it all sound to it.

"What's Ah?"

"I'll tell you in a minute," she says. "Firstly, I want to say that I've emailed my autopsy report to you and confirmed that cause of death was due to two blows to the head."

"Good. That tallies with Corinna's story." I'm glad to be talking shop again, back on neutral ground. It helps to calm me. "So there's no way that being kneed in the groin caused Ray's death?" I persist.

"No. Absolutely not. Particularly not in this case." Daisy's voice is strong, confident.

I let out a breath and sigh. "Thank God."

"Let's get back to the 'Ah'. I want to know about Jack." Bloody hell, she doesn't give up, does she?

"Jack? What do you want to know about him?" I ask innocently.

"You know what I mean," she says throwing a cushion from her chair my way. I watch with relief as it falls at my feet. I don't want another red wine spillage incident with my blouse. Was that really only last night? It feels like weeks ago.

"He's helping me with this Corinna and Ray thing. I texted him yesterday after I found the photo of Ben and me in Ray's house. He's a private investigator. He works part-time for Stuart and Jenny from The Lighthouse charity."

"And?"

"And what?" I ask innocently.

"I've got eyes, Steph. I can see perfectly well. That man has got the hots for you."

"Really? You can see that? What, are you psychic?"

We both laugh.

"It's still early days, don't make more of it than it is," I say honestly and with a serious tone. "I like him a lot, but it's taken me eleven years to get to this stage. Who knows how long it'll take me to get to the next?"

"I understand what you're saying, sweetie, but life is about taking chances or at least working towards your hopes and dreams. If nothing else, just use him for sex!"

"Daisy!" I try to reprimand her, but it comes out in a half giggle. My cheeks suddenly warm at the thought of using Jack for sex.

"Steph, Jack's a hunk, he's got that husky voice going for him and I don't think he's interested in anyone else. As Meg Ryan said in *Top Gun, 'Unless you are a fool, that boy is off the market. He's 100% primetime in love with you.'*"

Oh, Daisy. She does make me laugh. She's good for my confidence and I smile, taking another sip of my wine and absently twirl my fingers through my hair. "Does that make me Kelly McGillis?"

"Of course!" She laughs, winking at me. "He can be your Pete Mitchell, codename Maverick."

The topic of romance reminds me of the Chris and her situation. I'm just about to say something when Daisy's phone pings. I watch as she takes her phone from the nearby table and stares at it blankly for a moment before replying. Then she looks across to me and smiles.

"Don't tell me. Chris?" I ask, feeling rather smug with myself and impressed with my matchmaking skills.

"Yes. How did you know?" she asks before her phone pings again. She reads the text and replies.

"And?" I can't take the suspense. I stand up and walk over to her. Daisy holds on to the phone as though it's a priceless artefact.

"We're going out for a drink tomorrow evening at 8pm." She stands, her excitement evident in the way she throws herself at me.

"Finally!" I sigh with relief as I grip her shoulders in a sisterly hug.

The following couple of hours fly by as we catch up on events in our lives. Daisy leaves at 10.30pm because she's got an early start in the morning. I can't help but hold on to her for a little longer as we hug our goodbyes.

"Remember what I said," she whispers, "take a chance on him. He may turn out to be the one."

I close the door behind her and lean back against it, smiling and just simply enjoying the moment. The golden glimmer of hope that Jack has given me over the past couple of days settles to a warmer, sunnier hue. Or, I think cynically, maybe that's the wine dulling the edges.

I slowly head upstairs to see if the boys have managed to stay awake during the film. They are both snoozing on top of the bed. Ben's in his pyjamas and Jack's still in his red long-sleeved top and black jeans. His dark brown ankle boots are neatly placed on the floor next to the bed, with his black leather jacket and the empty Coke cans. The popcorn packets are thrown in the rubbish basket. My heart melts as I allow myself a minute to watch them at peace in sleep.

I was relieved and proud of Ben for telling me about the emails earlier, even if I had a sneaky feeling that he'd already told Jack. To have made recent contact with his dad and to then have that contact ripped away from him must mess with his head.

I move to the bed and gently stroke Ben's cheek. His eyes flutter briefly, then open.

"Sorry. I fell asleep," he says groggily.

"That's fine. Bedtime for you now, though."

Jack moves at the sound of the conversation and Ben and I both hold our breath watching him. As if he can feel us staring, he slowly opens his eyes and they begin to focus first on me, then Ben.

"Sorry. I nodded off."

"Me too." Ben smiles. "Thanks for chilling out with me tonight."

"No problem," Jack says, stretching his long limbs, standing up and watching Ben as he snuggles under the duvet.

"See you in the morning, sweetie." I kiss Ben on the forehead. Jack looks at me quickly and moves towards Ben, and in the sweetest, kindest moment he pats Ben's arm as it sits on top of the duvet. "Night, buddy. Sleep well."

I leave Ben to turn off his lamp as Jack and I slowly make our way down the stairs. I feel a little awkward, a bit like a teenager on a first date.

"You don't have to go home, you know. It's getting late and you're tired. We're both tired," I say in a quiet voice when we reach the living room.

"I'm pretty beat but I don't want to put on you. I can sleep on the sofa again."

"I'll get you some blankets and a sheet," I say, watching his reaction closely. He doesn't touch me. Just stands there and waits.

"Thanks." His husky voice sends a warmth down my spine until my whole body has a yearning to be held by this man.

And then I suddenly remember what Daisy said about taking a chance and Jack being my Maverick. The words that follow make me sound uncertain, but my heart knows the truth. I'm falling for this man. I'm falling hard and I need to give myself permission to trust and love again.

Jack is sitting on the sofa when I return to the living room and quickly stands up when I put the blankets and sheet next to him and help him to lay them across the sofa. When we've finished, we stand facing each other, neither wanting to break the silence.

"Well, goodnight then," I speak first, my arms hanging limply. Do I have the courage to touch him first?

"Goodnight, Steph," he whispers, his brown eyes boring into mine. "Sleep well."

What the hell is the matter with him? Why won't he touch me?

"Goodnight," I whisper back as I turn and move toward the stairs. And then I realise why he's not touching me, why he's waiting and watching. It feels like the universe just clicked into place. He's letting me make the decisions, allowing me to set the pace.

I turn swiftly, watching his silhouette, his long-sleeved top stretching across his back as he bends to move a cushion onto the arm of the sofa. Clearly, he looks after himself, keeps himself in good shape. He takes my breath away.

"Jack," I whisper, and watch him turn. I watch the surprise on his face when he realises that I'm still here. Be brave, Steph. Move forward not backwards. I hold my head up high which I hope will hide my lack of confidence and slowly walk to him. Everything is happening in slow motion, like a scene from a film when you know the heroine is going to get her man. I stop in front of him:

"Don't move," I say, watching his serious face with brows that are knitted together asking a question I'm not prepared to verbally answer. His lips are closed as he watches me. Lips that I need to touch. Because he's lit a fire in me that I haven't felt in a long time. Soft brown eyes look at me, waiting.

I lift my arm and snake my hand around the nape of his neck, relishing the feel of his warm skin. I don't take my eyes off him and watch his sharp intake of breath as I slowly pull him closer to me until our lips touch. I close my eyes and savour the touch of his lips on mine, then I put my free hand over his heart and gently tease his lips open with the tip of my tongue. Our mouths move tentatively together, exploring the feel and taste of each other, working to find a rhythm that fits us. I can't help the murmur of contentment as my hand moves from Jack's chest and reaches up to cup his neck. I pull away from him slightly, lean my forehead to his and say quietly: "Kiss me, Jack."

Warm hands take my hips and pull me slowly into his lean hard body. My fingers stroke his neck and reach for the base of his skull. "Don't hold back, kiss me," I whisper in his ear. His hands cupped my face as his eyes questioned me, asking if I was sure. I nodded. I couldn't think of anything worse than not kissing Jack and not having him touch me right now. I hold him close as he takes a deep breath and puts his mouth gently on mine. This time he doesn't hold back.

Chapter 19: The visit

Corinna

The cell at the police station is cold. I can't seem to get warm. The shivering usually starts as soon as I wake up and stays with me until I go to sleep. I sit on my bed with the grey blanket wrapped around my shoulders. I can feel the beginning of a cold coming on as my throat feels as though it's on fire and I started to sneeze last night. The peephole on the door is kept permanently open so I don't have much privacy, especially when I need to use the toilet. I don't think the police officers trust me. Maybe they think I'm going to hurt myself.

I see a familiar pair of blue eyes as PC Dawson checks on me through the peephole. The rattle of keys echoes in the silent cell and the door is suddenly pushed open. PC Dawson looks at me.

"Corinna, you have a couple of visitors."

"OK." I look at her, wondering if she's got a family to go home to. Or if she's on her own. Just like me.

"Are you alright? You look a little pale." She sounds worried and frowns as she looks at me.

"Yeah. Just a bit of a chill. I'll be alright," I say standing up.

"The nurse will come and check your stitches today. I'll ask her to take a quick look at you."

"No need," I say, looking at the floor and putting my hands out for her to handcuff me. The top half of my body feels sore and stiff when I move, the stitches across my chest tight as they hold my skin together. I hope that the soreness near my neck goes away soon. Apart from that I'm fine. I think.

The cold metal bites into my skin and an icy chill works itself up my arms until it makes my shoulders shake.

"Let's keep this blanket on you for now until you've seen the nurse." PC Dawson's eyes lift to mine, then drop suddenly as though she finds it hard to look at me. There's an aura of sadness emanating from her.

PC Dawson leads me to the interview room through a maze of corridors and up a flight of steps. As I walk into the room, I expect to see Steph, Jenny or Noah to talk through the Magistrate date and any new developments. But I'm taken by surprise by the faces I see sitting behind a white desk. I never expected to see my care leaver personal advisor, Jude Kilkenny, and Jules Walker, the caretaker for Richmond House. PC Dawson withdraws to the corner of the room and stands silently as Jude begins to speak.

"Hi, Corinna," Jude says. She hasn't changed much. I've known her since I was nine. Her wavy blonde hair fashioned into a shoulder-length bob-style is a little greyer, her short figure is a little plumper and she still wears long, flowing cotton dresses. Of course, they're too long for her so the material drags along the floor as she moves. Today her dress is dark pink to match her pink heart earrings. She'd been my social worker nine years ago, the person who'd supported Mum and me from the very beginning. She left for three years to have a baby and when she returned to social care, she retrained so that she could work in the adult sector.

"Hey, Jude," I say, and suddenly the soulful words of the Beatles song of the same title pops into my head: "Don't make it bad, Sing a sad song and make it better". I don't think anything will make this better. I close my eyes and silently pray for a miracle. As I sit down, slowly lowering myself onto the brown wooden chair, PC Dawson moves to my side to take my cuffs off and steps back to the corner of the room. I rub my wrists absently before resting my arms on the table. Instantly, I wonder what they're doing here.

Jude reaches out to pat my hand. I find it hard to meet her gaze, I feel like I've let her down somehow.

"How are you? Jules called me when he found out you'd been arrested. You know he's studying to become a social worker right and he's at Richmond House for hands-on experience?"

"No, I didn't know that." I turn to Jules and nod to him. "I hope I haven't got you into any trouble?" I ask him.

"No, of course not, Corinna. It's you we're worried about. How are you?" he asks me. He looks worried.

"I'm alright. A bit sore, a bit frightened…" My voice sounds soft, distant. "I didn't do it, you know. I didn't kill Ray. I pushed my knee into his groin to defend myself and get him off me. He was alive when I left him." There's a pleading tone to my voice. I desperately want them to believe me.

"We know. I've never known you to hurt a living thing," Jude soothes, stroking my hand. "When you were little you looked after your mum when you could have left her to fester in her own filth. I've known you for most of your life, Corinna. I know you couldn't have done this."

"Thanks for believing me," I say, with tears in my eyes. My fingers grip hers and hold tight for the briefest moment.

Jules looks worried. His blue eyes bore into me as if it's the first time he's seen me. He shuffles his seat closer to the table, his blue half-neck jumper loosens across his chest as he leans his elbows on the table.

"Corinna," he says, "I'm sorry, but I had no idea that you were in hospital and that you had been taken into custody."

"It's alright, Jules. How would you know? You're not supposed to be watching us twenty-four hours a day," I say. Really, it's not his fault. If it's anyone's it's mine. I don't really know much about Jules apart from the fact that he works as the caretaker for Richmond Court. He's nice-looking, too nice-looking for a caretaker, with his long, lean build and his blonde hair which is always held back in a ponytail. He reminds me of an explorer. I can picture him deep in the jungle saving wild animals from extinction or climbing the frozen mountains of Antarctica. For the month I dated Ray I was completely enchanted by him, his knowledge, his confidence, his ability to be happy in his own skin. I spent most of my time at his house or on dates. I never really saw Jules.

"Corinna, do you have legal representation?" asks Jules, pushing his hand through the top of his ponytailed hair. "Do you know how long they're going to keep you in custody before they charge or release you?"

"I've got a solicitor and his name is Noah Robinson," I tell them, concentrating my stare on the wall behind them. "He works with The Lighthouse charity. Jenny Greyson, who runs the charity with her husband, has been visiting and supporting me."

"Jenny Greyson?" Jude's eyebrows rise. "How on earth did you get to have such a prominent contact? She's well known and respected on the social care circuit."

I look at Jude and finally meet her eyes. I'm surprised there is no tell-tale signs of disappointment in her face. "DI Rutland knows both Jenny and Noah, she contacted them to help me," I explain. Thinking about it, I've been lucky to have them supporting me.

"How long?" Jules ask again. His voice has an edge to it. The scowl on his face looks anything but sympathetic.

"I've got ninety-six hours in custody before they charge or release me," I answer, annoyed with his curt manner. What the bloody hell is his problem?

"Jesus!" He pushes the chair back and stands up, pacing the room. Grey cargo pants brush together as he holds his hand against his forehead.

"Jules!" Jude admonishes, as he walks from one side of the room to the other with one hand over his chin. "Calm yourself. This is helping no one!"

"It's not your fault," I repeat, trying to calm him.

"I feel responsible. You got into trouble under my care. I should have taken more notice." He sounds as though he's berating himself, but I know it's not his fault.

"We need to do something to help you, Corinna," he says as he comes to a standstill beside me. "We can't leave you here like this! Tell me how we can help."

I look at each of them. Jules, who is standing next to me, is begging for a way to help me. He seems distraught for me and he doesn't even know me. Jude, who is sitting opposite me, has a sad smile and her soothing hand pats mine.

"Well," I say to my visitors, "the only way to really help me is if you find the person who actually killed Ray. And preferably find him or her before 2.30pm on Monday!"

Chapter 20: Dream on

Steph

My right shoulder is stinging. I think it's going to pop out of the socket. My arm feels like it's burning. I try to bump my shoulder into him to move him off me but he's too heavy. I can't think straight I'm in so much pain. Scream. Don't scream. Scream. Don't scream, you'll frighten Ben. In the end the pain is too much, searing and causing my brain to re-engage. I looked at him and screamed:

"Ray! Stop! You're hurting me!" My scream was so piercing it was hurting my head and I couldn't stop the tears that rolled down my face.

"You deserve to hurt. Look what you made me do!" he shouted, his face scrunched and distorted with rage. I took in the cold, menacing eyes of a man I'm supposed to love, cherish, honour and obey, who now stared back at me with such hatred. I look at the coffee stain getting darker as the liquid sinks into his blue T-shirt. This life of mine was no life at all. It was pure hell, something I wouldn't wish on my worst enemy. If I had somewhere safe to take Ben and myself I'd be out of here like a shot.

I think back to this morning and how this latest episode of violence had begun. It started off as a lazy Sunday morning. When you have a three-year-old child it is common to have interruptions during the night and Ben was no exception. He had a cold and his nose was blocked which meant that he didn't sleep for very long before waking up, uncomfortable and panicking through his blocked nose. I'd put Vicks VapoRub on his chest and pillow but that didn't help much. Of course, Ray had slept through everything, through the four times that I'd been into Ben's room. By 8am I was exhausted, and Ben was still fast asleep.

However, Ray wasn't fast asleep. He was wide awake. And he wanted sex. The moment I realised someone was rubbing my breasts through my red T-shirt nightshirt and kissing my neck I growled, opened one eye and pushed Ray's shoulders. I'd rolled onto my side away from him. I was so tired. I just wanted to sleep.

This was followed by groping hands pulling up my nightshirt, hands that were about to pull down my underwear. I swatted his hands away and moaned:

"Ray! I'm exhausted. I've been up half the night with Ben."

"So? Why are you moaning? It's not like you have to make any effort," he'd snapped at me.

"Please don't be like that. I'll feel better when I've had some rest." My voice sounded tired, even to my ears as I pleaded with him. I forced myself to stay calm because I didn't want to provoke him into one of his rages, so I turned toward him and stroked his face trying to remember the man I fell in love with. In one swift movement he'd pushed me onto my back and was on top of me, his body caging mine. I could feel his morning erection as he pushed me into the mattress and panicked, grabbing his arms.

"Ray," I begged in a pleading voice, my body stiffening. "Please. Can't you wait until tonight when Ben's asleep?"

He pushed a knee between my legs trying to open them and, for a moment, I saw a glimpse of excitement as he forced himself on me. Jesus! He's enjoying this, it turns him on. This knowledge is not good, it magnifies my fear of him tenfold. I don't think I can ever trust him after this.

"I'm not waiting for something that could be over and done within two minutes if you'd just shut up and let me get on with it," he snarled, his hands pushing my shoulders down holding me in place.

"If you do this," I spluttered at him, tears rolling down my cheeks, "I'll never forgive you."

"Oh, you will Steph." He gave a harsh laugh. "You always do."

"No, not this time, Ray. I won't." My nose ran and all I could think about was giving him what he wanted and getting it over and done with.

"Mummy! Mummy! Want you," Ben's three-year-old voice broke into our thoughts.

"Shit!" Ray spat. "The little sod has crap timing," he said, as he pushed my shoulders hard into the mattress and he rolled onto his back, throwing his arm over his head. He looked like a child having a tantrum.

"Mummy! Pwease! Want to get up." Ben sounds annoyed, he was probably standing by the safety gate at the open door of his bedroom. If he started crying Ray would get mad and shout at him.

I looked at Ray. "I'll go sort him out. Take him downstairs," I say, wanting to get Ben as far away from Ray's wrath as possible.

"Go!" Ray shouted, his hand already moving under the duvet to touch himself.

I quickly get up out of bed, pulling my nightshirt down over me. Living with Ray was exhausting, it felt as though I was walking on eggshells every damn day. I grabbed my cream kimono-style dressing gown, tied it quickly around my waist and collected Ben from the safety gate.

"Good morning, sunshine. How are you feeling now?" I hugged him close and felt a huge wave of relief as his little body wrapped around me, just the smell of him settling me.

"Mummy, are you sad?" He looked at me, the grey dinosaur from his green pyjamas peeking over the top of my arm. This son of mine saw everything that Ray didn't or refused to see. The pain and weariness of living this way. He'd lost some of his chubbiness and was a little boy now, with dark curly hair, curls that Ray was desperate to cut off. He was petite for three and had the cutest freckles which sat high on his cheekbones and sprinkled under his eyes.

"No, Mummy isn't sad, sweetheart," I answered, holding him tight as I took the stairs. "Not now anyway," I muttered quietly to myself.

"I'm sowwy," he smiled, and kissed me softly on my cheek. I had to bite back the tears.

"Baby boy, you've got nothing to be sorry for. You did nothing wrong," I reassured him with a gentle stroke of his cheek followed by a quick kiss to his nose. "Now, let's get you some breakfast." I wiped my watery eyes and put him on the living room sofa to watch cartoons while I was pulling myself together. Taking a deep breath, I began to prepare Ben's cereal and orange juice. How the hell was I going to get out of this situation? I have no one to turn to. My parents were addicts and I'd left home to live with my aunt, but she died when I was eighteen. I literally had no one. It's hard to keep going when every way I turn is a dead end. If it wasn't for Ben I would have walked out of this marriage and ended the cycle of violence for good.

I took the bowl of Shreddies and a cup of orange juice to Ben and asked him to be careful with the milk I'd put in the bowl. The kettle was hissing and bubbling away for hot drinks when I heard Ray coming down the green carpeted stairs. I'd finished making his coffee by the time he'd sauntered past the kitchen door. He was wearing old blue jeans and a blue long-sleeved shirt. He reached out to the nearby white painted windowsill, picked up the TV remote control and flopped down into a brown suede armchair. I watched anxiously, hoping that he'd managed to calm himself down.

The coffee was steaming hot as I'd carried the white mug across to him. I walked in front of him and touched his arm, handing him his coffee. "Here you go," I said.

Ray took the coffee from me and I think I may have filled the mug too full, because as the mug transferred from one hand to another the hot liquid spilled onto his top. He was as quick and silent as a panther as he threw the coffee mug at the wall, taking me firmly by my arms and beginning to shake me roughly. "Look what you made me do!" he shouted.

I don't know why his anger caught me by surprise, but a half cry came from my mouth as he shook from side to side, my vision became blurry and his fingers were pinching my skin. "It was an accident," I wailed. Out of the corner of my eye I saw Ben look my way and willed him to ignore me. Of course, he couldn't. It's not natural to ignore someone you care about when they're being hurt.

"Mummy!" There was panic in Ben's voice and his face scrunched ready to burst into tears.

"Ben, can you go and sit behind the sofa, sweetie?" I plead. "Ray, please. You're hurting me."

"Mummy!" Ben climbed off the sofa, his cereal bowl and cup slipping to the floor. "Daddy, pwease don't hurt Mummy." He rushed up to Ray and grabbed his leg. "Let her go."

"Ben!" I warned, my body stiffening and my stomach knotted in fear. "Ben, go behind the sofa. Please." I couldn't bear it if Ben got hurt. Ray kicked his leg at Ben, trying to release the hold his little hands had on his leg.

"Brat!" Ray shouted, spittle coming from his mouth.

"No, Ray," I shouted, my heart pumping in my chest. "Leave him alone." It was too late, for what I hadn't seen was Ben digging his teeth into Ray's leg. Ray let go of me and lashed at Ben's face, sending my brave howling toddler son tumbling in a flurry of limbs across the living room floor.

"Noooooo!" I shouted, angry and pushing at Ray with everything I had. "Noooooo!"

"Steph. Wake up!"

210

"Stop!"

For a moment I don't know where I am, but then strong arms take hold of me. They're warm and comforting.

"Steph. Wake up. It's me, Jack."

I wake with a jolt and look into dark brown eyes. Not Ray's eyes. They say the eyes are the window to the soul and I think they're right because all I see in Jack's eyes is concern and worry.

"Jack?"

"Yes?" he says, carefully folding me into his arms and rubbing my back.

"I'm a little thirsty. Can you get me some water please?"

I look around the room and realise that we're lying side by side on the sofa in the living room. My head had been resting on Jack's shoulder as I try to focus on why I am here on the sofa with Jack. I look at my watch. Bloody hell. It's 2am! And then I remember. The kiss. When I think of that kiss a warm contented feeling comes over me. Memories of Jack kissing me and holding me as if I were the most precious thing he'd ever touched, sends shivers down my spine, sending my nightmares away. For the moment.

A moment later Jack pushes off the sofa and walks to the kitchen. The lamp in the living room sends a soft glow over the room as I sit up and take the glass of water that Jacks offers. Taking several deep gulps, I let the cool liquid soothe my dry mouth.

"Thanks," I say, cautiously putting the glass on the nearby side table. My hand is shaking, and I watch as the glass wobbles onto the wood.

"I wish I could do something more to help you," he says, carefully sitting beside me. He turns his body so that he's facing me. His brow is furrowed, and his eyes dart about in concern. Clearly, he's worried about me and my nightmares.

I try to reassure him. "You're doing more than you know, Jack. Once the case is finished and we've done all we can to make sure that Ray's death is investigated properly, I think the nightmares will stop."

"Promise me," his tone is serious as he gently cups my chin to meet his gaze, "if they don't go away that you will see a professional to help you through the healing process. Please."

"I promise." I touch his cheek thinking how much this man is beginning to mean to me. "Now please hold me. I'm getting cold."

"Bossy woman!" he mutters, as he holds me tight and pulls me into his lean warm chest.

A feeling of contentment takes over me as we sit holding on to each other, relishing the warmth and togetherness, our eyes closed. I don't want to move but I know in my heart that I'm not quite ready for the next stage with him. I need to take things slowly, there's my job and Ben to consider, and that's nothing compared to the long road of rebuilding my trust in men. Getting to know Jack and learning to trust him is helping to rebuild my confidence in myself and my ability to make good choices, particularly where men are concerned. However, Jack and I have only known each other for a few days and Ray's murder has heightened our emotions, fast forwarding them tenfold. I can't deny this pull towards him though, the way he makes me feel when he talks to me, watches me, the connection that comes as naturally as I breathe.

"Jack?" I say quietly. "We both need to sleep. We have to be ready for work in a few hours."

"I know," he replies quietly without opening his eyes. "Time for you to head upstairs and get some rest," he says, opening his eyes and stroking my shoulder gently through the material of my long-sleeved top.

"How did you know?" I ask, sitting up in wonder that he'd anticipated how I'd feel.

"Steph," he says, pushing himself to a standing position and leaning down to take my hands. "You were in a violent relationship with your ex-husband and you're having nightmares." He pulls my hands firmly so that I'm standing in front of him. "On top of that I'm beginning to suspect that I may be the first man you've been interested in since Ray. Am I right?"

"Yes, you are," I say, feeling very vulnerable and wishing the ground would swallow me up.

"Then let's take this one step at a time and do it properly. There's no rush," he says, leaning into me so our foreheads are touching. "I'm not going anywhere."

"OK. You're right," I say, reluctantly pulling away from him. I take two steps back before my treacherous feet lead me back to him. "I think I'm falling for you," I say quietly, looking up. For a moment there's a dreaded silence, as though I've said something I shouldn't have. Shit.

"Goodnight, Steph," he drawls in his deep husky voice before brushing his lips against the side of my cheek. I close my eyes, remembering this moment and then slowly move away.

As I turn and walk to the door his voice stops me.

"Steph?"

"Yes?" I turn to look at him.

"I think I'm falling for you too," he says, his eyes glistening in the semi-darkness. I can't help but smile and feel a little giddy.

"Goodnight, Jack," I reply, unable to keep the smile from my face as I take the stairs to bed. "Sweet dreams."

The morning comes too soon, and I wake with a familiar heaviness in my body and mind. My eyes feel like they're sealed shut together with glue. I put an arm over my face, shutting the world out. A warm fuzzy feeling settles over me when I remember what Jack and I said to each other before we went to sleep. Memories of being in his arms and feeling contented flood through me, so I lie still and saviour the moment.

A banging on my door breaks the spell. My teenager is up and about.

"Mum! Have you seen my P.E kit?" Ben shouts loud enough to wake the whole street.

Peace is now shattered. I check the clock and it's 7.15am.

"Mum?"

"Hold on, Ben, for goodness sake. Give me a minute to wake up properly."

I pull on my pale pink dressing gown and head to the door. "Ben, can you keep the noise down, Jack is downstairs," I say, walking across the hall. "Did you check your room and the wash basket?" I ask him.

"Yes, no sign. Jack? Downstairs?" he repeats, following me in his Star Wars pyjamas.

Jack is softly snoring as we reach the living room. "Yes, it was getting late and he was tired. Hope that's OK?"

"Sure, he's a cool guy," he says. staring at the sleeping male lying on the blue living room sofa.

"Morning, sleepyhead," I say with a smile, waiting for him to wake up. There's movement and then a head pops up from under the blanket. There's a tiredness around his bloodshot eyes and an endearing large crease across his cheek where he's been lying. He rubs sleep from his eyes and mumbles:

"What time is it?"

"7.15am. Do you want tea or coffee?" I ask, walking through the dining room into the kitchen.

"Jesus! I feel as though I haven't slept," his husky voice grumbles as he pulls himself into a sitting position. "Tea, milk, one sugar. Please."

"Jack. Can I ask you something?" I hear Ben say.

"Sure, Ben. What do you need?" Jack's voice replies.

This doesn't feel strange at all, being side-tracked by my son for the man lying on the, sofa.

"There's this girl at school and her name is Molly."

The noise from the kettle prevents me from hearing the rest of their conversation so I concentrate on making the mugs of tea. When the drinks are ready, I check the cupboard under the stairs for Ben's P.E. kit and hey presto – there it is! I hoist the drawstring straps over my shoulder, find the tea tray and collect the mugs.

"One P.E. bag," I say, balancing the tray in one hand and dropping the bag from my shoulder onto the floor beside Ben. "It was in the cupboard under the stairs."

"Thanks, Mum," Ben replies, taking one of the mugs and grabbing the bag by the base. "I'll take this in my room. I've got a few things I need to do before school, but I'll make sure to grab some toast before I go."

"Just make sure you do," I shout after him, as I take two mugs of tea and offer Jack one. I sit beside him holding my hot tea on my lap. "Is everything alright with Ben?" I ask.

"Yep, all sorted. He just wanted some advice on a girl he likes," he says, in between sips of hot tea.

"Ah, well I hope you gave him good advice," I answer, shuffling a little closer. "About last night," I begin. "I'm sorry."

"Sorry for what?" He rests his mug on the top of his legs, holding it carefully with both hands and looks at me.

"For the nightmare and for making you sleep downstairs." I am apologising for the problems he has to contend with, by wanting to get to know me. My problems.

"Don't be," he says quietly, reaching down to put his mug on the carpet. "You worry too much, Steph." Then, taking my chin in his hand he leans in to whisper in my ear. "Step by step we said last night. I'll be here with you all the way."

"Good. Because I'm scared," I say, as his thumb caresses my lower lip.

"I know, sweetheart, but you need to know one thing about me," he says quietly, stroking my cheek.

"What's that?" I ask, my eyes closed, mesmerised by his touch.

"I'm a very patient man."

And then he takes my mug, puts it down on the floor and kisses me gently until I'm not scared anymore.

Chapter 21: A work in progress

Jack

I pull up a known police force contact on my mobile who is currently working at the Thames Valley station based in Banbury. I'm sitting in the Mazda outside my house having changed and put a spare clothes bag in the car, just in case. I'm chasing up some leads before I set off on my investigations.

"Max? Yes, I'm fine thanks. I wondered if you could do some digging on known loan sharks in the areas local to Wantage. Yes, I'm working on a case and I've found five thousand pounds deposited into a victim's account. Also, there's a guy called Dave Lewis, think he used to be on the job, he's got a private investigation business in Witney. Can you let me know if anything flags up for him? Cheers, I owe you one, mate." We chat for a couple of minutes before he hangs up. That's one thing ticked off the list.

I'm a great networker and in my earlier probation role I made some solid professional contacts – people who you could count on when it matters. In return I'm always happy to offer my services free for a good cause.

My mind wanders to Steph and how she's doing. It was nice staying with her last night, even though she had one of those flashback nightmares. That bastard Ray Delossi has a lot to answer for. I feel so at ease with her when we're together and I'm also beginning to care for her. A lot. I seem to have easily fitted into Steph and Ben's family life, he's a good kid and I'm growing attached to them both. She's done a brilliant job bringing him up on her own.

It's Friday morning and I'm glad that it's nearly the weekend. This week has been the strangest, most exhausting and yet best week of my life. I feel the change in me since meeting Steph and

Ben, a sense of belonging; they are taking over my daily life, my thoughts, my heart. I want to wrap them up and keep them safe. I want to show her that there are good men in the world, that there can be a happy ending.

Steph left for work at 8am, at ease in her black trousers, white blouse and black ankle boots. There was a calmness about her since we'd kissed and been honest with each other about our feelings, so the taking things slowly was working out well for us. She said she was meeting with her boss, Detective Chief Inspector Mike Jones, this afternoon. We're both hoping that he won't take her off the case because of her personal connection with the murder victim. Meanwhile, everyone is very aware that Corinna has until 2.30pm on Monday afternoon to be charged with Ray's murder or set free. The clock is ticking.

Ben left for school at 8.15am. I was tempted to offer him a lift but I didn't want to impact too much on his daily routine. He told me he often meets his friends on the way to school and I didn't want to embarrass him.

I turn on the ignition, put the Mazda into gear, and then set off for Ray's house to see if I can find out what he'd been up to for the past month or so. Following that, I plan to head to Lewis Investigations in Witney where I've booked an appointment with Dave Lewis for 11.30am.

When I arrive at Ray's, surprisingly, there is no police presence by the green front door. I decide it's safer to enter the house via the rear entrance therefore I walk around the corner of the property to the back. It's an end semi-detached house with a small front garden and a wall which graduates to six feet as it follows the outside of the house until you reach a dark green gate at the back. I try the gate latch and it opens easily, if a little stiff. The garden is well kept with large paved slabs that cover the entire area. There is a small patio table with four white plastic chairs pushed into it. The parasol has a green weather protection cover, as does the small free-standing unit which may house a barbeque.

Closing the gate behind me, I walk up to the green back door. Immediately, my eyes drop to the scuffs on the side of the door near the handle and the fact that it doesn't look closed, let alone locked. The lock has splintered. The door has been kicked in. This is not a good sign. There's been a break-in.

I look at my watch. It's 9.45am. I take out my phone and text Steph.

You free? Can you give me a quick call? J x.

I wait patiently for a response but I'm desperate to get inside before the plods arrive. My phone vibrates and Prince's "Purple Rain" starts to play. I must change that damn tone. I've had it for years and it's beginning to annoy the hell out of me.

"Hey, what's up?" says Steph's now familiar voice.

"I'm at Ray's. I was going to see if I could find anything else in the house that could help us. There's no police officer on the front so I went around the back and the gate is unlocked. The back door has been kicked open."

"Jesus! I'll be there in about fifteen minutes. I'll just finish debriefing the team and head over to you. Don't go in and don't touch anything."

"I won't. I'll wait in my car for you."

Fifteen minutes later and I'm getting fed up of the adverts on the local radio station in between the music, but I'm also too lazy to plug in my phone and set up some new music. I've called Dave Lewis and moved our appointment to 12 noon, just in case.

Steph pulls up in her dark blue Fiesta and climbs out of the car. She's got a man with her. He's tall with a head of dark-blonde hair and a slim build. He's not bad looking. He looks about thirty-five. I temper the seed of jealousy that grows in the pit of my stomach. Get a grip, Jack! This is probably her work colleague.

I climb out of my car and head towards them. I watch the work colleague carefully, noting the confident way in which he walks in his grey trousers, white shirt and loosened blue tie. He's wearing a think padded jacket. Interesting.

"Hey, Chris." Steph turns to her colleague and begins the introductions. "This is Jack, Jack Kinsey. He's a PI and is doing some voluntary consulting on the case." Steph fleetingly catches my eye and gestures her hand to myself and Chris.

Chris holds out his hand. "Hey, Jack. Nice to meet you." He smiles at me and it seems genuine. "I work with DI Rutland. She says you were with her on the night of the murder?"

"Chris," I say with confidence. "Yes, that's right. We were binge watching a crime series on Netflix." I look at Steph wondering if her cheeks will start to colour because I remembered what she'd told me and shake Chris's hand firmly.

"I'll talk you through what happened when I got here," I said, taking them to the rear garden entrance.

"There was no police presence at the front door, so I tried the gate to the back of the house. It was open. As I move closer to the door, I see the scuff marks of what looks like a boot being pushed against the door to kick it open. The door's been pulled forward to look as though it's closed."

"Right. Let's go in," says Steph. She motions both Chris and I to join her. I didn't expect her to let me go in with them and I'm grateful to her for including me. This almost makes a statement. I feel like she's almost claiming me both personally and professionally.

The kitchen blind is closed so the first thing we realise is how dark it is in here. The second thing we notice is the sickly stench of urine as it fills our nostrils and hangs in the air. There is mess everywhere, drawers pulled out and utensils have been thrown onto the floor. The kettle and toaster are in the sink and the microwave has been dropped onto the floor and its door is hanging off. Breakfast cereal has been emptied across the floor and urinated on. Jesus! People can be such cretins.

Chris speaks first: "Shit. Someone pissed all over the place. What a mess! Jesus, who did this?"

"I'm wondering if it's the loan shark," I reply. "Maybe he's come back to get his money?"

"Loan shark?" They both look at me as if I've lost my marbles.

"My guess is that the five K that Ray borrowed and deposited into his account a couple of months ago was from a loan shark and they wanted their money back with interest."

"How do you know about the five grand?" Chris asks, then shakes his head at me. "No, don't tell me. I don't want to know."

"As I said earlier, Jack has been doing some voluntary consulting for us," Steph says in a don't mention it again tone.

We move through the dining area of the kitchen and into the living room when Steph suddenly stops and points to a now empty TV cabinet in front of us. "There was a PS4 when we were here a few days ago and an Alexa smart home device sitting on the top. They're both missing." She moves past the overturned beech side table in the living room. "Another Alexa sat here," she pointed to the bookcase, "and they've taken the TV and Sky box too."

The sofa and two matching chairs have been cut with a knife as though someone hoped to find something valuable hidden within the foam. This looks bad, even desperate.

"Let's check upstairs," Steph says, taking out her phone as she begins to climb the stairs.

"Hi, DI Rutland here." Her voice sounds pissed. "Ray Delossi's house has been broken into and burglarised. I need SOCO over here dusting for prints. Can you also find out why there's no police presence at the house when I specifically asked for one to be here?"

There's a small landing with a dark wood balustrade leading to two bedrooms and, I suspect, a bathroom. We follow Steph into the nearest bedroom. It's plain and soulless as expected, with black and red stripy bedding, white walls and red curtains. No furnishings that help to make a house a home. There are several photos of Ray on the bedside cabinet to the right of the bed showing him as a boy: skinny, hungry-looking, and a few others as the man he grew into.

My thoughts wander to why there are no photos of his family. I read somewhere that there is a mum, dad and brother and make a mental note to confirm this and where they are. I know there was a photo of Steph and Ben too on his cabinet. It's all a bit odd.

The second bedroom was completely different. It was painted sky blue with football and fast car posters on the walls. There is a white metal bedstead with a football duvet on it and a small lamp on a bedside table next to the bed. To me it looked like the room of a young teenage boy with books and a desk. There were warm furnishings such as the soft grass effect carpet and duvet with matching curtains. With the hint of paint still in the air, I look at the room with the eyes of a parent who waits for their teenager to come home after a long absence. It's a room waiting for someone to occupy it.

A cold chill goes through me and paralyses me for a moment. I look at Steph. She's gone white, her face blank, and begins to shudder as though she too has been chilled to the bone, so I walk over to her and carefully guide her towards the bed. "Here, Steph. Sit." I gently push her down and I know it's not professional, but I put my arm around her shoulders anyway to rub some warmth back into her.

Chris looks at Steph, his brows pulling together in a frown, making his eyes smaller. He slips gloves onto his hands and pulls open one of the drawers in the desk. It's full of papers. That's strange. "Boss, you need to see this," he says, pulling the drawer completely out. There's an odd tone to his voice as he lays the drawer on to the bed beside Steph. "Holy Shit!" He pulls paper, newspaper cuttings, glue and scissors out and studies them.

Steph pulls several pairs of gloves from her handbag and hands me a pair as we join Chris standing over the bed. Chris takes the letter he's been holding. It's a plain A4 paper with newspaper cut out letters on it. A blackmail letter and it's addressed to Steph. He hands it to me. I hear Steph gasp in horror and her face becomes deathly white as I begin to read the words.

DI Rutland,

Your son has been taken. Don't try to find him.

We want five thousand in cash by Friday 13th October.

Wait for our call.

"Idiot! So he was going to kidnap Ben and blackmail you for his return," I hiss, passing the letter to Steph's shaky fingers. Chris and I watch in silence as Steph stares at the letter.

"Did you see the date?" she asks quietly as a look of disbelief spreads across her face. Her eyes are wide, her nostrils flare as if she's forcing herself to inhale air. Chris and I check the date on the paper.

"Shit!" I say stiffening, trying to keep my anger under control. "That's a week on Friday. He was really going to go ahead with it. What a bastard."

Chris pushes his fingers through his hair as he shakes his head. "I can't get my head around this," he says pacing the room. "I mean, if he hadn't been murdered, he would have kidnapped Ben. His own son. And ransomed him to you for five K."

"That just about sums it up," I say, my eyes not leaving Steph.

"You alright, Steph? You look a bit peaky," Chris says, his lips spread into a grim line.

"I'm so sorry," Steph puts her hand to her mouth and her eyes roll, "but I think I'm going to be sick," she says before rushing out of the room.

There's a silence in the room as Chris and I listen to the sound of Steph retching somewhere nearby.

"He was a real bastard her ex, wasn't he?" Chris says, looking at me.

"Yeah, the worst by the sound of it," I reply as I start walking to the door. "I'll go and see if she's OK." She's kneeling on the floor in the bathroom when I find her, dry heaving over the toilet pan. I kneel beside her, stroke her hair and hold it back off her face until she's finished.

As she stands up I grab a towel from the rail, hold one corner under the water until I can feel it run warm, rinse it and gently wipe her face. She stands still, letting me tend to her. Finally, I use the dry end of the towel to pat her face dry. I put my hands on her arms gently but firmly, dip my head and rest my forehead on hers. I can see the pain in her eyes.

"He was a bastard," I whisper, stroking her cheek. "He's gone now. Don't let him take you with him." I search her eyes for a sign that she's listening to me, then watch with relief as her hand rises and slowly touches my shoulder. I can see her coming back to me.

"Let's get Chris and get out of here. We've seen enough. Let SOCO do the rest," I tell her, taking her hand to find Chris.

"You alright?" Chris looks at Steph as we catch up with him on the landing. He's holding several full evidence bags that look like the contents found in the desk drawer.

"Yeah. Sorry about that," she says, lowering her eyes with embarrassment.

"No need to apologise," Chris says, waving his hand in dismissal of the incident.

We leave this mausoleum of a house with its stinking kitchen, broken door, slashed sofa and creepy bedroom, and step outside into the clean, crisp air. I walk along the pavement and look for

Ray's car, something else that doesn't seem right about this place. It's gone.

"It appears they took his car too," I say. "Perhaps we'd better check Delossi Car Sales to see if it's been hit too."

Steph looks at Chris who nods and takes out his phone.

"Call or text if you need me. I have to get over to Witney to see Dave Lewis of Lewis Investigations. I want to know just how far he was tailing and monitoring you and Ben. He'd better be forthcoming because I am in no mood to make small talk today. What Ray did was a game changer. I'm fucking mad as hell at him. Now I'm taking no prisoners."

Steph smiles and gives me the biggest, most appreciative hug and whispers in my ear. "I love that you're being protective, Jack, but don't do anything stupid."

"I'll be careful," I assure her with a shrug. "And text you if I find anything," I call to her as I get in my car. I put the postcode into my satnav for directions to Lewis Investigations and set off. This day is becoming more interesting by the minute.

***

Dave Lewis, alias Lewis Investigations, is situated above a Chinese restaurant on the High Street in Witney. The brownstone building matches similar buildings in the immediate area. I've parked near to the High Street and have given myself two hours to find Lewis and hopefully find out any relevant information.

I press the button on the intercom system. A sharp male voice answers, crackling through the system:

"Lewis Investigations."

"It's Jack Kinsey. I've got an appointment," I answer.

"Ah yes. Come up."

I hear the sound of the lock being released and I push the door until I find myself standing inside a dim hallway with a bright light shining above me. I follow the stairs in front of me until I reach a heavy blue door with an attached wooden plaque which reads "Lewis Investigations". It suddenly swings open and a portly, balding man wearing a brown suit and a big smile greets me.

I grasp his outstretched hand. It's firm. First impressions: I kind of like this man.

"Thanks for seeing me," I say, as he beckons me into his office. I follow and am surprised by how clean, tidy and professional it looks. I sit in a brown leather armchair which faces the mahogany desk and wait for him to seat himself. Lewis sits in the brown leather swivel chair behind his desk and looks at me. It looks as if he's contemplating whether he can trust me or not. I think he decides that he can because he begins to speak.

"You're here about Ray Delossi," he begins. "Obviously, client confidentiality needs to be taken into account, but as my former client is now deceased, I do have some flexibility."

"Ray Delossi was a bastard," I say bluntly, "we both know that."

"I don't know about that. Yes, he was short-tempered, but–"

"Do you know what he did to his wife?" I interrupted. "Do you know why she left him and had to live in hiding to keep her and her son safe? Do you realise that short temper of his resulted in her ending up in hospital bruised and battered numerous times?"

"No," he insisted, "I didn't know. I was asked to find them, follow them, take photos and gather information about their lives and routines."

"Did that not strike you as funny that a grown man would be asking you to do that, especially once you had found them?"

"No," he says again. "If I found that weird, I'd be out of a job."

"What about making sure that morally you're not putting someone in danger? I mean, look what he did to his latest girlfriend." I can feel my voice rising higher and try to calm myself down.

He glares at me and folds his hands onto his lap.

"OK." I put my hands up in a sign of surrender. "Let's go back to why I'm here. It would be good if you could answer a few questions for me."

"I'll try." He seems honest. "I never liked him, but I had no proof to say that he would be a danger to anyone. I want you to know that."

"About Steph and Ben. Did he say what plans, if any, he had for them?" I ask, trying to push for any information that could give me a lead.

"No. He said he just wanted to know where they were," he said, bouncing back slightly in his chair, his hands folded over his portly belly.

"Did you know that he put the photos you took in frames in his house to make it look as though they lived there? As though they were his family."

"Jesus! That's creepy. No, I never went to his home. He always came to the office."

"So, he never said anything about getting back in touch with Ben? Did you give him Ben's email address?"

"Yes, I'm afraid I did. I collected email addresses from the boy and a friend of his as he walked home from school, telling them that I worked for a teen mag and was collecting emails to enter youngsters into a competition. I said that the winner and a friend could win a day trip to London including a ride on the London Eye and lunch. Knowing what I know now I feel bad about it. But it's done."

"About his finances. They're not good. The car sales business is not making any money and it looks as though he's struggling. He had a loan from someone for five thousand pounds about two months ago. Do you know who that's from? And when did you do your last job for him? Did he pay you up to date?"

He stared at his fingernails. "I finished my last job with him last month, and yes, he paid me up to date. He said he was having some money problems at work but he was sorting that out. He had a friend in Basingstoke called Danny – he didn't say his last name – but he said Danny was helping him out. That's all I know."

"Danny. That's good." I'll tell Chris. I've got a name, something to work with. Maybe that'll narrow it down for Max's search.

"How's that young girl, uh, what's her name, Corinna?" Lewis suddenly asks. "I saw her once when he came to see me. He'd parked outside and she was sitting in the car. Pretty little thing."

"Well, she's going to be on trial for murder," I state, meeting his eyes, "but it looks like she was defending herself. Another life ruined by that bastard. If you saw what he did to her…"

I get up and hold my hand out. Lewis stands too and takes my hand. "Thanks."

"I hope she gets off. If there's anything I can do to help…" His tone seems genuine, his eyes sympathetic.

"I'll let you know," I say, before leaving the room. I'm focused on the mysterious Danny, who I'm thinking is the loan shark and start to text Max to let him know when my phone starts to play "Purple Rain". It's Steph.

"Hi, Steph. Any news?" I say as I push open the main door and start walking back to my car.

"Hi, Jack. I've spoken to DCI Jones and he's happy for me to carry on with the Delossi case, but I need to update him every day."

"That's brilliant," I tell her, feeling relieved.

"There's also a breakthrough for Corinna. One of the neighbours, Geoff Cross, who lives in the house opposite Ray, has confirmed that he saw her running from the house distressed and bleeding at around 10pm. He didn't tell us because he didn't want to get involved. He also says that he saw a dark figure walk into Ray's house about five minutes later and can't remember seeing the figure come out."

"Thank God!" I say, "that's great news for Corinna. With Cross's statement that's got to put Corinna on the back burner while we try to find the real murderer."

"Yes, we're bringing him in to work with the sketch artists to see if we can get any facial markings to go on," she says down the line. "It would be great if I don't have to charge her on Monday afternoon, but that would be asking for a miracle."

"I know," I say. "Unless the murderer walks into the station himself or herself and fully confesses to Ray's murder then we're still up against it." I didn't want to put a damper on things but we certainly needed a miracle to get Corinna freed from prison.

I tell her about my visit to Lewis and that I'll update Max to search for Danny, the loan shark, and that it might, if I'm lucky, lead us to our burglar and the stolen stuff. She hadn't heard back from the Delossi Car Sales place yet. Perhaps they won't need further funds. I'm not entirely sure what the debt stands at. The only thing I know I can count on is that it will definitely be quite a bit more than five K!

I hear a bleep and realise that I have a call waiting.

"Sorry," I say to her, enjoying our conversation. "I've got someone calling me on the line. Can I call you back in a minute?"

"Yes. No problem," she replies. "Speak soon."

I disconnect and answer the phone.

"Jack!" It's my mum's fraught voice. "Jack!" She's sobbing.

"What is it, Mum?" I ask. My heart almost stops. My mum never cries.

"It's your dad. He's had a heart attack. I'm at the hospital with him now. Please come," I hear the panic in her voice.

"Are you at the John Radcliffe?" I ask, hoping she'll say yes. I'm not too far from there, probably about twenty minutes.

"Yes," she sobs through her tears. "Please hurry, Jack. I need you."

"I'm on my way," I can hear my reply, but it sounds faint as if it doesn't belong to me.

I'm in shock and numb when I call Steph back. My fingers won't move properly as I hit several wrong buttons before I locate Steph's number. I'm half running to the car when she answers.

"Jack?" she questions. I think she can hear me running.

"It's my dad. He's had a heart attack. He's at the JR. I'm on my way there now," I blurt out in between breaths, my legs moving as fast as they can.

"Shit, Jack. I'm so sorry. Can I do anything?" she says softly, with concern in her voice.

"No. I just need to get there. Be with Mum and Dad. I'll call when I know what's happening," I tell her as I reach the road that leads into the car park.

"OK. Drive carefully."

"I will." I hang up as I turn in to the car park. Shit. Shit. Shit. It never rains…

Chapter 22: Saving myself

Unknown

My head is a mess. I walk the streets trying to clear the fog in my brain. Someone brushes past me, knocking my shoulder. It pulls me out of my reverie as I watch the medium height black chap who bumped into me in his black leather trousers and blue suede jacket, pull the woman with short blonde curly hair and wearing a bright pink blouse, slimline knee-length purple skirt and pink stiletto shoes roughly by the arm.

"Leon, you're hurting me," the woman pleads in a soft Irish accent. "Leon, slow down. I can't walk so fast in these heels."

"You're always wearing those damn shoes," Leon says, with anger in his voice. He's walking so quickly that he's almost yanking her arm out of the socket. "Which means you're always late for everything. Now shut up, woman, and keep walking or we'll be late for the theatre."

The fog in my brain turns to red. How dare that man talk to the woman like that. How dare he manhandle her. What is the matter with people these days? I follow them along the main street, biding my time until I come upon an empty side street to discuss the situation with him. Before they know what is happening, I push the man forcefully into the quiet windowless street. The woman whose arm he is firmly holding totters on her heels behind him.

"What the f…! Leon says, surprised.

"Exactly!" I say, casually pinning him into the wall so fast that it forces him to lose his grip on the woman. She stumbles slightly as I talk to the man. "What is the matter with you? Treating a woman like that, dragging her down the street like she's a piece of meat." I can't keep the sharpness from my voice. This man is a menace, has the making of another Ray Delossi.

231

"You're mental," he says with some bravado, but his eyes move erratically betraying his confidence. "Mind your own damn business."

The woman stands next to him. "Who's this, Leon? A friend of yours?" she asks in her Irish brogue.

"Shut up, Lynette!" he shouts at her, and I watch her recoil away from him when he raises his voice.

"Would you mind stepping back into the main street, Lynette?" I say, politely addressing the woman, "I need to have a private word with Leon." I wait until she's out of sight, ball my right hand into a fist, bring my bent arm back as far as it will go and punch the son of a bitch full in the face.

"Ahhh," he croaks as my fist hits his nose and cracks. He puts his arms up to his face to ward off another blow. "What the fuck, man?" he says, trying to talk through his blocked nose. "I'b gonna call de polib."

"Whatever," I reply. My hands are back on his shoulders and pinning him upright. I don't give a toss about what he does or doesn't do apart from if he's hitting women. The clock is already ticking on my freedom and my life, punching this guy isn't going to make a difference in the grand scheme of things. "You really need to reassess how you treat women and people who are physically weaker than yourself," I say to his stricken face. He is all talk and no action. Just empty threats. "If you have to pick on someone, try doing it to someone your own size. Or someone who will fight back. Otherwise, I'm coming back for you."

I let go of his shoulders and push my face right into his so that all I can see are the pupils in his eyes. "And next time you won't live to call the police."

Without another glance I walk back into the main street where I find Lynette hovering in front of a bookshop smoking a cigarette as if her life depended on it.

"If I were you," I say as I stroll past her, "I'd get yourself a new boyfriend, Lynette. Leon is nothing but a prick."

Bugger. I thought life was bad when Blip died, but I hadn't visualised the impact of what my killing Ray Delossi would do to anyone he was in contact with at the time of his death. Talk about making things complicated. When I get home, I think about texting an old friend of mine who happens to be working on the Delossi case, but then decide to hold my nerve. If I get involved, I may become a person of interest and that's the last thing I need. It's clear I should keep a low profile, particularly after what happened earlier in the side street and that other incident. There are just over two and a half days left to get Corinna off the murder charge, preferably without incriminating myself.

I can only see three ways out of this mess. One, someone needs to come forward, to give evidence that they saw Corinna leave and another person entering the house on the night he died. This information either leads them to me or enables Corinna to be charged on circumstantial evidence. Why the hell didn't I clean up anything suspicious and check the knife when I was there? I could have made it harder for the police to place Corinna at the scene of the crime.

The second choice is for me to hand myself in to the police and offer a full confession. The third and final option would be for me to write a confession to the murder and kill myself, but then I'd have to call the police before Monday afternoon before they charged Corinna.

There's no way I would cut myself, not after seeing the mess that Blip left for me to find in the bathroom. So, I guess my weapon of choice to do myself in would be to take pills, lots of them. People will think it's strange, talking about suicide with such calmness, but I feel like I've only been living half a life since Blip died. In the early days following her death I'd sat with a drug cocktail and alcohol more than once, sobbing like a child and telling myself to put an end to this misery. The only thing that stopped me, was the additional anguish it would put my parents through. How can you live knowing that both of your children had killed themselves? It was a burden I wouldn't wish on my worst enemy. I guess I'd best make the most of my last couple of nights of freedom.

Chapter 23: Time to focus

Steph

When I'm back at the office there are more pictures and documents added to the incident board, including the written timeline of the house break-in and the subsequent theft of Ray's car and other equipment. I dismiss the photos of my battered face and body that stare back at me from the board and continue looking at the information we have garnered about Ray over the past few days.

Chris and I start the debrief with the team, updating them with our findings from Ray's house and I also tell them what Jack said about Lewis. The evidence bags containing Ray's blackmail handiwork are sent to the labs for analysis. I explain to the group that Jack Kinsey is undertaking some voluntary consulting work for us and is looking into finding a loan shark called Danny who Ray knew from Basingstoke. Sam said he'd ask a friend who's on the force in Basingstoke about known villains and loan sharks in the area.

Sam walks forward in jeans and a smart dark blue shirt. He's holding a piece of paper. "I'm afraid Mick the sketch artist couldn't get much from Geoff Cross. He pins the paper to the board. It's just a shape of a head with a hood tilted over most of it. No hair, no eyes, beard, lips, earrings.

"Well, that narrows it down," says Chris as he shakes his head in frustration at the nondescript drawing. "That could be anyone. Man or woman."

"Yes," I say in agreement, "but this is definitely the person we should be looking at for Ray's murder. I can feel it in my bones."

"I agree," Justine says peering at the picture.

"Me too," Danielle says, before changing the subject to tell us about her earlier meeting with the bank manager of Ray's bank regarding his three accounts and shared her latest findings with the team. The situation is becoming more bizarre by the minute as she tells us that Ray has been putting one hundred pounds a month into a savings account for eight years, and it's in Ben's name.

"I've checked out Ray's car," says Justine as she steps forward, pushing a stray hair behind her ear. "He's got a black BMW 3 Series 2017 plate. I've put out a registration alert on it. Though, if it's been stolen the chances are that the plates will have been switched and a paint job done to it by now."

The fax machine springs to life and paper starts printing, so I walk over to collect the latest information. "I think you're right, Justine," I say, scanning the printed sheet. "We have confirmation that Corinna's DNA and fingerprints are on one of the two wine glasses found in Ray's house." I wave the paper absently and lay it on top of my pile of paperwork by the incident board. I feel despondent, I was really hoping for a lead on Ray but all I'm getting are dead ends. I study the information board in front of me hoping for a miracle.

"We need to go back to the drawing board," I say looking up at the team, "and double check everyone's alibi's for last Tuesday, 16th October, between 9pm and 8am. Check everyone we've come into contact with, man or woman, since Ray's murder and check their family history to make sure that Ray Delossi was not known to them. That includes the manager at Delossi Car Sales."

"Yes, Boss," Chris says. "I'll call the manager, Luke Pertwee, and check any CCTVs in the area. Justine and Sam, you take the neighbour Cross and the rest of the neighbours. Justine, can you also chase the lab for Delossi's house break-in and the blackmail stuff?"

I check my silver watch. It was 3pm. I look at Chris and he nods, so I add: "We'll get as much of this done as we can today. No more debriefs. Call me if you get any leads."

In light of what we found at Ray's house regarding the blackmail notes and undelivered ransom letter, it's fair to say that I'm pissed at Ray and don't want his bloody money. Even if it is for Ben. Shit! How do I keep the blackmail news from him? Again, it's just another piece of the puzzle that was Ray's life and the fall out that I am now left to deal with.

Danielle steps forward, brown tendrils of hair swirling down each side of her face as she moves toward me. She's holding a beige document folder in her hand and asks for a quiet word. Her eyes don't quite meet mine and her shoulders slump as she follows me into my office.

"This is delicate, Boss." She hesitates a little before closing the door quietly. I settle into my brown leather chair and look at her.

"You'd better sit then," I say, watching as she sits in the brown checked chair opposite me. She's wearing a denim collared tunic and black leggings. She looks good, so vibrant and young. God, I need to take up a hobby. Maybe I'll start jogging again when this case is over. I used to love that when I was younger, before I met Ray.

Danielle breaks into my thoughts. "As you know," she starts, "I've been going through Delossi's laptop and his bank accounts. I've also found an attached document on his laptop which is a copy of a will that he had drawn two years ago. This is the print off." She hands me the paperwork.

I'm not sure what I'm looking at until I see my name written in capital letters in black and white print on the document. He wrote me into his damn will. Why the hell would he do that?

"He cited you as his next of kin," Danielle states bluntly as I continue to stare at the document, silently fuming.

"He also cited you as his sole beneficiary of any property, businesses, cars and goods that were still in his ownership at the time of his death."

"Fuck!" I say quietly to myself, pushing my leather chair back and standing up. I rub my forehead to ward off the nagging pain in my head and open the office door to call Chris to join me in the office. He looks up, sees my face and walks quickly towards me.

"What is it?" he asks coming into the room. His blue cotton shirt sleeves are rolled up and his hands are in his pockets. He looks at Danielle and then his focus settles on me.

"Tell him," I demand, looking at Danielle – my head is thumping. "Tell him what Ray did!"

"It's the will. I printed it off," Danielle says pointing to the document in my hand. I hold it out to him and watch as he begins to skim read the pages. Danielle explains about the next of kin and beneficiary business until Chris puts his hand up to stop her.

"Holy Shit!" his voice rises in frustration. He looks my way. "Why would he try to blackmail you and then leave you everything in his will? I don't get it."

"Me neither, but after today I'll be needing that money for bloody therapy!" I mutter, facing the glass partition and watching the team going about their work.

"This is now a serious conflict of interest for you," he states, running his hands through his hair.

"I know, Chris. I bloody know that." I try to contain my anger but it's boiling inside me. I moved on with my life and didn't expect to have anything to do with Ray again. "I don't want anything from him. Hasn't he got any family who are alive?"

"No. His parents died very recently. His dad died in prison a month ago and his mum was involved in a hit and run near Tower Hamlets two weeks ago. His brother is in prison," Danielle says.

"Jesus!" I mutter in disbelief. If ever there's a time to focus, this is it. I nibble the inside of my cheek and rub my head.

"OK, we need to verify the will with the company who drew it up and then get our legal department to look at the document," I tell

Danielle. "This doesn't look good on me. Everything pertaining to money, savings and the will should now go through DCI Jones. I'll call him asap. How am I supposed to be the lead investigator on his murder case when I'm now his next of kin and sole beneficiary to all that he has?"

"Boss?" Justine shouts from her desk waving her hand, the landline phone in the other hand.

"Yes?" I say, wondering what else can ruin my day today.

"I've got Dr Soames on the line. She says Delossi's body is ready to be released and she wants to know if we know who his next of kin is?"

My head continues to throb as I look from Danielle to Chris and back at Justine who still holds the phone:

"Well, apparently that would be me, I'm his next of kin," I say, walking into the room. It sounds crazy just hearing myself say the words, so what the others think of it as they hear my statement is, frankly, anyone's guess. "I'll speak to her." I take the phone from Justine.

"Hey, Daisy. It's me," I say, closing my eyes as a sharp pain shoots across my forehead. I update her about my new responsibilities thanks to Ray Delossi and nibble my inner cheek when she starts cursing even though I totally agree with her. "My thoughts exactly. I'll source a funeral director and organise his burial. I'll be in touch when I've got things organised."

After the phone call I delegate this task to Justine. I feel a slight pang of guilt as though I'm passing on my mess for others to clean up, but then I argue with myself that this is still an official case and we have to tie things up and get closure. Justine needs to simply look for local funeral directors and find out the information for me.

Chris walks up to me carrying a plastic cup of water and two tablets.

"Here you go, Boss. Two paracetamols," he says handing me the tablets and water. "They'll help your headache."

"Thanks." I touch his shoulder briefly in appreciation before taking the tablets

"Boss." Sam looks up at me from his desk, his eyes bright with excitement. "My friend just came through with the loan shark thing. The guy we're looking for is Danny Devlin."

"Well done, Sam." I look at my watch and the wall clock. We're running out of time. "Call him now. Check his whereabouts for last Tuesday evening from 9pm onwards and verify that if you can. Book in to see him first thing on Monday morning. See if you can find the missing electrical goods from Ray's house. Chris has a list. It would be good to get the final amount owing from the debt."

"Thanks, Boss." He smiles with pride. "Will do." He strides towards Chris.

"I'll be in my office. I need to talk to DCI Jones," I say, turning to my quiet sanctuary, I close the door and rest my head against it for a moment. My eyes are closed. Crack on, Steph. Times a-wasting. I sit down at my desk, reach for the landline phone and call Mike Jones' number.

"Sir, it's DI Rutland," I say, moving the phone to my left ear and tilting my head to secure it in place, which leaves my right hand free to write notes.

"Hey, Steph. How are things?"

"There are some complications, Sir. Danielle has been going through Delossi's laptop and found several documents. One includes a document declaring me as his next of kin, and the other is a document citing me as his sole beneficiary. On top of that he's been saving money into an account for Ben for the past eight years."

"Bugger!" I hear my boss mutter over the phone.

"Precisely, Sir. I've asked Danielle to liaise with you over this. She will verify the documents' validity with the solicitor who drew it up and also with our legal department. Can you deal with this as it's now a conflict of interest for me?"

"Yes, of course." He sounds serious, worried. "Anything I can do. Sounds like you've got your hands full."

"Just a tad, Sir. Delossi's house was broken into today. When Chris and I went to investigate we found a pile of blackmail papers and a note in the desk drawer of the spare room. The letter said that he'd taken my son and wanted five grand from me for his release."

"Holy Mother of God!" he gasped, and I could just imagine his face screwed up in horror. "Off the record, Steph," he began, "Delossi was a bastard. He must have been a sad, deluded psycho to expect you to sort out his burial after what he did and planned to do to you and Ben."

"Off the record, Sir, he was a nasty piece of work and I would like nothing more than to get Corinna James out of that cell downstairs, bury Ray's sorry arse and get on with my life!"

"I'm with you there, Steph. I'll sort out the legal side and liaise with Danielle. I'll update you as much as I am able to."

"Thank you, Sir."

He's a good sort, DCI Mike Jones. One of the best. He has integrity and loyalty and I know he'll stand by me and support me whenever he can.

I text Ben. He's not finishing school until 4.15pm today because there's rugby practice and I tell him that I'll pick him up from school because we need to meet Jack. I haven't heard from Jack since his earlier call to say he was heading to the hospital. I hope his dad is alright.

We're at the hospital by 5pm and I check in at the busy reception to find out what ward Jack's dad has been admitted to. Ben stays close by my side, his arm almost touching mine as we walk. I don't think he likes hospitals too much and it doesn't help that it's built like a maze.

Finally, we reach the floor where Jack's dad is and I tell the plump, dishevelled, black-haired sister at the entrance desk to the ward that I'm Jack's wife (a little white lie but needs must) and therefore the daughter in law of his parents. The sister explains that Jack's dad has been put in a room of his own and she gestures with her hand to Room 3, points the way with her square chin and continues with her paperwork as we hurry past.

The bravado in which we rushed to the hospital suddenly leaves me. I can literally feel it draining from my body as I knock quietly on the door and slowly open it.

The room is in semi-darkness, it's dark outside and the curtains are drawn. There's a light shining over the bed which glares intrusively over the patient. An older woman with a head of greying brunette sits in a heavy chair holding her husband's hand. I assume that this is Jack's mother. I look at Jack who sits the other side of the bed, his hand resting near his dad's and talking quietly to him. Jack looks tired. Worried.

Jack looks up at us, his face in shock. Maybe I did the wrong thing. Maybe I shouldn't be here. I don't want to intrude. I put my hand on Ben's shoulder for reassurance. I'm not sure if I'm reassuring him or if he's reassuring me. Jack stands and walks slowly towards us.

"Steph," he says in his deep husky voice. "You're here?" His arms reach out to take my shoulders and pull me to him.

"We are. How is he?" I say softly, holding him tight. Ben stands next to me looking concerned. We've only known this man for a matter of days but the impact he has had on us is incredible. Jack looks down at Ben and my heart melts as Ben holds out his young arms and wraps them around both of us. I can't help but smile at this beautiful boy of mine as he grows into a courageous, generous and caring young man. I am so proud of him.

"How are you, Jack?" Ben asks and I see a lump in Jack's throat. It must be humbling for him to acknowledge that this boy cares for him the way he does.

"I'm fine, Ben." Jack squeezes Ben's shoulders in reassurance.

Someone clears their throat and I look up to see Jack's parents looking at us with bemused looks on their face.

"Are you going to introduce us, son?" His mum's voice, clear and steady, breaks the silence.

Jack disentangles himself from us and stands in the middle with an arm around each of us. He seems more than happy to introduce us.

"Mum, Dad, this is Steph... and this young man here is Steph's son, Ben."

Jack's mum stands up and walks towards me.

"Hello, Mrs Kinsey. Sorry for the intrusion."

"It's Kate, please just call me Kate. Hello, Steph. Lovely to meet you," she says with warmth as I go to take her outstretched hand. Suddenly, she seems to change her mind as she gathers me in a big, warm hug. The hug feels genuine and oddly comforting.

She turns to Ben and gives him a warm smile. "Hello, Ben. I'm Kate, Jack's mum. It's lovely to meet you."

Ben holds out his hand. He's still in his grey school jacket and trousers and white shirt. "Hello, Kate," he says seriously. "You must be really nice if you're Jack's mum. I like him a lot."

Kate smiles and shakes his hand gently. "I would like to think I am," she smiles.

Jack's dad, looking pale and attached to a drip, seems to brighten up as Kate introduces me to her husband. She looks adoringly at him and smiles. "He's given us quite a fright today. He has to stay in hospital for a few days so they can monitor him and to make sure his new medication is doing the job. The doctor says he's lucky it was only a minor heart attack. More like a warning."

"I'm relieved. You must listen to the doctors though," I say with a smile.

"You sound just like my wife and son!" he says, trying to laugh and then holds his chest as if the laughter is painful.

"Be careful, Peter. You're still sore." Jack's mum moves quickly to her husband's side and strokes his head. She sits next to him and takes his hand again, stroking over his knuckles and reassuring him that everything will be alright.

"We should go. I just wanted to pop by," I say, turning to Jack. "Just to make sure you're all OK and to see if you needed anything."

"I think we're fine, aren't we?" Jack asks his mum and she nods her head. "But why don't I take you and Ben for a cuppa? There's a Costa nearby."

It would be great to have just a few minutes with Jack so I look at Ben and we both nod affirmatively. I'm feeling a little tired and wound up about Ray's will and the next of kin thing. The "work" face that I show to everyone doesn't seem to fool Jack or Ben. They can see that I've got a lot on my mind but don't say anything.

"It's great to meet you both. Please take care, Peter. Don't overdo it."

Kate walks slowly towards me and holds my shoulders gently. "I can see why Jack likes you. Ben is adorable, a credit to you. I hope you come to visit again soon."

I can feel a pink blush rising up my neck at Kate's compliments. "Thank you, Kate. That's very kind of you." I feel emotional because his parents are so accepting of myself and Ben. I watch Jack kiss his mum goodbye telling her he'll be back soon and that he'll bring her a cup of tea on his return. Then he ushers Ben and I through the door and down the corridor to the lift.

Three steaming mugs sit in front of us in the coffee shop. We're perched on hard wooden chairs at a corner table listening to James Blunt softly telling someone that they're "beautiful".

The tiredness around Jack's eyes is still there. His face is still drawn but he seems reinvigorated somehow. Knowing his dad is going to be alright must be a huge relief but there's something else too. I saw it the moment Jack realised we'd come to him. The sight of us lifted him, gave him strength. He looks at me now and starts mouthing the words from the song as they come through the speaker. He knows I'll start to blush again. He knows I can't help it. A hand gently sits on top of my hand, a light touch that grounds me.

"Jack. Mum's face is going bright red," Ben smirks.

"I know, Ben. She's embarrassed because I'm singing to her," he says with a wink.

"She is pretty, isn't she?" Ben asks him as if I'm not present.

"No. She's more than that. She's beautiful," Jack replies instantly.

"Stop it, both of you. You're as bad as each other!"

They look at one another with big grins on their faces like two conspirators organising a coup. I miss this, I love it that there are two of us, Ben and I, but it would be even better if we became three one day.

"How did your afternoon go?" Jack suddenly asks.

I gave him Sam's information on Danny Devlin, the Basingstoke loan shark, and that Sam was going to see him on Monday to look for the stolen goods and to find out exactly how much he owed.

He studies my face. It is as though he can read my mind. "There's more?" he asks quietly.

"Yes, but I don't want to talk about that right now," I say a little too sharply. "I just want to chill with you guys." I smile and catch Jack's slightly raised eyebrow and gently shake my head.

Ben dips his long-handled spoon into the mountain of squirty cream and marshmallows on the top of his hot chocolate. "Well I've got some good news," he quips. "Molly let me sit next to her at lunch today. She's nice and easy to talk to."

"Well done, Ben," Jack says, patting Ben's shoulder carefully so that he doesn't spill his hot chocolate.

"Do you know how long your dad will be in hospital for?" I ask, wondering what Jack's plans are and if there is anything I can do to help.

"About five days to a week. I can't tell you how relieved I am that this was a minor one."

"I'm so relieved for you and your mum, Jack. Will you let me know if you need anything?"

He nods. "I'd better get that tea and get back to Mum. I'm not sure what I'm doing later. I'll text you."

"No problem," I say, taking my spare house key from my purse and giving it to him. "Just in case you need to crash somewhere tonight closer to the hospital. I'll leave blankets and sheets on the sofa."

He takes the key and doesn't say anything. He just stares at it as though it's a treasured gift. "Thanks." When he looks at me his eyes are shining.

We finish our drinks and Jack leans in to kiss me briefly on the cheek before patting Ben's arm and telling him to look after me. Then we go our separate ways.

On the way home it's quiet in the car. I concentrate on driving and Ben leans his head back and closes his eyes. "I like him," he says without looking up. His eyes are still closed. "I like him a lot."

"Me too, Ben. Me too," I answer softly, tears welling in my eyes.

"I think he likes us," he continues. "I wish I had a dad who loved me and wanted to live with me. If I could choose, I would choose someone like Jack to be my dad. He's kind and protective and he really, I mean 'really' likes you."

"Ben!" I nearly swerve the car. "First of all, these things take time and I wouldn't want to push Jack into a situation he isn't comfortable with, and secondly how do you know he really, really likes me?"

"He can't stop looking at you and touches you whenever he can." Our eyes meet in the darkness of the car.

"Oh. Does that bother you?" I ask cautiously.

"No. It's nice to see you happy."

"You know you'll always be my wingman, right?"

"I know, Mum," he says, as our eyes briefly meet.

The in-car phone shrills through our laughter as I talk to Justine on speakerphone.

"Justine, I have Ben in the car with me. Go ahead."

"Well, I've found a place near to you to sort out the meeting. I've had the package transferred already to the place and I'll text you their number and address so that you can check which dates you want to book the meeting."

"Thanks, Justine. See you Monday. Have a good weekend."

Much later after we've picked up a McDonald's from the drive-in on our way home, demolished it in front of the telly and caught up with the news of the day, we head to bed. It had been another long and exhausting day. Thank goodness the weekend was almost upon us and we could slow the pace a little. My head hit the pillow and I fell into a blissful sleep.

I don't know how long I'd been asleep when I hear the front door open and quietly close. Jack came back. And in the darkness, I fell back to sleep with a smile on my face.

Chapter 24: Hanging in there

Corinna

I think the bravado and encouragement of Dr Seuss' words are fading a little as I sit quietly in my cold, stark prison cell. I'm waiting to hear from Noah and Steph. I don't really know what's going on. All I know is that I'm being held until Monday afternoon when they will make the decision to charge me or free me. I've only been in here for a few days but I already miss work at the museum and my independence. What little I had left before Ray entered my life. When you're imprisoned in a strange, confined environment and your freedom has been taken from you everything becomes magnified as though your senses are letting you know what you're missing. And every day feels like a month, every minute feels like a week, and every second feels like a day.

The stitches are beginning to itch on my chest making me want to scratch at them and rip open the new scar tissue. Maybe it's pent-up anger that makes me want to scratch. I know I committed a crime, but a crime was also committed against me and I only hit Ray with my knee to defend myself. When will I ever get a break in this godforsaken life? When will I get a chance find out what I can make of myself? I splutter out a cough. Oh no, not again. I put my hand over my mouth. It's a tickly cough, the type you can't get rid of. It started not long after Noah and Jenny's visit, as if my body was telling me that it's had enough, as if it's protesting.

Noah and Jenny have been great but they're not the ones stuck in here looking at four white walls, a metal bed with a plastic mattress and matching pillow and a dirty-looking unit with a toilet and a wash basin. I've now got two grey blankets to keep me warm at night. Yeah! I lie back on the bed and fold my arms behind my head, looking up at the ceiling. My mind begins to wander back to eight years ago.

***

The doorbell rings and I go to answer it. I hope it's not the family social worker, Jude Kilkenny, with her blonde short bob-style and long skirts and dresses and an assortment of silver bangles that jingled whenever she moves. If Jude sees the mess, she'll be disappointed, and I don't think I can take the look of pity in her eyes today. Today is not my lucky day. I slowly lean my head around the open door and see one of her familiar blue boots step forward to keep the door open. A piece of green floaty material clings to another suede boot as the rest of the long dress follows Jude across the threshold of my home. Jude sweeps forward, she's in the hallway now and my heart sinks.

"Hey, Corinna," she says in a warm voice, one hand sweeping a strand of blonde hair from her face and tucking it behind her ear. "Can I come in?"

"Sure," I say, reluctantly. I know it's not my fault but that doesn't stop me feeling embarrassed at the state of the house and the way in which we live. "Mum's not having a good day," I explain as she walks through the doorway into the living room with the tatty old brown sofa and chairs, the threadbare, stained carpet and the old television that's seen better days.

Mum is sitting on one of the chairs staring at the blank television screen. I should be at school, but on days when she's not responsive I stay at home to make sure that she eats, drinks and uses the toilet.

"Hello, Julie. How are you?" Jude sinks into the opposite chair to Mum. I'm not surprised when Mum doesn't react or respond to Jude. She continues to stare at the screen.

Jude looks concerned as she starts to look around the room, taking in Mum's dirty clothes thrown on the back of the chair and twisting one of my old threadbare light brown teddy bears in her hands. *I'm doing my best!* I want to shout. *You try looking after a mentally ill mother when you're ten-years-old.*

I sit on the sofa. I'm tired. Life's such hard work sometimes. I suddenly remember my manners and feeling far older than my years I stand up and ask: "Cup of tea, Jude?"

"Yes please, dear," she says kindly, holding her black satchel bag with one hand and resting the other on the top of the sofa. She follows me into the kitchen and lays her bag on top of the counter. I've tidied a little but this morning I decided to leave the dishes in the sink and not wash them. Of course, they've now started to build up in the wash bowl. I was about to tackle them when Jude arrived.

"How long has she been this unresponsive?" she asks, taking the dirty dishes from the bowl and filling it with clean hot, soapy water. She picks up a small saucepan, dumps it into the water and scrubs it with a dirty looking scourer.

"This is her third day. I was about to call you," I say, raising my voice slightly over the noise of the kettle.

I put two mugs, teabags, sugar, milk and teaspoons onto the counter. I stand watching her with my back leaning against the counter with my arms folded. I appreciate how quickly she washes the rest of the dishes, rinses them and stacks them carefully on the draining board.

"I think it's time we think about getting her specialised help, Corinna." Jude gives me a swift look.

"But, Jude," I begin to protest. My shoulders stiffen and I start to panic. I watch in slow motion as Jude dries her hands using a nearby hand towel and walks toward me. Her hand softly pats my shoulder and I shudder briefly at her touch. I've been trying to avoid this conversation for months:

"She needs medical and physical care that you can't give her, Corinna," her words cut like glass.

"I know," I say as tears roll down my cheeks. Our eyes connect and hold for a moment and I see such sadness in hers as she talks to me. Tears drop onto the counter as I pour boiling water into mugs and finish making the hot drinks. "I've tried my best but it's too much."

"Corinna, you have done a brilliant job so far, but you never should have been given the task to look after your mum when your dad left the family home five years ago. You were… no, you *are* much too young for that kind of responsibility. You deserve a life."

"But she hasn't been this bad all of that time," I protest quietly, feeling numb. "She's got worse over the past six months."

"I know, dear, but now it's time for both of you to get the help you need," she says kindly.

I hold my mug in my hands, the scalding heat searing my fingers as tears fall down my face. I'm sorry, Mum, so sorry. But I can't do this anymore.

"OK, Jude. You're right. It's time," I say finally, wiping my face on the sleeve of my jumper. "But where will I go? What will happen to me? What will happen to Mum?" I ask, worried about the future of leaving the familiarity of my home.

"Don't worry, Corinna. There are policies put in place for situations like this. There are places where you can live, possibly with a foster family or in a group home. Wherever you go there will be adults there who will make sure that you have food to eat, a roof over your head and are able to attend school and make good choices for your future."

"But I'm frightened, Jude." That's an understatement. I'm terrified and I don't want to leave here and go somewhere new. I don't have a choice though.

"I know you are, dear," she says, putting her arm around my shoulder, "but I will try my best to keep in touch and support you where I can."

"Thank you," I whisper, holding on to her warmth. "What about Mum?"

"Your mum will be put into a residential nursing environment and given appropriate medication prescribed by the doctor. She'll be safe, fed and clean."

"I'm glad she'll be safe," I say quietly, looking through the open doorway of the kitchen at my mother who I might never see again. I'm so sad. I just want to go to bed, fall asleep and never wake up.

As I sit close to Mum for the last time, my tea in my hand, I think of the few belongings that I will need to take with me. My books. There are only a few that the teachers at school have kindly given me and Dr Seuss, my favourite from another life, when Dad was here and life was good. When I had birthday presents and Christmas was exciting. My clothes. Well, they're old, ill-fitting and falling apart.

***

As I look up at the ceiling of my prison cell I wonder where I'll find the strength to carry on. With an uncertain future ahead of me and a heart so weary I just want to curl up and die. I'm hanging in there, but only by the thinnest of threads.

Chapter 25: She's the one

Jack

I've never been a romantic person. If you had asked me a week ago, I'd have told you that I haven't got a romantic bone in my body. When I was younger, I was a free spirit, living life to the full, wining and dining girlfriends but never making a commitment. I told myself that loving life and being in a serious relationship didn't work together. That was before I met Steph, before I realised that things could be different. Our natural connection, the way our eyes catch over something trivial or important, it's liberating. Steph's touch calms me and thrills me at the same time. Like a hurricane she burst into my life and turned it upside down. My life before Steph was emotionally empty and I'd never noticed. Until now.

I met a beautiful redhead at university when I was studying forensic psychology. I'd always been interested in the link between psychology and the law and why certain individuals commit crimes. I am still committed to understanding the triggers that cause someone to commit heinous crimes such as murder, using torture to establish control, gratification, or to feel a high. I guess if Ray Delossi had still been alive he would have made an excellent subject. To interview him and discover why he physically and mentally hurt women he became close to would be fascinating.

But back to the beautiful redhead. Her name was Rachel and she and I were inseparable for about a year. Then she started to talk about the future; saving for a place together, getting married and having children.

From then on I lost interest. I liked Rachel, I really did, but I just wanted to live a little, be an independent spirit and travel the world. Since Rachel there have been a few relationships here and there but nothing serious. I'd focused on completing my degree, finding work experience in a probation office and finally finding the job of my dreams as a forensic psychologist.

I was lucky. After getting a First degree at Portsmouth Uni I managed to secure an internship in a probation office working with young offenders where I learnt the crafts of my trade. By understanding the psychology behind the criminal behaviour of young offenders we can try to reduce the impact of reoffending. That's the theory, but putting it into practice and eradicating repeat offending is an entirely different thing!

For eight years I advised the police at court and on parole boards and became head of my little three-man unit. Even so, I was beginning to feel that it was time to move on to something else. I thought it would be nice to be my own boss, answer only to myself, and work my own hours for a change. It was by chance at a benefit fundraising dinner I had been invited to where I was introduced to Stuart and Jenny Greyson which turned me in a completely different direction, from working with offenders to indirectly supporting victims of abuse. Wow! What they did for vulnerable people blew my mind.

I told them that I was thinking of a career change and they told me they were looking for someone that they could keep on a retainer to support the people at The Lighthouse.

Setting up "Kinsey Investigations and Services" was the best thing I have ever done. I freelanced as a consultant forensic psychologist and took several training courses for private investigators before adding that to my service list. It was a win-win situation.

The fee I charge clients is substantial and it allows me flexibility to help The Lighthouse charity whenever needed. I have time to indulge my interests such as working out at the gym, kickboxing, cars and women.

My parents are good people, they are kind and honest and have worked hard all their lives. I'm their only child. Mum was a senior nurse working in the Accident and Emergency Department at the local hospital, and Dad was a bank manager. They both retired a couple of months ago and had made plans to go travelling soon. Obviously, that was now out of the question with Dad's heart attack, for the moment at least.

And now I've met Steph with her quiet strength and determination, and I see the love she has for her son and her job despite everything she's been through. I see how she holds her head up high and keeps grasping what she can from life. And now I'm hooked. She is the most beautiful person inside and out. I guess what I am trying to say is that she's "the one" – the one I want to share my life with. I still can't believe that Ben asked me if I was OK at the hospital, he's an amazing young man and very mature for his age.

I dropped Mum home around 9pm last night, made us both beans on toast and went to sleep on the sofa with a blanket when she went to bed. I tossed and turned for about an hour or so until I picked up my keyring and looked at Steph's house key. I wrote Mum a note to say where I had gone and that I would pick her up at 9.30am to take her to the hospital tomorrow morning. Then I went to Steph's.

A sense of belonging and peace came over me from the moment I walked into Steph's house. I went quietly into the living room, taking in the small lit table lamp and the blankets and sheets neatly folded on the blue sofa seat cushion. I set a 7.45am alarm on my phone and drop it on the floor next to me. As I lay my head on the sofa cushion, pull the blankets over me and close my eyes, I can't help but feel as if I've come home.

Saturday morning. It's daylight. I open my tired eyes and reach on the floor for my phone. It's 7.30am.

"He's awake, Mum," says a familiar male voice.

"Let him sleep a little longer, Ben," I hear a distant voice call and what sounds like the kettle boiling. "He must be shattered."

"I'm awake and yes, I am shattered," I say, doggedly forcing myself off the sofa to a standing position so that I can stretch.

This sofa sleeping habit of mine is playing havoc with my back and shoulders.

Ben is in black and grey plain pyjamas and he's sitting on the sofa with my blanket pulled up to his waist. He's looking at something on his mobile. "Hey, Jack, check out this Facebook clip, it's gone viral."

I return to the sofa and sit down next to Ben as Steph comes in dressed in faded blue jeans and an oversized purple collarless blouse and carrying three mugs of tea. I take mine giving her a smile and settle the hot mug between my legs, holding it with both hands.

Steph put's Ben's mug on the side table. "Tea, Ben."

"Thanks, Mum." He gives her a sweet smile and then looks my way.

"So, there's this man," Ben begins with excitement, "he pushes this other man up a side street, punches him and walks away. He's like a vigilante hero because he was standing up for a woman who was with the man because he was hurting her." He begins to play the video, putting the sound on full. I watch the clip, the vigilante punching the bad guy and telling him what he thought of him. It's one of those moments in life where you wish you'd done the same thing, hitting back at someone who hurts others.

"You really need to reassess how you treat women and people who are physically weaker than yourself," the man's voice booms from the screen. I watch Steph as she moves to Ben's side to look at the clip herself.

"If you have to pick on someone," the man tells the bad guy with the bloody nose, "try doing it to someone your own size. Or someone who will fight back. Otherwise I'm coming back for you. And next time you won't live to call the police."

"Holy Shit!" Steph says, her eyes quickly catching mine before returning to the screen on Ben's phone. Her face has gone white.

"Mum!" Ben says.

"I know that man! That's Jules Walker, the caretaker from Richmond Court where Corinna lives." She walks to the windowsill and puts her mug down, her face screwed in concentration as though she's trying to piece together a puzzle in her head.

"Jesus!" I say.

"You know him?" Ben asks, with his face breaking into a smile. "How cool is that."

"It's not cool, Ben," she answers, walking towards him. "What he did is not right. You know you can't take the law into your own hands. No matter what the circumstances. Can you forward me that video?"

Ben shrugs and pushes himself up off the sofa. "I still think he's one of the good guys. He stood up for that woman." With that he wanders through the dining room towards the kitchen.

"I've got to pick Mum up at 9.30am to take her to the hospital," I say. "Want to come or have you guys got things to do?" I ask, trying to keep my voice light. I want her to come with me, want to have her by my side.

"I'd like to come, if that's OK. I'm sure Ben would like to meet your parents again too," she says, patting my shoulder.

A couple of hours later I've taken Steph and Ben with me to collect Mum and head to the hospital. Dad seemed a lot brighter, although he's still very pale and he becomes tired easily. The doctor was more optimistic and reassured Mum and I that, all being well, he should be ready to go home in another three days.

The news was a relief and Mum's eyes had filled with tears as she held Dad's hand and leaned over to kiss him gently on the cheek.

I sat beside Dad and patted his hand, giving a huge sigh of relief and a silent prayer to the man upstairs. I felt like a heavy weight had been lifted from my shoulders.

I think about Steph.

When they moved to Shore House, she told me that Ben was only three and there were things that he didn't need to know about, such as the extent to which Ray would beat her. That's not lying as such, it's just protecting him from the truth. What possible good would it have done to have given Ben explicit details about his dad's assaults on her and to know about her injuries? No parent wants their child to know that they were used as a punchbag, that they were unable to defend themselves against someone who was supposed to love them.

I offer to take Steph and Ben for an early lunch while Dad rested, and we left Mum with a cheese sandwich and a cup of tea. By midday we were sitting in Frankie and Benny's and checking out the menu. In many ways we looked like the average normal family, out on a chilly Saturday in October enjoying some quality family time.

A young, good-looking, dark-haired waiter came to take our lunch order of spaghetti carbonara for me, a lasagne for Ben, and for Steph a creamy chicken and mushroom pasta bake with garlic bread to share. I ordered a strong cappuccino because I was desperately in need of a caffeine fix. My lack of sleep was catching up with me and I hadn't had time to visit the gym. Steph ordered herself and Ben Diet Cokes and a jug of tap water for the table before excusing herself to make a couple of phone calls, one of which I think was to contact the funeral directors. She's been extremely calm since we found the blackmail letter and I need to find time to talk to her alone to see how she's really coping with everything that's happening. The drinks arrived as Steph returned to the table. I couldn't help but notice the grim smile on her face.

"Jenny is going to see Corinna this afternoon." She sits in between me and Ben. "I'm worried about her mental state. I'm hoping to visit her tomorrow morning. If something happens to her then that's one more person almost destroyed by that man."

"Who's Corinna?" Ben asks, looking at his phone and taking a sip of Coke at the same time.

"Just someone connected to this case," Steph says looking at him, "It's nothing for you to worry about, sweetie." She gives his hand a reassuring pat.

I nod in agreement and then slurp some of my coffee as Ben stands and makes his excuses to use the bathroom. I take this opportunity to lift my eyebrows, waiting for her to talk.

She nods slowly and begins to talk. "I've spoken to the funeral director and he says the earliest slot available for Ray to be cremated at Oxford Crematorium is a week on Tuesday." Her voice has a flat tone to it and her face shows no emotion. I think she's had enough of Ray Delossi and his life. I don't blame her. She continues: "Ray hasn't stipulated any preference for a burial, so I've opted for a cremation."

"I agree with you about Corinna," I say in response, as I take another sip of my coffee and begin to feel the caffeine kick in. My brain feels as though it's suddenly been switched on. "We need a break to find this person who went into the house after she left. And you know my thoughts about Ray. He deserves to have an unmarked grave. But I understand he was Ben's father and will support you with whatever choices you make." I put my hand over hers hoping to reassure her that I'm on her side.

It must be a strange feeling. Burying someone who you grew to hate, who hurt you physically and mentally. Someone who you used to be married to and who you briefly loved. I can't imagine what she's going through.

I spy Ben walking back to us and immediately wonder how he will take the latest news about his father. The man he never really knew.

I take another sip of my coffee before Ben sits down next to Steph.

"I'm starving," he says, his eyes wide as he spies the waitress bringing food over to another table.

"You're always starving!" Steph laughs and thankfully our food finally arrives. Ben's lasagne looks good as does Steph's chicken and mushroom pasta bake, but I'm happy with my spaghetti carbonara. The garlic bread arrives, parmesan offered, and thankfully it's time to tuck into the food.

Steph looks at me in a strange way as if she's contemplating a problem, and I'm not overly surprised when she addresses Ben in a serious tone in between mouthfuls of creamy rigatoni pasta.

"Ben, there's something I need to talk to you about. Something that Danielle found on your dad's laptop."

"Mm?" He looks up, a large chunk of lasagne speared onto his fork.

"We found several documents that are related to you and me. The first revelation is that he has named me as his next of kin."

Ben puts down his fork and the lasagne oozes slowly onto the plate.

"You're joking?" He laughs then studies her expressionless face. "Why would he do that? You haven't had anything to do with him for years!"

"I know." She looks down at her plate. She's got a slightly defeated look about her. "Which also means that it's my job to contact the funeral director and to organise his burial."

"What a prat! I can't believe he would expect that of you!" He looks slightly annoyed as he dissects a portion of lasagne and stuffs it into his mouth.

I look at Ben as he eats, his brows drawn together. His face has that baffled look of someone trying to work out the answer to life, the universe and everything. He's munching and processing the situation at the same time. I'm relieved that he doesn't look too upset though.

"The second thing?" Ben asks his mum.

"Well, the second thing is that he set up a savings account eight years ago and it's in your name."

"Oh, I like the sound of that!" He smiles.

"Ben!" Steph says sharply.

"Well, he didn't do much for me when he was alive, did he?" he mumbles with a mouthful of garlic bread.

I try to keep a straight face. Ben looks at me, an amused look on his face and we both start to laugh. Steph's face is a picture. I'm not sure if she wants to laugh with us, cry or tear us off a strip for not taking this seriously.

"Is there a third thing?" Ben asks his mother.

"Oh yes," Steph says in a slightly sarcastic voice. "He's named me as the beneficiary to everything he left behind."

"Holy Cow!" He's almost erring on the side of over excitement. "We are going to be rich!"

"Well, that's one way of looking at it!" Steph answers, her eyes catching mine.

I raise my eyebrows and shrug my shoulders. Not a bad way of looking at things.

"Don't forget, Ben, that this all needs to be verified properly by the solicitors and our legal team," Steph warns.

We sit in companionable silence for the rest of the meal, each of us exploring our own private thoughts, contemplating the different scenarios and wondering what the future holds for us.

It won't make any difference to me, money or not. I started to fall for her from the moment I met her, and I continued to fall for her when I saw her inner strength and vulnerability, despite the scars – mental and physical – that she's been left with. The nightmares, the memories, the way she commands respect in her work, even though I sense she's crumbling inside she deserves to be happy. Both of them do.

Chapter 26: Waiting

Steph

It never ceases to amaze me how people cope with the stress and strains of life. Not that there's such a thing as a "normal" family, but some people have it hard.

Looking after a child with disabilities can cause immense frustration, isolation and feelings of anger and panic. The death of a child or parent changes the dynamics of the family and causes indescribable heartache. The inner strength needed to cope and carry on following the loss of a child is nothing short of miraculous. I would like to think that I would be able to find the strength to carry on if I lost Ben, but realistically nobody knows how they will react until they've been in that situation.

Jem once told me when we lived at the refuge home, Shore House, that she was able to find peace and safety when she was with Noah and his gran. She explained how her sketching calmed her enabling her to escape from reality. They were the tools she used to keep herself going, to find some positives to counterbalance the negatives of her abusive home life.

Thank goodness I told Ben the latest news about Ray. It was eating away at me not being able to be honest with him. He is coping so well with the constant changes to his life. I always thought he was a strong, self-confident young man but the change in him as he processed the news about Ray, the savings, the burial and the bloody estate value, is amazing. He's growing up so fast, maturing in a way that makes me immensely proud of the young adult he's becoming.

After lunch Jack dropped us back home and called his mum to say that he was on his way back to the hospital. He said he'd return to us around 8pm once he'd dropped his mum home and made sure she was alright. Over coffee I explained to Ben when his dad's funeral would be and made it clear to him that I would support his choice whether he decided to attend or not. He'd just shrugged his shoulders, picked up his phone and gone to his room. I had no intention of telling Ben about the kidnapping and blackmail scheme Ray had been planning. There were some things better left unsaid.

Jenny called to tell me how her visit to Corinna had gone. Understandably, she was worried about Corinna and how she was coping. I felt the same way about Corinna, the guilt of not being able to find Ray's murderer eating at me. I needed something to distract me so, on a whim, I decided to ask Jenny if I could bring Jack to dinner with me when Ben and I visited their Chippenham home tomorrow.

"Of course, you can!" she replied, her voice rising in excitement. "It would be great to see him. How are things with you and Jack?" she asked.

"Good," I said. "We've been spending a lot of time together, grown quite close. He's good with Ben too."

"Oh, Steph, I'm so pleased for you both. Who knows, I may need to buy a wedding hat soon!"

"Jenny! Slow down!" I laugh. "Hopefully when Ray's case is closed, and things have calmed down a little we can see what a regular relationship looks like. It's been a rollercoaster ride so far."

"I know, sweetie," Jenny states in a soft voice, "but as I've already told you, Jack is one of the good guys. He's definitely a keeper."

"You and Daisy must be working together!" I say with exasperation. "She says the same thing."

"Then I must be telling you the truth!" she adds abruptly. "By the way, can you see if you can cheer up Corinna a little tomorrow? She's got a terrible cough and she seemed really down when I saw her today. I think she's expecting the worst."

I tell her I'll do my best before disconnecting the call. I stand and listen for a moment. Everything is quiet and I allow myself the time to enjoy the silence of my home while I can. Let the world take care of itself for a few minutes. When did everything become so hectic? Something has been niggling me and I can't quite put my finger on it. Jules Walker. I was going to wait until Monday morning to chase him, but due to time restraints I decide to contact him now. I quickly search my work notebook for his phone number and give him a call. The phone rings three times before a voice speaks down the line.

"Hello?" a male voice says.

"Mr Walker, Jules?" I ask.

"Yes. Who is this?" His voice is strong, questioning.

"It's DI Rutland from Thames Valley Police. We met the other day when you showed myself and my colleague to Corinna James's flat," I explain, trying to put him at ease. There's something about this man that doesn't add up, in addition to his sideline of becoming a vigilante viral sensation.

"Oh yes," he sounds wary, "I remember now. What can I do for you, Detective Inspector?"

"I saw your stage debut on Facebook," I tell him, waiting for his response.

"My stage debut?' He queries. "Sorry, you've lost me. I don't do Facebook and I don't know what you're talking about."

"On Facebook, the clip of you punching a guy because he was mistreating a young woman."

There's a long pause and a sharp intake of breath before Jules speaks.

"Shit!" He sounds angry. "How stupid am I? I should have realised that some bugger would be filming it on his or her phone."

"For what it's worth, Jules," I say, "a lot of people have watched your video footage and like what you did. You had lots of hits and comments on what they think. I wonder if it would be possible to come and see you first thing on Monday morning. Say, 9am?"

"I guess I don't really have much choice, do I?" he says in a flat tone.

"Not really, but I would appreciate your cooperation, all the same," I add.

"Of course. I'll see you at 9am," he says putting the phone down on me.

I hear Ben coming downstairs. He's singing to himself and the words become clearer as he gets closer. It's an Ed Sheeran song called "Perfect" and I smile as the lyrics to the song mirror his first feelings of being in love with a girl.

"Has Molly been in touch then?" I ask, as he wanders into the kitchen.

"Yep," he smiles, striding through the hall to sit next to me on the sofa in the living room, his phone still in his hand. "She just sent me a text wishing me a good weekend."

"That's nice of her," I say, putting my arm around his shoulder. "She's welcome here anytime."

"Thanks. Can I ask you something, Mum?" There's hesitancy in his voice and his hand rubs his cheek.

"Sure."

"If Jack really likes us, do you think he'd like to live with us one day?"

"Possibly. We'd have to ask him at some point, wouldn't we? It's still a little early for that though, don't you think?" I look at my son, wondering what was going through his young mind to provoke this conversation.

"I know it's early, but it just feels right having him around, being here. I've never had that sense of family… grandparents and stuff."

"Oh, Ben." I look at him and feel a pang of guilt to hear that my lack of a family has impacted on his life so much. "If I could change things, Ben, I would. You know when I met your Dad, I was glad to get away from home. My Mum was a drunk and my Dad was a heroin addict."

"I know, Mum," he says in a quiet voice. "You don't have to explain anything. I just like Jack is all." He's growing up so quickly now and I owe him the truth, well, some of it anyway to help him understand what happened.

"I lived on and off with my Aunt Lucy but then she became ill with cancer when I was eighteen," I continue, telling him my story. "After she died, I gave up college and my part-time job and moved away. It was stupid I know, but my parents were toxic, they were so wrapped up in themselves and where they would get their next fix that they didn't even know I existed. I left, got a job and met your dad a year or so later."

"Oh, Mum," he says, giving me a hug. "It's not your fault. You're the best mum in the world. You've always been there for me."

I hold him tight, my head resting on the top of his and rock slightly. "And you're the best son, Ben." I choked back the tears. "You kept me going so many times when I wanted to give up."

Hours later after dinner Ben and I are snuggled on the sofa, watching an action film on Netflix with empty cheese puff and popcorn wrappers scattered around us. It's 8pm and we're halfway through the film when Jack comes home.

"Hey, guys. What are you watching?" He stares at the flat television screen and his face breaks into the biggest smile. "James Bond, great." He walks to the sofa and I feel the cushion dip as he drops into the seat beside me and drapes his arm loosely over the back of the sofa. If this man doesn't like us, I'd be amazed. Every bone in my body is telling me that he's here because he wants to be.

The film finished about half an hour ago and Ben went up to bed. I've collected the empty wrappers and drink cups and disposed of them in the kitchen, made us both a mug of tea and settle myself beside him on the sofa with the sound of the television quietly playing in the background.

"I called Jules Walker this afternoon," I say, breaking the silence and turning to face him.

He looks at me, one eyebrow raised and a slight quirk to his mouth. "Why am I not surprised. Did you tell him about the Facebook video?" His fingers reach out to stroke the back of my hand.

"Yes."

"What did he say?" He turns to me, a look of concentration on his face as he waited for my reply.

"He seemed agitated, cross even that he'd been caught on camera," I say, threading my fingers through his and stroking my thumb across his knuckles. He smelled of sandalwood and citrus which calmed and excited me when he was close to me and made me acutely aware of his presence. "I'm going to see him at 9am on Monday morning."

"You don't think he's involved in Ray's murder, do you?" His eyes hold mine, asking the question that's been sitting at the back of my mind since I spoke to Walker earlier.

"I don't know. Possibly. I need to get a background check on him and look into his history to see if there are any connections between him, his family and Ray," I mutter, thinking out loud.

"Want me to do some digging?" he asks lightly, as though he's asking if I want a cup of tea.

"Yes please," I say. "Let's see if Jules Walker has any skeletons in his closet." I take my phone from my jeans pocket and call one of my work numbers to organise a police national computer check on Jules Walker. Then I text Chris and tell him to meet me at Richmond Court just before 9am on Monday.

Jack pushes himself up and walks to the dark mahogany dining table. He locates his laptop from the table and disconnects the charger plug. It should be fully charged by now. Jack pushes his chair closer to the table and I notice how quickly his fingers fly across the keyboard as it powers to life and follows his searches. No reply from Chris, he must be indisposed or asleep. My watch says it's 10.30pm. Why does each day feel so long? It's never-ending.

"Steph," Jack calls, looking through the open door to me, "you need to see this."

I walk over to him and stand behind him to look at the screen. It's an online article from the *Oxford Mail* dated four years ago. The article reports the death of a sixteen-year-old girl committing suicide in Thame. Her name is Belinda Karin Walker-Mason, her parents were Eric and Kerry. She had an older brother called Julian. Julian Walker. Jules. Shit. There's a photo of the family following Belinda's inquest and Julian's face screwed up in grief looks back at us. His blonde hair is shorter but there's no disputing the fact that it's Jules Walker. What on earth did Ray Delossi do to this family for the daughter to kill herself and for Jules to exact revenge four years later?

"Oh my God!" My whole body stiffens and a rush of cold air sweeps over me as Jack brings up another window. I'm not sure how he's done this but there are mortuary photos of Belinda on the screen, her young body enveloped in a bluish tint is covered with a white sheet to the top of her shoulders. The report says she cut her wrists, but there are clear marks of a fading black eye, bruised cheekbone and slight imprints around her neck.

"Oh my God! He hurt her and she killed herself," I say in a low voice that doesn't sound like mine. I push down the nauseous feeling that sits in the pit of my stomach. My knees feel weak, so

I step to the side and hold on to the cold surface of the dining table.

"The bastard assaulted her, a sixteen-year-old girl." Jack pushes back his chair and walks around the room, his face focusing on the carpet as he follows the rectangular shape of the table. He puts a hand to his head as if he's warding off a shooting pain. "I would have done that, Steph." His deep voice sounds pained. "Killed him, I mean. If he'd done that to my little sister, if he'd destroyed my family."

I step in front of him to stop him from pacing and put my hand on his shirt, over his heart. "I know you would. I know you would, Jack," I say, and can't stop the tears falling down my cheeks. "Still, this is just circumstantial, there's nothing putting him in the house on the night of the murder. I need to speak to him to confirm what happened. To confirm motive," I say without feeling. "I just don't think I can bear it if I have to arrest him." I'm overwhelmed with the trail of destruction that Ray's life and death has left in his wake.

Jack holds me close, strokes my loose curly hair and in turn I wrap my arms around him and hold on to the strength that he freely offers. "I know, Steph, I know," he whispers in my ear. Jack caresses my cheek with his free hand. "Make sure you take someone with you when you visit him. Chris or me." He watches me until I nod.

Jack's hand moves slowly to follow the contours of my neck. His thumb glides across my skin stroking and calming and sending unwanted shivers down my back. He leans his head against mine and says in a deep, quiet voice. "It's been a long week, DI Rutland. Do you think you could offer a quick goodnight kiss for a man in need of your touch before he settles down on your sofa for the night?"

***

I forgot how grim police stations are at the weekend. More so because it's the weekend when people want to be at home with their friends and families. The chairs are standard metal and wood, the type that are not particularly comfortable. We're in one of the interview rooms at the Oxford police station where I'm based and where Corinna has been kept for the past two days. It's Sunday morning and I'm very much aware that I'm hoping for a miracle so that I can free her tomorrow. I still can't reconcile what Ray did to Belinda Walker-Mason.

As I wait for Corinna to arrive, I consider how quickly this case could be wrapped up if Jules Walker confessed to killing Ray Delossi. I quickly type a text to the team, telling them to continue with their follow ups but that we'll debrief at 11am tomorrow instead because Chris and I would be at Richmond Court to speak to Jules Walker. Chris replied confirming that he'll meet me at Richmond Court at 9am. Sam needs to follow up on Danny Devlin and the CCTV came back with nothing. A zero from Ray's BMW too. I reckon that's gone towards payment of the outstanding debt for Danny Devlin. What I really need is a confession.

The off-white walls don't offer much warmth to a room that only has two chairs sitting either side of the table.

Corinna looks pale and a little withdrawn when she arrives and is seated opposite me by the Desk Sergeant, a tall gangly man with a receding hairline, brown moustache and crinkled face. I notice that Corinna still wears the standard grey jogging bottoms and sweatshirt while her clothes are being processed, and her hair hangs in unkept greasy locks to her shoulders. She has a tickly cough that surfaces mostly when she talks. She doesn't smile, just sits there with her hands folded and looks at the table.

"How are you?" I ask, leaning over the table.

"Fine," she splutters with a wheeze.

"You look a little pale. Are you eating?" I continue. It's important that she tries to look after herself.

"Yes," she says, forcing the word out before a cough can makes its way through.

"I know you're probably fed up, depressed even, but I need you to stay strong. People are rooting for you and trying to find the person responsible for Ray Delossi's death. I think we have a lead, but I need to check it out first."

"I'm trying." Her eyes continue to focus on the table in front of her.

"Have you seen the doctor about your cough?"

"No."

"I'm going to Jenny's for dinner tonight. Is there anything you want me to tell her?"

"No."

I'm getting worried and frustrated with her. She needs to find the strength to carry on and not give in.

"Stop it!" I say sharply, drawing her back to me, back to the living.

She suddenly looks up. "Stop what?"

"Stop letting him win. Do you think he felt sorry when he was using you as a punchbag, slapping you, cutting you?" I say in a harsher tone than I intended. "Do you think he felt sorry when he was emailing my son and sneakily trying to get back into his life? Do you think he was sorry for physically hurting me and God knows how many others? Why do you think I wear high neck tops? Look." I pull my jumper down a little to show the start of a scar.

Her eyes stray to the scar and recognition hits her.

"You weren't the only one, Corinna. But you were the one to fight back, even if all you did was knee him in the groin. For crying out loud, it's killing me that my hands are tied when I'm trying to help you. You need to know that Noah, Jenny, Jack, myself and my team – we're all working hard to find out who murdered Ray."

"I'm sorry," she says, struggling not to cough. Her eyes are a little brighter.

"Don't be sorry. Be brave, be strong. Do it for those people who suffer, have suffered and continue to suffer from abuse. Do it for all of us. Please." I'm almost pleading with her.

"I will, Steph. I won't let it beat me." She tries to smile.

On my way out of the station I speak to the Desk Sergeant and ask him to put Corinna on a fifteen minute watch because she seems depressed, and then tell him to get a doctor to see what he or she can do for that cough of hers.

As I'm about to leave for the hospital I receive a text from Jack telling me that his parents' friends are due to visit the hospital for the afternoon and he'd be happy to come with Ben and I to dinner at Stuart and Jenny's house.

Following an early lunch at home we arrive in Chippenham in Jack's red Mazda. It's a weird feeling being driven as opposed to driving. Both Stuart and Jenny acknowledge Jack warmly, while Stuart grasps his hand and pats him on his back. Ben and I walk into their loving family home and savour their warm hugs.

Stuart is the Sunday cook. He loves cooking the roast dinner. He's a real family man at heart. He and Jenny were unable to have children and instead dedicated their lives to helping others through The Lighthouse and other charitable projects. The people who they've helped over the years include Jem, Ben and I. We're all part of their family.

Jenny and I play catch-up about Corinna in the kitchen, making hot drinks for everyone and trying to keep out of Stuart's way. Jack catches my eye as he leans in the doorway, steaming coffee mug in hand. He looks chilled and confident and makes me blush as his lips form a warm smile. Ben is helping to chop carrots. It appears that Sunday dinner is mostly prepared by the males of the household, and you won't get an argument from me. I'm more than happy to sip my coffee and tell Jenny about my visit with Corinna. I agree that Corinna is becoming depressed and in need of support and quite a bit of luck.

As we sit down to roast chicken a little while later, I feel grateful for Stuart and Jenny's tactful way of not addressing our couple status. Let it happen naturally I keep telling myself.

"We've got some good news," Ben announces, spooning a slice of carrot into his mouth. He munches for a moment before continuing: "First, there's a girl called Molly at school and I think she likes me. And second…"

"Yes?" Jenny's voice breaks in, resting her knife and fork on her plate.

"Well, clearly Mum and Jack are getting on well together," Ben gestures to myself and Jack with his fork, "and Mum says he may move in with us one day, but we need to wait a while to ask him."

"Ben!" I say indignantly as the slice of chicken I'm chewing almost chokes me and I feel a warming blush settle across my entire face. My unease is not helped by Jack who decides to pat my back in mock support. Please let the earth swallow me up!

Jack looks slightly bemused and raises one eyebrow. I grimace and mouth "*Sorry!*"

I hear a chuckle and a clearing of throats as Stuart and Jenny try to hide their amusement.

"Is it too early to buy a wedding hat then?" Jenny asks, giving me a wink.

"Jenny!" I say. Honestly, this woman will have me married and with child by Christmas!

"Let's get Corinna sorted first," I calmly explain to Ben as I spear some broccoli onto my fork, "and your dad's funeral which is a week on Tuesday. Once the loose ends are tied up we can relax and talk some more," I say, looking at Jack. I study his face, looking for a sign to show how he's feeling. After the briefest moment his lips turn up on each side and he's giving me the most beautiful reassuring smile. I smile back, slowly breathing out.

Ben nods. "Alright, I'll wait until we've buried Dad." He looks at his plate and stabs at a small ball of sage and onion stuffing with his fork. He looks at me. "I've decided I do want to go to his funeral," he says solemnly, and pops the stuffing ball into his mouth.

"You do?" I ask. I'm not surprised. Ben is a brave young man and would want to say goodbye to his dad.

"Yes," he says looking down at his plate. "I just want to say goodbye. Jack, can you come too?" Ben asks quietly, his eyes focused on Jack.

Jack looks at me, then at Ben. "Sure, Ben. Whatever you need."

"If you two could come too, that would be great," I say, looking at Stuart and Jenny.

"Of course. Text us the details and we'll check the diary and see if we can shuffle a few things around," Stuart says in his deep steady voice.

"That's a very adult thing of you to do, Ben," Jenny says.

Ben nods. "I didn't know him well so it shouldn't be too bad."

So that's sorted then. No fuss, just a few words and the whole thing is arranged. I won't be writing a eulogy though.

Chapter 27: No way out

Jules

"Shit!" I fist my hand and hit my forehead. What was I thinking punching that idiot Leon down that side street? What is the matter with me? I am officially the stupidest guy in the country.

I walk to the mirror and study my face. "And that's how you keep a bloody low profile!" I say aloud. If only my other self, the one in the mirror, would talk some sense, once in a while things might have turned out differently.

And now that bloody DI is coming to see me on Monday morning. I need to start writing my confession. This is going to take a bit of time. I walk to my bedroom and stoop to the blue carpeted floor to pick up my laptop which has been charging at the side of my bed.

"I am such an idiot," I mutter as I buff up the pillows on my bed and shuffle up the grey patterned duvet until I'm sitting against the headboard and pillows. I pull the laptop onto my lap and turn it on. While it's coming to life with my password, I think of what my confession will mean to everyone, including my parents. To Corinna, it will be the miracle she needs to live a free and hopefully happy life. For my parents, it will bring sadness, shock and possible closure to Blip's death. For the police, it means that they can close their case and move on. For me. Well, that's another story.

I bring up a new Word document, look at the blank screen and start typing:

"I, Jules Walker, confess to the murder of Ray Delossi".

Chapter 28: The truth

Steph

I sit in my blue Fiesta with my phone playing The Rolling Stones at Richmond Court on Monday morning. I'm waiting for Chris. I check my watch. It's 8.50am. The day is grey and cloudy and cold. My black trench coat and brown crossover bag sit in the passenger seat, waiting.

I hear the rumble of a car and see Chris's silver Volvo pull into the car park through my rear-view mirror. He sees my blue Fiesta, notices the car parking spaces either side of me and brings the Volvo to a halt beside me. I check myself in the mirror. I'm wearing a soft white blouse with a tie front, my black trousers and black suede ankle boots. There's a hint of dark pink lipstick on my lips and my hair is tied loosely back with a brown jaw clip. I'm happy so I lean over, grab my coat and bag and leave the car.

Chris wears a dark grey woollen funnel neck coat. It's completely open, showing a plain white shirt tucked into his black trousers. His shoes are black and his tie a beautiful sapphire blue.

"Hey," he says moving towards me. "What have you got on Jules Walker?" he asks with one eyebrow raised.

"Hey, thanks for meeting me," I say, threading my arms into my coat and leading him to the door. "Jack and I did some digging on him. He hasn't got a record but four years ago his sixteen-year-old sister Belinda killed herself."

"Bloody Hell! Why?" He stops, looks at me briefly and then falls back into step.

"From the mortuary photos and records it looks as though she'd been assaulted," I say, in a detached but slightly raised voice that also holds a hint of excitement because the feeling I have in my gut is that our man is Jules Walker.

"Jesus! What led you to him?" he asks as we buzz flat number ten on the entry phone.

I hear a buzz as the intercom connects and Jules Walker's voice answers. "Yes?"

"It's DI Rutland and DS Jackson."

"Come in." The voice sounds muffled.

"Thanks," I reply as I wait for the door release and open it for Chris. "The Facebook video," I continue, "I guess you didn't see it. It came up on Ben's Facebook feed. A video of a man punching another man up a side street because he was mistreating a woman."

Chris stands next to me as we press the doorbell to the flat. "The video went viral," I say as the door opened. The man in front of me looks like Jules Walker but not the one I saw just a few days ago.

"Come in," says the pale faced stranger with the mass of uncombed blonde hair falling to his shoulders. He wears a blue T-shirt and black jeans which are stained with beans, breadcrumbs and butter, and his feet are bare. The stink of whiskey emanating from him is unmistakable. No, this is not the tidy, confident and casual Jules that we know. We nod and follow him through to the living room. There's an old brown sofa, a matching chair and a brown footstool. He motions for us to sit and we do. I take the chair and look around the room. Something doesn't feel quite right. There's an open baked bean can with a large spoon on the small metal table which sits between the sofa and chair. A handwritten envelope lies next to the can. On the floor is a half-eaten bowl of cereal, and next to the footstool lies two empty bottles of Jack Daniels. Shit. This is not good.

Jules slumps on the sofa, leans his arms to his knees and covers his face with his hands. Chris remains standing by the door as if he thinks Jules will make a run for it. Personally, I wonder if Mr Walker is fit to run anywhere.

"Mr Walker," I begin. "Jules. Are you alright?" I ask, hoping that he will find the strength to tell the truth.

There's a muffled sound from him. "On the floor, next to the chair."

I look around and notice a dark green photograph album jutting out from under my chair. We don't use photo albums much these days, but years ago it was all we had to remember who we used to be and the people we loved. I shuffle and lean over to pick up the album. I know what I'm going to find but it doesn't make it any easier. My heart is beating so fast as I slowly open the album and see the precious faces of the Walker family staring back at me.

Jules looks across at the album balanced on my knees and I look at photos of Belinda, of Jules, of their parents. I see smiles, concentration, scowling, action shots, memories that can never be replaced.

"Belinda," I say softly, waiting for him to acknowledge it.

"I always called her Blip. It was my nickname for her," he says sadly, his arms resting on his knees and his fingers pulling at each other. I stare at the photo of a young boy, perhaps five or six-years-old holding a small baby in his arms, a hospital incubator in the background.

"I loved her from the moment she was born," he says staring in to space. "I promised that I'd look after her. That's what older brothers do, isn't it?"

"Yes," I answer quietly, with a lump in my throat.

"Then she met him. Ray Delossi. And everything changed. She changed." He looks at his fingers as if he's never seen them before. His face distorts and he suddenly puts his hands to his face and howls like a wounded animal.

"Take your time, Jules. Do you want a cup of tea or coffee?" Chris asks, still guarding the living room door.

"No," he wipes the tears from his face with his bare arms, "nothing will make this better."

"What did Ray Delossi do to your sister, Jules?" I ask, turning the pages of the photo album, visually reading the life of the baby girl he called Blip with her big brother and parents until she was around fifteen or sixteen. Just before her death.

"He hurt her. She wouldn't talk properly about it, but there were marks to her eye, her cheekbone and around her neck. He ripped her necklace, the one I'd given her – ripped it off her bloody neck before he tried to strangle her. She wouldn't give me his address, wouldn't let me find him. Then she got so depressed she wouldn't leave the house. A few weeks after the assault I found her in the bathroom with her wrists cut open. She died the next day."

"I am so very sorry for your loss, Jules," I say sadly. "He should have been arrested for the assault. You and your family must have been devastated."

He nods, his dirty straggly hair dipping around his neck.

"How did you find Ray Delossi?" I ask, pushing him to tell me the truth.

"By accident." For the first time he looks directly at me. "I was in a bar in Oxford one night two weeks ago with some friends celebrating someone's birthday and I saw him. I was sitting at one of those high tables as he walked through the crowd to the bar, decked out in a dark suit and white shirt, open at the neck. There was no mistaking him and his bloody swagger. Couldn't believe my eyes. He was probably on the prowl for another innocent life to ruin."

Chris stepped forward, his hands in his pockets and face blank except for the flickering of his eyes.

"You followed him home?" he asked.

"Yes." Jules nodded and looked at me. "I followed him in my black Mini Cooper and knew what I would do to him. After an hour I decided to return home and make some plans. I planned to go back to Delossi's on Tuesday 16th October in the evening to kill him." His eyes were lifeless as he faced me, as though he was lost in a sea of pain and couldn't find his way out.

I looked at him. "You lied to us about the days and shifts you work?"

"Yes." his voice was flat. "Although I am on site much of the time, I am allowed to leave Richmond Court if I need to do something."

"So, Corinna James?" Chris's voice asks with a hint of anger. "Did you know Delossi was dating her?"

"No." Jules turns to look at him and his mouth drops to a grim line. "I had no idea. I saw a woman running from his house, I didn't know it was Corinna. It was too dark outside in the street and her hair was covering her face." He stands and brushes his hands down his dirty jeans. "I never meant to hurt her or anyone. Only Delossi," he says taking a step to the metal table and picking up the handwritten envelope. "This is my full written confession. I hope it's enough to free Corinna." He pauses and hands me the letter.

I put the letter on top of the open photograph album. It's addressed to me.

"I'm so sorry, Jules, but we're going to have to take you in," I say, placing my hand gently on top of the envelope and looking across to my DS. "Chris, can you call it in please?" I ask, checking the time on my watch. It's 9.40am.

Chris nods, walks to the dark hallway and takes out his phone. I can hear him speaking in a low tone but can't make out the words. "I wish there was another way to help you, Jules, but my hands are tied," I say quietly. "I do have a few contacts though, maybe they can help," I say softly, thinking of Jack and my adopted family.

"Don't worry," he replies in a low voice with his head down and shoulders slumped in defeat. "As long as Corinna is released, I don't care about myself."

Fifteen minutes later, the confession letter is in an evidence bag in my crossover bag and Jules has been handcuffed and put into the back of a police patrol car. I've called DCI Jones and told him that Jules Walker has confessed to the Delossi murder and that SOCO are going through Walker's flat in minute detail. I also text Jack and tell him that everything is fine.

I walk out into the cold day to my blue Fiesta with Chris by my side. My heart is heavy and my head aches. I absently chew the inside of my inner cheek. I look at the patrol car that will take Jules Walker to the station and look around to see the two police officers who arrived to escort him to the station. They're talking to a forensics officer, who is putting a small black case into the back of her white van. As we walk closer to the car I peer in, that's when I notice that the rear door has been opened on the far side. The car is empty. I look at Chris and we stare in disbelief.

"Bugger!" I say aloud, calling the officers back to their car.

Chapter 29: Laying ghosts to rest

Jack

God, it's cold in here. I shiver. Even in my long black woollen coat I feel cold. Why is there never any heating in these places? I am sitting on the front pew in between Steph and Ben, Stuart and Jenny sit behind us, and occasionally pat the dark padded jacket which covers Ben's shoulders. The funeral conductor, a short man in a black suit, white shirt and black tie, reads a poem and talks about how we should celebrate Ray Delossi's life. I don't think so, mate. That man caused unbelievable heartache to nearly everyone he met. In another breath I argue with myself I would never have met Steph if it wasn't for him. Despite what he did in life, his road led me to these two people who sit beside me.

If you're lucky you get to have a long, happy and healthy life. That's what I want with Steph and Ben and my parents and those people close to me. Sometimes you suffer by losing those closest to you or by being unlucky enough to live a long and painful life. At some point we all lose someone close to us.

There's nothing like a funeral to remind you of how fragile life is and how we forget to celebrate life as we're living it because we're always trying to achieve something better, or we're trying to cope with simply living our daily lives.

I feel a hand on mine. Ben's fingers are chilled. I look at Ben and grasp his hand tightly. Steph's hand searches for mine too. I feel like I'm grounding them to this earth, to the here and now. To me. I feel like I want to live a life that gives me joy, peace and a sense of belonging. Steph and Ben give me this.

We don't speak throughout the ceremony. It's very simple. There are no eulogies.

Chapter 30: Time to move on

Steph

"Keep your eyes closed," I tell Ben, holding my hands over his eyes and moving him towards the silver-grey car parked ahead of us. It's been a week since Corinna's release, and she is happily recuperating from her ordeal at Hope House. The difference between isolated misery and being surrounded by people who care for her has had an astounding effect on Corinna. She is smiling again.

It was a foregone conclusion that she would be released due to the full written confession from Jules Walker, which even stated where we would find the gloves and blood splattered clothes, he'd worn on the night he killed Ray. He'd buried everything in a small box in a patch of garden at the back of Richmond Court. Forensics confirmed the blood on the clothes belonged to Ray Delossi and that unequivocally put Walker at the scene of the crime. Despite extensive searches we still have no idea where Walker is or how he escaped from the police car. I want him to face charges for killing Ray, but I also think he's suffered enough and will probably continue to suffer until the day he dies. It's not easy to move on from the darkness that sometimes lies within our souls. Chris and Daisy enjoyed their dinner date and are now officially a couple. I'm so happy for them. Everyone deserves a chance to find the person they're supposed to be with.

Nothing came of Danny Devlin. I think he knew how to cover his tracks well. No witnesses to the break-in, no sign of the missing goods and a BMW that vanished into thin air. He told Sam Tribble that the five K loan had been repaid in full.

"What's the surprise?" Ben asks me, his hand on my arm.

"Wait and see." I can't contain my excitement. "It's something that Jack wants to show you."

Finally, I have him where I want him, standing in front of the car. Jack leans against it wearing grey jeans, black boots and a dark red shirt. He looks sexy standing there with a wide grin and his arms casually folded.

"OK. Open them," I say, looking forward to his reaction.

In slow motion I watch Ben as he recognises the car. His face lights up and he shakes his head:

"Wow! You've got to be kidding me! It's a bloody Aston Martin Rapide!"

"Ben!" I tell him, trying to not to smile.

"It is!" Jack smiles at him, putting his arm around his shoulder. "You guys ready for a ride? I've organised one more surprise."

"Hell, yes! I bet it drives like a dream." Ben's eyes light up with excitement and his smile is so big and genuine it makes my heart soar.

"It sure does. One day I'll teach you to drive it."

Ben opens the backseat door and clambers in. "Cool."

"Hey, you," I say, stepping into Jack's arms and gazing up at him with a smile.

"Hey, you," he smiles back.

We take a step closer to each other. He reaches out and cups my face to kiss me on the cheek. I put my hand on his chest before sliding both arms up to settle around his neck.

"Come on, you two. Plenty of time for that later," shouts the teenager in the background.

We pull away from each other and take our places in the car, still smiling. We snap on our seatbelts and I watch as Jack smoothly moves the Aston Martin away from the kerb.

"So, exactly where are we going?" I ask.

"Just a little surprise. Do you trust me?" Jack smirks my way.

"With my life." My heart races as I catch his gaze.

We chat throughout the journey, until about thirty minutes later Jack pulls into a large secluded driveway. I stare in awe at the grey detached Gothic-style house. There are six cars in the driveway. Some I recognise. I look at the two balloons hanging over the front door.

"This is my home," Jack says quietly, bringing the car to a stop and undoing his seatbelt.

"Wow, Jack! This is great," Ben says from the backseat, unclasping his belt.

The front door swings open and a flurry of familiar faces rush out of the door.

"I wanted to take you both on a special picnic, just the three of us. But it's too cold in November so I organised the next best thing, an indoor get-together with family and friends."

As I get out of the car Jenny rushes up and gives me a big hug. We walk arm in arm into the house where Stuart is waiting. He slaps Jack on the back and they both put their arms on Ben's shoulders.

"Oh wow," is all I can say, once we're inside. Everyone is there, Corinna, Peter and Kate, Lottie and her four-year-old son, Harley. My gaze catches a heavily pregnant Jem in a long floaty purple dress standing beside Lottie who looks happy in a longline dark blue jumper with a cowl neck and grey fitted jeans.

"Aunty Seph! Aunty Seph!" shouts Harley, hugging my knees. I smile, he still calls me by my nickname even though I'm sure he can actually say Steph. I lift him into my arms and kiss his soft cheek.

"Hey, champ! How are you?" I smile at him.

"Good. Mummy says I've got to be careful when I'm hugging knees. Just in case I've got chocolate around my mouth." My eye catches Lottie's and we stifle a grin. Clearly, someone has experienced the chocolate knee situation recently.

"I think your mum's right, champ. Just in case," I say, ruffling his short mousy hair and giving him a happy smile. I turn to Jem and make the shape of a round tummy with my hand to mimic her bulging pregnancy bump and ask her how she is.

She can't help but smile when she replies: "I'll be better when this little one comes out in four weeks. We must catch up soon."

I nod, putting my spare arm around her shoulders and give her a loving hug. Harley kisses my cheek and whispers in my ear: "You smell nice, Aunty Seph." I stroke his cheek, smiling, and turn back to say something to Jem. She's become distracted, searching the room for Noah. Her eyes find him and, as if they're connected somehow, he lifts his head from his conversation with Stuart to look up and gives her a dazzling smile. My eye catches Corinna across the room chatting to Jack. She looks good. Happy. Healthy. I'll catch up with her in a little while.

Jenny is walking around the room with a tray of half-filled wine glasses and is encouraging everyone to take a glass. Ben is following her, walking carefully with his tray containing small glasses of orange juice.

Harley wriggles and I carefully put him down so that he can run across the room to Lottie who is sitting talking quietly to Peter and Kate. Peter is looking much better, Jack says, he's much more like himself these days. I take two glasses of orange juice from Ben and give one to Jem.

Jack holds a wine glass in one hand and clears his throat. He waits until the room becomes silent before speaking:

"I would like to raise a toast or two. The first is to Corinna for coming through her ordeal and showing everyone what it means to stay strong. Secondly, I would like to raise a toast to family and friends and to the people we care about." Jack's gaze catches mine and holds me in place for what seems like a lifetime. And then he smiles, and I know he's won. He's won my heart so completely with his gentle encouragement, his support. He knew when to let me go, to give me space to find myself again. Slowly he turns to his father and gives him a quick nod of his head to acknowledge the importance of still having him with us. Family.

"Therefore, can you please raise a toast to Corinna, family and friends." His deep husky voice is confident as he raises his glass and takes a sip of wine.

"Here, Here. To Corinna and family and friends," a roomful of voices chant in unison. There are raised glasses, slurps and the odd cheer. Most of all there are smiles. Corinna's eyes shine as she looks at me and raises her glass. I smile and salute her with my own glass in a wordless thank you. Some things don't need to be said out loud. We each take a sip of our drink. Strength lies in love and friendship. Strength lies in shared experiences.

I catch Jack's eye and follow him as he walks to the kitchen. His arm reaches behind him to take my hand in his. His fingers are warm and steady as they link through mine. Suddenly he turns me about, so that my back is pressed against the countertop. His head tilts slightly as he swoops in with a soft kiss to my cheek, his forehead dropping gently to touch mine. Our eyes meet.

"There was something Ben mentioned a while back. Something about me one day wanting to move in with you both," he says, his breath warm on my lips.

"Yes?" I hold my breath.

"Yes," he gives me a small smile, "so what do you think?" His soft brown eyes hold mine.

"I think it would be a great idea. You?" I say, reaching up to touch his cheek and feeling rewarded when he leans into my touch.

"I would love to live with you and Ben – as a family." I let out a breath. A thankful, grateful breath for the strange circumstances that brought this man into my life.

"I don't mind whether it's here or at your place. Obviously, this place is bigger," he chatters on.

"I love this place from what I've seen so far," I reassure him, resting my hand on his chest.

"I'll show you both around later and we'll see what Ben thinks," Jack says, before leaning close to my ear. "I love you, Steph. I wasn't expecting it, I didn't think I wanted it, but I found it. I found love with you," he says quietly in my ear before he kisses me gently, his lips lightly touching mine. And then his tongue sweeps along my lower lip and our mouths fuse together in a whirlwind of exploration.

I was about to say it back but it's hard to think straight when your head is in the clouds and you're being kissed to within an inch of your life.

Epilogue: Eight weeks later

Steph

Ben bumps my shoulder as we finish eating our spaghetti bolognaise dinner around the glossy grey dining table of our new Gothic home. We moved in with Jack two weeks ago. This house is to die for. It's full of characterful touches such as old stone fireplaces, doors and windows, but it has been thoroughly updated to accommodate modern living. There's underfloor heating, a state-of-the art kitchen and a gorgeous dark ruby hallway with a sweeping wide staircase. There is space to grow as a family and a beautiful mature garden filled with bushy green shrubs, meandering pathways with privacy seating and a brilliant red climbing clematis over the wrought iron gazebo at the bottom of the garden. What more can I ask for? I put my house up for rent and a young couple moved in last week. I hope they'll be as happy there as Ben and I were.

Following the excitement of the past eight weeks, I decided to take that much deserved week off work to move into Jack's house. The solicitors are working their way through Ray's will and estate. I don't want the money. It was Ray's and I never expected to receive any financial compensation for being Ray's beaten wife. I simply wanted to forget about him and move on with my life.

Ben was so excited to move in here with Jack and their relationship continues to thrive. It's a joy to watch. We're creating new memories and, in my book, that's priceless.

Shopping for accessories to furnish Ben's new bedroom had Jack in fits of laughter as they took the Aston Martin for the shopping trip. Ben was smiling in the passenger seat as I waved them off, his passenger window down and shouting: "Floor it, Jack! Where's the ejector seat?"

***

Ben leans from his seat next to me and nudges me again, waking me from my daydream.

"What?" I ask.

He leans down to pick up an object from the floor and carefully lays it on the table. It's a grey Lego model of an Aston Martin. "Jack helped me to find it," he says, "but I put it together, I built it."

I smile and carefully touch the top of the car. "It's lovely, Ben, just like the real thing."

"It's for you." Ben's eyes light up.

"Thank you, Ben. I love it," I say, feeling grateful but wondering what was going through his mind.

"Open the door, Mum," he says, his voice quietening. "Look inside."

"OK," I say slowly, looking first at Ben and then at Jack who sits facing me. Jack's face is pensive, his eyes flicker to Ben.

I squeeze my finger through the window on the door of the small model and gently pull the door open. I can feel something small and soft sitting inside the car. I begin to pull out a piece of tissue, which is folded carefully into the tiniest shape. I lay the tissue on the table and carefully unfold it until a piece of circular metal clicks softly onto the hard surface of the table. The ring is a single diamond, white gold, and it glistens. I look at it and then I catch Jack's eye. He looks serious as he reaches for my hand.

"I love you, Steph. I want to spend the rest of my life with you and Ben," he says, as his hand moves to caress my face. "Will you marry me?"

My hand flies to my mouth and my whole body feels numb with shock. A marriage proposal. This was something I never expected to hear again. My mind goes blank. The pressure of Jack's fingers squeezing mine bring me back to reality and I meet his gaze, savouring the moment as he waits patiently for my reply. And then I smile, my heart soaring as I hold his hand against my cheek.

"Mum. Say yes, say yes!" Ben orders, his brown eyes bright with excitement.

"Yes. I mean, I would love to marry you, Jack." He gets up from his chair, takes the few steps to my side and puts his hands out to pull me to my feet. In a daze I grasp his hand and when I'm standing, he takes the ring from me, slips it slowly onto my finger and gives me the gentlest of kisses. A promise of love. The concentration slips from his face and the room brightens as he finally smiles, taking my breath away. There is a burning need inside me, a need to tell him how I feel, so I lean in and whisper in his ear: "I love you, Jack."

"Phew, thank God for that. I was worried the car wasn't going to be enough!" Ben's overdramatic declaration brings us back to reality. We smile at him.

"You did good, Ben," Jack says, patting him on the back.

I can't wait to see Jenny's face when I tell her. She'll have that knowing look on her face and a desperate need to buy a wedding hat. On second thoughts, maybe we will enjoy our new engagement in private for a few days. There'll be plenty of time for list making.

Ben walks into the hug and we enclose him, making sure he knows he plays a pivotal role in our little family unit. There's a contented silence as we enjoy the moment that seals us as a family. Ben shifts slightly, looking up at Jack. He wants to ask him something, I know that thoughtful look on his face.

"Jack?" Ben asks.

"Mmm?" he answers, turning his head to Ben. I hold on tight, enjoying the feel and strength of him. Who would have thought that I'd find myself able to love and trust someone again?

"Would it be OK if I called you 'Dad' sometimes?" Ben's cheeks redden slightly.

"I'd be honoured, Ben," Jack answers, studying Ben's face. "Really honoured." The look they share is priceless. For a moment I see Jack's eyes glisten with happiness and humility as though someone has given him the most precious gift. Jack glances at me, before catching the stray tear that escapes down my cheek with his thumb. I smile and lean into his touch. The future looks good.

Acknowledgements

Thanks to a huge bunch of people who help me along the way. To Lisa, Julia, Sheila, Denise, Cath and Janine who are awesome and give their time to read and offer feedback to my books and storylines. To Laura, who unwittingly manages to offer lots of help and guidance along the way. To James and his dry humour which motivates me to continually improve or ignore, depends on my mood.

A big thank you to the Cornerstone Art Centre who have supported me from the beginning. To all of you lovely readers who have bought my books and given fab feedback. Reviews on Amazon are always greatly appreciated.

Thanks to my local M&S and Boswells for keeping me in coffee, as I sit and tap away on the laptop.

Finally, to my hubby who is always on hand to support with IT stuff, and who steps in regularly to help with my 'I don't know what I did there' queries. And, no, you shouldn't be worried that I am googling emergency contraception!

The Lamp-post Shakers

The novella tells the story of Jem and Noah. Jem has suffered neglect, emotional and physical abuse from her mother since her father left the family home when she was five years old. Her best friend, Noah and his gran try to help, but their hands are tied. Following an upsetting episode at home, Jem decides to leave home. At fifteen, she is given a second chance when she meets Jenny and Stuart, who run The Lighthouse charity and several refuge homes for vulnerable women and children.

Jem and Noah move on with their lives, until Jem returns home ten years later, to face her demons following a shocking revelation. It is possible to find your soulmate when everything around you seems to be crumbling? This book can be read as a standalone or as part of The Lighthouse Series.

What readers say about The Lamp-post Shakers

"Fantastic read. Really enjoyed it!
Very well written and kept me gripped to keep reading more.
Look forward to reading the next novel!"

Donna

Read on for an excerpt of The Lamp-post Shakers

The Lamp-post Shakers

Chapter 1: Dangerous and daring: now (Jem)

I wasn't sure when it began or how I managed to get into this situation, but the first thing I remember when I look in the rearview mirror of my little Peugeot 207 was that I had gotten myself into a bit of a pickle. My ivory silk off-the-shoulder wedding dress is slightly creased from being bunched to fit into the front seat of the car and red blotches have formed around my neck and cheeks. My eyeliner and mascara has smudged so much, I look as if I have two black eyes and my short, curly dark hair looks a mess. The hair clips keeping my birdcage veil in place are hanging precariously askew, like an acupuncture session gone wrong, and, for the hundredth time today, I wished that I had more controllable hair. "For goodness sake, Jem, get a grip on yourself," I say to no one there. "You look like you've been dragged through a hedge backwards." Quickly, I pull out the hair clips and pull at the veil to free my unruly mop. Now, that feels much better.

So, back to my predicament, yes – I am currently sitting in my car in a wedding dress, on the verge of a complete meltdown, having left my would-be husband standing in the registry office among his family and our friends. "Shit…shit…shit…" I mutter. It's hard to be stoical when all you want to do is to burst into tears – but I am trying here. First thing though, I need to start driving and get as far away from here as I possibly could so that I can think straight and work out my next steps. I find the spare key, hidden in my well thought through hiding place in the glove compartment, and turn on the ignition. I'm putting the car into gear and take off the handbrake when a fist bangs against the driver's side window. Fuck! It's Craig, the ditched groom and he looks mad as hell.

"What the hell, Jem! Get out of the car and face me. What's going on with you?"

Craig keeps one hand on the top of the roof of the car, as if he thinks this will stop me from leaving. His face is red and matches his red ruffled spiky hair, he looks as though he's had electric shock treatment and the current is still on. I stare at him in all his wedding finery, trying to think why I believed I could trust and love this man in the first place. He wasn't really my type…but then what was my type, someone with dark hair and blue eyes?

Thinking back, there was always a feeling of dishonesty about him, but I couldn't quite put my finger of why I felt this way. So, in the end, I got swept away with the excitement of finally having someone to love in my life, and to finally having someone to love me for being me.

My instincts are to open the door and kick him in the balls or to do some clever martial arts move to his face. Whichever causes the most pain. Thankfully, I keep my instincts in check and take a deep breath. I stare at him, angry with him for being such a dick, and with myself for getting caught up in his web of lies that involve having contact with my mother.

He attempts to pull open the door, but I shake my head sadly and slowly start to drive. I drive as tears roll down my cheeks and I sigh with relief as my hands and feet respond automatically. I find myself heading to the only place that I think no one will look for me and that I have ever felt safe in my life. Shore House.

I can almost hear my mother's shrill voice shouting, "Jemima, what has gotten into you? How dare you do this to me? I'll be a laughing-stock."

"Yes, you and me both, Mother," I grimace to myself. "You and me both."

Is it too late to finally rid oneself of the fear that has haunted you for most of your life? Can I find the strength to move forward and be the happy, carefree, independent person who I feel I deserve to be? Well, I have made the first daring step, something that not even my clever mother would have dreamed in her wildest dreams that I would do. I have taken myself away from the danger, from the poison and from those who wish me harm, and now I am heading for my safe place. No "congratulations to the bride and groom", no wedding speeches and no sharing a hopeful future with someone who cares for me. Thanks for nothing, Craig.

Printed in Great Britain
by Amazon